Alfric turned. The man who had stalked unheard to well within killing distance was Nappy, a huffy-puffy individual of slightly less than average height. Nappy was pink of face and bald of pate and could often be seen hustling about Galsh Ebrek looking slightly comical thanks to his pigeon-toed gait. He was renowned for his sweet temper, for the jolly delight he took in all innocent pleasures, and for his work as a committee man. Nappy was famous in charity circles, and was known to be happiest at festivals when he could transmogrify himself into Mister Cornucopia, and dispense sweets for the children and kisses for the blushing virgins.

'I'm so glad to see you, Mister Danbrog,' said Nappy, extending his hand. Alfric took it and pumped it. Nappy's hand was soft and damp. A clinging, friendly hand.

'We haven't seen you here for ever so long,' said Nappy. 'I'm so, so very glad to see you.'

The sincerity of these effusions could not be doubted. That was Nappy all over. He was acknowledged as the happiest, friendliest person in Wen Endex. Which made no difference to the facts of the matter. Nappy was what he was and he did what he did, and there was no getting round that.

'Sorry I can't stay to chat,' said Nappy, shifting on his feet in that fluidly furtive manner which was his trademark, 'but I must be going now.'

And already Nappy was sliding, sidestepping, nimbling past Alfric's defenses. Alfric thought him shifting right, but he was gone to the left, sliding past and—

And—

And?

Alfric wanted to scream.

Nappy was behind him.

And all Alfric could think was this:

'Just let it be quick, that's all. Just let it be quick.'

Also by Hugh Cook

and published by Corgi Books

THE WEREWOLF AND THE WORMLORD

Hugh Cook

CORGI BOOKS

THE WEREWOLF AND THE WORMLORD
A CORGI BOOK 0 552 13538 0

First publication in Great Britain

PRINTING HISTORY
Corgi edition published 1991

This book is set in 10/12½pt Times by
County Typesetters, Margate, Kent

Corgi Books are published by Transworld Publishers Ltd.,
61–63 Uxbridge Road, Ealing, London W5 5SA, in Australia
by Transworld Publishers (Australia) Pty. Ltd., 15–23 Helles
Avenue, Moorebank, NSW 2170, and in New Zealand by
Transworld Publishers (N.Z.) Ltd., Cnr. Moselle and
Waipareira Avenues, Henderson, Auckland.

Made and printed in Great Britain by
BPCC Hazell Books
Aylesbury, Bucks., England
Member of BPCC Ltd

CHAPTER ONE

Touching that monstrous bulk of the whale or ork we have received nothing certain. They grow exceedingly fat, insomuch that an incredible quantity of oil will be extracted out of one whale.

Lord Baakan, *History of Life and Death*

It is an undisputed truth that a man with weak sight must be in need of an ogre; for, as all the world knows, ogres are by far the best oculists. Therefore it is not surprising that, on each of his annual visits to the Qinjoks, Alfric Danbrog took the opportunity to have his eyes retested and to get a new pair of spectacles ground to his prescription.

Shortly after his thirty-third birthday, Alfric made his fifth such venture into the mountains. On this occasion, the bespectacled banker took with him a large carven box. This was a gift for the ogre king; and inside there were twenty pink mice, five thousand dead fleas, thirty chunks of cheese and seven dragons.

Alfric's journey to the Qinjoks was made exclusively by night, which multiplied its many difficulties. However, young Danbrog was not just a banker but the son of a Yudonic Knight, and he pressed on regardless of danger. Once the many difficulties of the journey had been overcome, Alfric's first duty was to present himself to the ogre king. The audience took place in a deep delved mountain cave in one of the shallower portions of that underground redoubt known as the Qinjok Sko.

Before the meeting, the king's chamberlain cautioned Alfric thus:

'You will not address the king by his given name.'

The chamberlain, a small and nervous troll, had given Alfric exactly the same warning on each of the four previous visits the young banker had made to these mountains. But Alfric did not remind him of this.

'My lord,' said Alfric, 'I do not even know the king's name, therefore am in no danger of addressing him thereby.'

This was a diplomatic mistruth. Alfric Danbrog knew full well that the ogre king had been named Sweet Sugar-Delicious Dimple-Dumpling.

Among ogres, the naming of children is traditionally a mother's privilege; and female ogres are apt to lapse into a disgustingly mawkish sentimentality shortly after giving birth. Those who cleave to the evolutionary heresy hold that such a lapse is necessary to the survival of the species, for baby ogres (and the full-grown adults, come to that) are so hideously ugly that it is surely only the onset of such sentimentality which keeps their mothers from strangling them at birth.

Once the chamberlain had been assured on this point of protocol, Alfric was admitted to the presence of the above-mentioned Sweet Sugar-Delicious Dimple-Dumpling, king of the Qinjoks. The king, let it be noted, was nothing like his name. Rather, he would have better fitted the name his father would have liked to bestow on him: Bloodgut the Skullsmasher.

While the ogre and the banker met on cordial terms,

there stood between them a line of granitic cubes, each standing taller than a cat but shorter than a hunting hound. These were stumbling blocks, placed there in case Alfric should take it into his head to draw his sword and charge the throne.

Technically, there was peace between Galsh Ebrek and the Qinjoks. Furthermore, every expert in combat will tell you that it is theoretically impossible for a lone swordsman to overcome a full-grown ogre. However, the Yudonic Knights are what they are; and the king did well to be cautious.

'We trust your journey was pleasant,' said King Dimple-Dumpling.

'It was not,' said Alfric. 'The roads between Galsh Ebrek and the Qinjoks owe more to fantasy than to fact. The dark was dark, the rain was wet, and the mud was excessive in the extreme, quantity in this case quite failing to make up for lack of quality.'

So he spoke because his ethnology texts had taught him that ogres value honesty in speech above all other things.

Such scholarly claims are in fact exaggerated. There are many things an orgre values far more, some of them being mulberry wine, gluttonous indulgence in live frogs, and the possession of vast quantities of gold.

'So,' said the ogre king. 'You travelled by night.'

'I did, my liege,' said Alfric.

'Hmmm,' said the ogre king.

While the king puzzled over this strange behaviour, Alfric had ample time to study his majesty's surrounds. Ranged behind the king were racks of skulls; interlaced washing lines strung with scalps; and two vultures, each a triumph of the taxidermist's art. Carven draconites served

7

these beasts as eyes, and an evil light swashed from these gems as they caught the buckling flaze of torches. Flanking these beasts were skeletons in duplicate; while at the king's head was the mouldering head of a dragon. And, in pride of place at his right hand, a low bookcase crammed with philosophy books.

Alfric started to sweat.

Not because he was frightened, but because the cave was grossly overheated.

'So,' said the king. 'You travelled by night. Which means, does it not, that She walks again?'

'So it has been said,' acknowledged Alfric.

'It has been said, has it? And what do you believe?'

'That custom commands me,' said Alfric. 'Hence I walk by night. I can do no less. I am of a Family.'

'You belong to the Bank,' said the king, 'yet declare allegiance to a Family.'

'The Bank, my liege, lives within the bounds of law and custom; nor does the Bank seek to sever its servants from their rightful bondage to either.'

'I have heard otherwise,' said the king, almost as if he were accusing Alfric of mistruthing.

'My liege,' said Alfric, 'I cannot answer Rumour, for Rumour has ten thousand tongues and I have but one.'

'Hmmm,' said the king.

Thinking.

Then:

'You travelled by night.'

Alfric kept his face blank. This was no time to show impatience. But Alfric liked to do business in an efficient manner; and not for nothing was the king known as He Who Talks In Circles.

'Night is a strange time to travel,' continued King

Dimple-Dumpling. 'Particularly when night is Her chosen time.'

'My duty bids me to rule the night,' said Alfric. 'I cannot permit Her forays to keep me from the dark. I am a Yudonic Knight.'

'Who fears nothing,' said the king.

When one hears dry irony from the lips of an orgre, it is hard to credit ones ears. But Alfric, who knew ogres better than most of his kind, did not underestimate them. He answered deadpan:

'My liege is generous in his praises. I fear myself unworthy of such praise.'

'Why unworthy?' said the king. 'Do you think yourself a coward?'

A dangerous question, and one not easy to answer. In the halls of an ogre king, one does not confess to cowardice, for the ogres think pusillanimity to be a crime meriting death. Equally, in such a place one boasts not of courage, for ogres delight in supervising tests of the same.

'Well,' said the king. 'Are you a coward or are you not?'

'So far,' said Alfric, answering carefully, 'fear has not chosen to be my companion. But, in keeping with the teachings of the philosophers, I do not hold such companionship to be merely because it lies outside my own experience.'

An adroit answer, displaying the mental agility which had seen Alfric rise so far and so fast in the ranks of the Bank. It pleased the king.

'Well,' said the king, 'enough small talk. Now to business. Have you brought me my dragons?'

'I have,' said Alfric, and opened the carven box which had originally held pink mice, chunks of cheese, dead fleas and seven dragons. The mice were meant to keep the dragons warm, the cheese to feed the mice and the fleas to feed the dragons. A cunning arrangement, which had worked up to a point. Two of the dragons had survived the journey, and King Dimple-Dumpling was delighted.

The dragons were tiny, for they belonged to a breed which grew no longer than a fingerlength. Nevertheless, they were true dragons which could fly and breathe fire. Or, more exactly, spark fire; for the incendiary output from these untunchilamons was scarcely sufficient to threaten the life of a bedbug.

Untunchilamons they were called because they hailed from an oceanic island of that name. (Here let it be recorded that the untunchilamons were referred to by a small group of linguistic dissidents as the injiltaprajuras. However, the correct name is untunchilamon, for Galsh Ebrek's School of Heraldry so entered this new breed of dragon into the Registry of Pageantry.)

It was said by some that Justina Thrug had discovered the species on the abovementioned island; by others, that she had proved her powers as a witch by creating the genus *ex nihilo*. Here the term 'genus' is controversial, with many categorizers preferring to conglomerate the untunchilamons with more conventional dragons.

Yet surely the untunchilamons are not just a distinct species but a unique genus with claims, indeed, to being a separate one-species family. To mention no other matter, their method of reproduction strongly supports their pretensions to unique generic status; for, unlike other dragons, they eschew copulation in favour of parthenogenesis. All untunchilamons are female, and their opalescent eggs require no fertilization from any agency outside their own bodies.

Such a method of propagation has many advantages. However, sexual congress is a sovereign method for securing genetic diversity; and hence is most marvellously effective in allowing populations of both plants and animals to adapt to abruptions, dislocations and disease. In contrast, diversification among the untunchilamons was necessarily very slow, consisting as it did of occasional accidents in the parthenogenetic process.

As the island of their origin was tropical, the untunchilamons were woefully ill equipped to withstand the inclemency of the winters of Galsh Ebrek. Lacking the ability to diversify and adapt, their populations were constrained to dwell in or around fireplaces, chimneys and kitchen stoves, where constant combustion afforded them a climate somewhat like that of their ancestral homeland.

Alfric explained the environmental limitations of the beasts with great care.

'But they fly forth from their chimneys, do they not?' said King Dimple-Dumpling.

'Oh indeed, my liege. To a range of fifty paces or more, sometimes even a hundred.'

'And they ravage their enemies, do they not? Fleas, lice and bedbugs?'

'As advertised, my liege.'

'What about crab-lice?' said King Dimple-Dumpling.

Alfric did not even blink.

'That I do not know,' said he. 'I suggest that any experiment in that direction be made with care. In our experience, these dragons do not bite without extreme provocation. Nevertheless, they do on occasion assail their prey with fire, a potential problem should such prey be in, ah, a sensitive location.'

11

'Thank you,' said the king. 'We will meet again in eight days. Then the ransom will be delivered into your care.'

'My liege is gracious,' said Alfric, and bowed, and withdrew.

Alfric Danbrog made good use of the eight days thus granted to him, using the time to see his ogre oculist, to do some private research in King Dimple-Dumpling's library, and to indulge in some casual tourism. Of these activities, the ocular consultation was the most important. Alfric suffered from pronounced myopia combined with a degree of astigmatism; his handicap being such that his ogre proclaimed him to be deficient by a full ten diopters. A cruel fate, this; for it meant his chances of attaining supremacy with the sword were not of the best.

However, such genetic disadvantage is often accompanied by a collateral benefit; inasmuch as the type of ocular defect which Alfric suffered is positively correlated with high intelligence. In Alfric's case, an inexactitude of vision was accompanied by mental acuity of the highest order; his acumen and cleverness had allowed him to qualify as a Certified Genius, and thus to join the Bank.

And it was Bank business, rather than any concern for his organs of vision, which had ultimately impelled Alfric to dare the dangers of the journey to the Qinjoks. The delivery of a kindle of dragons to King Dimple-Dumpling had been but a minor courtesy. Alfric's true duty was to check the Annual Tribute of jade which the ogre king consigned to Obooloo; to uplift that Tribute; to convey it safely to Galsh Ebrek; and there in the presence of witnesses to deliver it unto a certain ambassador.

The eight days went swiftly, Alfric receiving his new

spectacles on the last of them. Shortly after accepting delivery of these precision instruments, Alfric was summoned into the presence of King Dimple-Dumpling at midnight. The ogre king sat in state, drinking of blood-red wine. (Or was it actual blood? Alfric was diplomat enough not to ask.)

'We have the treasure,' said the king, indicating the six small barrels of jade balanced upon the stumbling blocks. 'You have my permission to check the contents.'

Alfric then laboriously checked each item against the standard inventory.

'It is here, my liege,' said he.

'Good,' said the king. Then, generously: 'Choose something for yourself.'

Alfric blinked, momentarily disconcerted.

'My liege,' said Alfric, 'this belongs not to me, nor can it. This trove entire is pledged to Aldarch the Third, Mutilator of Yestron.'

Thus spoke Alfric Danbrog.

But the king insisted.

So, unwillingly, Alfric selected a single saladin ring for himself. He slipped it on to one of his fingers, held it to the torchlight, and smiled in mimickry of pleasure. Later he would take the thing from his finger and cram it into his pocket, not wanting to display such evidence of criminal activity in public. But one does not thus treat a king's gift in that king's presence.

The casks of jade were then closed and sealed in Alfric's presence. Then ogres took them away. He would not see them again until he left, which would be shortly. By then, the casks would have been loaded on to his pack horses.

Of course the ogres had no absolute need to yield up

such a ransom. Ogres have such a slow replacement rate that it is seldom wise for them to engage quick-breeding humans in outright war; however, the monsters of the Qinjoks did have the option of retiring to redoubts which could never have been stormed by human agency. But the ogres nevertheless thought it best to comply with human demands – up to a point. For the ogres were scientists; and, while the greater part of their number would have survived a war with Wen Endex, such a conflict might have had disastrous consequences for such unprotectable assets as their masterwork telescopes and their great tree breeding program (now already five thousand years old).

Besides which, the orks would have suffered greatly in any war. Ogres, like trolls, are by nature a troglodytical breed, and could have survived in the underground fastness of the Qinjok Sko for many months, if not for years. Orks, on the other hand, would swiftly have perished in such conditions. For, since they are unable to live away from water for any great length of time (they need not just enough to drink, but a sufficiency in which to immerse themselves on a regular basis) orks soon perish in cavebound confinement.

The ogres of the Qinjoks suffer from a surpassing sense of responsibility; an affliction which, as a rule, cannot be said to overly oppress the human race. Generations earlier, the ogres had placed the orks under their protection; and this protection they had since maintained, though at times it might have been politic for them to do otherwise.

Therefore let it not be said that the ogres paid their Annual Tribute out of fear. Rather, they did so out of love for that Science of which they had such great hopes;

14

and out of duty to the orks which dwelt in their care.

Once the six barrels of jade were out of sight, the king addressed Alfric anew, saying:

'You leave by night.'

'As my liege knows,' said Alfric carefully.

'Because She walks,' said the king.

'So it is said.'

'It is said! And you believe? Or don't you?'

'As custom commands me, I walk by night when such a duty is placed upon my people.'

'Of custom you have spoken, but not of belief,' said the king. 'What do you believe? Does She walk or does She not?'

'I reserve judgement,' said Alfric.

'But others do not,' said the king.

'My liege knows that many see hunting of any kind as great sport in its own right,' said Alfric. 'Regardless of whether anything actually exists to be hunted. Thus the enthusiasm with which Rumour has been greeted.'

'Rumour!' said the king. 'I thought there were Signs!'

'It has been said,' answered Alfric, now impatient to be gone.

'So you admit it,' said the king, as if they were in court and Alfric stood accused of a crime. 'What Signs has Rumour spoken of?'

'The carcase of an ox,' said Alfric. 'Its bones shattered by the clawed thing which gnawed its guts but left the meat untasted. Some claim also to have seen blood in the Riga Rimur.'

'Near Galsh Ebrek?' said the king.

'She will not come near the High City,' said Alfric flatly. 'That would mean Her certain doom regardless of Her power.'

'Aha!' said the king. 'Just then you spoke as if you believed in Her!'

'It would be foolish for me to do otherwise,' said Alfric. 'The Wormlord killed Her son. That was before the days of my generation, but it happened. It is a fact. Therefore I do not dispute claims of Her existence. Nevertheless, I am not necessarily convinced that She walks.'

'But you travel armed for war,' said the king.

'I would not walk the night otherwise,' said Alfric. 'She is not the only denizen of the night. Not by any means.'

'Who else do you fear, then?' said the king.

'Men, for the most part,' answered Alfric. 'Bandits and such.'

'So you fear men,' said the king. 'As the orks fear them.'

'My liege, the time when orks had cause to fear the people of Galsh Ebrek lies long in the past,' said Alfric, answering almost casually.

'It does?' said the king.

'So opinion runs in Galsh Ebrek,' answered Alfric, belatedly sensing unsuspected complications.

'Good!' said the king. 'For I have it in mind to send two ambassadors to that city. My ambassadors are orks. You can arrange for it?'

'Within the year, certainly,' said Alfric.

'You misunderstand me,' said the king. 'I wish to send my ambassadors now. With you. Tonight.'

'The wish of my liege is my command,' said Alfric.

Whereupon the chamberlain called in two orks, and introductions were made. One ork (Morgenstern by name) larger than the other (who was called Cod), but neither

16

could be considered small. The ork (otherwise known as the swamp-whale, or simply as the whale) does not reach the monstrous size alleged by Lord Baakan and others to be its birthright (perhaps Baakan confused the creature with the swamp giant). Nevertheless, though smaller than any full-grown ogre, the ork is rather larger than a man.

At least, the males are.

Alfric Danbrog had studied long and deeply in his ethnology texts, which had informed him that orks demonstrate pronounced sexual dimorphism, the males being big and bulky and the females (subservient to the males in all matters) small and shy. The standard ethnology texts also declared that the apparelling of orks is chiefly by way of wool, the male orks wearing trousers of coarse wool while the females adorn themselves in pleated skirts dyed in checkerboard patterns.

The days when the Yudonic Knights of Wen Endex had hunted orks for their blubber and oil were long in the past, but nevertheless Alfric felt more than a twinge of racial guilt as he was introduced to his new companions. He tried to dismiss such guilt by telling himself he was no longer a child of Wen Endex, or, really, a Yudonic Knight. Had he not thrown in his lot with the Bankers? Had he not even taken a new name, Izdarbolskobidarbix? Of course he had. And yet: the guilt persisted.

'I trust,' said King Dimple-Dumpling, 'that you personally guarantee the safety of my orks.'

'I do, my liege,' said Alfric. 'I guarantee their safety as far as Galsh Ebrek. After that, the Wormlord will doubtless take them into his care. As all the world knows, the Wormlord has the highest regard for the niceties of diplomacy.'

'It was once said,' said the ogre king, 'that the Wormlord also had the highest regard for his honour. He did battle with Her son on account of such honour. Will he not do battle with Herself?'

'My liege,' said Alfric, keeping his face studiously blank, 'word of the Wormlord's will is not in my keeping.'

But Alfric knew what Rumour had to say on that subject. The Wormlord was old, and his courage had failed along with his strength. Soon he would die, his death perhaps precipitating a struggle for the throne of Wen Endex.

Alfric Danbrog hoped to avoid personal involvement in such struggle. But, because of his genesis and breeding, that might prove very difficult.

CHAPTER TWO

After leaving the presence of the ogre king, Alfric trekked for half a league underground before he at last emerged on to a mountain path beneath a dark and moonless night sky. The horses followed, snorting as they came out into the skeletal wind, the bitter cold. Alfric would not suffer from that chill, for he had donned thick furs for the journey. These (luxury of luxuries!) were furs of the wolverine, hence would not freeze regardless of how cold the air became.

The orks came last. Morgenstern, whom Alfric had picked as a complainer, made no comment on the cold because he was insensitive to it. Cold such as this would not trouble the orks, for both were far too thick and fat, too oiled and greasy, too lubbery blubbery.

Standing sentinel by the cavemouth exit was the gnarled statue of an ancient ablach, illuminated by phosphorescence from smothering lichens. Both Cod and Morgenstern bent down and kissed the stone dwarf for luck. Alfric, who had no truck with superstition, checked the stowage of the six barrels of jade, inspected the ropes of walrus hide which linked each pack horses to the next, then said to the leading animal:

'Chok-chok!'

The horse started to move. The others followed. The orks, who had been having a little talk to the stone dwarf, hastily fell in behind.

19

Snow crunched underfoot and underhoof as the expedition began to descend the mountain trail. The sky was cloudy and the clouds, or so Alfric suspected from the feel of the air, more than a little moody. He expected bad weather, and soon. He was glad when the trail shortly plunged into a forest of winter-black trees, gaunt and leafless to the last branch, for the forest was comparatively sheltered.

The forest was dark beneath the clouded sky. Here and there, a star-lichen glowed, but apart from that there was precious little illumination. This was the dark where the timorous think of ghost and ghoul, of adhantare and revenant. But Alfric Danbrog feared not the dark. Rather, he feared the moon, the Great Sorceress which has overrule of the tides of sea and blood alike. Hence he welcomed the absence of the welkin-wanderer, and was if anything comforted by the shrouding shadows.

By rights, the near-sighted banker should have been fumbling blind in that umbrage, for his spectacles had no special powers to decipher the dark. And let the plain truth be stated here without equivocation: travelling through forest by night is dangerous and often leads to death. Indeed, to go a mere half-dozen paces into the woodlands by night is to risk disorientation, for nothing is more baffling than the dark.

But Alfric was not as other men. In proof of which, he found his way efficiently and without undue effort. The path itself helped guide him; it was a slightly concave track which became an impromptu stream whenever it rained, and now afforded him with a trail of soft and yielding mud to follow. The moment he deviated from the mud's guidance, rocks and roots would ruck beneath his boots, warning him to reseek his footing.

In addition to such clabber-footed guidance, Alfric trusted much to his ears, for there was a constant clackering from ghoul-fingered branches animated by the bitter malice of the wind. With trees to either side thus preaching the appetites of emptiness, Alfric was ever-assisted to find his way. Furthermore, eye-jabbing branches stood ready to correct him should he blunder from the path.

Yet it was not either underfoot mud or sideline tree-talk which ultimately secured Alfric's route. Rather, it was his eyesight. By day, thanks to the correction supplied by his spectacles, his vision was neither better nor worse than that of other people. By day, he could pretend to be normal.

But night—

Night was different.

Night meant changes.

Alfric Danbrog possessed night vision of uncanny capacity. The forest was not utterly dark, for, quite apart from the soft phosphorescence of the occasional star-lichen, there remained (despite the clouds) a dim filtration of almost subliminal illumination from the sky, and it is certain that Alfric's eyes were well-equipped to gather in that minimal light.

But that is not the entire story.

For, as he travelled that darkened path, Alfric Danbrog sometimes had occasion to probe the night with a special urgency. When he did so, he saw not dimly but well. On such occasions, he saw not perfectly, for the colours of things remained secret: but shape and form were instantly betrayed to his scrutiny. Thus, while Alfric moved through a world of shadows, those shadows yielded their secrets to his gaze on demand. Such

21

demand he made when the trail took him through a black and overbranched cutting, a place devoid of star-lichens and virtually hidden from the sky, a place more cave than path. And there he saw almost as well as when walking beneath the open sky.

A curious observer might almost have thought that Alfric's eyes sent out a light of their own, interrogating the dark with outpourings of wavelengths mostly invisible to unaided human perception. Furthermore, had such an observer been able to study the steadfast trailblazer at close quarters, a most disconcerting phenomenon would have made itself evident. In places particularly dark, Alfric's eyes took on a dull red hue which was visible at half a dozen paces. And once, when a stick-crack alerted his sword-hand to a possible ambusher, Alfric's eyes positively flamed as he sought his putative enemy.

With such a guide, the expedition leagued well through the night, until Alfric at last called a halt.

'What are we stopping for?' said Cod, who had already proved himself more ready with questions than his fellow.

'To make camp,' said Alfric.

'And about time,' rumbled Morgenstern. 'Grief of gods, my feet are halfway broken.'

'But why here?' said Cod, peering into the night which, for him, was almost featureless.

'We have a knoll,' said Alfric, indicating with a hand which Cod had not the slightest hope of seeing in the dark. 'That's for us, for our camp. Three can fight six from a knoll, or so it's said in theory.'

Alfric did not mention that theory also says that two can take four if the four be orks and the two be men. He was, after all, a diplomat; so, while he thought of his orks as a useless encumbrance and a potentially embarrassing responsibility, he addressed them to their faces as if they were valued allies.

'I hear water,' said Cod.

'Of course,' said Alfric, yielding marginally to an underlying impatience. 'I didn't stop here by accident. There's a stream down there. Nothing for the horses, but you can't have everything.'

'There's probably worms,' said Morgenstern, speaking of the stream.

'No,' said Alfric. 'No worms. It's deep, but it's clear water, I've seen it by day. Trust me, it's safe.'

So the orks ventured to the near-frozen water, and soon Alfric heard them disporting themselves in the stream. Their layers of blubber were such that they could happily bathe in water too cold to melt ice. Alfric tethered his horses, put up a tent, gathered wood and made a fire. It was the fire which allowed the orks to find their way to the knoll once their aqueous delights were at an end.

Once the orks had returned, Alfric went down to the stream himself. He stripped, washed crutch and feet, washed his armpits and splashed some water in his face. Then, shivering and shuddering, he dressed himself again.

Then waited.

Watching.

Listening.

Was anything out there?

Creeping, peeping, preparing for ravaging?

Nothing.

Just the desolate wind, the rick-rack branches of the winterworld forest, and, far off, a late-hunting parrot-bat.

The sky was growing grey as the rule of the Revealer drew near. This place was far from Her haunts. And, in any case, if She was still out in the night, then She would now be making for her home in a great hurry.

Alfric made his way back to the knoll, only to find that his tent had assumed a most unusual shape. It was swollen, bulging and close to bursting. For half a moment he thought it bewitched. Then he realized his orks had taken refuge within. He had expected them to sleep outside in the open. For, with their layers of oil-yielding blubber, they were equipped to endure such repose without undue discomfort.

So what had got into them?

Were they asserting their status as royal ambassadors?

Or were they scared of the dark, and of the possibility of being set upon by Herself in that dark?

Knowing orks as he did, Alfric was inclined to suspect that it was fear which had driven them inside the largely illusory protection of his canvas. And, while he was displeased at being thus exiled from his own tentage, he had to admire the ingenuity with which the lugubrious monsters had crammed their combined bulk into a tent of such modest size.

Besides, there was no point in arguing about it, because the orks were already asleep, as was evident from their strenuous snoring. Alfric knew from his ethnology texts that few tasks are more futile than trying to rouse a slumbering ork. So he wrapped himself in a goundsheet and settled against a tree to sleep.

Sleep, however, came not.

For Alfric began to worry about the difficulties that would beset him once they got to Galsh Ebrek. The more he thought about it, the less he liked the idea of exposing a pair of innocent orks to the dangers of that city, particularly when King Dimple-Dumpling might well hold him personally responsible for the well-being of the orks even after those creatures had been delivered to Saxo Pall. Since Alfric was the son of a Yudonic Knight, he was not in the habit of confessing fear. Nevertheless, he did not exactly relish the possibility of incurring an ogre's enmity.

The incidental hazards of Galsh Ebrek are bad enough, but in this case Alfric was more afraid of the active enmity of his enemies, most notably the three brothers Norn.

Pig Norn.

Wu Norn.

And Ciranoush Zaxilian Norn.

The trouble between Alfric Danbrog and the brothers Norn had started years ago, and it had started with Ciranoush.

Entry to the Bank was by competitive examination. While Ciranoush and Alfric were both Certified Geniuses, Alfric had won a marginal triumph in such examination, and therefore had been accepted by the Bank on the same day that Ciranoush was rejected. Ciranoush had promptly accused Alfric of bribing the Bank's examiner, and of forging medical records to conceal a scandalous genetic deficiency.

The passing years had done nothing to ease Ciranoush Zaxilian's jealous passion. Rather, Alfric's success had served only to increase his enemy's contumelious hatred; and Ciranoush had successfully joined his brothers Pig and Wu to a campaign of steady calumniation directed against his rival. So, in his thirty-fourth year of life, Alfric found himself almost in a state of feud with the brothers Norn.

Which boded ill for the welfare of Alfric's orks when at last they got to Galsh Ebrek.

CHAPTER THREE

The city of Galsh Ebrek, a muddy urbanization on the Riga Rimur River, was the Chivalric Centre of the Yudonic Knights and the capital of Wen Endex. Once Alfric and his orks reached the city they would be safe, at least from Her.

They set forth on the last march to Galsh Ebrek on a night of bitter cold. This final stage of their trek from the Qinjoks was dangerous, for they had to pass through a tract of wilderness where She liked to hunt, for She was close enough to the city to have hope of prey, yet far enough removed from its halls of power to have sure hope of escape after Her murders.

Alfric confessed to no fear, and gave his orks no hint of the danger. But he kept his sword loose in its scabbard. However, the journey was uneventful, and toward midnight they came in sight of the Riga Rimur and the city on the far side of the river. To close with the fast-flowing waters, they had to follow a gnarled track through rucked swamplands where marsh lights flared a ghostly blue-white in the night. Unlike many of his people, Alfric had no fear of the cold lilting flames of marsh-wisp. If anything, he loved the night: his greatest danger being that he would love it too well.

'So that's Galsh Ebrek,' said Cod, looking at the huddling houses and the huge upsurge of Mobius Kolb which lay on the far side of the river.

'It is,' said Alfric.

There was a whimpling on the waters of the Riga Rimur where the wind rucked the surface. Here and there, lights gleamed briefly in the liquid black and then were gone again. Those lights were signs of organic life: for in the river there swam fish with phosphorescent eyes.

'How do we get across?' said Cod.

'We swim,' said Alfric.

'Swim!' cried Morgenstern. 'But we can't!'

All orks can swim. Their blubber-burdened bodies are well equipped for enduring the cold of the rivers of Wen Endex in winter. Furthermore, since orks can breathe underwater, it is impossible for them to drown. However, the grey-skinned monsters are ever reluctant to dare fresh running water, for in most of the rivers and streams of Wen Endex dwell ferocious worms which eat orks.

'Relax,' said Alfric. 'I was only joking.'

'Joking!' said Morgenstern. 'You call that a joke?'

And the ork was so upset that Alfric feared he might have created a major diplomatic incident. But, slowly, Morgenstern's fright eased, and the ork at last accepted Alfric's apologies.

'But,' said Morgenstern, 'if we don't swim, how do we get across?'

'By ferry,' said Cod. 'It's coming for us already.'

And so it was. The ferryman looked at the orks in askance. Of course he would have to take them across the river. The ferryman was a commoner and Alfric a Knight, so that settled that. But there remained the chance that the ferryman would create a diplomatic incident by insulting Alfric's monsters.

'Greetings, my good man,' said Alfric, in the tones of hearty condescension with which a Yudonic Knight often addresses a commoner. 'Hurry us across to the further shore if you will. Our good king Stavenger is waiting for these his guests. The Wormlord will not be pleased if you delay us, for these are the ambassadors from the Qinjoks, the ambassadors for whom he has long been waiting.'

This was a bluff, but it worked. The ferryman made no untoward comments about the orks, but instead maintained a sullen silence as he took the expedition across on his creaking boat. Alfric and Morgenstern went on the first trip, Cod came across with a horse on the next, then the remaining horses were shuttled across the Riga Rimur.

As Alfric and his orks were waiting for the last of the horses to arrive, a zana came dancing toward them across the waters.

'Look!' said Cod. 'What is it?'

'A zana,' said Alfric. 'One of the wild rainbows of Wen Endex. Have you never seen one before?'

'No,' said Cod, watching the zana come nimbling up the riverbank.

The ork's unfamiliarity with this phenomenon is not surprising, for the zana are rare once one moves any distance from Galsh Ebrek. Zana are not really rainbows, for the colours displayed by the splay of a zana are red, gold, green, blue and pink. Furthermore, unlike rainbows they can be touched, though it is unwise to do so because they sting.

'Yow!' cried Cod, having just been so wounded.

'Did you touch it?' said Alfric.

'Yes,' said Cod. 'And it bit me!'

Morgenstern picked up a handful of mud and hurled it after the retreating zana. Hit by the mud, it hummed, shattered into spectral splinters, then reformed and slid onwards.

'Are you hurt?' said Alfric.

'Yes,' said Cod, who was not disposed to be brave.

So Alfric was forced to sympathize, and gentle the ork's hand to soothe the pain.

Meanwhile, he noticed they were drawing a lot of odd glances from the passing foot traffic. In theory, while She was on the loose, night was far more dangerous than day. In practice, since the Yudonic Knights were constrained by custom to walk the night until She had ceased her depredations, the nights were actually safer. With so many knights out hunting Her, bandits and such preferred to strike by the winterlight sun. Thus those who travelled favoured the dark.

Among those who went past were old men and older woman stooped beneath huge burdens of firewood. Others laboured past carrying buckets of water balanced on shoulder-poles, buckets filled from the river just upstream from the dungdump. Some muttered to themselves, but none insulted the orks to their faces. Still, Alfric was glad when the last of the horses came ashore and he was ready to proceed.

'What's in the barrels, master?' said the ferryman.

'A ransom of jade from the Qinjoks,' said Alfric. 'The annual tribute from King Dimple-Dumpling.'

'Wealth of the orgre king, eh?' said the ferryman.

'Yes,' said Alfric. 'You should have taken your chance. You could have been rich for life.'

Then both laughed, and Alfric led horses and orks towards the city gates.

As has been said, Galsh Ebrek lay on (and, when the rain had been exceptionally heavy, at least partially in) the Riga Rimur River. Once it had been a walled city, but the swampy ground and the periodic delinquencies of the Riga Rimur had conspired to defeat the stone-mason's art; with the result that nothing remained of the masonry of lore and yore but for the massive bastions of the Stanch Gates. In place of stonework battlements, a rickety pale enclosed the city, this enclosure being largely notional due to the extent to which the fence had been vandalized by lawless wreckers in search of firewood.

While the city proper was very much a lowland affair, it was backed by a huge upthrust of rock. Mobius Kolb was the name of this mountainous granitic crescendo, and its bare and barren slopes were notable for the majestic monuments to power which they supported.

Atop the lowest shoulder of Mobius Kolb there stood the monstrous battlements of Saxo Pall. There dwelt the Wormlord, Tromso Stavenger by name, lord of Galsh Ebrek, king of Wen Endex, emperor of the Qinjoks and ruler of the Winter Sea. Old the Wormlord was, so old that many thought him close to death; though others disputed this, saying the king was known to have purchased the secret of immortality in his youth.

Higher yet, on a ridge of rock exposed to the full force of the gaunt winds of the Winter Sea and the haggling rains of all seasons, stood the expansive outworks of the Flesh Traders' Financial Association of Galsh Ebrek. Set inside those outworks was the gaunt donjon of the Bank, the Rock of Rocks which protected the greatest secret of that organization.

The secret protected by the Rock of Rocks served to

maintain the wealth of the Bank, but there was no secret at all about the origins of the Bank's prosperity. The Flesh Traders' Financial Association had first become wealthy in the days when Galsh Ebrek had been a great orking centre. Those granite outworks were a monument to lucrative murder and ever-rewarding terror. Tales of those days of joyful slaughter were still alive and well in Galsh Ebrek. Thus Alfric knew, for example, of the piteous screams of orklings thrown into the blubber pots while still alive. He knew of—

But this is a hideous, shameful, disgraceful phase of history. And recalling the horrors of those days does nothing to resurrect the victims. Suffice it to say that Alfric felt more than a little uncomfortable when he looked upon those distant walls and contemplated the first source of the money which had built him.

But there was something else which made him more uncomfortable yet. On the very highest point of Mobius Kolb was something that looked very much like a full moon. So much so that Alfric shuddered when he gazed upon its swollen light, even though he knew it was no moon but the Oracle of Ob, an occult machine which had ruled the heights for time out of mind.

The rains of millennia had weathered the carapace of that ancient arcanum. It had been ancient even before the ogres first came to the Qinjoks. In their archives, the ogres preserved fragmentary records of a few of the many temples which had risen on the heights of Mobius Kolb, pretending to understand or even to control that artefact which was also called the Ob, the Gloat, the Tynox and the Vo Un Ala Ma Drosk. But all those temples had at last fallen into ruins, sometimes under circumstances which still disconcerted later generations.

31

The good which could be done by the Oracle was uncertain, whereas the disasters it could cause were certain indeed; in consequence of which, all shunned its presence. Alfric in particular had good reason to keep his distance, and so had never climbed the slopes lying uphill from the Bank.

'Is that the Oracle?' said Cod, pointing at the Moon of the Mountain.

'Yes,' said Alfric. 'Watch out!'

Cod ceased his Ob-gazing in time to save himself from extinction beneath the wheels of a heavily laden cart. It was piled high with seaweed, huge scorlins of the stuff. Not the old, dead, brackeny seaweed which is found shangled with sand and sheals on the sea's spumestrand. No, this was fresh. The best select seacow's greed. At the smell of the stuff (a briny smell tinged with a faint, ever so faint aroma of codliver oil) Alfric's mouth watered; and he thought of seaweed soup with sideplates of garlic cockles, raw oysters and mussels marinated in wine.

Alfric abandoned such fantasy as he and his expedition followed the cart into the city. For, as always, soldiers were standing guard at the Stanch Gates; and, as always, those soldiers were armed with ceremonial orking harpoons. The harpoons were painted a bloody black (for the blood of orks is closer to night than to fire). Worse, globs of tar dangled from the harpoons, these globs representing gouts of hardened black ork blood. Alfric had never really noticed these sentries before, but now he noticed them furiously, because Cod and Morgenstern had stopped to stare.

'Blood of the Gloat!' said one of the guards. 'It's an ork!'

32

'No,' said his companion. 'I can count, though your mother could not. It's two orks.'

True. And both the lubbery animals were crying shamelessly. How embarrassing!

'Two orks,' said Alfric roughly, 'and one Yudonic Knight.'

So saying, he drew his sword and planted it in the mud between his feet.

'A Yudonic Knight?' said one guard to the other. 'I see no Yudonic Knight. I see a—'

'Say it not!' said Alfric. 'I am a Knight. With me I have two ambassadors sent by the king of the Qinjoks to the lord of Saxo Pall.'

Alfric's open anger warned the sentries they had almost gone too far. They did not apologize, but nor did they proceed to venture an irretrievable insult. Instead, one said something softly to the other, mouth to ear. Both laughed. Alfric slapped the leading pack horse. It got a move on, and the banker led his still-weeping orks into the streets of Galsh Ebrek.

One of the first things they passed was a boggy pit in which three swamp dragons were mulching garbage. These creatures are not true dragons any more than an ork is a true whale, but the naming of things proceeds without regard for scientific taxonomy, hence dragons they were to Galsh Ebrek.

But to the orks they were something else altogether.

'Hunters!' said Morgenstern fearfully.

The next moment, the swamp dragons scented the orks. With fearsome roars, they flung themselves at the walls of the pit, struggling to get out. Such escape was impossible, but the orks fled regardless, mud splattering in all directions as they charged down the street.

'Pox,' said Alfric.

And abandoned his pack horses while he went in pursuit.

Alfric found the orks huddled under a dung cart, clutching each other and sobbing fearfully. Inwardly he swore, then squatted down and began to sweet-talk the distraught creatures until their fears eased. Then he went back to recover his pack horses, only to find a gang of street boys had taken them in charge. That cost him some coppers (and, given the lawlessness of the streets, he was lucky it didn't cost him silver or gold).

After Alfric had rescued his horses, one of the homicidal dandiprats asked him:

'What's in the barrels, grandad?'

'Qinjok jade,' said Alfric shortly. 'The ogres' tribute. So you're lucky you didn't steal it. All Galsh Ebrek would've been after your blood.'

'I'll bet!' said his interlocuter.

Then laughed, and led his dwarfish army away in search of other amusements.

Alfric then led his expedition through the streets towards the Embassy housing the mission from Ang. And where and what is Ang? Why, Ang is an upland region in the heartland of the continent of Yestron, far south of Wen Endex. In Ang we find the city of Obooloo lies in that region, and from there the Izdimir Empire is ruled.

The Izdimir Empire's current ambassador in Galsh Ebrek was the eminent Pran No Dree. Once, No Dree had been the weatherman of Babrika. But now he was Al'three's ambassador to Wen Endex, which was not exactly a sought-after position. Still, No Dree had survived his first year in Galsh Ebrek, and with a little luck he might last out a second.

'Where are we going?' said the ever-curious Cod.

Alfric told him.

'That'll make for trouble,' said Morgenstern gloomily.

'Why?' said Alfric.

'This No Dree is of Janjuladoola race, is he not?'

'Yes,' said Alfric.

He was puzzled. What was the problem? Was there some deep-seated orkish prejudice against the Janjuladoola folk? His ethnology texts had made no mention of any such prejudice.

'He's a greyskin, then,' said Morgenstern.

'Well, yes,' said Alfric, still puzzled.

'So,' said Morgenstern, 'six to one he'll think you've brought us along by way of insult.'

Alfric was about to say that this was nonsense. Then he thought about it. The grey-skinned Janjuladoola were notorious racists and not exactly slow to take offence. And, to be honest, a baggy and blubbery ork could be construed as a grotesque parody of a Janjuladoola. So No Dree might quite possibly take offence. But – what a remarkable feat of insight on Morgenstern's part! Particularly since the ork had probably never seen a person of the Skin in his life. Perhaps there was more to these orks than met the eye.

'I have to admit,' said Alfric, 'you've out-thought me on this one.'

'That's Wen Endex all over,' grumbled Morgenstern. 'Nobody gives an ork the credit for half a brain. You don't think King Dimple-Dumpling chose us by accident, do you? He chose the best. After all, we've important business to do.'

'What business?' said Alfric.

Since Alfric Danbrog was a Banker Third Class, he

had mastered the nuances of diplomacy. But, since he was a Yudonic Knight by birth and breeding, he was ever inclined to lapse into undiplomatic directness. Hence the bluntness of his probe. A probe which met with failure, for Morgenstern said:

'We can't tell you that!'

Alfric thought:

—Why not?

And was about to ask as much, but restrained himself successfully. Instead, he flattered Morgenstern by asking his advice, saying:

'Well, since your secret mission's so important, whatever it is, I'd like to do everything I can to ensure your welcome in Galsh Ebrek. Doubtless a row with a Janjuladoola would be the wrong way to start. But I have to go to the Embassy without delay. That's a duty I can't avoid or postpone. So how would you suggest we handle this little difficulty?'

'I suggest,' said Morgenstern, 'that we orks would be quite comfortable waiting in the Embassy stables while you go in to meet the ambassador.'

'But I want to see the Skin!' said Cod.

'You would,' retorted Morgenstern. 'You wanted to watch your mother's autopsy.'

'I did watch it,' said Cod. 'And it was very interesting.'

Morgenstern shuddered, and said, as if pronouncing an imperial edict:

'We will wait in the stables.'

And wait they did. Under Alfric's orders, stable hands took his six barrels into the Embassy. In the reception chamber, a representative of the Bank was waiting; for there was always a banker stationed in the Embassy when the ogres' tribute was expected.

The banker on duty tonight was the elderly Eg, a Banker Third Class like Alfric.

'Greetings, Iz'bix,' said Eg.

'And to you, greetings,' replied Alfric.

Then they had to wait while the ambassador was roused from sleep. No Dree was asleep? At night? Though She was on the loose? Yes, he was. He was shamelessly asleep. For Pran No Dree was not a Yudonic Knight, therefore did not share the burden of honour which compelled Alfric and his peers to guard the dark against Her depredations.

It was an uncomfortable wait, for Alfric and Eg had little to say to each other. Alfric's meteoric rise to Banker Third Class had made him no friends and many enemies. While his superiors smiled upon him, he had yet to find a welcome among the ranks of his peers, and it was unlikely that he ever would. Furthermore, the reception chamber was physically uncomfortable, since a blazing fire kept the room at sweat-heat. Alfric shed his furs, but still felt choked by the heat.

When the grey-skinned ambassador at last presented himself in the reception chamber, the seals of all six barrels from the Qinjoks were checked by Banker Danbrog, Banker Eg, No Dree himself and a full half dozen ambassadorial aides and attachés. After due consideration, it was agreed that the seals were intact. At a signal from No Dree, an aide began to open one of the barrels.

The lid came free.

Now the critical question would be answered: would the fortune of fragile jade have survived the journey from the Qinjoks intact?

The lid came off.

No Dree gasped.

'The jade!' said he.

In the barrel was nothing but a rubbish of broken sticks and autumn leaves.

'This cannot be!' said No Dree. 'Where is the jade, the jade?'

Alfric, with difficulty, kept himself from yawning.

'It is as we feared,' said Banker Eg gravely. 'The Curse of the Hag has struck again.'

'Curse?' said No Dree. 'What curse? This is unpardonable!' He turned on Alfric. 'You barbarian fool! You lost the jade. You got yourself robbed. Or did you steal it?'

Alfric withstood this insult without blinking or protesting. That was what he was paid for. No Dree plunged his hands into the barrel and began shovelling out handfuls of leaves and sticks. Stuck to one stick were a couple of snails, snug in their winter sleep. No Dree cursed the snails. Then flung them into the blazing fire. Alfric silently regretted this minor tragedy: for he had a soft spot for snails.

No Dree heaped curses on the taciturn Knight. Then began to threaten.

'I'll have you boiled alive,' said No Dree. 'I'll have you torn apart with hooks and pinchers.'

'My lord is merciful,' said Alfric, before he could stop himself.

'You joke?' said No Dree. 'You dare to joke? This is no joke, you barbarous piece of yak dung.'

And, because of Alfric's unwise indulgence in sarcasm, honour could not be satisfied until No Dree had ranted himself hoarse.

But the end result of all these histrionics was a

foregone conclusion. The ambassador at last had to admit (though with every show of reluctance) that the seals had not been tampered with. And he had to accept (to do otherwise would have been to precipitate both his own death and a disastrous war) that King Dimple-Dumpling's tribute had been sealed into those barrels in Alfric's presence; and, furthermore, that the said tribute had been converted to rubbish by the Curse of the Hag.

This Curse of the Hag, a foul and poxy malison if ever there was one, had thus afflicted Wen Endex for generations. But it was not just Wen Endex which was thus affected. It would seem that a variant of this curse operates in, among other places, Port Domax. There, many an unsuspecting person has paid good money for some bauble which the retailing merchant has then beautifully packaged to enhance customer satisfaction; the sorry outcome being that, when opened, the gift-package has proved to hold no more than a few broken stones or similar rubbish. However, in Wen Endex, the Curse of the Hag seldom struck except to hex the ogre king's tribute into rubbish.

It may be asked why the Izdimir Empire (as represented by its ambassadors) persisted in demanding the annual collection of this tribute when the Curse of the Hag inevitably converted it to garbage. The answer to any such question is simple. While the enterprise was empty of profit, the collection of this tribute and the delivery of the same to the ambassador from Ang allowed the Izdimir Empire to demonstrate that both Wen Endex and the Quinjoks were subject states obedient to the dictates of Obooloo.

By such diplomatic finesse was the need for war

avoided; for, thanks to such annual proofs of obedience, Aldarch the Third (like his predecessors before him) had no need to go to the trouble and expense of marching armies into the northernmost regions of the continent of Yestron to take physical possession of those lands he was so confident he ruled.

Thus, once No Dree had ranted himself into silence, the delivery of the tribute was accepted as a fact, its conversion to leaves and such rubbish was officially attributed to the Curse of the Hag, various papers were signed attesting to this fact and this attribution, then hands were shaken in accordance with the custom of Wen Endex, reverence was made after the Janjuladoola fashion, and Alfric, his mission over, was able to escape from the heat and hostility of the Embassy.

A light rain was falling outside, misting against Alfric's spectacles so that, had he wanted perfect vision, he would have had to cleanse those optical devices thrice in every sixty heartbeats. He did no such thing, having found it wiser to avoid such full-time occupation. Instead, he cursed a couple of times, then went and collected his orks and his pack horses from the barn.

'Where now?' said Cod.

'Now,' said Alfric, 'we find you two somewhere to sleep for the night.'

Alfric thought this should not prove too difficult. But, once his orks had been refused lodgings by five foul netherskens of the lowest kind, he began to revise his estimate of the difficulties involved in finding lodgings for a pair of orks in Galsh Ebrek in the dead of night.

'Don't worry about us,' said Morgenstern. 'We can sleep in the mud.'

Doubtless they could. But Alfric had more than a

rough idea of how the ogre king would react if he knew his ambassadors had been so insulted. The possibilities were appalling.

'No,' said Alfric. 'I'll find you somewhere to sleep. Somehow.'

Should he take them up Mobius Kolb? He had the option of presenting them to the Wormlord that very night. By rights the Wormlord should offer them the freedom of Saxo Pall. But what if the Wormlord refused them hospitality? That would be a dreadful blow to Alfric's prestige. Doubtless the Bank itself would quarter the orks if all else failed. But how would that look on Alfric's dossier? He was a Banker Third Class, not a miserable clerk or an appretice shroff. One of his rank was meant to be ambassador, negotiator and arbitrator all rolled into one. It would be a black mark against him if he came whining to his superiors complaining that he couldn't find a couple of spare beds in the largest city in Wen Endex.

Then inspiration struck.

'The Green Cricket, that's the place.'

He had to go there anywhere, to return the pack horses he had hired.

'What place?' said Cod.

'It's an inn,' said Alfric. 'An inn in Fraudenzimmer Street.'

With orks in tow, Alfric ventured to the backlands of Galsh Ebrek, to Fraudenzimmer Street and the dark-gabled frontage of the Green Cricket. There Alfric delivered the pack horses into the care of Brock the Ostler.

'How are you for beds tonight?' said Alfric.

'That,' said Brock, eyeing the orks doubtfully, 'is something you'd have to ask Herself.'

So Alfric took his orks to the front door and knocked. The overhang of the second storey sheltered the doorway from the downfalling rain. Under that overhang was a huge iron cauldron, a relic of the orking days of yore. Its bottom had rusted out years ago, but it remained a potent token of the horrors of the past. To Alfric's disgust, both Cod and Morgenstern burst into tears at the sight of it.

'Gods,' muttered Alfric.

He banged on the door of the lushery, demanding an entry. He wanted to be gone, gone, away from these embarrassingly over-sensitive animals. However, his unsubtle overtures drew no response from the Green Cricket.

'Allow me,' said Cod the ork, wiping away his tears.

And Cod fisted the door until its timbers shivered.

A dwarf-hole level with Alfric's knees opened abruptly and a dwarf looked out.

'Who is it?' said the dwarf Du Deiner.

'Myself,' said Alfric.

'And who's that?' said Du Deiner, who was looking from candlefire brightness into the murk of an overhung night.

'Myself is Herself,' said Alfric. 'I come from bog, my body drenched with blood but my appetites unsated. I seek a dwarf. I yearn to ravage its flesh for its liver, to gouge out its eyes and pull off its ears for my porridge.'

'Oh, you,' said Du Deiner, belatedly recognizing the voice. 'Hang about, I'll open the door.'

The dwarf was as good as his word, and shortly laboured the door open with some help from his colleague Mich Dir.

'Come in,' said Du Deiner.

'In, in,' urged Mich Dir, for the draught from the open door was making the candles flaze.

In went Alfric with his orks following on his heels.

'No!' said Du Deiner, when he saw the first of the monsters. 'They can't come in. They're—'

'They're friends,' said Alfric, inverting the dwarf.

Du Deiner kicked, struggled and bit. When he bit, Alfric dropped him.

'Stop that!' This command came from Anna Blaume herself, she bedizened in flame-coloured taffeta, she enshrined in state behind the battlements of her bar. She followed up her order by saying: 'Why, it's Ally!' Then, cheerfully: 'Come in, come in!'

'I am in,' said Alfric, somewhat vexed that this blowsy publican should name him 'Ally' in public.

Izdarbolskobidarbix was the name he preferred. Failing that, Mister Danbrog. Or, as a minimum courtesy, Alfric. He had told Ms Blaume as much on many occasions; but she was immune to lectures.

'Do you drink?' said Blaume, speaking not to Alfric but to the orks.

'Beer,' said Cod.

A wide-eyed Morgenstern said nothing, but looked in askance at the roistering room where drunks sat in each other's laps or lay on the floor, hammered artificial flatulence from empty wine skins, and made popcorn in a huge wok perched atop a charcoal brazier. A drunk tossed a handful of popcorn skywards. A velvety green vogel swooped from the rafters and snapped one nipplebit nicely. Then it settled on Morgenstern's head. The ork clawed at it in a frenzy.

'Skaps,' said Blaume, sharply.

The vogel launched itself into the air, circled thrice,

then hooked itself on to a smokey rafter and chittered with malicious laughter. The vogel is the parrot-bad of Wen Endex, a creature noted more for misbehaviour than for speech.

'She'll have a beer too,' said Cod, putting his arm around a much-shaken Morgenstern.

'He,' said Alfric, by way of correction.

(Did orks have their own native tongue in addition to Toxteth? Or did they, like the ogres of the Qinjoks, acquire that language with their mothers' milk? A question worth pursuing, but not now.)

'Hello Anna,' said Alfric, as beers for all were served.

'Hello,' said she. 'Good to see you again.'

Then Anna Blaume broke off to talk to her child, little Ben Zvanzig (son of Sin Zvanzig), who was crying.

'There now,' said Blaume, giving him a tea-towel. 'Dry your pepper-weepers and don't be poorly.'

'But it bit me,' sobbed Ben.

'Well, that's what they do, my dear,' said Blaume. 'Any time you try to strangle them, at any rate. Sheila, my love. Taken Ben upstairs and put him to bed.'

Whereupon little Ben Zvanzig was led away by Anna Blaume's girl child, a slip of a thing who was aged eleven. (And who was her father, then? That must remain one of the smaller but nevertheless insoluble mysteries of the universe, for even Anna Blaume herself had not the slightest idea.)

'Well, Ally,' said Blaume. 'What have you got for me, apart from trouble?'

'This,' said Alfric, pulling a saladin ring from his pocket.

This had cost him nothing, for it was a gift from the ogre king. (Strange, that it had not been converted to

44

treefall rubbish like the rest of the Qinjok tribute – but perhaps Alfric's pocket was possessed of magical properties which protected its contents from the Curse of the Hag.) Though the gift had cost nothing, it was a handsome present even so; and Alfric experienced a certain amount of painful regret as Blaume took it from him.

'That's lovely,' said she, and lent over the bar to kiss him.

'I'm glad you like it,' said Alfric, kissing back politely.

As he did so, he caught Blaume's smell, which was that of a well-greased frying pan; for Anna Blaume regularly rubbed her skin with lard to check the progress of a discomforting disease of the integumentary system.

'Will you marry me?' said Blaume.

'I've told you before,' said Alfric, 'I'm married already.'

'She's no good for you,' said Blaume. 'She's a bloodless thing bereft of passion.'

'But so am I,' said Alfric.

'So in combination you're naught but disaster,' said Blaume.

Then leant across the bar and kissed him again. But he was not tempted, not tonight; so he brushed her away.

Anna Blaume was a red; or, to put it more politely, a person of Ebrell Island descent. However, she had not the red hair so typical of that breed; instead, her hair was yellow. It was so filthy that its texture was that of coarse straw, and it was streaked with blue dye and green. Is it any wonder that Alfric was not attracted? What attracted him was the thought of a warm bed, a good long sleep without tree-roots ribbing into his back, and then work at the Bank. Ah yes, the Bank.

'So you're not in the mood,' said Anna Blaume.

'I'm not,' said Alfric. 'Not tonight.'

'But you came here for something. Not just to bring back the horses, I'll warrant.'

'You're right,' said Alfric.

'You want a favour, I suppose. Let me guess. You want me to quarter these orks.'

'If you would,' said Alfric.

'Of course I would,' said Blaume. 'I can't have you taking them home, can I? You might cook them – like you cooked the last lot.'

Anna Blaume laughed uproariously as a shocked and terrified Morgenstern clung to Cod for comfort.

'Never mind, love,' said Blaume, reaching out and patting Morgenstern on the arm. 'You won't get eaten here.'

'They'd better not,' said Alfric, with feeling. 'They're ambassadors. Ambassadors from the king of the Qinjoks.'

'Oh, ambassadors, are they?' said Blaume. 'You'd be an ambassador yourself, by the looks of it. An ambassador from the realms of the dead, if I be a judge. Time you were home and in your own bed, if you're not going to jump into mine.'

'I won't argue with that,' said Alfric.

Then Alfric Danbrog and Anna Blaume exchanged goodbye kisses, and Alfric started for home, leaving his orks in the care of the proprietor of the Green Cricket.

Of Alfric Danbrog's domestic relations, the less that is said the better, for the subject is a sorry one. However, some comment must necessarily be made.

There was trouble when Alfric reached home. First, because his thoughts were all for the various despatches from the Bank which awaited his arrival. Second, because he had brought his wife no present from the Qinjoks. Third, because he answered her welcoming kiss in the most perfunctory manner. Fourth, because he supped her hot soup hastily, reading a despatch from the Bank as he did so; his lack of appreciation being so great that he quite failed to realize that this was the very seaweed soup he had lusted for as he drew near the Stanch Gates.

Is it any wonder that a quarrel shortly ensued?

The quarrel became a raging row. And, in a moment of blind anger, Alfric lashed out and caught his wife with a four-knuckle punch which laid her out on the floor. He tried to apologize, but that did him no good and her less; and when at last they retired to bed, she made her body a flesh-clothed skeleton, and rejected his every advance.

Not that he advanced too strenuously, for he was weary, and his greatest lust was for sleep.

CHAPTER FOUR

Early the next night, Alfric Danbrog woke from sleep, took his breakfast, then set forth for the Bank. As he tramped through the backways of Galsh Ebrek, making for the slopes of Mobius Kolb, he was armed as if for war, and with some reason. Galsh Ebrek by night was not the safest of places, as anyone could have guessed by listening to the brawl-bawdy uproar of the taverns, or by inspecting the massive iron bars with which the merchants of that city habitually invest their windows.

As Alfric went down Tupping Way, the door of a lushery was thrown open. A drunken lantern lurched, sagged and went down as a drunk collapsed in the mud. The hapless inebriate lay there, doomed to become the prey of mutchers unless rescued by a selfless citizen. Alfric, lacking the time to be such a citizen, pressed on regardless, leaving the drunk to his doom.

Alfric reached the foot of Mobius Kolb unscathed and began to ascend that huge upthrust of rock. He passed beneath the monstrous battlements of Saxo Pall then laboured upward toward the granite outworks of the Bank. At the gates of the Bank he paused. Higher yet, on the utmost summit of Mobius Kolb, the Oracle of Ob shone moon-bright. As always, Alfric found it disturbing to look upon that alluring light by night. As always, he was tempted to ascend, to close with that light and confront.

As ever before, Alfric resisted the temptation, turned from Ob and went in through the gates of the Bank.

'Your pass, sir,' said a sentry.

An unavoidable formality, even though sentry and banker knew each other by sight, and had done so for years. Bank security was second to none, and for good reason. Yielding to the dictates of that security, Alfric pulled out his pass and unfolded it. This document identified him as Izdarbolskobidarbix, Banker Third Class, his affiliation being with the Flesh Traders' Financial Association. His details were there given in a dozen different languages; and, on the back, there were both his palm-prints and his footprints.

'Welcome, Iz-bix,' said the sentry, handing back the pass.

'My greetings to the greeter,' said Alfric formally, then passed within.

As always, Alfric was tempted to chastise the sentry for abbreviating his name. Izdarbolskobidarbix was no idle monicker but a very formal name which should not be idly perverted by wageslave minions. He would let it pass for now. But once he made Banker Second Class, then things would change!

In the vestibule, Alfric divested himself of boots, leathers and weaponry, donned silken robes and slipped his feet into warm felt slippers. He was entering another world. He was leaving Galsh Ebrek, city of clumsy warriors addicted to dreams of beserker blood; and he was entering upon the organized sanity of the Bank where click-clacking abaci measured the constant increase of power and of influence.

Once changed, Alfric set forth for his office. To his surprise, in the lantern-lit corridors he passed Justina

Thrug, who gave him a casual nod as she went by with her escorts.

Banker Eg was waiting in Alfric's office.

'Good morning,' said Eg.

Of course it was night. Still, it was the beginning of their working day, so a 'good morning' was not entirely illogical. Besides, Eg was speaking Toxteth; and that coarse and violent language is robust enough to survive a great deal of abuse and misuse.

'Good morning,' said Alfric, taking off his spectacles and polishing them with a clean white cotton handkerchief. 'I just passed Justina Thrug in the corridor. What's she doing here?'

'I believe she came in for a loan,' said Eg.

'A loan!' said Alfric. 'Against what surety?'

'I said she came for a loan,' said Eg. 'Not that she was granted one.'

As everyone knew, Justina was the daughter of Lonstantine Thrug, a knight who had emigrated with his family to foreign parts. The entire family had died or disappeared in a series of overseas disasters; whereafter Justina had returned to Wen Endex, alone and penniless. (And almost toothless, for she was well past the first bloom of youth, and had abused her dentition in tropical climes by an over-use of sugarcane.)

'Well,' said Alfric, rummaging through his in-tray, 'I hope she doesn't get a loan. Or, if she does, that I don't have to enforce its collection.'

'Don't worry,' said Eg. 'You're not likely to. I hear a whisper that you're in line for promotion.'

'Perhaps,' said Alfric casually. He had heard that whisper too. 'But then, we're all in line for promotion. Eventually.'

'Some of us,' said Eg, 'are getting a little too old.' Eg was speaking of himself. 'Anyway,' he said, 'that's not what I'm here to talk about. I've got a message for you, from Xzu.'

'Xzu?' said Alfric in surprise. 'Does he want to see me?'

'No,' said Eg. 'He wants you to see your father.'

'My father?' said Alfric. 'What's happened to him? Is he in jail?'

'No,' said Eg. 'What on earth made you think he might be?'

'If he's not in jail,' said Alfric, ignoring Eg's question, 'then what? In debt, is it? How much has he borrowed from us?'

'Nothing,' said Eg. 'Or nothing I know of. You're to see him, that's all.'

'Tomorrow night, then,' said Alfric decisively. 'And then only if I can chop through this paperwork. Oh, and my report. On the Qinjoks. I've got to write a report.'

'No,' said Eg. 'This takes precedence.'

'What does?' said Alfric.

'Your visit to your father.'

'Joking aside,' said Alfric, 'this report's important. The ogre king has sent ambassadors to Galsh Ebrek.'

'Ambassadors!'

'Yes. So my report—'

'Xzu was very clear,' said Eg. 'You're to see your father. Straight away. No matter what. Those were his orders.'

'Are you serious?' said Alfric, in something close to amazement.

'I am,' said Eg.

'Well,' said Alfric, dubiously, 'if that's so, I don't have

51

time to draft out a report. So I'll have to see Xzu right now to give him a verbal accounting. About the ambassadors, I mean.'

'You can't do that,' said Eg.

'Why?'

'Because,' said Eg, 'Xzu is Elsewhere.'

'Oh,' said Alfric.

Then said no more. For the inhibitions ran deep, and he found it difficult to talk about visits Elsewhere even when he was in the company of a fellow banker.

'I tell you what,' said Eg, 'why don't you give me a verbal report and I'll précis the same to Xzu when he's back.'

'Oh, all right,' said Alfric. 'The ambassadors, well, they're a couple of orks and—'

'Orks?' said Eg, it being his turn to be amazed.

'Yes,' said Alfric. 'Orks, orks. Don't look at me like that. It wasn't my idea! Anyway—'

Alfric gave Banker Eg the gist of the matter for ontelling to Comptroller Xzu. Then, reluctantly, Alfric left his office, retreated to the vestibule, changed back into his boots and battle-gear, and set off for his father's home. He went on foot, for there was no road for horses, not where he was going.

After Grendel Danbrog had been formally banished from Galsh Ebrek, he had settled in a house which stood atop a crag uplofted above some woodlands a full league from the city. Alfric was all mud, muck and sweat by the time he reached his father's dwelling place, for much of the going was boggy, and the uphill labour needed to ascend the crag was heavy work in his furs.

Though She was said to be on the loose, Grendel's house stood in little danger of attack by Herself. For no man or monster would choose to assail Grendel Danbrog, warrior amongst warriors. The house backed on to the rocks which formed the upmost tooth of the crag. It was approached by a narrow path which zag-zigged upwards through overgrowths of evergreen thorns. A deep ditch filled with such vegetative teeth guarded the final approach to the house, a single creaking plank providing a somewhat perilous crossing.

Alfric crossed.

Knocked on the door.

'It's open!'

His mother's voice.

Alfric shouldered the heavy door ajar and went in. His father was nowhere to be seen, but his mother was working by the whimpling flaze of a single candle flame. He entered, taking care where he put his feet, for the floor was rotten. The place smelt as if something else was rotten as well, but the smell was merely that of Alfric's parents, unwashed since the day they were born.

'Shut the door,' said Gertrude.

Alfric obeyed, and the flame steadied.

'What you doing?' said Alfric.

'What does it look like?' said his mother.

Gertrude Danbrog was a heavy woman, a woman no longer in possession of even the last rags of her beauty. She was busy making a casserole. As Alfric watched, she took an onion, cut free its roughish root, skinned it, chopped it, then tossed it into a fire-blackened pot. Then she took the corpses of a couple of small animals. Rabbits? No, they were ferrets. Deft was her hand as she skinned these beasts, whistling tonelessly all the while.

'May I sit down?' said Alfric.

'No,' said Gertrude.

53

Alfric was not surprised. This was more or less the unwelcome he had expected.

'Where's my father, then?' he said.

'In the barn.'

'What barn? You haven't got a barn.'

'We have now. Built it last moon. Down by the Yarn Pool. That's where he is. Off you go now.'

Alfric was not minded to stay, for already he had endured the stench of that dwelling for as long as he could. So off he went, down to the Yarn Pool, where he found a new barn standing. It was built of logs. Had his father a tree-cutting permit, then? Probably not. Grendel Danbrog lived for the most part in defiance of the law, for none would dare bring complaint against him without the most grievous of reasons.

When he neared the Yarn Pool, Alfric stopped. Could he see the barn? He could. And also: something else. Something sitting on a sharpened stake. The head of an animal. What? A goat. The sight made Alfric hesitate. Grendel had moods when it was better to avoid him: perhaps this was one of them. But the night was getting bitterly cold, and his sweat had cooled to chill; the wind hissed and fluthered, savaged and swept, and the thought of the barn's comfort was positively appealing.

So Alfric opened a side door and went in.

Inside, voices drowned the suthering without. For here was a gathering of Yudonic Knights, several of whom were competing in story-telling. At Alfric's entry, they broke off and saluted his arrival.

'Here's Alfric!'

'Alfric, my boy. Come sit beside me.'

Then there was much handshaking and back-slapping, all of which was somewhat to the bewilderment of Alfric

Danbrog. For, even though he was personally acquainted with most of these men, he scarcely counted himself the friend of any; and never before had he received any especial mark of their favour.

Once the boisterous greetings were done with, the Yudonic Knights went on with their stories, their heroic saga-tellings. One told of a dragon vomiting fiery gobbets as it rushed upon a hapless hero, lashing the air with roars of wrath; and, naturally, in this telling of the tale the hero triumphed, for all that he was armed with nothing more than a letter opener.

Many such stories the knights retailed. Of dragon and basilisk, of bills and byrnies, of blood and decapitations. And, though they were amateurs, they brought to their tales all the professional enthusiasm with which a scop bards any account of murder and mayhem.

At last, Grendel called a halt.

'Enough of talk and tales,' said Grendel. 'Let's get down to business.'

Business? What was he talking about? Something to do with the Bank? Were these ruthless marauders after loans for something? If so, they'd probably be out of luck.

'Alfric,' said Grendel. 'Step forth so all can see you.'

Alfric did so.

'Behold,' said Grendel. 'My son.'

One Knight leaned close and removed Alfric's spectacles. The banker felt a momentary panic as these so-essential instruments were removed, for his nearest spare pair was back in Galsh Ebrek. With the spectacles gone, Alfric's world disintegrated into a blurred collage of colours, each sharp-featured face collapsing into a porridge of flesh.

'So this is the son,' said the Knight. 'I could tear it limb from limb without blinking.'

'If you feel that a profitable way to spend your night,' said Alfric coolly, 'then feel free.'

The Knight laughed, then peered closely at Alfric's eyes, and was satisfied with what he saw.

'They're not red,' said he. 'Not red at all.'

With that, the Knight replaced the spectacles. As he was slightly drunk, he jammed them on, hurting the already reddened skin-patch on the bridge of Alfric's nose. The lenses were blurred, smeared, greasefingered; but Alfric, though angry at this malhandling of his property, realized a well-meaning ignorance was to blame.

Usually, he would have taken off the spectacles immediately to remedy the damage. But here he did no such thing, for he was on display. So he put his hand to the hilt of his sword and said:

'No red you see because none there is to sight.'

With Alfric's normality thus vouched for, the joviality of the gathering increased markedly. Soon, everyone was in a mood for a story, so Grendel Danbrog began upon a tale.

Grendel told of the Wormlord's father, and how that man had marched against Her son with a company of Knights. When father and companions failed to return from their expedition, nobody in Galsh Ebrek had been willing to follow in their footsteps. Nobody except Tromso Stavenger. Daring much, he had tracked through the wilds until he came to a gorge where his father and companions had been ambushed.

A terrible doom had come upon them in this narrow place. Here lay weapons barbed with blood, killing-irons of surpassing strength which had not availed against the fury which had fallen upon the Knights. Torn were the mailcoats and hewed the helmets. A shield lay in fragments; it had burst asunder, one piece driving deep into the heart of an oak.

And the dead!

The condition of the dead is best left undescribed, but Grendel described them regardless.

'That was what the Wormlord found. Then he knew his father had fallen victim to Her son. The monster had struck, destroying all. Other mortals would have fled in despair, but the Wormlord did not. Instead, he vowed to seek out Her son, to meet him in combat and tear him asunder. This he did.'

At that, the side door opened; and, as if on cue, the Wormlord entered. A great silence descended upon the Yudonic Knights. Their king looked them over, then spoke.

'Grendel,' said Tromso Stavenger. 'Which is Alfric?'

'This one, my lord,' said Grendel, pointing at Alfric.

The Wormlord advanced upon his grandson.

'So this is Alfric,' said Stavenger.

'It is,' said Grendel.

'A good-looking boy,' said the Wormlord.

Other compliments and queries followed, and all in all a great pretence of a family reunion was made. Alfric participated in this microdrama without knowing why it was being staged. Though the world might not know it, Alfric was no stranger to his grandfather; for the Banker Third Class had sometimes had occasion to discuss Bank business with the Wormlord, and more than once the two had taken wine together in private quarters. A little reflection convinced Alfric that this play-acting was being done for the benefit of the assembled Yudonic Knights.

'A good-looking boy, as I said before,' said Stavenger. 'A child of a Family. A good match for any girl. But I hear he's married, though. A commoner. Why so, boy?'

'I work for the Bank,' said Alfric. 'It is Bank policy that one must marry. To do otherwise is to invite either the perils of debauchery or those of neurosis.'

'Neurosis?' said Stavenger, genuinely puzzled. 'What be this neurosis?'

'An obscure foreign ailment in which the Bank believes though I do not,' said Alfric. 'Still, married I am, and lamenting the matter will not change it.' He sought for a way to change the subject and found one: 'But come, my lord. Enough talk of myself. Let's have a toast, a toast to yourself if I may be so bold. Then a toast to us all, if this barn can boast of a drink for your indulgence.'

A tankard was produced for the Wormlord, who joined in the second of Alfric's toasts – but cautiously, for he was too frail to countenance intemperate indulgence.

Tromso Stavenger still wore his horned helmet, as was his invariable custom. The helmet was of ancient iron, stained by weather and use. The Wormlord himself was nearly as ancient, though he hid it well. Before he moved, gestured or spoke, it was his custom to pause to gather the necessary energy needed to pursue his purpose with heroic amplitude. By such habitual recourse he gave a good (albeit spasmodic) imitation of a warrior in the years of his strength.

But age, age, age was writ everywhere in the Wormlord's lineage. Was written so clearly that even the illiterate could see it. The little hair that tweaked out from beneath his iron skullcap was grey, as was his shapeless beard. Likewise grey was his moustache, which curved down around his mouth in twin horns which mirror-echoed those of his helmet. One eye was opaque, a white cloud, useless. And everywhere his skin was furrowed and rucked, folded and buckled and mottled with liver spots, those manifestations of age which an obscure poet of Wen Endex has described as 'leaves of the bodyweather's autumn'.

A little liquor served (though cautiously imbibed) to loosen the Wormlord's tongue, and soon he was persuaded to tell of his hunt for Her son and the killing which followed their encounter.

'Is it true about the blood?' said Grendel, still happy to hear the details though he had heard them all a thousand times before.

'It is,' said Stavenger. 'When I cleansed the gore from the noble iron, each splotch of blood burnt purple in the night as it dripped to the ground. As home I rode, a storm came up. Clouds swept the moon from the sky. Grey were those clouds, grey and writhing, a flood of wrath which consumed the heavens and then unleashed a ruthless fury of windstorm rain.'

Strongly spoke the Wormlord, and great was the enthusiasm with which the assembled Knights attended to his words. Still, Alfric thought this woodland barn to be no place for the old man, who was fit for little more than to spend his evenings deciphering his hearthfire's labyrinth. To make him act as hero-king was farcical, and a cruel farce at that.

After much tale-telling, the Wormlord at last began to say his goodbyes. He worked his way round to Alfric.

'Tell me, boy,' said Tromso Stavenger, gripping Alfric by the shoulder. 'What do you want to make of yourself?'

'What I can,' answered Alfric.

'Well said,' said the Wormlord with a nod.

Then he departed, going out into the night alone. A reckless thing to do, surely; but he was still fearless for all that he was old; and, if She were to fall upon him in the dark, he would accept that ending without complaint.

After that, the meeting began to break up, the Yudonic Knights dispersing in twos and threes. At last, Alfric was left alone with his father.

Grendel Danbrog looked upon his son, then belched prodigiously.

'Ah,' said Grendel, slapping himself twice on the gut, 'that feels better. Well, my son, how did you enjoy your evening?'

'It was passable,' said Alfric, still mystified as to why he had been summoned here.

Something was going on, obviously.

But what?

'Passable?' said Grendel. 'Is that all you've got to say? The Wormlord met you. Is that not a great honour?'

'I'm no stranger to my grandfather,' said Alfric.

'Oh, you've met him privily, that I know. Wasn't I at the first of those meetings? Of course I was. But for him to acknowledge you in the presence of the most trusted of his Knights, ah, that's something else again. It holds great promise for the future.'

'Doubtless,' said Alfric, by way of politeness. 'However, the present also has its demands. If you'll excuse me, I must be getting back to Galsh Ebrek.'

'No,' said Grendel. 'You're staying here the night. On tomorrow's night, we go together to Saxo Pall.'

'Together?' said Alfric. 'Whatever for?'

'You'll find out when we get there,' said Grendel.

'Look,' said Alfric, starting to get angry. 'I don't know what you're playing at, but you have to realize I've got responsibilities. I've got a busy schedule. My in-tray is bulging, my—'

'Enough,' said Grendel, silencing him with a gesture. Then he reached into a small pocket originally designed to hold a miniature whetstone, pulled out a grubby piece of paper, unfolded it and handed it to Alfric, saying: 'Read this.'

The letter, which was of recent date, was signed by Comptroller Xzu of the Flesh Traders' Financial Association. It commanded Alfric, in the name of the Bank, to obey his father and do whatever his father commanded.

Alfric was bewildered to receive such a letter, but knew he had best do what it said.

'But,' said Alfric, 'what's it all about? What's going on?'

'Peace,' said Grendel. 'Wait. And tomorrow night, you will know. Oh yes. Then you'll know all.'

And with that, Alfric had to be content.

CHAPTER FIVE

On the next night, father and son went to Galsh Ebrek, climbed the slopes of Mobius Kolb and dared themselves to the gates of Tromso Stavenger's castle.

Alfric was most unhappy at entering Saxo Pall. He had often ventured to the Wormlord's stronghold on Bank business. Nevertheless, that did nothing to alter the fact that he was technically liable to instant execution every time he intruded upon the royal castle.

When Grendel had been accused of bearing a lycanthropic taint, Tromso Stavenger had exiled him from Galsh Ebrek with these words:

'You are to leave this city immediately, never to return. Furthermore, you, and your sons, and the sons of your sons unto the fifth generation, will not set foot in Saxo Pall. On pain of death.'

Thereafter, Grendel had abjured the family name. On marrying a female of the Danbrog family, he had taken to himself the name of that clan. Thus Alfric, Grendel's eldest son, styled himself Alfric Danbrog.

But for the unsubstantiated allegations of lycanthropy, Grendel would have been in line to inherit the throne of Wen Endex, and his eldest son likewise. What would it have been like to be a prince of the royal blood, heir apparent to the kingdom of Wen Endex and all its powers? Alfric thought about that, sometimes. Oh yes. Little as he liked to admit it, he thought about it.

When father and son had been admitted into the forbidden stronghold, Guignol Grangalet was summoned. The Wormlord's Chief of Protocol hastened to meet these most unwelcome guests.

'What are you doing here?' said Grangalet, when he saw Grendel.

'I'm here to see my father,' said Grendel. 'Show me to the old monster.'

Heated words then followed between Guignol Grangalet and Grendel Danbrog. But at length the Chief of Protocol yielded to the will of the Wormlord's son.

'I'll take you to see him,' said Guignol Grangalet. 'But only you. Your son must wait as a hostage.'

'You're not putting him in a cage,' said Grendel harshly.

'Perish the thought!' said the Chief of Protocol. 'Your son can wait in the Hall of Shields.'

And Alfric shortly found himself alone and abandoned in that place of spiderweb draughts and guttering lanterns.

A great many death-branded shields were hung on the walls of this hall, for the honour of all the Ruling Families of Wen Endex was here represented. One shield displayed a decapitated head, its hair held by a grasping hand with blood-red talons. Other themes? A rain of blood. A sea of blood. A bloody wound. A pyramid of skulls, fountains of blood spurting from the eyesockets of each. A heap of amputated hands. And many more in a similar vein.

While Alfric was renewing his acquaintance with the culture of the Yudonic Knights, someone came up behind him unheard. He almost leapt out of his skin when he heard a bright and cheery voice say:

63

'Hello.'

Alfric turned. The man who had stalked unheard to well within killing distance was Nappy, a huffy-puffy individual of slightly less than average height. Nappy was pink of face and bald of pate, and could often be seen hustling about Galsh Ebrek, looking slightly comical thanks to his pigeon-toed gait. He was renowned for his sweet temper, for the jolly delight he took in all innocent pleasures, and for his work as a committee man. Nappy was famous in charity circles, and was known to be happiest at festivals when he could transmogrify himself into Mister Cornucopia, and dispense sweets for the children and kisses for blushing virgins.

'I'm so glad to see you, Mister Danbrog,' said Nappy, extending his hand.

Alfric took it and pumped it. Nappy's hand was soft and damp. A clinging, friendly hand.

'We haven't seen you here for ever so long,' said Nappy. 'I'm so, so, so very glad to see you.'

The sincerity of these effusions could not be doubted. That was Nappy all over. He was acknowledged as the happiest, friendliest person in Wen Endex. Which made no difference to the facts of the matter. Nappy was what he was and he did what he did, and there was no getting round that.

'Sorry I can't stay to chat,' said Nappy. Shifting on his feet in that fluidly furtive manner which was his trademark. 'But I must be going now.'

And already Nappy was sliding, sidestepping, nimbling past Alfric's defences. Alfric thought him shifting right, but he was gone to the left, sliding past and—

And—

And?

Alfric wanted to scream.

Nappy was behind him.

And all Alfric could think was this:

—Just let it be quick, that's all, just let it be quick.

But it was not quick, it was slow stretching to forever, so at last Alfric cleared his throat as if to ask a question. Then found he could not speak. So he turned around. Nappy was gone. Alfric bareswept the hall with his eyes. Nothing. Nobody. Whereupon Alfric walked to the nearest window, opened the single shutter, leaned out as far as he could and, without further preamble, was efficiently sick.

Alfric's vomit slurped down the stones of the window's venting thickness, some sticking to the warding rock, some sliding at last to the open air, nightfalling to the rocks of Mobius Kolb. And Alfric found himself shuddering. His silken robe was wet against his back and his legs were weak; and still his stomach knotted and churned. He closed the shutter and began to walk up and down the Hall of Shields; and was still walking when Guignol Grangalet returned to collect him.

'You look like you've seen a ghost,' said the Wormlord's Chief of Protocol.

'No,' said Alfric. 'No, not a ghost.'

'What, then?'

'Nothing,' said Alfric, who very much wanted to forget. 'I think I must have eaten something that disagreed with me, that's all.'

And Alfric made no further comment on his recent trauma as Guignol Grangalet led him to the throne-room, which was much-crowded with a great many Yudonic Knights.

'Stand here,' said Grangalet, placing Alfric not far from the throne.

Close by were the Norn brothers: Pig, Wu and Ciranoush Zaxilian. To minimize the chances of trouble starting, Alfric studiously avoided eye contact, and concentrated on his grandfather. On his throne sat Tromso Stavenger, Wormlord of Wen Endex. At his feet his twenty-seventh wife, the delectable Lilian. This pretty little thing, who was but thirteen years of age, was playing with a golden bangle. Sitting on a chair to Stavenger's left was his daughter, Ursula Major.

Tromso Stavenger had fathered only two children. The eldest was Grendel, accused of lycanthropy and hence denied his inheritance and exiled from Galsh Ebrek. The younger was female, Ursula Major. Younger? Yes, she was much younger. For a full five lustra separated the birth of Ursula Major from the nativity of Grendel Danbrog; and Ursula was Alfric's coeval.

Since Ursula Major was the only one of the Wormlord's children who was fit to inherit the throne, she was next in line for kingly power. When Tromso Stavenger died, Ursula would rule Wen Endex. She was dressed for the role already, for she wore a glittering helm and carried a shield displaying a woman's wound armed with a great ferocity of razorblade teeth. A sword she had also; the result being that she looked for all the world like a shield maiden of legend. However, her accoutrements were not of iron. Rather, they were lightweight toys of beaten tin. And it was widely known in Galsh Ebrek that Ursula was unfit to rule, for she was more a clothes horse than a horse-mastering warrior.

Ursula Major was technically a very beautiful woman, a blonde with well-defined mammary glands, luxurious curves and lips to match. But on this occasion she looked distinctly sour. Why?

And why was there a second chair to Ursula's left? That chair was not unoccupied. Instead, the matronly Justina Thrug was seated on that chair. With, of all things, a pet owl seated on her shoulder. Alfric was intensely irritated. What was the Thrug-thing doing on a chair of such honour? He turned to ask Grangalet about it, and—

And Grangalet was gone, silently replaced by Nappy.

Alfric's stomach lurched and his gorge rose. He controlled himself. Just. But sweat bulged from his forehead and his kneejoints almost gave way beneath him.

'What a happy occasion,' said Nappy happily. 'How nice to have you back in your grandfather's hall.'

'Yes,' said Alfric. Then: 'What is that Thrug female doing sitting beside Ursula?'

'She is Ursula's advisor,' said Nappy. 'Hence it is her privilege to be so seated.'

'Oh,' said Alfric. Then: 'But—'

But he could say no more, for Guignol Grangalet was calling for silence.

Once the Yudonic Knights had settled to silence, the Wormlord began to speak.

'I have little to say,' he said. 'And that will be said quickly. As you know, She walks the land. It is because of Her that we gather here by night. As king, I have a duty to march forth against Herself. But as king, I also have need to see to the administration of Wen Endex.

'I am old. I know this. I am old, and near death. Long have I struggled against the infirmities of age, but the struggle availeth naught. In my early days, a wise man sold me the secret of immortal youth. He was a wise man indeed, for he prospered exceedingly.'

The Wormlord paused. Alfric suspected this was to give the assembly the chance to laugh. But nobody did so.

'Wise indeed,' repeated the Wormlord. 'For he grew rich while others died.'

Then he paused again. Now most of his auditors understood that a joke was being made, but they did not laugh. Instead, an embarrassed silence prevailed. It was not the done thing to laugh at a joke at the king's expense. Not even when the joke was made by the king himself.

'He grew rich,' said the Wormlord wearily, 'and I grew old. Now I am near death. It is no use pretending. I know myself to be mortal, and know that others know as much.

'Though I am old, death still holds its fears for me. This surprises me. In my youth, I thought fear of oblivion to be the exclusive property of the young, of those with so much to lose. Now I am old. My bones hurt, my teeth are gone, and of my bowels the less said the better. Still, I have something to lose – my life. Life is still life, even though one be the age one is.'

What age was that? Alfric did not know. Alfric was 33. His father, Grendel Danbrog, was 58. Which meant his grandfather was unlikely to be much younger than 72, and was more likely to be aged over 80.

The Wormlord continued:

'While fear of death still appals me, nevertheless I cannot hold to life much longer. Once I have found a suitable successor to the throne, I will march forth against Herself.'

Tromso Stavenger glanced sideways at a frozen-faced Ursula Major then said:

'My daughter is not a suitable successor. I have discussed this with her.'

Alfric could imagine the nature of that discussion.

'Ursula will naturally inherit the throne if I die before a suitable champion has proved himself better suited for that seat,' said the Wormlord. 'However, you all know I have the right to appoint such a champion to succeed me. Written law and the dictates of custom give me such a right. There are ample precedents.'

The Wormlord allowed himself some silence. Was this to give his words time to sink in? Or was he wearying from the effort of speaking? Alfric was inclined to think it was weariness which had compelled Stavenger to pause. Certainly the old man's voice was much stronger when he continued:

'The champion must be from one of the Families. That is my rule. The champion must perform three feats of courage. That is my rule. To be precise, the champion must recover the three saga swords and bring them here to me in Saxo Pall. Once this has been done, I will yield my throne to the champion, then march forth to do battle with Herself.

'You all know what the saga swords are. Likewise, you all know where these weapons are to be found, and what dread dangers will confront the questing hero who dares to seek their possession. I trust that I have no need to remind you of the special conditions attached to any quest against the dragon Qa.

'Well then. Do I have a volunteer?'

Did he?

No.

A great silence prevailed in the throneroom.

As Tromso Stavenger had rightly stated, all present

were familiar with the difficulties of questing for the three saga swords. Alfric, who had attended memorial services for some of the would-be heroes who had dared such quests, was far too sane even to think of volunteering his flesh for such lunacy.

But others must have been thinking on his behalf, for Grendel Danbrog spoke into the silence, saying:

'My son chooses to dare himself upon this quest.'

The strongspoken words echoed about the throneroom.

'Bravo,' murmured Nappy.

Alfric was about to protest, but Ciranoush Zaxilian Norn spoke first, saying:

'No minion of the moon can sit upon the Wormlord's throne.'

'I will vacate the throne in favour of the victor,' said Tromso Stavenger. 'Regardless of who the victor might be.'

By now, Alfric understood all. Tromso Stavenger had repented of the rage with which he had driven his son from his house. Now the Wormlord was going to make amends by allowing his grandson to claim the throne. Alfric looked from Grendel to Stavenger. Both were smiling upon him.

But—

The three quests were suicidal, and Alfric knew it. He knew too that the life of a Yudonic Knight was not for him. He had no taste for drinking, brawling and debauchery; and was reluctant to admit to any desire to rule over people addicted to such activities. So he spoke up strongly, saying:

'My father has nominated me as a questing hero, but I do not accept this nomination. I will have nothing to do with any such quest.'

Then Alfric turned on his heel and departed from the throneroom. Some of the Yudonic Knights spat on him as he passed, but he escaped from Saxo Pall with his life and liberty unimpaired.

At least for the moment.

CHAPTER SIX

When at last Alfric left the fastness of Saxo Pall and
began the descent of Mobius Kolb, he expected to make
his way back to Varnvelten Street, there to join his wife
in a meal and, later, in sexual congress.

But this was not to be.

For Alfric was still descending the slopes of Mobius
Kolb when he was intercepted by a messenger who
directed him to report to the Bank. This he did, though it
meant a weary trek up to the heights.

The light of the Oracle of Ob shone strange and strong
from the utmost peak of Mobius Kolb. Once again,
Alfric felt the lure of that light. He was glad to escape
inside, into the vestibule of the Bank, where once again
he made the change from boots and leathers to robes and
slippers.

To his surprise, Alfric was then directed to the office
of Comptroller Xzu, a Banker Second Class who was
responsible for Alfric's supervision. Many feared Xzu,
but Alfric did not. For he had something on Xzu; he
knew Xzu had accepted bribes in the past, and, what's
more, he could prove it. If the need arose.

On arrival at Xzu's office, Alfric received another
surprise; for the office sent him on to the Survey Room,
a hallowed chamber high in the Rock of Rocks, the
gaunt donjon which served the Flesh Traders' Financial
Association as its ultimate stronghold. Only the mightiest

managers of the Bank worked out of the Survey Room; and Alfric had never visited it before except to deliver messages.

To the Keeper of Secrets went Alfric Danbrog, ascending many weary stairs to reach the Survey Room. The habit of housing the high and the mighty in upper-storey rooms was neither practical nor desirable, but it was nearly unshakeable: even though it properly belonged to an earlier era when (this much the legends acknowledged, and more) dignitaries could be whisked to the heights by magical means or their mechanical equivalents.

At last Alfric reached the door guarding the final few stairs leading up to the Survey Room, negotiated his safe-passage with the guards who stood sentry there, then ascended to the utmost heights of the Keeper of Secrets and entered the Survey Room. This capacious office was lit by a full two dozen lanterns. It had four windows, each guarded by a single sheet of glass; but precious little could be seen of the world outside.

Comptroller Xzu offered his guest a little wine. Alfric sipped cautiously, tasting, testing. He calculated interest rates in his head, thus assuring himself that his mental faculties were not being subtlely impaired. Thus he had been taught by the Bank; for the Bank had dealings with people from many cultures, some of them renowned for the use of subtle and swift-acting poisons.

'While you're here,' said Xzu genially, 'you might care to admire the view.'

Alfric knew not whether his superior was drunk; or deluded; or was making a joke; or mistakenly thought the view to be of interest. Rather than try to puzzle out this conundrum, Alfric dutifully peered through the nearest window, which showed him mostly his own reflection. He looked closer, using his hands to screen out lantern light. He caught a glimpse of a malevolent red light flaring in the depths of his own eyes: and jerked away abruptly.

Had Xzu noticed his disconcertment? No. The Banker Second Class was engaged in pouring some more wine.

Xzu looked up.

'What did you see?' said he.

'Not much,' said Alfric, who felt under no compulsion to lie for the sake of politeness.

'Ah,' said Xzu. 'A pity. You should come here by day. It's a good view then. The bulk of Mobius Kolb stands between us and a perfect viewscape. Still, what we do see is remarkable.'

'One suspects the vista is truly worthy of admiration,' said Alfric cautiously. 'Yet the fragility of glass is surely not entirely compatible with the requirements of security.'

'This is,' said Xzu.

And rapped his knuckles against the window, then invited Alfric to do likewise, which he did.

'We bought these panes of glass three generations ago,' said Xzu. 'From the ogres of the Qinjoks, as it happens.'

'Truly?' said Alfric in wonderment. 'I did not know they had such skill.'

His opinion of the ogres was thus much enhanced, though this enhancement was spurious. In point of fact, the ogres had not made those windows: they had found them. Each window had once been the windshield of a Raflanderk IV All-Terrain Assault Vehicle, a product of a civilization long since destroyed and forgotten.

74

'What skills the ogres do or do not possess is a moot point,' said Xzu, who rightly suspected the miraculous windows to be a relic of antiquity. 'The point is,' said Xzu, 'the windows let us enjoy the view.' Then, a little pointedly: 'As it happens, I've often enjoyed the view.'

Only then, belatedly, did Alfric realize what Xzu was trying to tell him. Xzu was highlighting his long familiarity with the Survey Room. Xzu was making a power statement. Usually, Alfric would have picked up this subtlety immediately, without needing to have it hammered home. But renewed acquaintance with his father's world had temporarily lessened the enthusiasm with which he usually attended to the nuances of conversation.

It would be overstating the case to say that rebellion stirred in Alfric's heart. Still, on this occasion he found himself impatient with the posturing, the over-intricate manoeuvring and sidelong statements of oracular ambiguity which attended life within the Bank. For the first time in a long time, he found no delight in his own understanding of the shadings of suggestion and the implications of unstated comment.

'Our masters live well,' said Alfric.

This was a subtle statement in its own right; for Alfric was pointing out that there were powers in the Bank far greater than Xzu.

'So they do,' said Comptroller Xzu. 'Happily, for the moment I share their privileges, since I have been temporarily raised to the rank of Banker First Class. I am also temporarily without peers, since our Masters are Elsewhere.'

Alfric knew the meaning of this, and was not so indiscreet as to ask 'where'.

Instead, he sipped his wine and pretended to admire the view as Banker Xzu, temporarily a Master, continued the lengthy verbal preambles with which he was choosing to preface whatever business it was that he wished to conduct.

The Yudonic Knights of Wen Endex tend to see verbal intercourse as a form of rape, whereas the bankers view it more as an exercise of the arts of seduction. Hence, whereas the Knights will settle swiftly to the meat of a matter, the bankers are not so hasty. Rather, they choose to exercise their eloquence as if for its own sake. A procedure not without reason, for each Bank, by the nature of its Secret, is intimately connected with other great financial institutions in cultures greatly dissimilar from each other; which leads to the need for the diligent cultivation of delicacies of diplomacy, lest sensibilities be needlessly affronted when business is done.

At last Banker Xzu got to the point:

'Sometimes in this life one finds oneself progressing towards quite unforeseen goals. Do you not agree?'

'One would not lightly venture to disagree,' said Alfric cautiously.

'Furthermore, it is immature – is it not? – to be obsessionally addicted to a certain line of action. Surely flexibility is a mark of maturity.'

'It has been said that firm resolution is admirable,' said Alfric. 'Nevertheless, I take your point.'

Then, to Alfric's surprise, Banker Xzu produced a legal document some years old, and invited Alfric to read it. Of course he recognized it immediately. It was a treaty he had signed when he entered the Bank. The treaty committed Alfric to try (should the Bank so direct it) to win the throne of Wen Endex: but only if the

76

Wormlord should die or should be appearing to die.

Alfric had signed that treaty because at the time (how could he have been so naive?) he had genuinely believed Tromso Stavenger to be immortal.

'Interesting,' said Alfric, perusing the contract. 'Such a luxuriance of words speaks of great expense undertaken by lawyers and their clerks. It speaks of a serious investment in myself. An investment on the part of the Bank, I mean. Surely that investment was not meant as a preparation for death. Or is there some nuance in the multi-layered complexity of the present situation which I have missed? Is this contract being evoked to secure my death?'

'I have not said that the contract is being evoked at all,' said Banker Xzu gently.

'Then why show it to me?' said Alfric, with a flash of anger.

'To . . . to refresh your memory,' said Xzu. 'It does exist. It could be evoked. Should we choose. But we would prefer . . . we would prefer a volunteer.'

'You want me to volunteer, do you? To volunteer to quest for the saga swords. But why? If you want me dead, why choose such an elaborate method?'

'Alfric,' said Banker Xzu, 'we do not want you dead. We want you to succeed. To make yourself king. Were you to become Wormlord, there could be a very favourable alliance between the throne and the Bank.'

'But the quests are suicidal,' said Alfric. 'All three of them. Why, hundreds have been killed by the dragon alone.'

'Not so,' said Banker Xzu. 'The dragon has so far killed fewer than sixty people.'

'Fewer than sixty,' said Alfric. 'So I exaggerate, do I?

77

Many questing heroes have gone against the dragon. All have died. So you will grant, surely, a mortality rate of 100 per cent.'

'I grant it,' said Xzu. 'But you are not as others. Come, let us descend to the lower depths. The Bank has gathered together certain experts who, we believe, can instruct you in methods whereby you may attempt the quests with every hope of success.'

'That's as may be,' said Alfric, 'but I beg permission to go home before attending a meeting with any such experts. My wife will be worried if I don't come home soon.'

'Return you cannot,' said Xzu. 'You must stay here until it is time for you to go to the palace.'

'To go to the palace?'

'Yes. To go to the palace to formally nominate yourself as a questing hero.'

'You command,' said Alfric, 'so I must obey. Still, my wife will be worried.'

Actually, Alfric thought Viola could take care of herself; but he was nevertheless at pains to emphasize his concern, for the Bank placed a high value on marital stability, and Alfric knew the most casual comments sometimes find their way into a personal dossier.

'Never mind about your darling Viola,' said Xzu, in tones so soothing that Alfric momentarily wondered if the man was drunk. 'A messenger will be sent to tell her you are delayed, and why.'

'Is it wise for us thus to disclose our business?' said Alfric.

'Your wife will be . . . adequately informed,' said Xzu. 'Meantime, let us go and meet our experts.'

So Alfric Danbrog went and met with experts who had

been gathered together by the Bank. And much did Alfric learn about the fighting of dragons, the braving of giants and the habits of vampires. Then he presented himself to the Wormlord. In the presence of Tromso Stavenger and his ministers, in the presence of Ursula Major and a full fifty of the Yudonic Knights, Alfric Danbrog committed himself to a heroic quest, this quest being to recover the three swords of saga and bring them to Saxo Pall in proof of the performance of his courage.

'Well spoken,' said the Wormlord, once Alfric had said his piece. 'Usually, we would treat you to a congratulatory banquet before you set forth. However, on this occasion that is not appropriate.'

'Why not?' said Alfric.

'Because your courage is not certain,' said the Wormlord. 'You accept the quest now, but you refused it earlier. Ride forth, my boy. Kill the dragon and recover the first sword. Return with that blade and then we will grant you a banquet.'

'So you doubt my courage,' said Alfric.

'I do,' said Stavenger. 'You've something to prove, and prove it you must if you want to be king.'

'His humanity,' said one of the Yudonic Knights, interrupting unexpectedly. 'That's what he's got to prove.'

'Who speaks?' said the Wormlord.

'I do,' said Ciranoush Zaxilian Norn, muscling forward.

'What is your quarrel with Alfric Danbrog?' said the Wormlord coldly.

'My quarrel is simple,' said Ciranoush Zaxilian. 'The thing is not human. It is a shapechanger like its father. The father is a werewolf, and the son likewise.'

79

'Alfric,' said the Wormlord. 'Speak to this accusation.'

'I am not a werewolf,' said Alfric with dignity. 'I cannot be. It is known that no person tainted by lycanthropy can enter the Bank. Before entering that organization, I underwent medical tests which proved me free of any such taint.'

'You bribed the medical examiners,' said Ciranoush Zaxilian. 'Just as you bribed—'

'That's enough!' said the Wormlord.

Ciranoush Zaxilian fell silent.

'Soon,' said Tromso Stavenger, 'I will die. Whoever succeeds me will face grave dangers, for these are difficult times for Wen Endex. As you know, every year we recover a great tribute in jade from the Qinjoks. But each year the Curse of the Hag reduces this tribute to so much rubbish.'

So spoke the Wormlord, then paused for effect. Alfric guessed that the pause was inviting a laugh: but nobody dared express levity. So Stavenger continued:

'As you know, the lords of the Izdimir Empire are not happy to receive a box of old sticks and leaves as tribute. Long have they demanded jade, and every year their demands grow more strident. The Demon of Ang is not easily appeased, as you know. I fear that Wen Endex will soon have need of the leadership of a hero.'

Tromso Stavenger paused again. Nobody even thought of laughing. The Wormlord was talking of the possibility of war, outright war between Wen Endex and the Empire to which it nominally belonged. That was a thought which sobered even the fiercest of the assembled warriors.

The Wormlord went on:

'Our nation needs a hero as king. Whoever wins the

saga swords will prove himself a hero by such endeavour. If Alfric Danbrog can win those swords then he will be the hero the times demand. Ciranoush Norn speaks as if he would dispute the right of Alfric Danbrog to go questing.

'Very well then. I speak to you, Ciranoush Zaxilian Norn. I give you the right to quest for the three swords of saga if you so choose. If you wish it, I will restrain Alfric Danbrog while you try your chances against the dragon, the giant and the vampires. I will not release him from my grip until you have either succeeded or failed. Does that proposition appeal to you, Ciranoush Zaxilian Norn? Do you wish to seize this chance to make yourself a hero?'

Silence.

'Answer me,' said the Wormlord. 'Do you or do you not choose to quest for the three swords of saga?'

Now Ciranoush Zaxilian Norn was not a coward, not exactly; but he was a realist. Ciranoush did not expect Alfric to return alive from the first quest, for the dragon Qa was a most reliable consumer of questing heroes. And Ciranoush, should he attempt the first quest, would have no better chance of survival.

So . . .

'Answer!' said the Wormlord.

'I answer in the negative,' said Ciranoush.

'Then let it so be recorded,' said Tromso Stavenger grandly. 'Ciranoush Norn was offered the chance to be hero and king. He declined. But Alfric Danbrog accepted. Surely it is no accident that Alfric is my grandson.'

Then the Wormlord paused.

And the Yudonic Knights this time did what their king wanted them to do.

They cheered.

Meanwhile, a banker by the name of Eg was undertaking certain diplomatic initiatives at the behest of the Flesh Traders' Financial Association. Let it be said that Alfric Danbrog, Banker Third Class, was entirely unaware of these initiatives; and, furthermore, would not have approved of them had he known about them.

To be precise, Banker Eg was making his way to Varnvelten Street with malice in his mind. When he arrived at Alfric Danbrog's house, he knocked on the door. Viola Vanaleta admitted him, and they were soon deep in conversation. About Alfric.

'Let me not prevaricate,' said Eg. 'Rather, let me settle to business immediately. And let me be honest with you. It is said that a resilient conscience, a yielding conscience, is an asset in a Banker. But, despite the odium we have long endured, we are not all of us possessed of easily mutable ethics. Lies and distortions come not easily to all of us, least of all to me. So let me be truthful.'

'Is – is Alfric in trouble?' said Vanaleta.

'My sweet and delectable Viola!' said the Banker. 'Fear not for the valorous Danbrog.'

Whereupon Vanaleta, like a timid maiden who fears to be defrauded of her virginity, began to be apprehensive on her own account.

But, after many circumlocutions, Eg disabused her of the notion that she was intended as his prey. Instead, he came up with something much more shocking:

'What are you trying to tell me?' said Vanaleta.

'Alfric,' said Eg, 'has a chance to marry Ursula Major and so acquire the throne.'

'But – but he can't!' said Vanaleta. 'He's married to me.'

'I know,' said Eg gently.

'Besides, it – it's – it'd be incest.'

'Such things are commonplace in royal families,' said Banker Eg, 'personal sin often being preferred to the disintegration of the body politic. Alfric recognizes as much.'

'You – you mean he—'

'He demands,' said Eg, 'a divorce.'

CHAPTER SEVEN

Alfric was rigorously quarantined by the Bank until he rode forth on the first of his three quests. Therefore his darling wife Viola Vanaleta was not able to tax him about the divorce he was demanding; and, indeed, Alfric for his part presumed himself still happily married.

Such was the state of affairs as Alfric Danbrog, son of Grendel Danbrog and grandson of Tromso Stavenger, rode out through the Stanch Gates. He was fated north to the island of Thodrun, there to dare the sea dragon Qa, to kill that dreaded worm and remove the revenant's claw from the monster's barrow.

Alfric was not entirely happy with this mission, for, quite apart from the dangers that were involved, the idea of being renowned for the murder of a famous bard did not exactly appeal to him. Qa was such a bard, a singer of songs, a praiser of kings, a recorder of heroes, a skop whose fame had once exceeded that of Greta Jalti himself.

It happened that the sea dragon Qa had once dwelt in Galsh Ebrek, there winning great fame as a poet. But tastes change.

Here the tastes in question are not those of the audience but of the artist. Long had Galsh Ebrek rejoiced in sagas of butcher-sword brutality; and the appetite for such epics remained constant. But Qa, at first a willing appeaser of such tastes, had at last grown bored with the composition of such bloodclot confectionery.

The dragon's ennui had first been displayed at a formal banquet at which, in place of the usual paean of praise to some head-hacking reaver, the poet had recited a narrative poem dealing with the lethal outcome of a drinking competition. Qa had expended some five thousand lines of *terza rima* on this theme. It had proved an acceptable novelty. Thereafter, the dragon had amused himself for the better part of a year by much droll doggerelizing on beer drinking competitions and brothel performances; and the Yudonic Knights had come to think of him as quite the best of their poets.

After all, other bards yet retained an interest in organized phlebotomy, and so were happy to compose stanzas about blood-drenched heroes and sword-slaughter armies. So Qa's diversions into other areas of chivalric culture were tolerated and, for the most part, actively welcomed.

But at last things went sour.

The dragon Qa wore out his interest in booze and brothels, and began to fancy himself as a mystic philosopher. Unfortunately this led him to compose verses of ever-increasing complexity and obscurity which were not at all to the taste of Galsh Ebrek. At one famous banquet, a good three-score Yudonic Knights displayed their scorn for philosophy by throwing things at their draconic skop: old bones, burnt boots, dollops of mud, sklogs of hardened manure and curses by the dozen.

In the days that followed, a much-mocked Qa became morose, then bad-tempered; then so forgot his manners as to begin to eat people. First the dragon had devoured a wood-cutter; then a couple of beggars; and after that a ferryman. Such peccadillos had been tolerated for a time, for the Yudonic Knights knew that artists are not as other people, and some allowance must be made for their occasional deviation from accepted standards of behaviour. Providing the people who were eaten were mere commoners, nobody was going to get too upset about it. (Except the friends and relations of such commoners – but they, they didn't really count.)

However, on one fine night in high summer, the dragon Qa had got more than a little drunk and had eaten of the flesh of the Wormlord's latest wife, a child no more than eleven years of age. Then Qa had fled – knowing that he had gone too far. Such was the wrath of the ruler of Saxo Pall that he had ordered a dozen of his knights to do a critical demolition job upon the reckless firedrake. Armed with swords, those heroes had set forth in hot pursuit. But Qa had ambushed them in a gully much overgrown with trees. These the dragon had set alight, and all the marauding Knights had been burnt alive.

Out of vanity, Qa had attempted to eat the lot. But biological limitations had defeated wilful gluttony, so in the end the dragon had been forced to leave a few bones and much-crunched skulls for the heroes' heirs and assigns to bury. However, while some such physical fragments had been left, the bloated and unrepentant sea dragon had made off with the ironsword Edda; the loss of which had been ever afterwards lamented in Galsh Ebrek.

For some time, nothing had been heard of the dragon; until at length it was learnt that Qa had taken up residence on Island Thodrun. Whereupon many heroes had been eager to close with the monster and exact revenge for the ghastly murders it had committed. But the Wormlord, declaring he could not afford to lose his Knights a dozen at a time, had ruled that none could quest against the dragon without royal permission. Anyone granted such permission must go alone, armed with only a sword.

Over the years, many of the brave and the beautiful had dared the attempt; and one and all had met with universal disaster.

In keeping with the Wormlord's law, the new champion rode forth alone with no bosom-comrades to stand by him in battle. Like those who had gone before him, Alfric Danbrog carried a sword. But he was confident of victory, for he was a Banker Third Class, and hence surely able to outwit a mere firedrake.

A full league short of Island Thodrun, Alfric left his horse in a grove of trees standing amidst the sand dunes. Anna Blaume would be most upset if her dearest Nodlums got eaten by a dragon; and, besides, Alfric wanted to preserve the beast in good health so it could carry a hearty load of dragon-treasure back to Galsh Ebrek.

'So long, horse,' said Alfric, giving the creature a perfunctory pat which was meant to be friendly.

Then the banker shouldered his pack, which was very heavy, and set forth along the beach, striding out to warm himself, for the night was bitterly cold. Though it was night, the bright beacon of Thodrun gave him more than enough light to see by. Thodrun's beacon was ancient, as old perhaps as the Oracle of Ob; but no legends surrounded it. All presumed it had served the ancients as a seamark, and thus it was used in Alfric's day. It was a globe of cold fire which sat atop a skeletal pyramid of a metal immune to corrosion; and it lit all around with a light greater than that of a full moon.

White shone that light on the sands of the shore; and white alike it shone on the waves of the sea, the full tide seas which stretched between Thodrun and the shore. Having no boat, and lacking any inclination to swim the distance, Alfric must perforce wait for low tide. Which he did. He dumped his pack well above the surfswash, then walked backwards and forwards, trying to keep warm, kicking at discards of clam shells and gaunt fragilities of driftwood deep-mined by seaworm, eroded by sandscour and windwork, scorched by fire or otherwise shaped and channelled by the servants of time.

As Alfric waited for the tide to recede, a growing impatience possessed him. The Bank had taught him (too well, perhaps) that time is money; and Alfric was ever inclined to thriftiness. He tried to be economical by drilling himself in the Janjuladoola tongue. He was fluent enough in that language, as he had proved in encounters with Pran No Dree. But there was always room for improvement. And it was important to improve; for, once he won promotion, he would be dealing regularly with Obooloo, and a mastery of Janjuladoola was essential for success in such dealings.

Despite this incentive, Alfric found himself unable to concentrate on mental revision. Obooloo was remote, distant, a dream. What was real was the here and now: sand underboot and the nightwind on his face. Momentarily, he wished his father was here to see him playing the Yudonic Knight to the full. A credit to his family and his people!

Then such thoughts ceased, for—

Something was coming.

And Something commanded his attention to the full.

Something sparkled and sharkled in the sea-shifting turbulence. It was a dragon, and it was swimming. Alfric's first thought was:

—How small it is.

Small it was indeed, for it was no larger than his horse. A little smaller, if anything.

At first, he wondered if the dragon had seen him, for it swam back and forth as if for no particular purpose. Then he began to suspect it was showing off. Particularly when it started indulging itself in some body surfing.

Such surfing at length brought the dragon into the shallows. It then waddled out of the waves and started up the beach. It halted at a cautious distance from the Banker Third Class, then shook itself like a dog, scattering water in all directions. A few stray flecks splattered against Alfric's spectacles, much to his annoyance.

'Hello,' said the sea dragon Qa. 'Have you come to kill me?'

'I have,' said Alfric.

'Where's your horse, then?'

'Pardon?' said Alfric.

'I asked after your horse,' said Qa.

'I don't have one.'

'Oh, come on,' said Qa. 'You don't expect me to believe that. You're a Yudonic Knight. Of course you have a horse.'

'How do you know I'm a Yudonic Knight? How can you be sure? I could be a commoner.'

'Commoners don't go in for dragon hunting,' said Qa.

'There's always an exception to every rule,' said Alfric.

'Yes, but you're not one of them,' said Qa. 'You're Alfric Danbrog, son of Grendel Danbrog. You're here to kill me so you can rescue the ironsword Edda.'

'How do you know that?' said Alfric, startled.

'Oh, I have my sources,' said Qa, sounding immensely pleased with himself. 'Now where's your horse?'

'I told you I don't have one.'

'Don't be like that,' said Qa. 'Your horse is my legitimate perk.'

'Your perk?'

'My perk, yes. Or my pay, that's another way of putting it. That's all part of my contract.'

'Your contract?' said Alfric in mounting amazement.

'Yes. My contract with Saxo Pall. I get paid, you know. You don't think I'm in this for my health, do you? I'm guarding treasure. So I get paid just like any other guard.'

'Dragons,' said Alfric, 'hoard treasure because that is their nature. They're a breed of creature given to thieving because that's how they're born. Like magpies. They like the bright and the shiny.'

'Oh no,' said Qa, sounding greatly offended. 'You've got it all wrong. That's land dragons you're talking about, those great hulking brutes with much fire but no brains. Those are the ones who operate from instinct. But I'm a sea dragon, which means I'm at least the intellectual equal of every person in Wen Endex.'

'You still hoard treasure and kill questing heroes,' said Alfric, determined to win this debate.

'Yes, yes, but not because I have any natural inclination to do any such thing. I do it because I get paid. I'm on an annual salary with a bonus for every questing hero duly killed and eaten. As for the horses, those are a perk. A legitimate perk! So where's yours?'

'Wait a moment,' said Alfric. 'What do you mean, you're on a salary? Who's paying you?'

'Why, the Wormlord, of course,' said Qa. 'Who else would pay me?'

'But – but you're a – a – you're an enemy of the state. A marauding monster. An outlaw.'

'No,' said Qa. 'I'm a royal dragon. It increases the Wormlord's prestige enormously to have me in Wen Endex.'

'You're talking the most absolute nonsense,' said Alfric, starting to get angry. 'The Wormlord doesn't league with renegade monsters. The very idea is – is—'

'Monstrous?' suggested Qa.

'Well, yes, monstrous.'

'Next thing you'll be saying I'm monstrous!' said Qa. 'Listen here, Danbrog. Haven't you learnt to think yet? How many men does it take to kill a dragon?'

'You're not immortal,' said Alfric.

'Blood of the Gloat!' said Qa. 'I invite it to think and all it does is threaten. It must be a Yudonic Knight, for all that it thinks itself a banker.'

'Today I'm a Yudonic Knight indeed,' said Alfric. 'Hence I come with my sword to kill you.'

'Why with a sword?' said Qa.

'Because that's what tradition decrees,' said Alfric.

'And why do you come alone?' said Qa. 'I suppose you're going to tell me that's traditional as well.'

'I can hardly tell you otherwise, because that's the truth,' said Alfric. 'Tradition is what tradition is.'

'And where does tradition come from, eh? Why don't men go hunting dragons with crossbows? Eh? Ask yourself that, Danbrog. A dozen men with crossbows and I'd have no hope at all. The Wormlord sends people solo with swords because he wants them dead.'

'That's absurd!' said Alfric.

'Is it?' said Qa. 'Think about it. It's a perfectly reasonable way for the king to get rid of dangerous young men with more ambition than sense.'

'Reasonable!' said Alfric.

'Oh yes,' said Qa. 'And merciful. I mean, they die with honour and all that. Better still, there's no feud between the king and the families of the deceased.'

Alfric's mind was positively boggling by now. But . . . what the dragon was saying made uncommonly good sense. And Alfric, thanks to his studies and experience with the Bank, knew all things are possible in politics. Weakly he asked:

'Do you think this arrangement is strictly ethical?'

'Ethical?' said Qa. 'Oh yes, it's ethical to ensure the orderly management of the affairs of state. Power is always challenged. You have to handle the challenges somehow.'

'There are other ways,' said Alfric.

'Of course there are,' said Qa. 'You could have democratic elections like the pirates of the Greaters.'

'Democratic elections?' said Alfric. 'What are you talking about?'

The sea dragon Qa explained.

'Oh,' said Alfric, 'now I know what you mean. Voting and all that. No, that'd never work in Wen Endex. The Knights would never stand for it. We'd have civil war. Besides, if we had one of these election things, the Wormlord might lose.'

'So he might,' said Qa. 'So he doesn't have elections. He has me, instead. I fulfil a very valuable social purpose. Consider. Someone threatens the Wormlord's throne. If he kills that person, he risks feud and social disorder. So he sends the challenger here, to be eaten. Result? Order, stability and enhanced social cohesion. Plus the surviving relatives of the deceased are enormously proud of their fallen son, nephew, father or brother, as the case may be. I give them their pride.'

The dragon Qa said this with great pride of his own. Alfric felt weak at the knees. Was it true? Could it be true? It certainly made a lot of sense. It explained a lot of things.

'Do you always tell people what's going on?' said Alfric, wondering how other questing heroes had reacted to the dragon's revelations.

'Oh no,' said Qa. 'Usually they're mostly grossly unmannerly. They don't have any time for talking at all. They come here drunk, you see. Most of them, at any rate. One or two have offered to share a drink with me, but unfortunately that's a no-no.'

'Why?' said Alfric.

'Because I'm an alcoholic,' said Qa sadly. 'Haven't had a drink for years, but I'm still an alcoholic. I can't fool myself, not now. Anyway, that's how it is. They come here drunk, haul out their swords and hack away. Straight into it! Don't even introduce themselves most of the time. Of course, I know who they are anyway.'

'Why?'

'I get told in advance, who's coming, and usually when. I was expecting you. They told me you'd be here by night. But why night? I didn't think to ask. But now I think of it, it's most unusual. They usually come by day, you know.'

'I walk the night because She walks the night also,' said Alfric.

93

'Oh,' said the sea dragon Qa, as if it didn't like the sound of that one little bit. 'She walks, does She? Well, nice chatting. I have to go now.'

And the dragon started to back off toward the surf.

'Go?' said Alfric. 'But we've business to conduct. Listen, I'm here to kill you, but it doesn't have to end that way. I've got a proposition.'

'Then bring it to me in the cave,' said Qa, the swash of dying surf washing around the rearmost of his four feet.

'The cave?' said Alfric, pursuing the dragon down the beach. 'Why can't we settle things here?'

'I can't kill people on the beach,' said Qa. 'That wouldn't be lawful. My charter's quite specific. All killings to be done on the island. In the cave, in fact.'

'Couldn't we make an exception?' said Alfric. 'Just this once. I mean, it's all the same to me whether I die here or on the island. And anyway, I'm not really expecting to die. Or to kill you. As I say, I've got a proposition.'

'That sounds very, very interesting,' said Qa. 'But I can't afford to violate the terms of my charter. One violation and it's all over, you see.'

Water broke and buckled about Alfric's ankles. It was cold, and flooded into his boots through flaws of which he had previously been unaware. Yet he did not retreat, for there was much he wanted to know. Instead, he demanded:

'Your charter?'

'My agreement with the Wormlord. Oh yes, I got a formal written agreement, you can be sure of that. Not that I keep it here. My solicitor has it safe in Galsh Ebrek.'

'Your solicitor!'

94

'That's right,' said Qa. 'Anyway, I'll see you in the cave.'

'I'm not swimming out to the island,' said Alfric.

'I'm not asking you to,' said Qa. 'The sea goes in and out twice a day. Tides, that's what it's called. Influence of the moon and all that. Oh, but you'd know about the moon. You being a werewolf and all that.'

'You called me a what?' said Alfric.

'A werewolf.'

'A werewolf!'

'Yes,' said Qa. 'Because that's what you are. Aren't you?'

'No!' said Alfric, hotly. 'I am not a werewolf. That's a base slander. A vile and gratuitous untruth. A rumour utterly without foundation. My father was smeared, that's what it was. I—'

'All right, all right,' said Qa. 'Sorry I spoke. Well, must be off now. Much swimming to do. Doctor's orders, you know.'

'Doctor's orders? You have a doctor as well as a solicitor?'

'Oh yes. Olaf Offorum. The Wormlord's personal physician. He sees to me as well. Comes here twice a year to check me out. Told me to do more swimming. Oh, and to eat more horsemeat as well. Where is your horse?'

'I haven't got one,' said Alfric.

'You mean you marched here all that way with that great big pack? I don't believe it. Not to worry, though. Mostly they bring their horses here, but when they don't I usually look in the forest.'

'The forest?'

'That's what I call it, but it's only a few trees really.

95

You know. Down the shore. About a league away. Anyway, that's all for now. See you later!'

With that, the dragon began to backtrack in earnest. A wave caught it, knocked it off balance and tumbled it up the beach. But on the second attempt the creature made it out into the surf. Alfric walked up the beach and sat down on his pack. His feet were cold and sodden, but he gave them little thought, for the sea dragon Qa had given him much else to think about.

The dragon's story rang true.

It was undeniable, for instance, that ambassadors from Ang were always enormously impressed by tales of the dragon's ferocity; and, come to think of it, by accounts of other dangers which existed in Wen Endex. It was something of a local tradition to brag of such hazards when speaking with an ambassador; and, for the first time, Alfric wondered whether that tradition was of spontaneous genesis, or whether the kings of Galsh Ebrek had carefully nurtured the custom.

Alfric Danbrog was starting to realize that there was much more to this business of kingship than met the eye. He had always thought the Wormlord did very little but sit on the throne: but obviously there was much more to learn.

Learn he would.

If he got to sit on that throne.

If he won all three saga swords.

If he secured Edda.

If he lived to see the morrow.

Alfric started to shiver, and not just because of the cold. He was starting to get nervous. He didn't like the sound of this dragon–king arrangement one little bit. It all sounded far too organized: very much like organized murder, in fact. So did the Wormlord really mean him to live? Or to die? Whatever the truth of the Wormlord's intentions, Alfric wished he could rush across the waters to Thodrun, forge his way into the cave and get it over with. Now.

But the tide was up.

So he would just have to wait.

Wait he did, until at last the skimmering skime of seawet sands stretched between Thodrun and the shore. Occasional waves still flirted across this sandstrand, but Alfric was not disposed to wait any longer. So he shouldered his pack and marched toward the island.

Up close to the rocks of Thodrun, the light from the island's beacon was so bright that colours could be seen in the rocks, which were wet with water and riven with streaks of quartz, splashed with the glitterdust of iron pyrites and stubbled with weird and inexplicable crystals of coppery hue.

Alfric did not pause to admire these colours.

First, because he was not in the mood.

Second, because he was knocked over by a wave.

Up from the depths of the sea it came, and swirled its way around the flanks of the island, stirring the seaweeds of the shore. Kelp and blubber weed gave themselves to its dance; mermaids' delight and seacow's greed joined the rhythms of its delight; and at last that energy-surge wrapped itself around Alfric Danbrog and swamped him entirely.

He was lucky to escape with his life.

However, he showed no gratitude for such luck; instead, he cursed most obscenely as he struggled up the island's rocks, still burdened with his pack, and dared himself into the dragon's lair.

'Who is it?' said Qa, as Alfric entered the cave.

'Myself,' said Alfric.

'Advance, myself, and be recognized.'

Alfric advanced, and stepped into a puddle, which proved to be waist-deep and exceedingly wet.

'Aha!' said Qa. 'The puddle-trap! You fell for it!'

'I have to admit I did,' said Alfric, struggling out of his pack.

'They usually do,' said the dragon complacently. 'If they've been particularly rude to me, I kill them then and there.'

'And if not?' said Alfric, throwing his pack well clear of the puddle.

'Then I give them a second chance,' said Qa.

'That's very sporting of you,' said Alfric, hauling himself out of the puddle.

'Oh yes,' said Qa. 'But it's in keeping with my status. I'm an honorary Yudonic Knight, you know.'

'That's nice,' said Alfric.

He was trying hard to remain polite, but this was a struggle; for, being exceedingly wet and very cold, Alfric had little time for dragonprattle. He looked around.

The cave was capacious, but not enormous. It was, in fact, not much bigger than the average haybarn. There was a solemn drip-drop of water, some of it falling from the roof, but rather more descending from Alfric himself. These drips splashed into puddles and stirred faint echoes from the living rock of the cave. There was not much sign of treasure. A few oddments here and there, yes, but no sign of the unlimited wealth of which legend had so generously rumoured.

Here and there were piles of skulls carefully assembled into pyramids. Skulls? Alfric looked more closely. They were skull-sized rocks. Strange.

'That's strange,' said Qa.

'You read minds?' said Alfric, startled.

'No,' said Qa. 'I use my eyes. That's how I saw.'

'Saw? Saw what?'

'The red light from yours. Your eyes, I mean.'

'You must be imagining things,' said Alfric; then slapped his arms vigorously against his chest, trying simultaneously to warm himself and get rid of some of the surplus water.

'Oh, I don't imagine things,' said Qa. 'I'm a trained observer, don't you know.'

'If you say so,' said Alfric, squatting down on his hams.

'I do say so,' said Qa. 'I saw you looking at one of my piles of rocks. You wouldn't be able to do that if you were an ordinary human.'

'And why not?' said Alfric.

'Because it's pitch dark in here, that's why,' said Qa.

'Then how can you see me seeing things?' said Alfric.

'Because I'm a sea dragon,' said Qa. 'Sea dragons can see in the dark. Not light, but heat. That's what they see, I mean. Heat. But I didn't see heat when I saw your eyes. No. I saw light. Red light. I can see it now. Anyway, enough of that. This debate isn't getting us very far. Let's get down to business. You've come to kill me.'

'In theory, yes.'

'In theory?' said Qa. 'What do you mean? You're going to run away? It's a bit late for that, isn't it?'

'Well, yes and no,' said Alfric. 'As I said before, I have a proposition.'

'Then what say you fetch your horse?' said Qa. 'We

99

could eat it here. Share it between us. Have a barbecue. Awfully jolly, what?'

'As I told you before,' said Alfric, 'I don't have a horse.'

'Really?'

'I give you my word of honour as a Yudonic Knight.'

'You're a liar,' said Qa. 'After I left you on the beach, I swam along the shore to look for your horse. I found it in the trees. That's where they always leave the horse.'

'You did no such thing,' said Alfric. 'You're just testing me. Consider me tested. I had no horse, and that's the truth. I walked here with my pack.'

'If you say so,' said Qa, mimicking Alfric's accents.

'I do say so,' said Alfric staunchly. 'And now let me say, with the greatest of sincerity, that I am familiar with your poetry, and admire it greatly.'

'Oh,' said Qa, in surprise. 'Do you?'

And, from the way the dragon spoke, Alfric knew that he really had its interest.

'Yes,' said Alfric. 'I hold your poetry in such high regard that I've committed some of it to memory. Would you like me to recite?'

'Please do,' said Qa, with the most genuine of enthusiasms.

So Alfric cleared his throat and began:

'Phenomenological stone.
No lapis lazuli but rock.
Your silence a rebuff to snakes.
In gutterals the wind
Gambles in dialects.
In marshland muds
(Cold codfish their taste, their scent

100

Deprived of ubiquity)
Stork critiques frog with a skewer.
You wait.
Phenomenological stone.'

'Marvellous stuff,' said Qa. 'Marvellous stuff, though I say it myself.'

'Such is your right,' said Alfric generously. 'After all, you created the stuff, so you're in the best position to appreciate its intrinsic genius.'

'So I am, so I am,' said Qa. 'But what about yourself? Do you really think you can appreciate it properly? Do you even know what it means?'

A note of suspicion had entered the dragon's voice, warning Alfric that he had better be careful.

'What it means?' said Alfric, striving to keep his teeth from chattering with the cold. 'Not exactly. But it speaks to me in a – a special way. When I hear those words, I feel as if I'm looking at the world through glass.'

All this and more said Alfric Danbrog. None of it was exactly spontaneous. In preparing himself for this mission, he had invaded a salon of poetasters in Galsh Ebrek, had studied the phrases by which the dilettanti flatter each other, and had invented some of his own just in case.

'You know,' said Qa, 'you're the first of my visitors who's known about my poetry. I usually ask them about it. Before I eat them, I mean. But the results have been most disappointing. Till now.'

'It is unfortunate,' said Alfric carefully, 'that poetry must struggle hard to preserve itself in the absence of the poet. For poetry can only come to full life through the genius of the voice of the original creator. I would be most privileged if I could hear you recite some of your verse.'

'My pleasure,' said Qa.

And, without further ado, the dragon began to recite:

> 'Slush, said the sea.
> Slush, slush.
> Slush blashimmer.
> Plash!
> Then the sun pursued biology
> And the world was dark.'

Alfric listened in respectful silence. Was there more to come? Apparently not. He wanted to scratch his backside, where wet cloth was crumpled against his skin. He was also experiencing the anal urgency of incipient diarrhoea. But he controlled his sphincter out of respect for the poet.

'That was good,' said Alfric. 'That was very good.'

'Ah,' said Qa. 'But do you know what it means? Or do you find all my poetry ultimately incomprehensible?'

'I – I'd hazard a guess that it says something about entropy. The heat death of the universe.'

The dragon's eyelids flickered.

Had Alfric said the right thing or—

'I see that for once I have the kind of audience I deserve,' said Qa.

'True,' said Alfric. 'I'm a great fan of yours. Since that's so, it's always hurt me to think that much of your genius is going to die with your flesh. You're going to die sooner or later. If you don't mind me saying so, it's probably going to be sooner rather than later. And, well, there's no collected edition of your works extant. Most of what survives exists in autograph form only, and may soon perish unless properly published.'

'Publication,' said Qa, 'costs money.'

'I am well aware of this,' said Alfric. 'So that's where my proposition comes into it. Subject to your compliance with certain terms, the Bank is prepared to pay for publication. A hundred scribes will work for a year to replicate your works so that your name will live in honour for ever. Life is short, but art is long. If art is properly collected and published in the first place.'

There was a pause, while the sea dragon Qa brooded about mortality, and about what a properly organized edition of the collected poems could do to perpetuate the memory of Galsh Ebrek's greatest poet.

'You're tempting me,' said Qa. 'Aren't you?'

Alfric mastered his now frankly chattering teeth and answered:

'Yes. The Bank wants me to succeed in this quest. So, if you hand over the ironsword Edda, the Bank will organize the publication of the poems.'

'I suppose,' said Qa, 'they'd also want me to let you kill me.'

'Well, yes,' admitted Alfric. 'That does come into it. I mean, technically I only have to recover the sword. But it'd look much better if I killed you into the bargain. From the point of heroic legend, I mean. If I'm going to be king, I'll have need of such a legend to support my rule.'

The dragon sighed, outbreathing warmth. Alfric wished it would sigh again, for he was sure he would shortly die of the cold. But it did not. Instead it said:

'The deal you offer me is no deal at all. While I'm proud to be an honorary Yudonic Knight, I know the limitations of the breed. They never accepted my genius in life, so they're not likely to in death. There's no point in publication, for the volumes would be torn apart to be used for lighting fires, or for – for purposes worse.'

'But,' said Alfric, 'distribution of your works will not be limited to Galsh Ebrek. Rather, the whole world will learn of your genius.'

'The world?'

'The Bank has authorized me to tell you about the Circle of the Partnership Banks,' said Alfric. 'Of this we do not usually speak. But let it be known that the Flesh Traders' Financial Association is linked to the rest of the civilized world by a series of Doors arranged in a Circle.'

'That's all Janjuladoola to me,' said Qa, using an expression in the Toxteth used to convey incomprehension.

So Alfric explained about the Circle of the Doors, a Circle controlled by a star-globe held by the Safrak Bank of the Safrak Islands, a place which was linked to the Monastic Treasury of Inner Adeer, itself in turn communicating with the Bank in Galsh Ebrek.

'By going through our own Door,' said Alfric, 'we can reach the Bondsman's Guild in Obooloo.'

Then he explained the rest of the Circle, and how the Doors opened up the entire world to the Bank. Qa listened, fascinated.

'You see,' said Alfric, in conclusion, 'your works will not be confined to Galsh Ebrek. Instead, your fame will spread throughout the world.'

'It's a thoughtful offer,' said the dragon. 'But I refuse.'

'Why?' said Alfric.

'Because I have a philosophical objection to suicide.'

'There is another way,' said Alfric.

'What's that?' said Qa.

'You don't really have to die. You could just disappear.'

'What? You mean, leave my barrow and swim off into the sea? Oh no, I couldn't do that. This is my home. It may not be much, but it's all I've got. I couldn't bear to leave it.'

And, at the very thought of leaving his much-loved domicile, Qa began to cry. Alfric was sorely embarrassed. The dragon was as wet as an ork!

'Look,' said Alfric, 'you've got it all wrong. I'm not asking you to – to just swim off into nowhere. Remember all the different Banks I told you about. Richest of all the Partnership Banks is the Singing Dove Pensions Trust of Tang. You remember what I told you about Tang?'

'Tell it to me again,' said Qa.

So Alfric told, enlarging on the wealth of the place, and the high regard in which poets were held by the populace.

'It sounds marvellous,' said Qa dreamily. 'I wish I could go to a place like that.'

'But you can, you can,' said Alfric earnestly. 'The Bank's arranged it all for you. We can smuggle you into Galsh Ebrek on a seaweed cart then let you through the Door. This time tomorrow, you can be in Tang.'

'Where I'd probably be killed as a marauder,' said Qa.

'No, no,' said Alfric, sounding shocked. 'Not at all. Your fame has gone there in advance. Here, I have an official invitation from the Emperor of Tang himself. You're invited there to be court poet. They admire poetry of your kind. Phenomenological stones. They

105

broke into open applause when they heard about it.'

Perhaps Alfric overstated the case somewhat. Nevertheless, the substance of what he was telling the dragon was true. The invitation was genuine. The Flesh Traders' Financial Association very much wanted Alfric to succeed in his quest and make himself Wormlord, so an immense amount of trouble had been put into cooking up a deal which would appeal to the sea dragon Qa.

'There remains,' said Qa, 'the problem of translation. I don't imagine they speak Toxteth in Tang.'

'No,' said Alfric, 'they don't. Scarcely anyone does, once you get outside Wen Endex. They speak Toxteth in Port Domax, of course, but I don't think it's heard in many other places.'

'So all my poetry would have to be translated.'

'Well . . . yes.'

'So my true genius could never be properly appreciated. It can't be, you know. Not in translation.'

'But you'd have a most admiring audience,' said Alfric, trying to be encouraging. 'Anyway, you could always learn the stuff they speak in Tang.'

'No,' said Qa. 'I can't. I'm too old to learn another language.'

'But,' said Alfric, 'sea dragons are famous for their intellectual agility. I'm sure you'd soon adapt. Come on. You can do it!'

'No,' said Qa, despondently. 'I'm too old, and I know it.'

Then the dragon began to cry once more, and a most melancholy sight it made. Alfric lost patience. He got to his feet.

'What's this?' said Qa. 'You want to get down to the fighting and killing?'

'No,' said Alfric, stamping his feet. 'I want to get warm. I'm soaked to the skin and in danger of dying of hypothermia.'

'Well then,' said Qa, 'warm yourself up quickly, for we really must get to the fighting bit.'

'Oh, I wouldn't say that's exactly essential,' said Alfric.

'I'm afraid it is,' said Qa. 'Honour and all that. It's all I've got left, you see. My honour as a Yudonic Knight and a loyal servant of the Wormlord. What do you want to use as a weapon? You've got your own sword, of course, but there are a few other weapons lying about. They usually want to use the ironsword, but it's rusted, as you see.'

'I can't, actually,' said Alfric. 'I mean, I don't know where it is.'

The dragon pointed it out.

Strangely, the hilt of the ironsword Edda was undamaged; it appeared to be made of a metal more durable than the rest. But the blade had suffered bitterly from the seasalt, which had reduced the weapon's striking strength to a wavery slither of black-buckling metal.

'So they usually go against you with their own swords,' said Alfric.

'Usually, yes.'

'And you kill them. Usually.'

'No,' said Qa. 'Not usually. Always. It's very simple. I breathe fire into the water, you see.' The dragon dabbled its claws in one of the puddles, demonstrating the prodigious quantities of water which were conveniently to hand. 'That fills the air with steam,' said Qa. 'So they can't see. Even if it's daytime. There's cracks in the rocks above, you see. If it's daytime there's light in the cave. Anyway, the steam blinds them. Usually they flail around a bit with their swords. Then I attack.'

'How?' said Alfric.

'Well,' said Qa, 'in my younger days, I used to bite off heads. Of course I broke the occasional fang on an iron collar or such. Then the rest of my teeth fell out with the onset of age. So these days I usually stand back and throw things.'

'Throw things?' said Alfric.

'Well, rocks,' said the dragon.

So saying, Qa secured a skull-sized rock with his talons.

'See that helmet?' he said.

'Yes,' said Alfric.

The helmet sat atop a dismal pile of shattered bucklers and mangled armour. Qa threw the stone with great speed and accuracy. The helmet was smashed back against the wall of the cave.

'That's . . . that's remarkably good throwing,' said Alfric.

'Also a demonstration of intelligence,' said Qa. 'That's what makes a sea dragon dangerous.'

'Dangerous indeed!' said Alfric. 'Quite frankly, I don't think I've got a chance of besting you in combat.'

'I'm sorry to hear that,' said Qa, 'because I rather like you. You're much more polite than the average Knight. I mean, they usually rabbit on no end about me eating that child and all the rest. Well, maybe it was a breach of etiquette, but I don't see that it was a sin. After all, something has to keep down the human population, doesn't it? Humans have no natural predators to keep their numbers in check, so if it wasn't for the occasional maneating dragon and such, you'd have a thousand million people or more living in Yestron alone.'

Alfric knew this was quite impossible, but nevertheless shuddered at such a nightmarish thought. A thousand million people! A ludicrous notion. But imagine . . .

'What about sea dragons?' said Alfric. 'Is there anything that eats sea dragons?'

'Oh, all kinds of things,' said Qa. 'Sharks, for example. Though sometimes we eat back. I've killed a good many sharks in my time, I'll have you know. Used to make a sport of it. Then there's sea serpents. Oh, and krakens of course. You know. The usual run of sea monsters.'

'That sounds very interesting,' said Alfric. 'What say you tell me about it while we have a little meal? If I'm going to die, I'd like to die on a full belly, and to listen to some more of your poetry before I expire, if you don't mind.'

'Why, that sounds a capital idea,' said the dragon. Then, mournfully: 'But I'm afraid I don't really have anything to offer you. It's not much of a life here, you see. Seaweed, that's what it mostly comes down to. Eating seaweed.'

'Actually,' said Alfric, 'I'm partial to seaweed.'

'Of course you are,' said Qa, 'you being a child of Wen Endex and all. But you like it cooked, don't you? Humans can't eat much of the stuff raw, oh no, I know that from past experience. I used to try keeping the occasional captive, when I had two of them. I sometimes did, you know. They didn't always come alone, even though that's the law. So I'd try to preserve some of the meat on the hoof. But they always complained most bitterly about the diet.'

109

'As it happens,' said Alfric, 'I've some food in my pack. Pork, actually. I have heard it said that sea dragons are partial to pork. You're most welcome to share it with me.'

'Why, that's very gracious of you,' said Qa.

So Alfric opened up his pack and the pair began to banquet upon pork, with Alfric taking care to select the very best bits for the dragon. While they ate, they discussed Galsh Ebrek. Qa had heard of the untunchilamons, and was most interested in the progress of that breed of miniatures.

'Maybe I could get one,' said Qa. 'As a pet. I've never had a pet, you know. It's a pity I have to kill you, otherwise you could fetch me one.'

'Doubtless you'll get all you deserve in time,' said Alfric. 'Would you care for some more pork?'

'Please.'

'You've got quite an appetite,' said Alfric.

'Yes,' said Qa. 'Since this is winter, I have to eat extramuch. Otherwise I'd have to hibernate. Most sea dragons do, you know. All through winter. Of course, extramuch mostly means great quantities of seaweed. Fortunately, I'm able to vary the diet from time to time.'

'How?' said Alfric.

'With Yudonic Knights, of course,' said Qa. 'And their horses. Would you like some fresh horsemeat to go with your pork?'

'I'd like that very much, if it were available,' said Alfric. 'For I'm rather partial to horsemeat. But unfortunately there's no horse available.'

'There is, you know,' said Qa.

Then the dragon went to the back of the cave, dipped its talons into a generous crack in the rock, and hauled out something which smelt very much like fresh meat. It proved to be the haunch of a horse. A horse very recently dead, if Alfric was any judge – and he thought himself a good one.

'You see,' said Qa, 'I did swim to the forest. I did find your horse.'

There was a pause.

Really!

This was most difficult!

'I – I'm sorry I lied to you about the horse,' said Alfric. 'But the rest is true. About the poetry, the invitation to Tang. All true.'

'I wish I could believe you,' said the dragon. 'But I can't. You're a liar, you see. Never mind, we won't let that stand in the way of our friendship. Which will last at least until the meal ends. Perhaps you're in the mood to listen to some more of my poetry. Are you?'

'Most definitely,' said Alfric.

So Qa began to recite. On and on went the recitation, the dragon at length abandoning food in favour of unrestricted concentration on poetry.

But it was too late.

For the dragon had already eaten more than it should have done.

And, soon enough, its eyes began to lull, its words became slurred, and it was struggling to keep its balance. Suddenly it fell over to one side. And then was abruptly sick.

'Oh,' said Qa, mournfully. 'I haven't been sick like that for years. Not since they fed me opium. At a banquet, it was. Done for a joke. There was opium, wasn't there? In the pork. The bits you fed me.'

'Yes,' admitted Alfric.

'You did well,' said the dragon. 'But not quite well enough. I've still the strength to kill you, you know. You'd better run while you've still got time.'

'You're bluffing, I'm afraid,' said Alfric. 'What's more, I know you're bluffing. Furthermore, it's time for me to kill you.'

'Just one thing I ask,' said the dragon.

'What's that?'

'No lectures, please,' said Qa. 'Not while I'm writhing in my death agonies. I couldn't bear it. Lectures, I mean. About eating children and all that.'

'Oh, that's perfectly understandable,' said Alfric, who detested children. 'No, I'm not killing you for any moralistic reasons. I'm killing you out of enlightened self-interest. How would you like to be killed?'

'A blade in the heart would be quickest,' said Qa, rolling over. 'Stick it in here.'

So saying, the dragon tapped its belly with a set of talons, indicating the location of the heart. Then it closed its eyes, as if waiting for death.

Alfric cautiously stepped back, away from the dragon. Stealthily he picked up a skull-sized rock. Then tossed it. So it landed on the dragon's belly.

Instantly the creature exploded into wrathful action, clawing with all four taloned legs, fire ravaging the air as it roared its anger. Then it realized it had been tricked. It had been fooled into expending its best energies on nothing more than a rock. It screamed, incoherent with rage. Scrabbled to its feet. Charged at Alfric.

But stumbled, tricked out of its balance by opium. Slithered. Fell. And Alfric drew his sword and leapt forward, stricking, hacking, slashing, plunging. Then struggling, struggling, struggling to draw out the steel which was stuck in the flesh, flesh he was kicking and cursing.

Badged with blood the ravager at last got free his blade. Then hacked. Then hacked again. Then stepped back to watch his enemy die.

'It hurts,' said Qa. 'It hurts.'

Alfric stood watching, panting harshly.

'It hurts,' moaned Qa.

Voice failing, fading.

A wisp of smoke escaped from the dragon's nostrils. One last firefly-rivalling flicker of fire showed at its mouth. Then it was dead. It was most clearly and obviously dead. Though Alfric nevertheless hacked off its head to be absolutely sure.

And then—

Then he bathed his hands in one of the puddles, for they had got scorched by fire in the course of the battle, and were very sore.

For a long time he squatted by the cold water, hands engulfed in that darkness. As he waited there, his battle-anger cooled away to nothing, and he was left alone and very lonely. The cave was dark, dark and cold, and very lonely. And Alfric began to weep for the dead dragon and its lonely vigil, and for the bitterness of this cold universe where things lived in holes, crawling forth at intervals to fight each other and die, each yearning for comfort yet afraid to trust the other, the dreaded other which might provide that comfort.

At last Alfric withdrew his hands from the water, cleansed his sword, sheathed his sword, picked up the shrivelled iron of the saga sword Edda, then left the cave. His pack he left behind, and also any and all other treasures which had belonged to the dragon.

Waves were sweeping across the sandstrand which stretched between Thodrun and the shore, either because the seas had got up or because the tide had started to come in while Alfric was in discourse with the dragon. The wind's icy blast in freezing squalls drove the racing combers with fury, but Alfric plunged into the water, unaffrighted, and struggled toward the shore. Only when he stepped clear of the sea did he realize how close he had come to losing the ironsword Edda to the wrecking waters.

Under the dead stars he walked toward the dunes, icy iron in his hand, bones creaking as his flesh animated itself toward its destination. He felt, at that moment, that he would not have cared even if he had lost the sword. For his guilt was upon him. He had killed, he had slaughtered a poet, and his shame would be upon him for ever. He had murdered Qa. He had been forced to. Because the dragon had not trusted him. If he had not lied about the horse, then he might have won the creature's trust. The dragon would have gone to Tang, and all would have ended happily ever after.

Instead, Alfric Danbrog would have bitter memories to bear for the rest of his life. But at least he was alive, yes, he was alive, and returning to Galsh Ebrek as a hero.

CHAPTER EIGHT

After killing the sea dragon Qa, Alfric tramped along the coast until he came to an abandoned croft. By that time, the night was nearly at an end. He laid himself down inside the ruinous crofthouse and dropped off into an exhausted sleep.

When Alfric woke, it was still night. Was he at the end of his dragon-fighting night? Or had he slept right through the day to the start of a new night? He could not say, for clouds obscured the sky, denying him the timetelling stars. Regardless of how long he might have slept, he felt weary, his body aching like a resurrected carcass. Pain still dwelt in his dragon-scorched hands, and to this annoyance was added a pressing hunger which he had no means of satisfying.

Hunger-driven, Alfric resumed his journey, at length passing between the Stanch Gates and entering Galsh Ebrek. Then he stopped in the nightmud street, momentarily unsure of how to cope with his many conflicting priorities. He wanted to rest, to eat and to drink; he wanted, also, to signal his success to Saxo Pall; and he should by rights report his successful return to the Bank.

Very well.

He was a Yudonic Knight, was he not?

Of course he was!

With that settled, Alfric backtracked to the Stanch Gates and acted like the Knight he was. He ordered one of the guards to the Bank to deliver a message, and directed another man to take a despatch to Saxo Pall.

'My lord,' said one of the men so commanded, 'where will we look for you if there is a reply to your messages?'

Alfric considered. He didn't want common guardsmen tramping into his own house.

'You can leave any reply to my messages at the Green Cricket,' he said.

A good choice, this, since Anna Blaume was a reliable holder of messages, and since Alfric meant to call round to the inn in any case to check on the progress of the orks.

With duties of communication thus satisfactorily discharged, Alfric took himself off to his own house, where he hoped a meal would be waiting for him. But it was not. Nothing was waiting for him. Not even his wife. Alfric foraged for food, eventually finding and consuming two (cold) baked potatoes and a cup of (equally cold) half-cooked moon beans. Then he went in search of his missing spouse: but his enquiries were fruitless.

What now?

Why, he must go to the Green Cricket, of course, to see if there were any messages for him.

When Alfric entered that insalubrious inn, he found a great many people within. But the place was not lively, for most of the patrons were in a near-corpse-like state in the aftermath of a party. What had occasioned such celebrations? Alfric did not ask. He was near collapse: though he knew not whether the cause of his suffering was indigestion, fatigue or emotional stress.

'Hello Alfric,' said the ork Morgenstern, addressing him from behind the bar. 'How are you?'

'Not very well,' said Alfric. 'Where's Anna?'

'In bed,' said Morgenstern.

116

Alfric had taste enough not to ask: who with? Instead, he said to Morgenstern:

'What puts you behind the bar? A career change?'

'No, no,' said Morgenstern.' 'I like it here.'

'Good,' said Alfric, for the sake of politeness. 'Has anyone been here tonight?'

'All kinds of people,' said Morgenstern. 'Many of them yet remain.'

So saying, the ork gestured at the sleeping drunks.

'That's not what I meant,' said Alfric. 'I meant messengers.'

'You didn't say messengers,' said Morgenstern.

'I say it now,' said Alfric, resisting an impulse to hit the soft and blubbery animal. 'Has anyone been here tonight? With a message, I mean? A message for me? Or a letter, a scroll, a parchment, a despatch, or anything else for me for that matter?'

'No,' said Morgenstern.

So much for that.

Alfric wondered what the orks were still doing at the Green Cricket. Had Tromso Stavenger refused them lodgings in Saxo Pall? Or had they proved too timid to present their diplomatic credentials to the Wormlord? Or—

Earlier, he had been most curious to discover the fate which had met the orkish Embassy; but his weariness had increased considerably since then. He decided it was best that he stay resolutely uninvolved. He had enough to cope with on his own account without getting involved in any actual or potential diplomatic disasters.

'Give me a beer,' said Alfric.

'Certainly,' said Morgenstern. 'If you've got the cash.'

'Put it on the slate,' said Alfric.

'You have one?'

'Of course,' said Alfric. 'I come here often.'

The ork hunted around among the slates, found Alfric's, chalked up a beer. Alfric took it to a seat by the fire and drank slowly. He felt oddly deflated and depressed. Maybe it was just the result of so much nightliving.

'How did your quest go?' said Morgenstern, who was polishing the bar.

Alfric looked up.

'So-so,' he said.

'Did you kill your dragon?'

'Yes,' said Alfric. 'But I'd rather not talk about it, if it's all the same with you.'

Thereafter Morgenstern left him alone. Alfric drank in silence, watching a band of untunchilamons making warfaring forays from the fireplace. Time and again the miniature dragons descended on slumbering drunks, raiding hair and clothing for whatever livestock they could find. Occasionally, in an excess of enthusiasm, a dragon singed human skin while crisping a hapless louse: which occasioned some sleepy swearing and ineffectual dragon-swatting.

In due course, Alfric started on a second beer. An unusual procedure, this, for he usually stopped at one. Alfric Danbrog valued self-control above all else, and feared ill consequences should he ever lose his grip on his will thanks to alcoholic intoxication.

The self-controlled banker was halfway through his second mug when a woman came down the stairs. Anna Blaume? No. Viola Vanaleta!

'Viola!' said Alfric, upsetting his mug as he started to his feet.

The woman momentarily looked startled, but recovered her poise almost immediately.

'Why, Alfric,' she said, coolly, 'what a surprise. What are you doing here?'

'Looking for you, as it happens,' said Alfric.

'Are you?' said Vanaleta. She turned to Morgenstern and said: 'Did he ask after me when he came in?'

The ork looked uneasy.

'Well?' said Vanaleta. 'I take it we can say your silence means no. Alfric, you didn't come here to look for me. You came to get drunk.'

'If I did,' said Alfric, 'such is my privilege. Just as it is my privilege, or should be, to return to my own home in every confidence of finding my wife in residence within.'

'You have lost yourself that privilege,' said Vanaleta.

At this stage the appropriate question was: why?

But Alfric did not ask this question, hence remained unenlightened. Instead he said:

'I don't like the tone of your voice. Let's go home and sort this out.'

'Home?' said Vanaleta. 'I'm not going anywhere with you.'

'Your abstraklous contumely ill befits you,' said Alfric coldly. 'You are my wife. My handmaiden.'

After that, things went from bad to worse.

Both Alfric Danbrog and Viola Vanaleta were in moods most unreasonable. Alfric because he was suffering from fatigue, and from a murderer's guilt, and from fear of his uncertain future. Vanaleta because she believed Alfric to be in the process of divorcing her, and thought his intemperate attempt to command her to be most unreasonable. Finally, Alfric was roused to such an anger that he tried to use force on his woman.

All things being equal, Alfric would have overwhelmed Vanaleta and would have dragged her home in triumph. But things were not equal. Before Alfric knew it, two dwarves had joined the battle. Du Deiner had him by the ankle while Mich Dir was doing his best to apply a stranglehold.

'Unhand me, you filthy ablach!' said Alfric, trying to kick away Du and claw away Mich.

He was still trying when two more people came down the stairs: Anna Blaume and Cod the ork. Shortly, Alfric found himself being set upon by one ork, two women and a pair of dwarves: a state of affairs which left him with no option except to surrender.

'Get up then,' said Blaume, 'and I'll get you a drink.'

A drink she got him, and then a second; and of the drinks that came later there is no counting. At one stage Alfric heard her say:

'One observes that the thumb is second cousin to the left foot.'

Then she laughed; but what the joke was, Alfric had no idea.

'Did I imagine it,' he said, 'or did you just say—'

'What?' said Blaume.

For Alfric's speech had become quite incomprehensible thanks to the prodigious importation of liquor into his system. While he thought himself quite lucid, his ears were garbaging what was said to them, and his tongue was rubbishing his every word to a mulching slather. Even his vision was starting to fritz, for the outlines of reality were blurring and bifurcating in a way which had nothing whatsoever to do with any optical deficiency.

Nevertheless, Alfric was sensible enough to recognize Pig Norn when that mix of brawn and flabber came crashing through the front door with Muscleman Wu close behind him.

'Jabraljik!' said Pig, or seemed to Alfric to say.

This Alfric took to be a distortion of his name: and, taking this distortion to be a challenge to battle, he got to his feet. His feet he tripped over. His face he recovered but his spectacles were missing, and by the time he had groped his way to his sight's salvation, the battle was well underway.

Pig and Wu were trying to spear orkflesh with their swords, but close-clinging dwarves and battering women were making this feat of chivalry difficult. Skaps the Vogel was swooping overhead, screaming in shrill-voiced anger. Some of the drunks, woken by the brawl, were fighting among themselves, or trying to.

'Stop!' said Alfric.

But nobody did.

So Alfric picked up a chair, or tried to. But his balance was betrayed by a draught from the fireplace, and he had to lean on the chair to keep his balance. He tried again, was more successful, and broke the chair over Wu's head. While the chair definitely suffered – it was asundered into woodwarp and wormdust, dowelling and splinters – Wu fought on, dauntless and dentless.

Alfric took off his spectacles, put them into a beer mug for safety, then threw himself into the battle. With Alfric deadweighting from his neck, Muscleman Wu began to tire. Then a couple of guardsmen entered, and, thanks to their intervention, both brothers Norn were overcome and were booted out into the street.

Full of the vigour of war, Alfric pursued them. He stood in the doorway of the Green Cricket and swore prodigiously at a much-battered Pig Norn who was even then picking himself out of the mud.

'You want a fight?' said Wu Norn. 'A real fight?

Then come out here and we'll settle things.'

'I will,' said Alfric.

But Anna Blaume and others grabbed him from behind and dragged him back to safety. Viola Vanaleta recovered the spectacles and shoved them on to Alfric's face, and the guardsmen delivered their message.

'Compliments of the Wormlord,' said they. 'Your presence is desired at Saxo Pall. Tonight is the night. All the Yudonic Knights are being ingathered for your banquet, which starts as soon as you present yourself.'

'Impossible,' said Alfric. 'I'm drunk.'

But Anna Blaume gave him a drink which made him throw up, then fed him some revolting black stuff, then burnt some white powder and made him inhale the fumes, then marched him to his home to recover the ironsword Edda, then escorted him to Saxo Pall and handed him over to Guignol Grangalet, and very shortly (or so it seemed to Alfric, whose time sense had become grossly distorted ever since he had breathed the fumes of the white powder) the young banker was in the throne-room in audience with the Wormlord, with a mass of Yudonic Knights in attendance.

'You have done well,' said Tromso Stavenger.

'Have I?' said Alfric, too dazed to know whether he had or had not.

'You have done very well,' said Stavenger. 'For you have brought us the ironsword Edda. Give it to me.'

In obedience to this command, Alfric presented the king with the saga sword. Some of the onlookers tittered when they saw what a rubbishy thing it was, but only Ciranoush Norn was bold enough to challenge the presentation.

'My lord!' said Ciranoush.

'You wish to be heard?' said the Wormlord.

'I will be heard!' said Ciranoush. 'Edda was a hero's weapon. But this? Some refuse-iron! The hilt intact, to be true, but the blade a stump of rotten rust. How know we this to be Edda?'

'I know,' said the Wormlord.

Then, to Alfric's astonishment, the king unscrewed the top of the sword's pommel; and from the hollow hilt the Wormlord poured a glitterment of diamonds, emeralds and rubies. One last thing rattled out. A single chip of lapis, incongruous against the glory of the jewels.

'The sword,' said the Wormlord, 'has proved itself.'

As Ciranoush stared at the jewels in dumbfounded silence, Alfric steadied his head for long enough to add:

'If further proof is demanded, seek it yourself on Island Thodrun. Qa lies dead, his body butchered, as other bodies will be before all differences in this kingdom are settled.'

'Other bodies?' said Ciranoush. 'What mean you by that?'

'You will not ask that question!' said the king. Then he tossed the chip of lapis to Alfric, who surprised himself by catching it neatly. 'A souvenir,' said Tromso Stavenger. 'I might give you another souvenir before the night is out. A head. A head for you to take home. The head of one of the brothers Norn.'

'My lord,' said Ciranoush, 'how has the family Norn excited your displeasure?'

'I am told,' said the Wormlord, 'that your brothers Pig and Wu have been brawling with the orks who happen to be ambassadors from the king of the Qinjoks.'

'Then I will see that apologies are made,' said Ciranoush.

Without further ado, Ciranoush called his brothers

forth from the mass of Yudonic Knights gathered in the throneroom. A sullen Pig and a slowvoiced Wu made formal apologies to the king.

'I am not necessarily entirely satisfied by your apologies,' said the king. 'It may be that I will make an example of one of you. I do not say that this is necessarily so. Only that I reserve the right to so act. Any offence against any ambassador is a most serious matter, whatever the nature of that ambassador. What I need from you now is a peace. A peace between the brothers Norn and the family Danbrog. Is there a peace between you? Alfric?'

'There is,' said Alfric.

Pig hesitated, then said:

'Yes, there is.'

And Wu:

'My brother speaks for me as well.'

'Good,' said Stavenger. 'Then you will all four of you sit together as a token of mutual trust and alliance. The three brothers Norn and Alfric Danbrog. Come, let us retire now to the banqueting hall.'

That they did, and soon a most uncomfortable Alfric Danbrog was seated at table with the three brothers Norn. Pig was seated to Alfric's left and Ciranoush to his right, with Wu a further place to the right. A four person Trough of Friendship was brought forth and set in front of them, that they might all eat from the same dish in token of the truceship to which their king had bound them. A select portion of a gigantic river worm (a worm which was all of a horselength from nose to tail) was placed in that dish, and vegetables mounded on top of it.

A great heat rose from the river worm; and heat likewise flushed forth from the brothers Norn; and further heat assailed Alfric from the hall itself, a hall heated by a full half-dozen blazing fireplaces. It is scarcely surprising that he found himself sweating, and that his neighbours were similarly afflicted.

Certain formalities then took place; then the Worm-lord took out his false teeth and wrapped them in a silken handkerchief, and all knew they were free to eat, which they did.

As the banquet got underway, Alfric did his best to ignore the brothers Norn. Easy enough to do, since Justina Thrug was seated opposite, and she was enough to take anyone's mind off his neighbours. She was a phenomenon.

Justina Thrug was a meaty woman with the most abstraklous history of debauchery. On this occasion, she was rigged out in flame-coloured taffeta most unfitting as wear for one who was a daughter of Lonstantine Thrug. In a further offence against custom, she had brought her pet owl to banquet. The name of the creature was Aquitaine Varazchavardan, a fact which Alfric Danbrog could not help but learn, since Justina often addressed the feathered beast by this name.

(The owl, for its part, said precious little in return.)

It was said that Justina Thrug was truly her father's daughter, and that nothing could abash her dauntless courage; but Alfric found such rumour hard to credit when he was confronted by this overloud and overweight female, a woman hardly overyoung.

Alfric was glad when the traditional banquet-time storytelling began, for it drowned out the Thrug. The tales that were told were all the usual, traditional stuff. Heroes venturing against those monsters which inhabit the wastelands. The glut of slaughter from the great battles of land and sea. The glory of the poets of the past who won deathless fame by fabling the heroes of such tales. The sacrifices made by those who, eager for fame, paid scant heed to the safety of the house of flesh. The plight of an outcast doomed by the betrayal of his king.

On and on went the storytelling, some in prose and some in verse, but all noble, heroic, inspired by visions of grandeur.

Listening, the Yudonic Knights indulged themselves in heroic ecstasies. They were no longer the inhabitants of a muddy little city in a minor province of the Izdimir Empire; they were not the denizens of an insignificant land half-engulfed by swamp; they were not the members of a bullyboy class dedicated to exploiting the labours of a subdued and sullen peasantry. Rather, they were lordly heroes in a land built for the accommodation of such men; their houses were palaces; their bad-tempered wives were compliant maidens who delighted in braiding broidered silk and looming fleeces for the comfort of their men; their estate was great, and their destiny to be greater yet.

At last, the Wormlord himself got to his feet, and (still without his teeth) began his tale of how he had marched against Her son, had met that monster, and had defeated him.

'My making was not by way of words moth-eaten. Rather it was through deeds that I became the man you see before you.'

Thus began the Wormlord. And by like boast he continued, until at last his tale was done.

Other boasts followed. Recitals of ancestral sovereignties; of lordly deeds which had set the world aflame with admiration; of the splendour of gold and the open-handed kings who had oft won fame by their dispensing of the same; of savage foes who had marched against the kings, only to be broken and defeated and backdriven by the might of the righteous.

And, for a while, Alfric was buoyed up by this stuff. But after a while it all got too much, and he wished he could leave. But he could not. This was his banquet, put on especially for his honour. If he left before it was finished, he would be insulting his king and his fellows.

In the end, Alfric dared himself away from the table long enough to take a piss – this itself a breach of custom, but he was past caring – only to find another flatulent hero-belcher in action when he returned.

On went the night, full of the wind of words. Of ring-prowed ships; of men in bearskin gloves manning such ships, the masts and sails of the same sheeted with ice; of swords adorned with coiled gold; of steeds with plaited manes, brave beasts which outran the wind; fell monsters encountered and defeated on a murky moor; horns heartening heroes as men graced with deathless courage met their end in contest with onswarming hordes of heartless reptiles; war-arrows embedded in corpses strewn upon steep rocky screens, discarded at the foot of precipitous crags, lying derelict in waters bloody and disturbed.

Of this sang the song-singers; and they sang also of the undisturbed valour of men who died without complaint though they were pierced to the vitals by deadly-barbed boar-spears; and of the outlandish grief which doomed the hero Hroblar to an uncouth death when his hand-meshed battle-corslet animated itself and ate through his flesh to the bone.

Also they sang – there was no stopping it, though Alfric would have been content to see all of creation come to an end rather than endure any more of this stuff – of the weapon-smiths of old and the weapons of their making.

Ah, the weapons!

Iron agleam in moonlight. Deathblades tempered in the blood of warfare. Ripple-patterned damascene slicing through the flesh of alien creatures ravenous for blood. The fighting fangs of heroes. Twist-patterned steel which had dared the hearts of heroes. Swords which lopped hands, which chopped feet, which shortened legs at the knees, which gouged out hearts and vivisected horses, which dissected the aorta and tasted the filth of the lower bowel.

Of such the poets sang, much to the delight of this company of heroes.

Of swords they sang, and of armour.

Buckler's proof against a basilisk's breath. Meshed mail. Gaunt helms topped with boars and dragons.

And the journeying, the endless trekking and marching and climbing endured by the thousands of heroes of legend, all of it to be described a footstep at a time, complete with descriptions of the texture of the mud through which they walked, and the very length of the leeches which there battened upon their flesh.

Earth was their way. Mud was their way. Wind was their way. Fire was their way. Ice was their way. Toes and hamstrings. Shins and shoulders. Corpses stretched lifeless. Lordless men manning the bulwark battlements. Heroes doomed to perish from the fiercest of griefs, dying encumbered by battle-harness, fighting in death in honour of their battle-vows, vaunting their boasts with the blood of their lungs on their lips.

Then at last the boast-telling was over, and serious drinking began. Alfric drank himself, in defiance of his custom. Heard but parts of the tabletalk, that talk rapidly mounting to uproar. Loud, over-loud, striving above all other voices, was that of Justina Thrug, asking a question.

'What,' asked Justina, 'is a virgin?'

Someone volunteered an explanation.

'Oh!' said she. 'Now I remember!'

Then she looked across at Alfric and said:

'Well, sweet wag, are you happy eating with your friends at that great big blood-brother plate?'

'Happy enough,' said Alfric.

Though in fact he was most unhappy at being reminded of the existence of his meal companions. He had (somehow) almost managed to forget about them entirely. Remembering their existence was unpleasant, for they were disgusting. Ciranoush, just to his right, repeatedly regurgitated his food, chewed the mouthfuls then swallowed again. As for Pig, why, Pig had drenched his food with a most revolting sauce, which was supplemented by a steady drip-drop of sweat which oozed from the bulky face of that entity. Right now, Pig was eating a chicken's arse, teasing away the delicate flesh, and, into the bargain, eating the yellow knobs of well-cooked yellow chickenshit.

'More beer, young sir?' said a waiter.

'Please,' said Alfric.

Then realized the waiter was no waiter, no, it was Nappy, Nappy was there, at his elbow, his side, and Alfric was near-paralysed with terror, for he had no help, no chance, no hope, he was doomed, he was done, he was dead, there was no getting away.

But nothing happened.

Nothing happened to Alfric.

Nappy filled Alfric's mug from a big jug. Then put

down the jug. Then Pig Norn was groping at Pig Norn's throat, clutching and clawing, writhing and striving, but it was no good, no good at all. The garotte was of wire, thin wire deep-biting hard, and Nappy was hauling on the wooden toggles which were tightening the wire.

In desperation, Pig Norn began to thrash about in his chair, trying to overbalance it. But the chair was heavy, solid oak was its weight, and Nappy was strategically positioned, behind Pig and immune to Pig's fistings and flailings. And Pig's feet were starting to drum, to drum, to drumbeat their death, and Pig's eyes were bulging, swelling, swollen, horror-glazed, hands spasming—

And—

And the legs spasming also, the drumbeat a death-rattle, a nothing, with bowels and bladder giving way in the aftermath, and stench rising to an absolute silence, all and everyone transfixed, horrified, all but for one old man singing tum-ti-tum-ti until someone hit him on the head with something hard and he collapsed unconscious.

Nappy loosened the garotte.

Alfric looked (he could not help himself). The line, hard line of the wire, deep-bitten, a red line, red, inflamed, blood oozing actual red where the wire had cut the skin, strength sufficient and you could take off a man's head, or could you? No, probably not, cutting through the actual spinal column would be too much, and anyway there's much meat there, a lot of meat, meat stronger than you might expect, stronger—

Alfric looked away.

The Wormlord was swilling some water round his mouth.

The Wormlord spat into his empty soup bowl.

The Wormlord unwrapped his false teeth and inserted

those oratorial aids into his mouth. He had not used them earlier when boasting of the exploits of his youth, but this was a more serious matter.

'Ciranoush Norn,' said Tromso Stavenger. 'It is to you I speak. Wu Norn. It is to you I speak also. Earlier I reserved the right to make an example of a molester of ambassadors. Now I have made such an example. Let this be recorded. We do not permit ambassadors to be molested within our domain. We hope the point is made. Permanently.'

Ciranoush Norn replied:

'It is.'

His voice was not steady. Even so, Alfric did not doubt the courage of the valorous Ciranoush. The present circumstances would have unsteadied anyone.

'Good,' said the Wormlord. 'Let the banquet resume.'

Diffidently, talk began again. Waiters descended upon the corpse of Pig Norn, rolled it up in a spare tablecloth and dragged it away. The soiled chair was removed and a fresh one substituted; and Nappy seated himself in the fresh chair, and began to banquet himself.

Nappy picked up the chicken's arse which Pig Norn had been eating. Nappy finished it off with every sign of enjoyment, and washed it down with ale from Pig's half-empty mug. Nappy wiped his greasy fingers on the tablecloth and beamed in delight.

'Well,' said Nappy, 'this has been an eventful evening, hasn't it?'

'Yes,' said Alfric unsteadily, trying to remain polite.

And, to Alfric's mounting horror, Nappy insisted on making further smalltalk. And still the banquet continued, with Alfric a prisoner of the proceedings since those proceedings were in his honour.

At last, knightly carcasses began to slide beneath the table, the victims of an overconsumption of liquor. As uproar ended and talk lulled away, various untunchilamons came forth from the banquet hall fireplaces to plunder the remnants of the feast. Nappy persuaded one to perch on his finger, and showed it to Alfric.

'It – it's beautiful,' said Alfric awkwardly.

True enough. The tiny dragon shone, glittered and forthblazed like a living gem.

'It likes me,' said Nappy simply.

Smiling, smiling.

He was so happy.

He was such a happy fellow.

'Yes,' said Alfric, trying to coax sincerity into his voice. 'I'm sure it does like you.'

'Most people do, you know,' said Nappy, 'once they get to know me.'

'I'm sure they do,' said Alfric. 'And I'm glad I'm getting to know you now.'

This may not seem much of a speech, but it cost Alfric immense effort. He was glad when Nappy was diverted by the spectacle of half a dozen dragons lapping at dregs of spilt ale with their tiny tongues. Soon there were a great many drunken dragons blundering about the banquet table or tracing erratic flightpaths through the air. One maniacal monster started feuding with a candleflame, a sight which Nappy found so droll that he laughed until he cried.

The surviving Norn brothers, Ciranoush Zaxilian and Muscleman Wu, did not laugh.

Nor did they cry.

But Alfric could imagine what they were thinking.

132

CHAPTER NINE

The next night, Alfric Danbrog rode forth on his second quest. His task was to dare go to the Spiderweb Castle which was guarded by the swamp giant, and there recover the silver sword known as Sulamith's Grief. Abuneheid was naught but cloud; no glimpse of the welkin wanderer was possible. But Alfric sensed that the moon was above; and sensed too that the moon was swelling, girthing, giving itself to acresce.

He rode alone, but did not consider himself lonely. Nor was he unhappy. For the moment, he welcomed the solitude which gave him the liberty to explore the solipsistic universe of his own thoughts.

The night through which he rode was empty of all human life except his own, which did not displease him. He remembered the absurdity with which the sea dragon Qa had conjured: the spectre of a thousand million people in Yestron. It was impossible, of course. And yet . . .

What if some nightmare should make it true?

Imagine.

Imagine the people ranked in their tens of millions, their hundreds of millions. Their clattering laughter littering the streets. Their sewage flowing in rivers. Their hair, the growth of it filling warehouses between dusk and dawn. The sheet-sheath growth of their fingernails, a mere fraction of a night's extension being sufficient to pave a mansion. Sebum and semen, a hundred barrels of each produced each night. The moon's bloody flux, a stenchtide ravaging through the streets, a periodic disaster itself sufficient to drive the sensitive insane. The very beaches of the Winter Sea bricabraced with goatskin condoms and unwanted abortions, evidence and aftermath of lust.

A thousand million people.

No wolf-haunt wilderness any more, only roads and houses, houses and roads, neighbours forever at squabble over each other's pigs and chickens, farms pocket-handkerchiefed by the everdivision of inheritance, one man's water fouled by his neighbour's leakage, and no act or decision free from scrutiny and interference, the very fact of inevitable observation being a most telling form of such interference.

Nightmaring thus, Alfric shuddered.

It was true that Alfric had his uses for the world of human voices, of beerbreath taverns and vaginal beds, of eyefriendly faces and laughing teeth, of saliva nipples and corrugated ears. Yet, even so, he often resented the existence of other people; and, though he knew Galsh Ebrek to be a small city, and knew Wen Endex to be a land virtually unpopulated, he often felt crushed to a state of claustrophobia by the everpressure of other flesh and other psyches; and, in imagination, conjured with worlds in which he would be the sole inhabitant, graced by the gift of many years of unimpeded meditation and optional exploration.

In many ways, life in the Bank was ideally suited to Alfric's temperament. Money is a set of abstractions, and he much preferred abstractions to people; he enjoyed scheming with the unreal, the essentially metaphysical, to create power; and it sometimes seemed to him miraculous that such abstract delights could prove so remunerative in practical terms.

True, Alfric's job involved a certain amount of human (and inhuman) contact, for as a Banker Third Class he was both diplomat and negotiator.

But a banker need not necessarily treat humans (or inhumans) as if they have any authentic existence in their own right. Rather, they can for the most part be treated as abstractions. As production units, consumption units, statistics to be manipulated by the Equations of Leverage.

And when Alfric negotiated with anyone on behalf of the Bank, he never (or, at least, very rarely) became involved with that person on an emotional level. Thus, though he had made several visits to the Qinjoks, and had dealt effectively with King Dimple-Dumpling on such visits, he was not to any extent personally embroiled in the king's affairs.

An ideal state of affairs!

But . . .

If Alfric were to become Wormlord, charged with the governance of Wen Endex and the welfare of all the people of the nation, then things would change. He would inevitably be inextricably tangled in the meshwork of loyalties and responsibilities which characterizes kingship.

There are empires in which the emperor is a living god and his people are as living trash in his presence. Nevertheless, the reality of the existence of such human garbage is not denied. There are slave states in which the slaves are seen as animals, and are treated as such; or, in some cases, worse treated. Even so, the slaves are real, inescapably real, unavoidably real, the psychic pressure of their existence amply demonstrated by the very complexity of the polite code of manners which makes their sufferings unmentionable.

But . . .

Maybe it would be possible to develop a kind of politics in which the great mass of the people would no longer be people at all. In which they would not be even animated rubbish or a lower form of animal life. Suppose one were to create a politics in which people became mere abstract symbols to be manipulated as one manipulates money. Thus a stinking beggar, a leprous thing of rags and ulcerated bones, would no longer be an entity to be either cherished or scorned, helped or rebuffed. Rather, the beggar would be reduced to an abstract token, a necessary side-effect of the mathematics of prosperity.

Was it possible?

Was it possible for a ruling politics to be so detached from reality?

Was it possible, in other words, for politics to be reduced to the painless manipulation of a web of symbols, an exercise of the intellect totally removed (in an emotional sense) from any realworld consequences?

For a moment, Alfric thought it was possible, and thought too that he might be able to bring about such a state of affairs. But he dismissed the thought as an absurdity.

Then began to reconsider.

It happened that the Partnership Banks had already gone a long way to creating the necessary philosophical underpinning of any such politics; for the manipulating of money already proceeded in a largely abstract arena

136

substantially divorced from all physical realities. Thus one very large and complex confederation of interlocked organizations was conducting its affairs, to a very considerable extent, as if it functioned in a symbolic field rather than a physical universe made of earth and air, fire and water.

As money is today, so the world can be tomorrow.

Thinking thus, Alfric shuddered; and knew then his own true capacity for evil.

Evil?

Yes.

Surely it would be evil in the highest degree to treat the real world as a solipsistic dream to be manipulated for symbolic satisfaction; and, on the level of practical affairs, to deny the existence of the real in favour of the mechanics of daydream. To puppet humans as if they were but shadows. It would be evil, yes.

But it was infinitely appealing.

The result would be – in effect – the abolition of the world. Even if Alfric became king, he would be able to retreat from existence into a world of symbols.

Thus thinking, thus brooding, Alfric went slowly through the forests of night. He was in no hurry; and, besides, apart from the horse he was riding, he had four pack horses, all heavily loaded, and this made haste impossible. So he went slowly, fantasizing, abstracting, politic-creating, reminiscing and hopeconjuring.

In the course of such thoughtwandering, it happened that at last Alfric began to meditate upon his relationship with his wife, his darling Viola Vanaleta. This he did with some reluctance, for his seven years of marriage had not been happy. The reason for this was not hard to find. Alfric was selfish, especially with his time. Through the years of his marriage, he had dedicated his efforts to his career and his own aggrandisement. Worse, the very foundations of his marraige were unsound; for Alfric had married simply to appease the needs of the flesh, and (despite his denials) his wife had long suspected as much, and had long resented being used as a convenience of lust.

The subject of marriage was also painful inasmuch as Alfric's occasional outbursts of anger had left him with much to be ashamed of. He remembered the last time he had hit her. It was so easy! And it happened so quickly. The wrathrage making his fists manic. The terrible, inexplicable, unreasonable anger seizing his flesh. In such a mood, he could quite happily punch glass, splinter wood, or gouge, squeeze, tear and strangle.

In such a mood, he might one day kill someone without thought, giving himself over to his murderous rage for the sheer bloody pleasure of slaughter.

And—

And what if such an anger came upon him when he was king?

It happened that he often hated the rest of the world for simply existing. It happened that the mere presence of other people was often enough to exacerbate the temper-fits which sometimes came upon him.

So—

But enough of the future.

Let the future look after itself, for what mattered was the present. The journey, and then the matter of surviving the great dare at journey's end.

A long journey Alfric had of it; and, before the end, thought deteriorated to mere imagespasm as exhaustion set in. His flesh was equal to the tasks which faced it, but his much-burdened mind was still suffering from the events of the last few days. Suffering from murdershock guilt, from deathfear assault, from the sudden and unexpected complexities which had entered his life. The Bank had long been his refuge against reality and the world; but now the Bank had forced him to enter the arena of active politics, thus exposing him to all manner of danger and uncertainty.

Consequently, towards the end of his journey Alfric was mazed with fatigue, fullblinded by moments of dream in which eldritch figures clumped from the hulkbulk trees, the dark-dwindle ditches. Though the dark yielded to his vision, it was ever an effort to find his way; and, even when the skycurrents stirred the cloud-seas sideways, the moon remained hidden, and all he saw was a scattering of stars, stars bright-burning, orange and green, poisonous confectionary, the heaven-tree's lethal nightfruit.

The forest thickened and the path narrowed, until at last Alfric had to dismount and lead his horses on foot through an overgrowth wilderness of gnarled and buckling vegetation, of broken limbs and staggering crutches.

At last he stopped, for the way was almost impassable, and he was more than half-minded to turn back. Then he smelt something. The low, slow, muddy smell of sedgeswamp, of mouldrot and vegetative decay, of duckweed and frogweed. It was near, it was near.

Thus guided, Alfric pressed forward. The undergrowth thinned, and he found himself by the shores of the much-dreaded Swamp of Slud. He made out the causeway which stretched from the shore to the distant night-humped mound which could only be the Spiderweb Castle.

Now Alfric was all business, his braindeath fatigue conquered entirely by the quick excitement of action. He unloaded his pack horses. As he hefted the heavy barrels of his baggage into a heap, he did his best to ignore the gnawing cries of anguish coming from a nearby clump of swampgrass. With the horses unloaded, Alfric led the beasts a safe distance into the forest and tethered them carefully. He clothed each with a blanket so it would not get too cold while it waited.

Then he went back to the swamp and waited himself.

But for the crying grass, all was silent.

As Alfric waited, the skyrug clouds drifted apart and the moon appeared, a moon not very far from the full. Alfric was startled by that white-blazing circle of light. How could the moon be so full so soon? He had calculated things otherwise: but one look at the sky told him his calculations were out by a matter of days.

The moonlight gauzed the light mist which lay across the swamps and the far-stretching causeway. Alfric durst not start out along that causeway until he had dealt with the swamp giant Kralch, Eater of Babies; the monster who, by tradition, was welcome to any unwanted flesh which was brought to the swampside.

As Alfric waited, the bawling baby began to get on his nerves. He did his best to ignore it. Maybe it wasn't a baby at all. It could be some trick of magic, perhaps – the grass itself crying out in anguish. Or a mutant frog. Or – well, a monkey. Or something. As long as he didn't look, he didn't know. As long as he didn't know, he wasn't guilty of anything.

Still, it did make for a long wait.

At last, the head and shoulders of a huge and slovenly beast came slurching out of the swamp.

'I am Kralch, Eater of Babies,' said the giant, clearvoiced across a distance of a hundred paces.

'Hi,' said Alfric. 'I'm Alfric Danbrog.'

He pitched his voice as if for battle, and loud and clear it carried through the night air.

'Have you brought me a baby?'

'Yes,' said Alfric. 'Can't you hear it crying?'

'Faintly,' said the giant. 'I'm somewhat deaf.'

'Oh,' said Alfric. 'Sorry to hear that.'

So saying, Alfric took the bung from the first of his barrels and kicked it over. A light and combustible oil (distilled at great expense from the flesh of riverworms) spilt outward and spread across the swamp.

'What are you doing?' said the giant.

'Pouring out a libation to the gods,' said Alfric. 'It's a form of sacrifice.'

With that, he unbunged and overturned a second barrel.

'Libation or no libation,' said the giant, 'I'm coming for the baby. If you're still there when I get there, I'll have you too.'

'Thanks for the warning,' said Alfric, and unbunged and kicked over a third barrel.

Kralch waded forward. Then the swamp shallowed, and the giant started to crawl. As it did so, it began to pant in a most hideous way. The truth was, the huge and hideous creature was in danger of expiring as soon as it dragged itself from the supporting watermuck of the swamp; and it put its very life in danger every time it came to claim a baby. One thing was certain: though the giant could crawl, it was totally incapable of standing up and supporting its weight on its legs once it was out of the swamp.

As the giant drew near, Alfric kicked over the last of his barrels. Then waited.

'I did warn you,' said the Eater of Babies. 'If you're going to run, you'd better start now.'

'Oh,' said Alfric coolly, 'I think it's you who's going to do the running.'

So saying, Alfric produced a small jar and a pair of tongs. Alfric reached into the jar with the tongs and pulled out a small piece of metal. The metal looked grey by moonlight; and, had a stronger light been available, its hue would have remained unchanged.

As Alfric shook away the last drops of water, the metal burst into flames.

Alfric touched the flaming metal to his oil slick, which ignited. The swamp erupted. The giant screamed, engulfed by fire. It convulsed in agony. Kicked, clawed, howled and thrashed, and fought its way back into the depths of the swamp.

'So much for that,' said Alfric briskly.

Then he shivered, and set forth along the causeway.

Endless seemed that causeway, but at last the steps of the Spiderweb Castle were before him. Alfric climbed those steps and entered that place of death, the Castle of the Curse. As legend alleged, this was a place of the dead. Cold they were, their corpses ageless, frozen for centuries in the same positions.

The guards who held the castle gate never blinked as Alfric walked between them. He walked within, passing elders gathered in twos and threes in private conference; young lovers exchanging kisses and blisses in shadowed places; servants locked for ever in the hurry-scurry attitudes of hard-driven servitors.

At last, he entered the Grand Hall.

Again, legend was confirmed, for here candles shone with a ghostly phosphorescence, and the candles were not consumed by their own burning. It was silent, utterly silent. Alfric heard his own breathing, the creak of his own leather boots, the dry friction as a *frisson* of nervousness agitated his fingers to a spiderkick shuffle. His footsteps stirred the dust which rose, half-swirled then settled.

As legend said, there was the royal family. Alfric recognized them, just as he recognized their friends and retainers; for each was dressed according to rank and attainments. And there was the Princess Gwenarath; and, as legend said, she was passing fair. So fair that Alfric was moved to touch her cheek. He yielded to this impulse, but found the flesh cold, yes, cold, and as hard as marble. And he saw the dust of ages had gritted in the royal eyes, had settled in the folds of the royal cloak.

But she was fair regardless, and Alfric, despite himself, began to weep; for here a great evil had been done, and for this evil he had no remedy.

Alfric squeezed the tears from his eyes, and, angry at himself for thus sentimentalizing, he got down to business. Where was the queen? There. Proffering the mead to her husband. And he, a half-smile on his lips, was making as if he would take the cup from the gold-decked woman. A noble pair they made, and—

'Let legend do the weeping,' said Alfric, with willed and conscious brutality.

So saying, he went to the empty chair which stood beside the royal couple. And there was the sword, just as legend claimed. Sulamith's Grief, a silver sword in a silver sheath. Alfric drew the blade, and it burnt brighter than the candles.

And—

Did the Grand Hall change?

Did he hear a faint whisper of the noise of revel? Did people silent for long centuries stir, if only by an eyelash? Did—

'I imagine it,' said Alfric loudly.

And knew it was true, yes, he had been imagining it. There was no noise, no life, and no hope of either. These people were long dead, however perfectly preserved their appearance might be.

Then—

Something did move.

Alfric saw it not, but heard it. A wrenching sound as metal tore free from metal.

Alfric nearly leapt out of his skin.

'Who's there?' he said.

He drew Sulamith's Grief and discarded the scabbard. The silver sword quivered in his hand. His heart quick-kicked. His eyes blazed red, alert for murder.

'Who?' he roared. 'Who's there?'

Nothing.

Nobody.

But something—

There!

Alfric saw it.

The sword.

The weapon was sheathed at the side of a swarthy warrior of undistinguished appearance, but it was sticking out from the hilt by a good fingerlength. Unless he was sorely mistaken, that blade was the thing which had moved. It was a plain black blade which had leapt (if Alfric was guessing correctly) from a plain black sheath.

Carefully, Alfric recovered the scabbard which he had

dropped. He sheathed Sulamith's Grief. Then he unbuckled the swordbelt belonging to the swarthy warrior. Gingerly, he drew free the plain black sword. Briefly, letters flamed green against the black of the blade. Alfric barely had time to read them, but read them he did, and what he read he would never forget:

'Bloodbane be my name. A risk to all, not least to he who holds me.'

Alfric shuddered. He knew the history of this sword – for what Yudonic Knight could live in ignorance of the legends which told of its murders?

Still . . .

Alfric tested the heft of the weapon. While he put it to no test of strength, already he knew that the old iron was no wise weaker for all the ages it had lain here, derelict and abandoned. He knew. For the sword was speaking to him, its assurance wordless yet warm.

'Hear me,' said Alfric, swordhanded as he spoke grim-voiced to Grand Hall. 'You who are dead. You who are living. You who are yet to be. Hear me. I come not as a thief. I come not as a looter. I come as a hero, and what I claim I claim as mine by right. I am the son of Grendel. I am the grandson of Tromso Stavenger, Wormlord of Wen Endex. I am rightful heir to the royal throne. By such right I claim this weapon.'

His voice died away.

Leaving Alfric standing there, alone and unanswered.

He smiled suddenly, wryly amused by his own heroic conceit; then he sheathed Bloodbane and buckled on the swordbelt which sustained the weapon's scabbard. Then he picked up Sulamith's Grief, and left.

On the steps of the Castle of the Curse, Alfric paused. The moon shone bright upon the swampland wastes, and he could feel the allure of the moon and his own swelling strength. On a whim, he drew the blacksword Blood-bane, and the old iron ran with white fire as he saluted the moon.

Alfric was still standing there in salute when the swamp giant Kralch erupted from the swamp not fifty paces away. Mud and water streamed from the monster's shoulders as it slurred its threat:

'You! I see you! You die!'

A stupid threat to make at that time and place, for it would have been the easiest thing in the world for Alfric to run back into the shelter of the Spiderweb Castle. But run he did not, for the bloody spell of the sword was upon him.

'The moon approaches full,' said Alfric, his voice clear-carrying across the strength. 'Know you who I am? Know you what? The moon grows, and my strength likewise. My Change is almost upon me. My Change can be willed if thus I wish.'

Thus spoke Alfric Danbrog. He was drunk, intoxicated by the moon, by the sword's own slaughter-lust, by a beserker-born rage of exultation. All this was plain from his voice, and the giant sank back at the sound of it, for the monster was a cowardly creature at hear.

'Come!' said Alfric. Challenging. Demanding. 'What stands against you? This?' So saying, Alfric brandished the blacksword Bloodbane. The blade ran with silver and with fire. 'Come,' said Alfric, 'this is nothing to fear. It is but a splinter.'

But the giant, frightened of this battle-boast warrior, submerged and withdrew.

'Well,' said Alfric, in disappointment. 'Be like that, then.'

And then he sheathed the sword, and sanity returned, and he began to shudder, and a cold sweat broke out on his skin. Then he picked up Sulamith's Grief – he had dropped that weapon while focusing on his challenge – and set forth for the swampshore.

When Alfric reached the shore, a nagging crying was still coming from one particular grassclump.

'Oh well,' said Alfric, with a sigh. 'I suppose I can't leave the thing.'

And, with the greatest reluctance, he went to investigate. As he had feared, there was a baby lying in the grass. It was swaddled in some dirty sheeting and cradled in a basket.

Alfric picked up the basket. The handle promptly tore free, precipitating the baby to the ground. There it bawled prodigiously. Alfric chided himself. He should have known nobody would be so foolish as to waste a good basket on a surplus baby.

What now?

If he picked up the basket then the rotten fabric would probably tear apart. If he took the whining creature from the basket then it might well excrete liquid wastes all over him.

'A curse on copulation,' said Alfric.

Then he went to his horses, cut up one of the horse blankets, and brought back a piece the right size for baby-wrapping. He lifted the still-squalling thing from its basket. Its enfolding sheeting was damp, and smelt faintly of ammonia. Alfric shuddered, and quickly wrapped the creature in the blanket so only its face was exposed.

Then a voice roared:

'You! This is your doom!'

Alfric turned, and saw the swamp giant Kralch standing far out in the mudmuck. A moment later, Kralch hurled a huge handful of mud in Alfric's direction. Dodge? Duck? Alfric did not dare to do either, for the baby might have come to grief had he indulged in athletics.

Instead, Alfric turned his back to meet the mud, holding the baby close to his bosom.

Sklappersplat!

The mud burst around Alfric, nearly knocking him off his feet. The reek of it almost made him throw up. A fish kicked on the moonlit grass not half a dozen paces away, displaced from its home by the mudthrowing.

Alfric hastened into the cover of the trees.

The giant threw another handful of mud, but this time missed. Nevertheless, it screamed in triumph, slapped the swamp with its three-fingered hands and howled obscenities to the night air.

'How childish,' muttered Alfric.

When he got to his horses, he dumped the baby into one of the saddlebags, and was shortly on his way home.

Though he did not know it, his homeward journey was not to be uneventful.

CHAPTER TEN

Alfric was only halfway back to Galsh Ebrek when he met with a stranger.

The circumstances of their meeting were thus:

Alfric was riding along when he saw the surface of the path had been disturbed. Such disturbance would have been invisible to any ordinary human by night, at least in a place so dark and overhung by trees; but to Alfric it was very clear.

Presuming that it was possible that bandits might have hastily dug a pit in that place, Alfric swung down from the saddle and drew the silversword Sulamith's Grief.

In open ground, Alfric might have stayed in the saddle. But here his options were limited. He could not spur his horse forward, because a suspected pit lay ahead. He could not retreat on horseback, either, because the pack animals behind him quite blocked the narrow path. Nor could he ride into the forest to either side, because the path ran between banks too steep for a horse to climb them; and, besides, the forest was low-branched and undergrowthed, which would have made riding either impossible or suicidal.

Warily, Alfric scanned the trees to either side, and shortly spied a single figure almost hidden by the undergrowth.

'You!' said Alfric. 'Step forth!'

No response.

149

Alfric stooped, picked up a stone and shied it at the figure. The stone clattered through the branches, barely missing the stranger.

'I see you well enough,' said Alfric. 'Step forth, or I'll cut you to pieces.'

Moving slowly and furtively, the figure crept into the open. Did it have longbow? Crossbow? Throwing stick? No. A sickle, that was all.

'Drop the blade,' said Alfric.

The figure dropped the blade.

Alfric advanced.

His opponent retreated.

Alfric stepped on the sickle, trapping it under his boot.

'Now,' he said, 'I will kill you, for you are doubtless a bandit. Do you wish to make a confession before I lop off your head?'

'Master,' said his intended victim, speaking in an old man's voice. 'Master, lop me not, for I have treasure in my cave. Treasure to make you rich.'

'You have, have you?' said Alfric.

'Truly.'

'You'd better not be lying. If you are, I'll cut off your sex and leave you to bleed to death.'

'Oh, I'm not lying, master, not lying at all.'

'Then tie up my horses while my blade keeps watch. Then lead on to this cave. Is it far?'

'A hundred paces, no more.'

As the old man was tying up the horses, the baby began to cry.

'What's that?' said the old man.

'What does it sound like?'

'A baby.'

'Why, and a baby it is. If you've any more stupid questions then keep them to yourself.'

'If it's a baby,' said the old man, 'I—'

'It is a baby! I've told you that twice, now.'

'My, you haven't half got a temper!' said the old man. 'All I was saying was maybe we'd best bring it inside.'

'I'll do that,' said Alfric. 'You keep your hands off it. And remember – I've a hand free for my sword.' He picked up the blanket-wrapped baby. 'Very well. We're ready. Lead on.'

The old man was lying about the distance to his lair, for the cave proved to be a good 150 paces distant. But Alfric forgave him for that.

The cave itself proved to be a most comfortable place. The elements had been walled out, and a door gave entry to a lantern-lit place complete with truckle bed, table and four-strong chairs. At the back of the cave were half a dozen strongboxes.

'Where's the treasure?' said Alfric.

'In the strongboxes,' said the old man. 'Before I open them, would you like a beer? Beer and cheese?'

'Beer, no,' said Alfric. 'Cheese, yes.'

'That's in the strongboxes too,' said the old man.

'Very well,' said Alfric. 'Let's have it.'

Alfric set the baby down on the table then sat himself down. He watched intently as the old man opened one of the strongboxes. Unless Alfric was much mistaken, there was some treachery afoot here. But what? As Alfric watched, the old man lifted a large cheese from the strongbox. He brought it to the table and cut a piece. Which he offered to Alfric.

Just as Alfric was reaching out for the cheese, he saw a

sudden gleam of triumph in the old man's eyes. Alfric jerked back his hand.

'It's poisoned!' he said. 'Isn't it?'

'No, master,' said the old man. 'It's perfectly good cheese. It's not poisoned at all.'

'Really?' said Alfric. 'Then you'll be happy to eat some for me.'

The old man hesitated.

'Eat it!' roared Alfric.

With every evidence of reluctance, the old man began to gnaw at the cheese. Then suddenly his attitude changed, and he wolfed at the stuff savagely. Moments later, with the strength of the cheese within him, the old man began to Change.

Alfric kicked away his chair and leapt backwards as his enemy swelled, girthed, heightened, haired and bruted, becoming monstrous, hands becoming paws, arms becoming legs. A musty smell filled the cave, a smell which Alfric somehow associated with . . . with . . . hamsters?

Down on four legs dropped the monster. Then it bared its teeth and chittered at Alfric in a battlefury. It was a hamster indeed, but it was a hamster the size of a bear, and surely the equal of any warrior in battle.

'Blood and bitches!' said Alfric.

Then tossed aside Sulamith's Grief and drew the blacksword Bloodbane. The intoxication of murder swelled his voice to wrath as he challenged the werehamster:

'Die if you must, for die you will if you take but one step toward me. I hold the blackblade Bloodbane. This weapon gives no mercy.'

As Alfric was so saying, the monster rushed toward the table. It paused, its whitesavage teeth but a hair away from the baby's head.

'Leave,' said the werehamster. 'Leave, or I will kill the child.'

'Feel free,' said Alfric. 'I found it an embarrassing encumbrance.'

The werehamster hesitated.

'Come on!' roared Alfric. 'Make up your mind. Kill the baby then die yourself. Or change to a man and beg my mercy.'

The werehamster chose to Change, and was shortly shrinking and shrivelling, deflating and wrinkling, becoming a man again. Once thus reconfigured, it said:

'What are you going to do to me?'

'By rights I should kill you. That is the rightful fate of all shape-changers.'

'But I'm – I'm not one of the Evil Ones. I'm only a werehamster.'

'That's evil enough for me,' said Alfric.

'Who are you, then?' said the werehamster man.

'I am Alfric Danbrog, son of Grendel and grandson of the Wormlord Tromso Stavenger.'

'Then who are you to talk? You're a werewolf!'

'I am not a werewolf,' said Alfric. 'But even if I was, it would make no difference. You are a bandit, a shameless marauder, a disturber of graves, and eater of live meat and dead, an evil hag-thing.'

'I am not,' said the werehamster man.

'You are,' said Alfric. 'At the very least, you are a bandit. You bring people here to kill them and steal their gold.'

'I do not.'

'You do,' said Alfric implacably. 'There is gold here. I can smell it.'

So saying, Alfric stared at the strongboxes, and his

eyes flashed wolfblood red. The werehamster man shrank back, terrified, fearing that this Yudonic Knight with his homicidal hero-sword was about to launch an assault upon his host.

'Well,' said Alfric. 'What's it going to be? Either I get your gold or your head. But I'm not leaving here empty-handed.'

This threat proved profitable, for the old man thereupon produced seven bagsacks of gold from his strong-boxes.

'That's all I have,' said the werehamster man anxiously.

'Is it?' said Alfric. 'It's not much.'

'It's all I have. I'm telling you!'

'All right,' said Alfric. 'I don't want all your gold. A bag will be quite enough.'

'Are you sure?' said the werehamster anxiously.

'Quite sure,' said Alfric.

Though the blackblade Bloodbane was urging Alfric to murder, he had already decided to spare the werehamster's life. So he thought it best to leave the thing with the better part of its money.

If Alfric were to take all the werehamster's treasure, then the thing would surely go marauding until it had redeemed its loss. Or, alternatively, if – as Alfric suspected – it had grown too old and feeble to make an effective bandit, then it might die in miserable poverty.

Both outcomes could easily be avoided by leaving the brute with some of its gains, however ill-gotten they might be. As for himself, why, Alfric was a Yudonic Knight, and so would never starve, for the ruling class had first claim on all that was good in Galsh Ebrek. Alfric was also in receipt of a banker's salary, which was well worth having. And, since he was being forced to contend for a kingdom, he lacked the patience to trifle with a werehamster's loot.

Under Alfric's supervision, the werehamster emptied one of the bagsacks on to the table. Once Alfric had assured himself all the gold was gold indeed – as a point of honour, he was determined not to let himself be swindled by a werehamster – he watched as the stuff was repacked. Then he made the werehamster carry both gold and baby out to the forest path, and supervised the miserable creature while it filled in the deathpit dug in that path.

Then Alfric rode on his way.

Thus did Alfric Danbrog triumph in one of the greatest tests of knighthood: a confrontation with one of the dreaded shape-changers. A warm glow of self-congratulation possessed him as he rode back to Galsh Ebrek. But this dissipated abruptly when he saw two men waiting for him at the Stanch Gates: Ciranoush Norn and Muscleman Wu.

'Good evening,' said Alfric, dropping his battlehand to the hilt of the blacksword Bloodbane.

The brothers Norn made no answer, but also made no move towards him. And Alfric, realizing that the inevitable feud-death confrontation was yet to come, pulled his hand free from the weapon which wished to claim it for murder, and rode on to the Green Cricket.

Why had the brothers Norn been waiting for him at the Stanch Gates? Obviously: to let him know his death was intended. They would not kill him in public, no, for the Wormlord would revenge him. The death of Pig Norn must have taught him that. But they would kill him sometime, somewhere, somehow – or at least try to encompass his death.

And they wanted him to suffer a nightmare or two before his doom befell him.

At the Green Cricket, Alfric checked in his hired horses at the stable, then went inside the inn. Anna Blaume was serving at the bar, helped by her daughter Sheila.

'A baby,' said Alfric, putting the squalling thing down on the counter.

'So I see,' said Anna Blaume.

Alfric dumped his bagsack on to the same counter, spilling gold across the beerspit wood.

'It's patrimony,' said Alfric.

'Is it a boy or a girl?' said Sheila.

'How would I know?' said Alfric.

'You mean you haven't looked!' said Anna Blaume. 'That means you – oh Alfric! The poor thing's probably been wet for – grief, men!'

'Blood of the Gloat,' muttered Alfric. 'A hero's welcome, is it? Give me a beer.'

While Alfric was drinking, his wife came downstairs on the arm of a common-born bruiser. The pair sat on a table. Du Deiner brought them drinks, and caught Alfric's eye, and smirked. This was an invitation for Alfric to make a scene: to threaten the bruiser and perhaps to kill him. With Bloodbane in his hands, Alfric could kill every man in the inn if he chose to go to war.

But . . .

Alfric found himself totally incapable of rousing himself to the fury which convention demanded. If his wife was committing adultery – what of it? Such wilful disloyalty suggested she wanted a divorce. Very well. She could have it. Alfric felt marriage had been a mistake, a descent into organic life which had distracted him from his career.

Besides, Viola Vanaleta was lowborn, and he could not have her as his wife if he was to become king. As king, he would need a wife from one of the Families; for only thus could he truly command the loyalties of the Yudonic Knights. If Alfric won the throne, Vanaleta would have to go whether she liked it or not, for to keep her would be to insult every Yudonic Knight in Wen Endex. So, at this stage, a complete abscission of their relationship would not be untimely.

With that decided, Alfric finished his beer then left the Green Cricket, sparing not a glance for Vanaleta as he strode from the inn. Once out in the night, he looked around warily, just in case the brothers Norn might be waiting in ambush. But they were not. So down the street he went, the murder-blade Bloodbane sheathed at his side and, swaggersticked in his hand, the scabbarded silversword, Sulamith's Grief.

As he walked along, he saw nothing unusual. As his fear of the brothers Norn faded, he became buoyant. Moonglitter brightened mudpuddles and mullioned windows alike, and the moon sharpened his every sense. So that, when passing one sidestreet—

He smelt something.

Something female.

Strong was that scent, and he knew what it was, and knew he should not venture into the sidestreet shadows, and knew what he would find if he did. But the brightburning moon commanded him, and, helpless to resist, down the sidestreet he went, and found what he had expected, a cart heavy-laden with the corpse of a huge wolf. Black was the fur of the beast, and black was the blood which had thickened on the fur around the heartwound, and black was the stump of the quarrel which had found the creature's heart.

The crossbow which had hurled that lethal bolt had been tossed into the cart, and by the wolf it lay. And Alfric smelt the stench of the killer upon the crossbow, and was afraid, and full of hate.

Then—

Sudden as the savagery of his fist-battering angers—

The fit was upon him, and, unable to help himself, he threw back his head and howled. Deep-throated the sound, bloodbarbaric, the gut-threat challenge of a forest marauder. And scarcely had the howl died away when a doorway nearby was thrown open with a bang. Out stumbled a man with a hatchet in one hand, a lantern in the other.

And Alfric was minded to savage the fork-legged thing on the spot, to skullcrunch its head and scrabble its guts, to maul it and gnaw it, to take revenge for the murder of the she.

'What was that?' said the citizen, wide-eyed with alarm.

And Alfric smelt the man, smelt his stale sweat, his beerbelch breath, his rich-larded fat and musty stupidity; smelt adultery's grease and buttock-cleft filth; and knew this, this, this thing had killed the she, with his stupid concoction of warped wood and wire he had killed her dead, and for that he deserved to die, surely, it would be but the work of the moment to rend him and tear him.

So Alfric—

—shuddered and—

—closed his jaws decisively.

Then shuddered again, got a grip on himself and spoke:

'It was a dog. A dog at the meat. I kicked it away. Now I bid you guard or remove this animal, my good man, or I'll have you arrested for creating a public menace.'

So saying, Alfric touched the hilt of his sword; and a bloodlust urge from the deathsword Bloodbane incited his heart to murder. But that he resisted easily, for he knew it was the sword speaking to him. And, once he had seen the citizen remove the wolf to a barn and secure it against dogs and such, Alfric went on his way.

As he stalked through the streets of Galsh Ebrek, Alfric kept his head down, deliberately ignoring the moon, and by the time he reached his home he felt more like a man and less like a wolf. But the shock of what had very nearly happened was still upon him; and he decided, in a coldblooded way, to drink himself into oblivion. For otherwise he did not think he could sleep.

However, he was only in the early stages of this project when his father arrived. Alfric explained what he was about – though he did not say why – and Grendel Dranbrog expressed a wish to join him. When Grendel made it clear he thought his son's drinking was the consequence of woman trouble, Alfric did nothing to disabuse him of this notion. So the two of them drank together, and ran down women as they did so.

'If only,' said Grendel, in a moment of unprecedented misogamy, 'they could all be killed as we kill Herself.'

'Have we killed Herself?' said Alfric.

'Not yet,' said Grendel. 'But that will come. In time. The Wormlord's sworn it, has he not?'

'So he has,' said Alfric. 'So I swear it too. With all

159

three quests complete, I'll march with the Wormlord. I'll dare Her lair and hack off Her head.'

'I'll hold you to that,' said his father.

Alfric realized he might have committed himself unwisely, but he scarcely cared. For surely killing Herself would be but a small feat compared to that which awaited him next. For next he must dare the vampires in their lair and rescue the third of the saga swords.

CHAPTER ELEVEN

When Alfric presented the silversword Sulamith's Grief to the Wormlord in Saxo Pall, the king of Wen Endex gave him in return the bright blade Chalingrad, arbiter of many deaths. This was a blade truly blessed with success, for well the weapon knew the bloody kiss of victory. And it was this ring-embellished sword that Alfric took with him when he rode forth on his third and final quest.

Chalingrad was doubtless a lesser weapon than Bloodbane; but, after due consideration, Alfric had decided to leave the deathblade at home, for he deemed the thing to be as much a menace to the owner as to anyone else. He would not be able to outfight the vampires, however valorous his swordarm; so a sword which was ever tempting him to murder would not be an asset on this quest.

For the expedition, Alfric had been given a broken-down horse not possessed of a name, which suggested that Anna Blaume did not expect him to return alive from the vampires' lair. Fair enough. He had his own doubts about his survival.

But he put those doubts out of mind as he rode through the globble-glubble mires of the streets of Galsh Ebrek, and then by the nightwaters of the Riga Rimur River where waterworms dwelt in dreams of drenching, and then down a shatterstone road through winterfallow farmlands. Then forest claimed him, cold forest where ice broke krintalkrastal beneath the hooves of his horse.

His journey was long; and before the end he was weary, and chilled by the night's bitter cold. The ground's stones and the sky's stars alike were hard and comfortless, tokens of an inimical cosmos. He tried to keep himself awake by revising the lemmas of ursury, the delicate mathematics of enrichment. But he began to sleep in spasms, dreaming brief dreams of seasalt fish and tromping elephants, waking time and again to save himself from tumbling from the saddle.

Alfric at last reached the cliffs which were his destination. Tall and gaunt they rose; with, beyond them, rising huger yet, derelict mountain upthrusts where humans never ventured. Somewhere, high amidst the mountains, a scarf of colour gleamed into life, whirled thrice about a peak of stone, and then was gone. What was it? Something equivalent to the zana, the wild rainbows of Galsh Ebrek? Or something different?

Alfric put it out of mind. Working in accordance with the instructions he had been given, he began to search for the door into the vampire depths, which he located after a long and weary search. This was clearly going to be a night for the long and the weary, and he only hoped his negotiations with the vampires would not prove too protracted.

The door was at the top of a steep flight of steps cut into the living rock of the mountains, so Alfric tethered his horse to a convenient tree, then began to climb.

As Alfric Danbrog advanced upon that door, warfaring men in battledress began to march out of it. Armed with old iron they were, their faces fell and silent. In an access of terror, Alfric clasped his ring-embellished sword and prepared to die – then realized the onmarching men were nothing but ghosts. As they flowed through him and around him, he imagined he heard a ghostly horn calling them to battle.

Then the men were gone, and Alfric Danbrog shrugged off his shock and, single of purpose, strode towards the door to the vampire depths. Striding thus, he tripped over a rock, which almost threw him off balance.

A rock?

On a night like this in a place like this, something which looked to be a rock could be anything. Alfric, remembering childhood tales of Grapter the Wishtoad, kicked at the rock until he had determined it was stone indeed.

A rock, then.

Rock qua rock.

A phenomenological rock?

Perhaps.

Alfric realized he was procrastinating. He willed himself away from the rock which had suddenly become so fascinating, and marched on the stonemade door to the vampires' lair. Alfric knocked upon that door, but the mountain answered him not.

'Open,' said Alfric sternly, 'or my sword will shatter your soul.'

The door gave no hint of opening, so Alfric swung at it with Chalingrad. To Alfric's surprise, the arbiter of many deaths splintered against the unyielding rock.

'Stroth!' he said.

Then examined the wreckage of the blade with care. Unless he was greatly mistaken, the weapon was made of cast iron. Not for the first time, Alfric began to wonder whether the Wormlord wanted him dead.

As the sword was useless for attack or defence, Alfric cast it aside, and thus was alone and unarmed when the door lurched open. At which stage his courage deserted him, and he would have fainly retired – but it was too late, for the door was fully open.

'Well?' said a ratcheting voice, a voice all stonedust and corncrake. 'Are you coming in or aren't you?'

'I am,' said Alfric.

Then swallowed, and strode into the tunnel which yawned in front of him. The door closed, shutting out the night, and leaving no light whatsoever; but Alfric, his eyes a venomous red, deciphered the blackness at will.

'Have you come here to die?' said someone behind him.

'No,' said Alfric. 'I've come here to offer you a deal.'

'A deal?'

'Don't sound so amazed. I'm Izdarbolskobidarbix, a Banker Third Class from the Flesh Traders' Financial Association. I'm authorized to make you a proposition. I suggest you take me to your Council Chamber.'

'Not till I know your name.'

'My name I have given you already,' said Alfric in irritation. 'Izdarbolskobidarbix is my name. Some of my peers have taken the liberty of shortening that title to Iz'bix on occasion; I will not resent it if you avail yourself of a similar privilege.'

'No name thus tongued was ever born in Wen Endex,' said the vampire voice doubtfully.

'Still,' said Alfric, 'it is how I call myself.'

'Then,' said the vampire, 'leaving aside the question of how you call yourself, who are you? Really?'

'Oh, all right then, if you really must know, I'm Alfric Danbrog, son of Grendel Danbrog and grandson of the

164

Wormlord Tromso Stavenger. You want to hear more? Gertrude Danbrog is my mother and Ursula Major my father's sister, hence my aunt. My paternal grandmother was—'

'Enough,' said the vampire, cutting him off. 'You have told me enough. Your naming makes you a shape-changer. Thus you are welcome, thrice welcome, ever welcome in the halls of blood.'

Alfric wanted to protest that he was not a shape-changer at all, but thought such objection unwise: hence allowed himself to be escorted to the Council Hall, where fresh blood was served to him while he waited for the Elders to gather.

At first, Alfric indulged his curiosity by scanning the assembling Elders. Under the interrogation of his probing eyes, they revealed themselves to be ancient, their skins clinging very close to their skeletons. Close proximity to the warm-blooded Alfric Danbrog inspired the vampires with appetite. They opened their mouths and drooled. Their teeth were sharp, very sharp, and many. Alfric abruptly ceased scanning the dark and settled back to wait.

At last, the Oldest of the Elders spoke:

'Greetings, Alfric Danbrog. We hear you have a proposition for us.'

'I do,' said Alfric. 'I come here as a representative of the Flesh Traders' Financial Association. We wish to do business.'

'The Bank has rejected our business in the past,' said the Oldest. 'Why should it change its mind now?'

'Policies change when needs change,' said Alfric. 'Our needs have changed. We have also grown more . . . more realistic over the years. The absurd prejudice

165

against bloodfeeding is no longer to be found among our ranks.'

'What of Yaf, then?' said the Oldest.

'Yaf is dead,' said Alfric bluntly. 'He's been dead for a hundred years.'

'But he can't be!' said the Oldest. 'It was only yesterday that he rebuffed me.'

'Was it?' said Alfric. 'Consult your memories.'

Silence.

Then, from out of the dark, the voice of the Oldest:

'You are right. It is my age. The years are so short after the first thousand or so. Besides, I've slept most of that time.'

'It is a pity that your sleep was not profitable,' said Alfric. 'But, with 3 per cent compounding interest, your sleep could be profitable indeed. We would of course be prepared to pay the interest in a form convenient to you, that is, not as gold but as virgin females to the equivalent value.'

'Details, please.'

'Interest would be credited to your account annually,' said Alfric. 'An initial deposit of 100 talents of gold would be worth 103 in a year's time. In two years, your investment would have grown to 106 talents plus a 900th of a talent. In three years—'

'Thank you,' said the Oldest, cutting him off just as he was getting enthusiastic. 'I am familiar with the wonders of compound interest. What you propose is similar to what I myself proposed to Yaf when I ventured to Galsh Ebrek.'

'I know,' said Alfric. 'I have seen the files. You offered Yaf some very good business. He was wrong to turn you down. Future generations have lamented his foolishness.'

166

The vampires had proposed to make a massive investment of gold with the Bank, then come to the Bank once every ten years to claim their interest in the form of so many virgin slaves. But Yaf had apparently experienced some moral scruples which had prevented him from concluding this bargain.

Why?

Alfric had no idea.

After all, a great many people invest their money in banks, and there is nothing to stop the investor spending the interest thus gained on buying slaves to be slaughtered, or in paying assassins, or in purchasing weapons of war. So surely it makes no moral difference if the bank (on the client's behalf) makes payments for similar purposes.

'You do guarantee,' said the Oldest, 'that you will be able to pay interest in the form of virgin slaves?'

'At the standard rate, yes,' said Alfric. 'I guarantee it with my life.'

'That's no guarantee!' said the Oldest. 'Not when you die so quickly.'

'I am only thirty-three,' said Alfric. 'The years of my strength are only half gone. Assuming you collect your first interest payment in ten years' time, I will still be in the prime of life.'

'If you were a human,' said the Oldest, 'I would not trust you. However, fortunately you are a werewolf. Therefore we can bargain.'

Alfric was enraged by this accusation. But he smoothed diplomacy into his voice and said:

'The terms I can offer you are good. But there is one thing I must have if we are to conclude any bargain whatsoever.'

'What thing is that?' said the Oldest.

'You have a sword here,' said Alfric. 'You have the sword known as Kinskorn.'

'Yes,' said the Oldest, acknowledging possession of that mighty blade.

'I require it,' said Alfric.

'Why?' said the Oldest.

Alfric sighed, tired already, and wearied further by the prospect of having to explain himself yet again. He tried to keep it short.

'As you doubtless know,' said Alfric, 'my grandfather, Tromso Stavenger, is the Wormlord. He denied all rights of succession to his eldest son, Grendel. I am Grendel's oldest son, but cannot inherit the throne in the ordinary way because my father has been cast out of the royal family.

'As things stand, Ursula Major should inherit the throne when the Wormlord dies. But he has repented of his choice. He regrets the wrath with which he exiled his son. He wishes to redeem himself by letting his son's son inherit the throne. I am his son's son.

'That I may inherit the throne with honour, the Wormlord has set me the task of salvaging the three saga swords. Two I have. I dared the great dragon Qa in his burrow. Long and hard I fought with him in his deep and smokey lair. Great were the gouts of flame he hurled against me, but my sword was strong, and the old iron availed where the iron of others had failed.'

Unconsciously, Alfric was slipping into the rhythms of the storytellers of Wen Endex, his phrasing drifting into the vocabularies of legend as his own tale took hold of him. Despite his determination to be succinct, he had given himself fully to wordy poetry by the time he came to tell of his battle with the swamp giant Kralch.

'Then,' said Alfric, 'I rode back to Galsh Ebrek. But my journey was not yet over, for—'

He paused.

These were vampires, outcasts, blood drinkers. They tolerated him only because they thought him a werewolf, an accursed shape-changer. Alfric had been about to boast of his duel with a ferocious werehamster, and the aplomb with which he had brought that baby-threatening monster to heel. But such a victory might not win him favour with this audience.

'For?' said the Oldest, in an encouraging manner. 'Go on.'

'For my horse fell lame,' said Alfric lamely, 'and I had to walk the rest of the way home.'

'Oh,' said the Oldest.

He was greatly disappointed. Being a vampire is one of the most tedious of all possible modes of existence, since it largely consists of sitting in the dark for many months at a time doing virtually nothing. Hence vampires make an enthusiastic audience for songs, poems and legends of all descriptions; a fact which allows any fluent-voiced prisoner of these monsters to survive until sleep or hoarseness prevails.

'Anyway,' said Alfric, 'you know how it is, and how it must be. I rescued the ironsword Edda, the revenant's claw. I dared the Spiderweb Castle for Sulamith's Grief. Now I must have Kinskorn to complete my sweep of the saga swords and secure my claim to the throne of Wen Endex.'

'Once you have all three swords,' said the Oldest, 'how soon will they make you king?'

'Immediately,' said Alfric.

'Immediately?'

'Yes,' said Alfric. 'For She has once more ventured from her lair. The Wormlord has sworn to surrender his throne and march forth against Herself as soon as the third of the saga swords has been delivered to Saxo Pall.'

This drew a rustling murmur of comment and speculation from the assembled Elders. Vampires are not afraid of much, but even they stand in fear of Herself.

'This is true?' said the Oldest.

'If it were not true, I would not have said it,' answered Alfric. 'I am not just a banker. I am also a Yudonic Knight, born and bred. We do not deal in falsehood.'

'Perhaps not,' said the Oldest. 'Very well. If Kinskorn is a necessary part of our bargain, then you must have it. But there is a quid pro quo.'

'Speak,' said Alfric.

'The virgin blood which constitutes our interest must be delivered by agents of the Bank to our very door.'

'That we can do,' said Alfric.

Comptroller Xzu had warned Alfric that the vampires would be very reluctant to venture within crossbow range of Galsh Ebrek, either to deposit their gold or to collect their interest. And Xzu had assured Alfric that the Bank would be perfectly happy to purchase virgin females on behalf of the vampires (in Tang, or Obooloo, or wherever the best price was to be had), to bring that livestock through the Door, to smuggle it out of Galsh Ebrek and to deliver it to the bloodfeeders.

In due course, both Alfric and the vampires were satisfied. Documents were sighted and signed, arrangements were made for delivery of gold and counter-delivery of interest, the brave sword Kinskorn was

170

delivered into Alfric's hands, and then he was led back outside.

Alfric said goodbye to his hosts, reclaimed his horse, and, with Kinskorn sheathed at his side, he set forth for Galsh Ebrek. As he went, he began composing a hero-song to tell of his great battle with the vampires in the echoing underearth halls of horror. He began to sing little bits of it to the night air.

It was a very exciting song, and Alfric became quite enthusiastic about it as he told of a fierce-voiced encounter in the vampire's Council Chamber, of the driblets of blood which spilt from a foul and stinking chalice as the Oldest drank, of the beserk rage with which Alfric Danbrog fell upon his enemies, of the swingeing sword-strokes with which he hack-chopped the monsters, of the waters of an underground river suffused with the phosphorescent green of the battle-spilt blood of a dying vampire, of the regal courage with which he hazarded his strength against a foe most fell.

Oh, it is great stuff, great stuff, this telling of knightly deeds! Doughty weapons clash; blood spurts; and reeking combat-sweat fouls the air. A hero stands solo against the deadly malice of demonic monsters. Dragon-decorated is the hero's helm, and flame is the blade he wields in the raven-black night as his martial deeds.

Imagine now the banquet; imagine now the hall. The great are beerdrinking from dragon-wreathed goblets, tossing chicken bones at the untunchilamons which go flirting through the air as the singer bards his deeds. The skop is inspired, knowing he is watched by men wise in years and noble of lineage, men who have tales of their own to tell. Stories of voyages in ocean-roving ships, of the swashbuckling waves of the tawny oceans, of landings on shores destined to run red with the blood of mortal onslaught.

And when the singer is done, those other tales begin, and so we hear of such ships and such beaches, and then of other things. Battles, swords, dragons, giants, blood, sinew, thigh, thew. Journeys fraught with misery. Kingly men in ample mail-coats striving to secure renown with bloody iron. Battle-honoured heroes ensnared and at last brought down to ruin by the conspiracies of the marriage bed.

And then, surely, ultimately we must hear of the Wormlord and his quest, of Tromso Stavenger and the way he fought Her son, met him face to face amidst the wolf-infested hillsides, the gloom of the crags. Met him, dared him, fought him, conquered, killed . . .

With such imaginings high-singing in his head, Alfric rode his broken-down horse through the forest wilds. The moon was riding high by now, the swollen moon mazed by broken branches as it filtered through the forest, layering mosaics of silver upon the gutteral black of the water of the streams which laced through the forest.

At last, Alfric's elation at daring the vampires and winning the brave sword Kinskorn began to wear off. His song-singing ceased, as did his imagining; and he began to take account of his saddle-sore backside, his nagging hunger, the bone-chill of the night, and his own weariness. At least he could do something about the hunger, for he had a loaf of bread in a sack tied behind his saddle.

Alfric stopped and dismounted.

'Don't go anywhere,' he said to his horse.

Then looped the reins around a branch so the animal

couldn't go anywhere. Then stamped his feet, shuddered at the cold, fumbled open the breadsack and took out the loaf, which was wrapped up in a bag of salmon skin where it was safe from rain and mist, and from the sweat of his horse.

The bread had been hot when purchased but now it was cold. Alfric tore the crust apart with merciless talons and wolfed into the soft and yielding flesh, his teeth savaging its substance as if seeking to tear bones from their anchoring tendons. Eating, feeding, tearing, gulleting, he looked like a wild thing; and, in the rage of his appetite, felt like one.

He chewed too little and swallowed too greedily; and bread lumped into a hard and painful bolus as his muscles worked it slowly down his throat. Then he ravaged the loaf anew, and, without warning, a quicksilver pain agonized through one of his rear teeth. He stopped chewing abruptly. Strange, this pain. He never got it when eating hard things, no, only when masticating sticky stuff like bread. He eased the mulch-mush of bread to the other side of his mouth, stuck a finger into his mouth, and cautiously felt the offending tooth.

No pain.

At least: his touch elicited no pain.

With great care, Alfric began to chew again. Then stopped. For he heard something. What? Unless he was mistaken, what he heard was a horse's hoof as it went crunch-crack through a crust of frozen mud. Then he heard a scattering of breaking twigs. What would break branches like that? Not a man, surely, for a man would be careful of his face. Unless he was armoured for battle, his helm protecting him from the fingering wood.

Alfric abruptly lost his appetite.

173

He spat out the bread in his mouth.

Then, as the moon caught them, he saw them, two of them, mounted men in the forest, and they saw him, for the larger challenged him:

'Danbrog!'

Alfric knew the man by voice. Wu Norn. Muscleman Wu. Swordsman, axeman, fistman, killer.

Alfric tried to respond. But found himself without voice. It was the shock of the sudden which had done it. He was unmanned as if by ambush. Had thought himself safe, home, successful, victorious, the slaughter-dare in the vampires' lair nothing more than a bad dream. Was not prepared for this, was not prepared at all, and already the smaller man had swung down from his horse and was coming at the charge, running over the buckle-buck of the ground, weapon out and rage in his throat, and—

Alfric drew Kinskorn.

And the wisdom of the weapon taught him necessity, taught him in time, and the blade balanced perfectly as it met shadow with shadow, iron with iron. Sparks screamed, ice cracked, a branch broke, and something—

Something was thrashing on the end of Alfric's sword, and Alfric drove his weight against the something, drove the sword deep, drove the sword home. And then, panting, sweating, cursing, tried to pull the sword out again. But the blade was stuck, or so it seemed to his sweating hands. But the man was dead, he was dead, was killed, Alfric had killed him, or Kinskorn had.

'Dansbrog!'

Thus roared Muscleman Wu. Then spurred his horse, crashing the beast through the nightgrowth, heedless of any damage which might be done to the brute which bore him or to himself.

Alfric waited to hear no more, but flung himself on to his own horse and spurred the beast. Off they went. Then the animal lurched violently as the reins restrained it.

'Stroth!' said Alfric, tugging at the reins.

But they would not come free and the branch would not break. So down from the horse he leapt, meaning to unknot the leather, remount and respur. But there was no time. Wu Norn was almost upon him, his sword already out for a slaughter-spree. Then Alfric screamed in frustrated rage, then punched his horse, then swore in blubbering panic and fled.

Bent low he ran, bent low, stooping at speed into the thickest of the forest, running, panting, running through the lowgrowth undergrowth, the snaggle-hook trees too thick for pursuit, too thick for Wu to follow unless Wu dismounted.

Wu did dismount.

When Alfric stopped, he heard Muscleman Wu. The killer of men was not far behind. Alfric was weaponless, had no way to fight. But could not run, could run no more, for he was unfit, out of condition, that was the truth of it. He sobbed for fear of his death, then—

—Mud.

So thought Alfric, and grappled with a handful of the stuff, hissing with the pain as ice-splintered muck packed into his palm. But the pain was good for the pain steadied him, sobered him, and he began to think, it might be a little late but he was thinking at last, and he eased his breathing as best he could, and sank low, and sheltered himself in the shadows, and heard Wu Norn swear, and remembered.

Moon was the night, but still the shadows were many,

yes, many many, here in the forest, the forest all stilts and crutches, all masts and fishing rods, and he was crouched in the thickest of those shadows, and the bafflement of the dark was sufficient to hide him, at least for the moment, yes, surely this man had lost him. Yes. But.

—But keep back!

Yes, he must keep back in the deepest of the shadows, for it was all too easy for the moon to catch the lenses of his spectacles and betray him by a splinter-flash of a light brighter than starlight. If he kept to the shadows, he would be safe, safe, at least for the moment.

—But.

But Muscleman Wu was not going to give up that easily. Wu began to quarter the ground, stabbing at logs lest they have livers inside them, kicking at softbogs in case lungs be laired within. Often he stopped. To listen.

So.

—What now?

—Retreat?

But this was no night for shadow-sneaking, no night for silent withdrawals. It was a night of frost-sharpened sounds, of sticks awaiting their rupture, of ice crusted that weight might break it. Alfric heard a night-hunter clitter through a litter of undergrowth rubbish a good two hundred paces distant. Wu Norn's head swung round, and moon spiked briefly from the warrior's eyes as he considered the sound and the distance.

Then Wu resumed his quartering-hunting.

'Danbrog!' roared Wu.

Then:

'Grendelson!'

Then:

176

'Come out, you whore! Iz-boliks, you banker-slut! Come out!'

But Alfric answered not to Iz-boliks, or to whore, or to Danbrog, or to Grendelson. However named, he would not answer. Instead, he lay still and thought.

Wu was formidable.

The warrior was wood-wise, could tell man from animal, and had hearing good enough to alert him to the need to tell. And Alfric, despite his thinking, had no bright ideas at all, and so was still lying there, still waiting, the cold of the mud hurting his hand, and he had no ideas, no ideas at all, for the mud was but a whim, for what could it do for him?

—Blind him.

But Muscleman Wu would kill him even if blinded by a faceful of mud. With sword in hand, Wu would kill him. Blade describing whirlwinds as it chopped through the night, slaughtering, fractioning, seeking, finding. At close quarters, a blinded man is still a killer if he knows what he's doing. And maybe Wu would blink at the right moment, or the mud would go wild, or the mud would find its mark but would blind the enemy for no more than an instant.

—No hope.

—No hope without weapons.

—A stick, then.

Alfric reached for the nearest branch which looked weapon-weighty. But the thing was stuck to a tree, was growing out of a tree, and he could not pull it free, not without filling the air with the sound of wrangling wood, of warp-woe and tree-splinter.

Alfric paused.

Momentarily defeated.

Then rage possessed him.

No! He would not fail! He would not die! Not now, now, when he was triumphant, victorious in questing, and close, yes, close to the throne, very close, to ride to Galsh Ebrek was all it would take to make himself king, and to ride he must kill, and to kill needed weapons, and weapons he had, yes, teeth and claws, claws and teeth, and the weight of his haunches, the strength of the moon.

And the moon.

And the moon—

And the moon was swelling, girthing, growing, becoming hot, yes, hot, and tumescent, yes, misting from silver to blood, and a prickling sensation thrilled through Alfric's arms as he willed the Change, his hands becoming clumsy, hairs thickening and darkening on the backs of his wrists, and already the moon was silver no more, but, rather, a smouldering fire.

The smells deepened, thickened and became more dangerous, their range increasing by several octaves. Hearing likewise prospered, so Danbrog Grendelson heard the thin whistling of the high-pitched bats, and heard too the whispers of the men who thought themselves stalking him.

—Quick, quick!

He tossed his spectacles aside, then tore free his boots and shuddered out of his clothes before his flesh could burst those accoutrements, then the pain took him, the spasms, the agony of the full force of the Change, and he thrashed in the shadows, heedless of the noise, helpless to save himself.

A voice:

'Gralaag?'

Unintelligible that voice, a question lurching across the octaves.

Then Alfric kicked away the last spasm and lay still, lay on his back and stared at the bloody moon, and when the voice spoke again he understood it, yes, though the voice was warped and distorted, deepened and thickened, made barbarous by ears atuned to a different blood:

'Grendelson? Is that you?'

Alfric rolled on to all fours and lurched across the forest floor. He was clumsy, finding four legs momentarily harder than two. But he was remembering, oh yes, remembering swiftly, remembering what he had learnt from a full three months spent running wild in the Qinjoks, and he hit his stride in less than a dozen paces.

'Maf!'

Thus Muscleman Wu, swearing in strangled shock as the huge wolf charged toward him.

Then:

'Norn for ever!'

Alfric heard the battlecry, saw the sword, and swerved, jinked, and ducked into the undergrowth, then was running full tilt, and thinking as he ran, thinking.

—Iron against bone and iron must win.

—But the man has a horse and no horseman will walk.

Thus thinking, Wolf Alfric ran at full pace, careless of noise. Then stopped abruptly and began to ghost through the forest, slinking from shadow to shadow, making for Wu Norn's horse. There was no wind to carry wolfsmell or othersmell, no wind to warn or make the beast uneasy, so Alfric feared not discovery as he went into hiding barely fifty paces from Muscleman Wu's abandoned horse.

Then Alfric lay still.

Wolf Alfric waited, a shadow hidden by shadows. Black, he was black, a beast of the night and hence hidden by the night, the underdepths of trees concealing him completely, all but for the eyes, the eyes as bloody as the moon which ruled him.

At last, as Alfric had expected, Muscleman Wu came shifting through the forest. Delicately went Wu, yes, as quietly as he could, but still he was noisy, for it is nearly impossible to move without sound on a night both still and icy-clear.

Alfric slitted his eyes, and then – it took an effort of will, but he managed it – closed them entirely to mask the moonburning fire.

Then he waited.

Listening.

Let the man walk past him.

Then—

Opened his eyes.

Then—

Moving with scarcely more sound than a vogel makes as it eases itself from one tree to the next, Alfric slipped out of the shadows in which he had been hiding. And fell in behind Muscleman Wu. The footsteps of the man masked the stealthy-stalking of the wolf. A moment to savour, this, yes, a moment to savour.

'Ya, Fom,' said Wu, greeting his horse.

Alfric caught the relief in Wu's voice, knew the man was glad to be back with his beast, knew the warrior Norn had no appetite for stalking a gigantic black wolf through this forest of ice and shadows, knew Wu wanted only to be gone, yes, gone, and quickly, to run back to Galsh Ebrek and settle his fears with a mug of good ale in company.

180

Then the brave horse Fom caught a whiff of something alien, threatening, and snorted, and pawed the ground. And Wu, alert to the nuances of such behaviour, guessed at what was behind him, and turned, but turned too late, for the weight was launched already, and Wu turned in time—

In time to be met, thrown back, thrown down, and—

Bone to be jaw, jaw to be teeth, teeth to be blood—

And Wu was struggling, wrestling, fighting the wolf which ravaged for his throat, and trying to Change as he fought, but he was too slow, too slow—

For Wolf Alfric tore his throat apart then rolled free—

Rolled free in time to watch.

Muscleman Wu was strong, as were all the Norns, and even in his death he found the time to Change, his clothes bursting and breaking as his Shape fought against them, jerkin ripping, belt snapping, chain mail coming apart.

And Alfric knew, then, that Wu had known his own nature, must have known. For chain mail will not break during a Change, not unless its web has been especially weakened to accommodate such an emergency. The mail worn by Muscleman Wu did so break, meaning that the Norn had always been prepared for this.

But—

It was too late.

For, as Muscleman Wu became wolf, the last of his strength left him, and he died.

Wolf Alfric sniffed around the corpse of his fallen foe, making sure. The wolf-corpse was more than a little ludicrous, lying there with its hind legs loose in a warrior's battle boots, lying in a raggage of clothes variously tight or torn, lying there very much dead.

Alfric wanted to laugh, but—

His flesh would not accommodate laughter, no, he had learnt that in the Qinjoks, for three months he had never laughed once as he had run wild in those mountains, hunting, seeking, tasting, listening, daring and mating, stalking and fighting, testing and training, learning and exulting.

Why had he come back?

Because, in the end, it had not been enough to be wolf, because wolves have no laughter, no voices. But otherwise, oh, otherwise it had been sweet, sweet indeed, and nothing before or since had compared to it, nothing till now.

Then Alfric, a live wolf by a dead wolf by a bloody moon, threw back his head and howled, bayed the bloodsong, sang the lifesong, and Wu's horse was affrighted as was Alfric's own, but fear was not sufficient, and there was some bloody business with horsemeat before Alfric was finished.

And then—

Then the madness claimed him, as it had that first time in the Qinjoks, and he ran as a beast with the moon burning in his blood, and he knew not where he ran or how.

In the Qinjoks, he had run that way (the first time, yes, only the first time) until exhaustion had claimed him. But tonight things were different, because, in time, his madness eased, and he became aware of something (or someone) calling him, summoning him. A compulsion was upon his will, and he did not understand the nature of this compulsion, and fought against it. It was none of the wolf things and none of the human things. It was not lust or hunger, was not fear or (even) the urgings of curiosity. Instead, it was a command from without, a command which mastered his will to its own.

And, fight against it as he would, Alfric had to obey the summons, and follow it where it compelled him.

A long running marathon he ran, a shadow fleeing through shadows to shadows, until at last the forest eased away to sand beneath his feet, and he broke free of the last trees, the gnarled evergreen pines of the dunes, and ran over the sandwaves and on to the open shore, where a fire burnt as bloody as the moon.

There were women gathered by the fire, women with strange marks on their foreheads and strange words in their mouths. And Alfric listened to the words and did not understand, but was compelled even so, and his Change came upon him, and, though he did not wish it, he was commanded from wolf to human.

Drunk with a sudden fatigue, Alfric Danbrog stood swaying by the balefire, his vision blurred, the flames smeared daubs of colour, the faces indistinct globs of mass and form, and either the women were chanting in a foreign language or else there was something wrong with his ears (his mind?) for he could not understand them.

Then—

But after that, what happened to him became incoherent, because he drank without thinking from a cup which they offered him, and his world blundered into something not far different from a dreamscape.

'Well met,' said the first hag.

'By night with the moon abune,' said the second.

'By starn and stone,' said the third.

'Bring her forth,' said the first.

'Step forward, my darling,' said the second.

'Here she is,' said the third.

Then it happened (or did it happen?) that Alfric Danbrog was face to face with a woman whose face was a mass of scars, burnt hideously by a balefire blaze like that which now made the sundering seas run red with reflected fire. Her face was cinders, ashes, desolation, scarred as the moon, but he accepted this, for a command was upon him. He did as she wished, and her blood broke, suddenly, yes, it was all over very suddenly.

When the girl was released, she went to the waters of the ocean and washed herself. And Alfric, feeling very weary, lay down by the fire. The old women covered his body with a blanket. Then the girl, washed cold by the waves of the Winter Sea, rejoined them; and the old women departed with the girl, leaving Alfric sleeping by the sea.

He dreamt, that night.

He dreamt of bones weeping for flesh, and of wind crying for the bones it thought it had once possessed. And then he dreamt of plum-petal pie, of untunchilamons by the thousand unquilting an eiderdown, and then (dreams shifting to nightmare) of gangrenous plague and carnivorous seals, of long-stretched scorlins in which lubbery kelp was entwined promiscuously with pungent blubber weed and the soft fronds of mermaids' delight, of those skorlins becoming corpses, of the corpses walking, of a war of walking corpses, of a fish swinging on a string as it rotted, of waves breaking scales of encrusted moonlight from the flanks of shuttling rocks, and of fire, of fire—

Of fire, yes, for he was burning.

CHAPTER TWELVE

For night after night, Alfric Danbrog lay in his father's house, shuddering with fever. In his illness, he endured incoherent visions, few of which were pleasant. Fragmentary ghosts smeared his cheeks with heated honey, spiked his bones with splinters of steel and whispered inscrutable words of wisdom into his ears.

'The best and worst,' said one. 'The best and worst of blades alike know that blood will have blood and blood.'

'What?' said Alfric.

And his mother, intruding upon this dialogue with delirium, said:

'There now, there now. Lie back. Rest. Don't worry. You'll be all right.'

But Alfric was not all right.

He was mortally ill, and he was living in torment.

In fever he imagined himself become a zombie, enslaved by witchcraft; his drudgery it was to be a corpse yet have to shift black wood and water until his bones neared breaking point from the strain of labour. At other times, he thought himself mutilated, staring at the world with one eye solo; and so convincing was this delusion that he tried to pluck out his rotten eye with his groping fingers.

Then, in one rare episode of peace, his hallucinations took him into a wonderwolf of pastoral bliss. It seemed to him that he spent an entire afternoon on a mellow-misty lakeside lawn, watching the wings of a bird making tracks upon the water. Then dark raindrops fell, and storm drenched down, and Alfric's world dissolved to water.

Then to fire.

He lived with fire and in fire, and watched fire consume the hush of a bird's egg, the bird itself, the bird's nest, the tree which held the nest, and then the world which held the tree.

Such was the heat of Alfric's fever that he imagined himself to be that world-burning fire. Wide he swelled, then shrank, diminishing in strength and freedom until at last he found himself burning in the confines of the hearth of a great hall, listening to bold singers declaring the deeds of dragons and telling of salamanders lapped in flame.

Later, he thought himself one of those singers; and imagined he stood by that fire. While thus standing, he saw the deathblade Bloodbane bury itself in the blazing hearth. It hurt him to see that weapon shrivelling amidst the fire-fretted wood. So Alfric, loathe to see such many-splendoured death destroyed, reached for the weapon and took it by the hilt.

For a moment he held it.

Then the sword turned to an eel, which writhed in Alfric's hand, wet and slippery.

Alfric reproved himself:

'This must stop. For this hints of neurosis, and my bank account cannot withstand the assault of any ailment so expensive.'

Obediently, his mind abandoned neurosis for madness, and he found himself plunged into an underhall deep in the earth where he fought against uncouth creatures of orange and umber, struggling long with nightmarish foes until at last he escaped to the world above.

Where was he? Dark thronged the shadows in a fastness of forest haunted by the deep-soughing song of millennial winds. Those winds began to weather and wither Alfric's flesh as he quested beneath dead, creaking branches. He was looking for a path, a track, a road. But none such he found. The cold wind blew through the rags of his clothes, flirting with the ghosts it found in his pockets. The wind was mauve and tasted of lemons. Lemons?

'None such grow in Wen Endex,' said Alfric. 'So these—'

But even in his fever-dreams he could not bring himself to speak of the Secret of the Partnership Banks.

'Freeze,' sang the wind.

Alfric thought its malice superfluous, for he was sure to freeze effectively without any such invitation.

Or was he?

By dint and endeavour, Alfric found a glowing ember – plucked it from the flesh of a toadstool and fanned it to life with a stuffed flamingo – and with that ember lit his own fever and fanned it into fire, until he was once more flame, and, thus incarnated, flourished skyward as an avatar of the sun.

At last, after much such turbulent adventuring, Alfric Danbrog slipped from fever into honest dream, and dreamt of bones scattered amidst the greyskull stones of a beach below the cliffs of the Winter Sea. There he stood, sadly contemplating life, time and mortality.

—Ever we die.

Thus thought Alfric Danbrog.

Death is the common fate of all. The fate of cowards and the fate also of those brave men and bold who seek to win a long-lasting glory with steel-edged swords. As even the heroes have found, to elude death is not easy. Even the mightiest, in time, must concede their wills to mortality. While the generosity of the flesh which allows the spirit to pursue its designs through many a year, each of those passing years is but a stay of execution, with the ultimate outcome unchanged.

But such knowledge led Alfric not to despair.

All men are dust; all men are bones. Yet, even so, much is allowed to the moment. Yes. Though all hopes are ultimately vanity, and though every reward is transitory, each moment is worth winning in its own right.

—The goodness of the moment for the moment suffices.

So thought Alfric Danbrog; and, imagining that he had a great truth to tell to the world, strove to wake from his dreams. But he could not wake, for the fever was coming upon him again.

Fever modulated dream to nightmare, and Alfric found himself trapped in a confused montage of overlapping epics, a world of monsters and heroes, sword-shields and blood. It was so exaggerated that he knew it at once for a dream.

—I'm dreaming.

So thought Alfric. But, try as he might, he could not awaken. For what seemed like forever, he was doomed to live through a sagalife of questing and battling. Swords splintered. Shields split. Castles rose and crumbled. Monsters weltered into blood. Ancient hatreds stirred to fresh murder, the blood of which was almost sufficient to drown him.

The swirling blood of a great feuding lapped round Alfric's ankles then rose to his knees, swirled round his waist then ascended to his neck. Then Ciranoush Norn loomed over Alfric and pushed him down, down into the blood which was welling all around. And such was the heat of the blood that Alfric's own blood boiled, and he screamed, though his scream was muffled as he could not breathe.

At last, such nightmares eased; and Alfric enjoyed sweet dreams again, for his blood was cooling, and he dreamt of big seas billowing to a misty shore, swamping against dunes and booming into the sea-caves of granitic cliffs. Of that he dreamt, and dreamt too of a cleft rock where there was a peace which sheltered him from wind and rain alike.

He hid himself in the warmth of that rock as the world cooled. At last the world grew so cold that there was ice sufficient in the world to bridge the oceans, and bridged indeed they were.

Then Alfric found himself sitting on the shore by the frozen sea, watching old women watching fire eat wood while they spun their spells. To his horror, Alfric dreamt himself drawn toward the fire by those spells. He knew he was going to be plunged into that heat, to be melted and baked, his shape to be changed, and his flesh to be fated—

Knowing what fate awaited him, Alfric struggled mightily to escape. In a rare moment of wakeful lucidity, Alfric found himself struggling with his mother by the household hearth.

—So I live.

Thus thought Alfric, waking entirely.

And such was his relief that he fainted clean away; and

his mother gathered up his feverish flesh and returned it to its sickbed.

Seven days and seven nights passed in such turmoil before Alfric's illness eased one last and final time. The result of that easing could well have been death, but his constitution was fundamentally strong, and he lived.

Just.

When the fever abated, Alfric did not ask what had happened. Not at first. But his mother put his spectacles in place, which told him, at the very least, that someone had found the slaughter-sight, and that something at least had been recovered from the forest.

Later, when Alfric was feeling stronger, his father came to his side. And Alfric at last asked what had happened. He thought it best to ask until he knew what other people knew. Once he knew that, then he would know what lies he would have to tell, though he hoped he would not have to lie to his father.

'You quested against the vampires,' said Grendel Danbrog. 'Do you remember that?'

'That, yes,' said Alfric. 'I remember that much.'

'You succeeded. You must have. For the sword Kinskorn was recovered from the forest.'

'Recovered?' said Alfric.

'I found it myself,' said his father. 'When you did not come back, I went looking for you. I tracked you through the forest. I came to a scene of fight and of slaughter.'

'Oh,' said Alfric.

He remembered.

Despite his fever, he remembered very clearly. All was clear until the time he had come to the fire by the sea. After that, things were nightmarish. Either he

190

had or had not been summoned to the shore by a coven of witches. Either he had or had not embraced a woman with a face too desolate for love. Either he had or had not been summoned to the sea for that precise purpose.

'A wolf was there,' said Grendel.

'A wolf?' said Alfric.

'In the forest,' said Grendel. 'Its throat torn open.'

'Oh,' said Alfric. 'Yes. A stick. I did that with a stick. Sharpened with a knife.'

'I guessed as much,' said Grendel. 'The wolf was clothed in the ruins of garments belonging to Muscleman Wu, so I had it brought back to Galsh Ebrek and named as Wu's corpse. The family Norn has not sought to deny it.'

'You had it brought back?'

'My comrades helped me. A dozen of the staunchest of the Yudonic Knights.'

'Good,' said Alfric, weakly. 'Good.'

'That's shut them up, I can tell you,' said Grendel. 'Not much noise from the Norns now one's proved a shape-changer.'

'Norns, plural? Surely Ciranoush is the sole survivor, singular.'

'Is it a pedant I've bred? For sure, Pig Norn is dead and Wu Norn likewise. For sure, Ciranoush Norn was one of three. But brothers have fathers and cousins and uncles and nephews and cousins once and twice and thrice removed, and I bid you tread carefully unless you want to embroil us in feud.'

'I'll tread very carefully,' said Alfric, shrinking more than slightly from his father's anger.

'Good,' said Grendel. 'Good.'

'I didn't . . . I didn't choose battle,' said Alfric. 'Not then. Not in the forest.'

'I guessed that,' said Grendel. 'But regardless of what you chose, you did well. Another corpse we found. The corpse of Pulaman the Tracker. You know him?'

'No,' said Alfric.

'That's no loss,' said Grendel. 'He was a nasty piece of work. Good with his tracking but reckless in combat. A sword was in his guts. Kinskorn was that sword. You must have killed him.'

'I did,' said Alfric. 'I remember.'

It was true. He remembered perfectly. And was disappointed to learn that he had killed a stranger, this Pulaman the Tracker of whom he had never heard. He had really thought it was Ciranoush Zaxilian Norn who had died on the end of Kinskorn, and life would have been much simpler if Ciranoush had died.

'I pulled free the sword and brought it back here,' said Grendel. 'I knew it to be yours to claim.'

'You have it here?'

'I do,' said Grendel.

'May I see it?'

'But of course.'

The sword was produced, and Alfric fondled it lovingly, and only broke off his fondling when his mother started ladling soup into his mouth.

'I would have thought,' said Alfric, speaking between mouthfuls of soup, 'that you would have taken this blade already to Saxo Pall.'

'Think less and eat more,' said his mother.

Soup engulfed Alfric's vocabulary.

'To take in the sword is your privilege,' said Grendel. 'Thus I kept it here for you.'

192

'How long have I been here?'

Grendel told him.

'You were found on the beach by the seaweed scavengers. You were by a fire. Amidst footprints. Who was it found you?'

'I've no idea,' said Alfric.

'But you have a mouth,' said Gertrude. 'Open it!'

Alfric yawned, was souped, swallowed.

'You were nine parts dead when found,' said Grendel. 'A blanket upon you, but nothing else. And a fever had you, oh yes, a wicked fever. But they brought you to me and we've cared for you nicely since.'

'How was it,' said Alfric's mother, 'that you came to be naked?'

'I thought they had dogs,' said Alfric. 'The hunters, I mean. I heard them. Tracking me. I took off my clothes, meaning to confuse the scent. Mud, that was going to be next. Mud on my flesh for warmth and disguise. Slip round behind them, mud in the shadows. Finish the men, the dogs.'

'But there were no dogs,' said Gertrude.

'Peace, woman,' said Grendel. 'We weren't there. We don't know what there was or wasn't.'

'Maybe there weren't dogs,' said Alfric. 'Maybe I imagined them. But imagining's no crime, is it?'

'No,' said Gertrude. 'But it's a crime to starve when there's food here in plenty. Come on. Open your mouth!'

Alfric obeyed, and was fed, and thus began the completion of his recovery; and three nights later he felt strong enough to march upon Saxo Pall.

So forth from his father's house went Alfric Danbrog, returning to Galsh Ebrek to declare his triumph in the third of his quests. A triple triumph! That meant he was king. The Wormlord would receive his gift; would praise him and crown him; and then would ride forth to meet his death at the hands of Herself.

So thought Alfric, exulting in visions of his own grandeur as he strode through the mud of the streets of Galsh Ebrek. Such was his intoxication that he walked right into a zana, and the wild rainbow stung him savagely. That sobered him somewhat; and he was sobered more to find no welcome in Saxo Pall, but, instead, hostile servants and surly guards.

'What is going on?' said Alfric, when Guignol Grangalet came forth to meet him. 'Have I offended the throne in some way?'

'That is not for me to say,' said the Chief of Protocol evasively. 'Best we go to the throne room.'

'Indeed!' said Alfric.

So there they went. But there was no sign of the Wormlord. Instead, a blonde and full-breasted woman sat upon the throne. It was Ursula Major, the Wormlord's daughter. Alfric was outraged to see her thus seated, but controlled his temper nicely.

'Good evening, aunt,' said Alfric, knowing full well that Ursula Major hated to be addressed as aunt. He bowed slightly then said: 'Lo! I have brought the brave sword Kinskorn!'

Loudly he declaimed those words; loudly and proudly. But, somehow, they fell flat.

'Thank you for the sword,' said Ursula coolly. 'The gift is welcome.'

'The gift has a price,' said Alfric. 'The price is the chair in which you sit.'

'You have no chairs of your own?' said Ursula. 'How

194

sad! Never mind. If you're truly here to beg for a bit of furniture, no doubt my good man Grangalet can find you a stool to take home.'

Alfric did not appreciate this clumsy joke. He was starting to get angry.

'I claim the throne,' he said. 'I am now rightfully king of Wen Endex.'

'The king, are you?' said Ursula Major.

'I am,' said Alfric, 'unless the Wormlord has repudiated his words. Where is he? Where is the Wormlord? Is he dead?'

'He is poorly,' said Ursula Major.

Her dulcet voice was cool, controlled. Even so, Alfric heard her fear. She was frightened. Of him.

'Poorly or not,' said Alfric, 'the king must see me, for I have brought him the third of the saga swords. We have an agreement.'

'I know your agreement,' said Ursula Major. 'I know it, as does all of Galsh Ebrek. Like the rest of the city, I think it a madness. The kingdom cannot be ruled by a lunatic's whim. So.'

'So you've got the Wormlord under lock and key,' said Alfric, half-misbelieving his ears.

'My father is ill, yes, and confined to his bed,' said Ursula Major. 'When he recovers – if he recovers – he may have something to say to you. We are not pleased with the shameless way you have abused his mental weakness. Doubtless when he is in his right mind, he will be similarly displeased.'

'You have no right to do this!' said Alfric.

'My lady rules as regent,' said Guignol Grangalet. 'She has every right.'

Alfric almost lost his temper entirely, then and there.

But he was a Banker Third Class, and thus a trained diplomat; and so had wit enough to temper his tongue to preserve his skin, and to retreat from Saxo Pall with all possible speed.

Once Alfric was free of the Wormlord's castle, he marched up the slopes of Mobius Kolb to the Bank, where he shortly presented himself to Comptroller Xzu.

'So,' said Xzu, 'here he is. The wolf-killer.'

'You know about that?' said Alfric.

'All Galsh Ebrek knows about that,' said Xzu. 'Your father displayed a dead wolf in the marketplace. He claimed it to be the corpse of Wu Norn.'

'It was,' said Alfric. 'I met him and killed him. He had a partner, too. He was . . . I'm sorry, the name escapes me.'

'Pulaman the Tracker,' said Xzu, who clearly had all the details written on his fingernails, as Bank parlance has it. 'So you killed Pulaman. And Wu. A pity that Ciranoush Norn remains on the loose.'

'Ciranoush, yes,' said Alfric. 'How is he taking it?'

'In silence,' said Xzu. 'These days he's much given to brooding, or so my spies tell me. Anyway. To business. You delivered the third of the saga swords to Saxo Pall, did you?'

'I did,' said Alfric. 'I left it at Ursula Major's feet, she being the regent, or so she claimed.'

'Regent she is, at least for the moment,' said Xzu. 'Our problem now is how to get rid of her. Once she's gone, we can place you on the throne and nobody will protest.'

'There's no way we can get rid of her,' said Alfric.

'Don't be so defeatist!' said Xzu. 'If necessary, we can bring in mercenaries and have the bitch murdered.'

Alfric could scarcely believe his ears.

'Yes,' he said, cautiously, 'but civil war might be the result. If one of the royal family is to be killed, it would be better if the Yudonic Knights did the killing.'

'Then you must rally the Knights for that purpose.'

'I – I lack sufficient stature. As yet. They might follow me in some things. Perhaps. But not in murder. Not murder of the king's own daughter.'

'Hmmm,' said Xzu, thinking. 'Well . . . does the Wormlord lack stature?'

'I believe most of the Knights to hold him in high regard,' said Alfric warily.

'Then they will hold his will in high regard, doubtless.'

'Yes,' said Alfric. 'But he has said nothing about murdering his daughter. Not to my knowledge. Nor do I believe I could successfully pretend that he has said any such thing.'

'I do not ask you to,' said Xzu. 'Rather, I suggest you repeat the Wormlord's own words to the Yudonic Knights.'

'What words are those?'

'Why, the man swore he would march forth against Herself, did he not? As soon as the saga swords were won, he would march.'

'He did,' said Alfric.

'Then summon the Knights. Tell them the saga swords are won. Tell them it is their knightly duty to help the Wormlord to fulfil his oath. Play upon their dreams of heroic grandeur. Sing them songs. Bard them the deeds of heroes. Skop the swordblood. Make each man a man indeed. You know the way of it. You know your people.'

'To a point,' said Alfric uneasily.

197

'Better still, go to your father. Ask him to do the barding and talking, the blood-stirring and the glory-boasting. He has the knack of it.'

And Alfric remembered the Yudonic Knights who had gathered in Grendel's barn at his father's behest. Yes, his father could summon and rouse those men. His father knew the way of it.

'Then,' said Xzu, starting to get enthusiastic, 'the Yudonic Knights will release the Wormlord from his confinement in Saxo Pall. He will march against Herself. And you, of course, will march with him.'

'Me?' said Alfric, startled.

'But of course,' said Xzu, smoothly. 'You must win yourself a share of the Wormlord's glory. Otherwise how can you rightly claim the throne?'

'But . . . but the Wormlord will die.'

'Will he?'

'Yes,' said Alfric, trying to conceal his fear, his anger. 'Nobody can contend against Herself.'

'Oh, come now,' said Xzu, sounding amused. 'You've dared against monsters thrice. Monsters are nothing. You dared against them solo, yet survived. Survived? You triumphed!'

'With help, yes,' said Alfric coldly. 'But She is not a foolish sea dragon or a brain-damaged giant. No. She is Herself, and She is nightmare.'

'Nightmare?' said Xzu carelessly. 'The word has been used of the vampires, you know.'

'Yes, I know, I know,' said Alfric. 'But the vampires were easiest of all. They wanted to deal with us, and we knew it. The same does not go for Herself. Or have you a secret to tell me? Has She been to the bank to ask for a loan, for a mortgage? Does she want to build herself a

198

nice little cottage with carpets clean on the floor, a housecat by the hearth?'

Xzu made no answer to this sarcastic sally.

Instead, he pushed a parchment across his desk.

'A promotion,' said Xzu. 'Your promotion. From Banker Third Class to Banker Second Class. You will note it is conditional. It becomes effective as soon as you return from a quest against Herself. A quest, please note, which you must undertake in the Wormlord's company.'

Alfric took it, read it, pushed it back.

'I'll think about it,' said he.

'Take your time,' said Xzu. 'But make sure your time isn't too much time. We'll see you back here once you've . . . once you've made a contribution to our welfare. Go now, friend banker, and may the Spirit of the Ledgers go with you, and may the Seven Demons of Usury confound your enemies, and may the power of the Great Schroff be with you.'

The invoking of these imaginary entities was a ponderous joke, a jejune joke of the kind that both Alfric and Xzu had outgrown long ago. Nevertheless, it was a Bank joke, confirming the pair as bankers in league against the world; and Alfric smiled, heartened by the comradeship the joke implied.

He rose, and went to the door.

Just before Alfric exited the room, Xzu spoke again, saying:

'Good luck, Alfric.'

'Thank you,' said Alfric, and left.

But though Alfric had thanked Comptroller Xzu for that parting benediction, the way it had been framed was not altogether to his liking. For Xzu had addressed him as 'Alfric'.

Izdarbolskobidarbix was the name he chose to use in the Bank; and, though he had long pardoned the occasional use of 'Alfric' or 'Danbrog' by his peers and superiors, he nevertheless resented such inaccuracy. He felt (perhaps he was wrong, perhaps he was over-sensitive, but what he could not deny were his own feelings) that Xzu had been deliberately putting him at a distance by calling him 'Alfric', and that Xzu's use of that name constituted, in some sense, a subtle casting out.

Certainly Alfric was being exiled from the Bank, at least for the moment. Exiled until he had 'made a contribution' to the Bank's welfare. He was under orders, then. He had to rouse the Yudonic Knights to action, to free the Wormlord from his imprisonment, then march with the Wormlord to do battle with Herself.

Alfric felt this to be grossly unfair.

Surely he had done enough already.

The odds had been in his favour when he had fought with the sea dragon Qa. Nevertheless, a single mistake could have seen him killed. As for the swamp giant – that encounter had been more dangerous yet. And the vampires were not exactly harmless.

'Still,' said Alfric, 'I'm not being given any choice in the matter.'

So he went to see his father, and, a night later, the pair met with two dozen of the most knightly of the Yudonic Knights. The site of this conclave was Grendel Danbrog's barn.

Here the Yudonic Knights, with drinking horns in hand, celebrated the hero-feats of Alfric Danbrog.

'Grendelson!' they roared. 'Grendelson! Hero!'

And Alfric, though he was slightly embarrassed by their enthusiasm, acknowledged this homage gracefully.

Then his father called the meeting to order.

'As you know,' said Grendel Danbrog, 'Ursula Major has imprisoned her father in his sickbed.'

'Shame!' cried someone.

Then others cried aloud, saying foul things about the virginal Ursula. Grendel hushed them down a low roar, then went on:

'This we know to be wrong. Above all else, the matter of Herself and Her doings is much on my mind. For too long has Her hideous hymn of triumph dominated our dreams. It is time for us to take in hand the ancient iron and pursue Her to Her lair, and there to hack and hew Her flesh until She is dead.'

Cries of enthusiastic applause greeted this proposition.

'But,' said Grendel, 'we cannot go alone. We need a leader. Only one man has the strength to be that leader. And that is Tromso Stavenger, our beloved Wormlord.'

Then Grendel launched himself into the much-beloved story of the youthful feats of the Wormlord, who had dared Her son, and had wrestled that monster to a standstill in a fight in which sinews had snapped and bone-joints had broken freely, and who had then killed Her son and cut off his head.

'That is our leader,' said Grendel. 'A hero true. That is the leader we must have if we are to dare ourselves to Her lair and engage ourselves in loathsome strife with Her strength.'

The Yudonic Knights had no trouble at all in convincing themselves that a scorning of peace well becomes a man; that they were made for death and danger; that their king was a hero and would lead them to deathless glory; and that launching a savage assault upon Herself

201

would be a truly enjoyable experience once they got into it.

Soon they were joying in the deed as if it had already been accomplished.

'It is a foul offence to life and honour that we should let Her live when Her death can be so easily accomplished,' said one, his boast representative of ruling opinion.

Alfric sat down in a corner and closed his eyes in something like despair. So they were really going to do it. So he could not return to the Bank and say they had refused.

He had a vision of what would really happen. When they came face to face with Herself, the Yudonic Knights would run. Their fathers had done as much on similar expeditions in the days of the past, so why should the sons be any different? Then She with Her baleful glare would transfix any fool who still stood against Her, then She would advance, and conquer, and kill, and glut Her greed on the flesh of the fallen.

So thinking, Alfric was minded to sever his own throat on the spot. To die in a warm and comfortable barn. Far better, surely, than to go wandering through the fens in search of Herself, and meet a hideous death when Her grisly rounds brought them into confrontation.

But Alfric's father had no such fearful thoughts. He was boasting with as much enthusiasm as the rest of them.

'Words and deeds,' said Grendel, quaffing good ale which he was far too drunk to appreciate. 'Great words and great deeds to match them. Of such is the life of men.'

Then Grendel began to sing the old songs, songs of

202

fresh-tarred ships and voyages across the Winter Sea to wars in foreign lands; songs of kings with boar-heads rampant on their helms, kings armed with iron fire-hardened; songs of heroes and their conquests.

While his father sung thus, Alfric remembered other songs: funeral dirges mournful in mood, telling of the death of lordly ships, the wailing of bed-mates, the burial of fallen kings, the wrath of battle-surge flames consuming the fallen. Such things happened. Even acknowledged heroes did not always triumph in their quests.

But no such thoughts spoiled the triumph of Grendel Danbrog, who boasted now of the great deeds of the past as if they were his very own:

'In Melrik's time we fought the dreaded Yun. By ocean's margin we withstood the warriors who crossed the Winter Sea to do battle with our forces. When the Yun poured forth from their ships, there we stood in our war-gear, keen for adventure.

'Melrik was our leader, Melrik our king. Proud was the weapon-stack of his wide-boasted hall. Prudent he was, yet brave, for he was ready to dare the nicors in their lair.'

On and on went Grendel, telling of the mangling of flesh, the sweetness of victory and the din of celebratory revelry, and of the Golden Age in which the triumphant Melrik ruled Wen Endex, 'land of sweet song and shining waters where all men lived in gladness'.

When Grendel Danbrog had exhausted himself by overindulgence in such epics, other Yudonic Knights took up the work. And it was late indeed before they got down to business in earnest.

But get down to business they did.

In the end.

'These last twelve weary winters I've watched our lord decline,' said Grendel. 'I know and you know that this is his last chance. If he is to march against Herself then he must do so now. But he needs our help. Will he have it?'

And the Yudonic Knights roared their answer:

'Yes!'

In short order, plans were agreed. The Yudonic Knights would storm Saxo Pall, release the Wormlord then march against Herself in the company of their lord.

As there was some organization which needed to be done – horses must be obtained and journeypacks filled, wills must be brought up to date and lovers kissed goodbye – the actual storming of Saxo Pall was set down for the following night.

Alfric did his best to conceal his infinite weariness as he parted from his father and those of the Knights who were doing the organizing.

'Where are you going?' said Grendel.

Alfric was actually going to the Flesh Traders' Financial Association to report to Comptroller Xzu on the plans which the Yudonic Knights had hatched. However, he did not think his father would like these plans being thus revealed. So he said:

'Home, that's all.'

'Stay,' said Grendel, in his lordliest voice. 'We need you here.'

Alfric was desperate to get away. He wanted the Bank to know that he had done as the Bank wished. That he had successfully roused the Yudonic Knights to action, and that soon the Wormlord would be freed to do battle with Herself. The sooner the Bank knew, the better, for such political ructions could affect everything from the price of firewood to the ninety-day interest rate.

Belatedly, Alfric remembered that he was married; and, moreover, that his wife had absconded from home, and was on the loose in the city, cuckolding him (for all he knew) with every drunk in every tavern in Galsh Ebrek. Actually, this mattered so little to Alfric that he had almost forgotten about it already. But it certainly gave him an excuse to be gone from the barn.

'I – I am a married man,' said Alfric.

'So you are, so you are,' said his father.

'And – and my wife—'

'Oh yes,' said his father. 'That. She's still running wild?'

'She is,' said Alfric. 'But I think I know where she'll be tonight. I think I can bring her to heel.'

'Then off you go,' said his father, approving this course of action instantly. 'Off you go, my boy, and do the best you can with the wench.'

CHAPTER THIRTEEN

Thus it happened that Alfric Danbrog leagued it home and prepared himself for an audience with Comptroller Xzu of the Flesh Traders' Association. He dreaded the thought of what might happen when the Yudonic Knights stormed Saxo Pall; and was fearfully afraid of joining the attack on Herself; but, nevertheless, his pride was great.

—Were it not for me, this would not be happening.

Thus whispered Alfric Danbrog to himself, and could not help but be mightily pleased with himself.

In his house in Varnvelten Street, Alfric washed himself, dried himself, dressed in clean clothes then shaved himself in front of his mirror.

This was an ancient mirror, a family heirloom. Inset in its surface was a small image-disk in which dwelt the portrait of a smiling girl with a face whiter than chalk and lips redder than blood. Her lips moved ever and ever, for she was whispering something. If the mirror were kept near fire, that whisper would strengthen to audible language – a song of some kind – but what the girl might be singing was ever a mystery. This mirror was one of the old things from a past long forgotten, and nobody knew how it had been made, or when, or where.

Alfric had owned the mirror for so long that, usually, he never thought of the girl; did not even see her as he pursued his own thought while shaving. But tonight he paused and studied that soundless face. Someone had made this mirror and had there delineated the features of the girl. And Alfric wondered, as he watched her smiling and singing, if she had really existed or whether a canny artist had created her marvellously detailed portrait from pure imagination.

And wondered, too, if even the slightest trace of his own existence would remain to the world after his death. Would someone, somewhere, hold some fragment of his face, words or work in memory? Or would all disappear, soapbubbling to zero in a world where even rocks were fated to be nubbed down to nothing?

'Morbid, morbid,' muttered Alfric, and hurried through the rest of his shaving, and would have cut himself badly in his haste had his razor not been excessively blunt.

Once these preparations were complete, Alfric made the trek to Mobius Kolb, entered the Bank, and was soon in conference with Comptroller Xzu.

Xzu listened impassively as Alfric – barely able to conceal his pride in his own achievements – told how the Yudonic Knights had been won over.

'They will do it,' said Alfric. 'Just as the Bank wants. They will storm Saxo Pall. Release the Wormlord. Then march upon Herself.'

Comptroller Xzu listened to him impassively.

Then sighed.

Then said:

'You are not a narcissist, are you?'

'A narcissist?' said Alfric in bewilderment.

He was taken aback by this tangential assault. What was its meaning? Had he been indulging in unseemly boasting? Well, perhaps a little . . . but that was pardonable, surely, under the circumstances.

'What I'm asking you,' said Xzu, 'is whether you put too great a value on the importance of satisfying your own ego.'

Alfric considered this.

Then said:

'I scarcely know how to answer a question so wide reaching when it is asked as if apropos of nothing. Of course I could indulge myself in rhetoric if pushed to justify my approach to life, or I could produce any number of apologias to justify the same . . . but such activity would scarcely have any point unless I know the details of whatever accusations are being made against me.'

Alfric paused. He was aware that most of what he had just said was nearly meaningless, and that he should say no more lest he make a fool of himself.

But he could not stop himself.

He was weak from illness, and feeling defensive; and so, as a squid squirts out meaningless scrolls of ink when disturbed, so Alfric squirted out words. He went on:

'However, whatever my incapacities, please be assured that I am unconscious of any error I have made. I have always served the Bank to the best of my ability, and it is my desire to do so in the future.'

Thus Alfric.

Comptroller Xzu smiled.

'You defend yourself well,' said Xzu. 'However, you are not under attack.'

'I'm not?'

'Whatever gave you the idea that you were? Have I indulged in curses or fulminations? Have I quoted unpleasant anecdotes against you? Have I made any critiques whatsoever? No. I have not.'

Not for the first time, Alfric realized that Comptroller Xzu no longer possessed a native's fluency with Toxteth. Xzu had spent so much of his life living in foreign parts that his use of the syntax and vocabulary of his birth tongue had become strangely stilted.

Really, Xzu was scarcely a citizen of Wen Endex at all. Rather, he belonged to that strange meta-nation created by the Partnership Banks; he lived in a world where market movements and currency fluctuations in Dalar ken Halvar or Chi'ash-lan were as present and as important to him as any events taking place in riverside Galsh Ebrek.

'While I have no criticism to make of you,' said Xzu, 'I do have a demand. My demand – which is the Bank's demand – is outlined in this document which I would like you to read.'

Alfric suspected that something uncommonly unpleasant was afoot. Bankers often committed to paper that which they were loathe to voice.

With great apprehension, Alfric took the document which Xzu extended to him.

And read.

The document was long and windy, but the gist of it was simple. Basically, it asked Alfric to delay the freeing of the Wormlord and the campaigning against Herself by seven days. Why? Because of certain unspecified 'diplomatic contingencies'.

Alfric read it once.

Read it twice.

Then—

He should by rights have read it a third time, to give himself opportunity for reflection. After all, in diplomacy, time spent in meditation is never wasted. So it is written in the Bank's Book of Wisdom, and the Bank should know.

But Alfric, at that moment, was in no mood for meditation. The demand the Bank was making was outrageous. How was he to delay the Knights? Those heroes were enraptured by enthusiasm for the project the Bank itself had schemed up, and no amount of rhetoric was likely to halt them.

'You know,' said Alfric, anger making him uncommonly audacious, 'this demand puts me in a very difficult position. In fact, it might almost have been calculated to cause me the maximum difficulty. What is this? Some kind of half-arsed test of my ability?'

'No, Alfric,' said Xzu. 'This is not a kind of practical examination. For reasons which I am currently not at liberty to reveal, certain complications have arisen *vis-à-vis* our plans to put you on the throne. These complications can doubtless be resolved in due course, but, for the moment, we need to call a halt to the action. We need you to stop the Yudonic Knights from doing what they plan to do.'

'What the Bank planned for them to do!' said Alfric.

'The Bank made certain plans, yes,' said Xzu. 'But now these have changed. And surely it is a banker's duty to change when the Bank does. You would not put personal ambition ahead of your duty to the Bank, would you? Or would you?

'This is where my earlier question is pertinent. I asked if you were a narcissist. I asked whether you put too great a value on satisfying your own ego. You answered in the negative. You made yourself out to be a loyal servant of the Bank, and expressed a desire to serve the Bank always to the best of your ability.

210

'That is how you spoke when our debate was being conducted on a purely theoretical level. Do you now wish to revise your commitment when you come face to face with the practical application of theory? Talk is easy, and you talk most beautifully. Deeds are another thing. Are you going to flinch from the exertion that deeds demand? Where is your honour, Alfric?'

So spoke Xzu.

Then sat back, leaving Alfric struggling with wordless frustration.

Despite his undiminished anger, Alfric had to admire the cunning of the great Comptroller Xzu. Oh yes. Xzu had manoeuvred Alfric nicely, prompting him into making declarations of loyalty. And now Xzu was using those declarations of leverage, speaking of 'honour', the watchword by which the Yudonic Knights wished to live.

Xzu was using Alfric's knightly heritage against him.

And Xzu had also reminded Alfric that the Bank existed for its own purposes – for the increase of its own wealth, power and influence – and that personal ambition and ego meant nothing to the Bank. If Alfric wished to rise in the Bank, then he must do what the Bank wished, regardless of how outrageous that might be.

Never before had Alfric faced that truth so clearly.

Of course, it was something he had always known. The marginalization of personal concerns is a characteristic of every large organization, and the Partnership Banks were as large as they come.

Even so, Alfric was almost stupefied to find himself being manipulated so shamelessly, tossed about like a cork on the storm-seas of politics. One day the Bank demands the release of the Wormlord. So a Danbrog must be commanded to arrange it. A little later, political concerns (What political concerns? Alfric was almost ready to kill to know!) demanded that the release of the Wormlord be delayed. So a Danbrog must arrange that, too, regardless of the difficulties and embarrassments involved.

'Well?' said Banker Xzu.

'I wonder,' said Alfric, 'if you have the slightest idea of the enormity of what you're asking.'

'Enormity?' said Xzu.

'I have given my word to my father and all the Yudonic Knights who were gathered together with him,' said Alfric. 'I have allied myself to their grand adventure. I have—'

'Yes, yes, I know all that,' said Xzu. 'I was born and raised here, the same as you were.'

'Then you know that you're being totally unreasonable,' said Alfric. 'I can't make and break my word to my father and my father's peers just because your policies change as – as casually as the weather.'

'Can't you?' said Xzu.

The waxen composure of this banker-comptroller was making Alfric steadily more angry. He was a Danbrog. A man in his own right. Not a thing of putty to be moulded into whatever shape the Bank chose. Or was he? Once again, he was brought face to face with the uncompromising nature of the organization. If he wanted to rise in the Partnership Banks, then he would have to surrender all personal freedom. His subservience to the organization would have to be absolute.

No formal bonds of slavery had been laid upon Alfric Danbrog, but, thanks to his ambition, he was a slave regardless, bound to the Bank with ties almost as strong

212

as those of blood. Because he wanted to rise in the organization, he had to measure his every public word (and most of his private speech) by what the Bank might think. Because of his status in the organization, he was never entirely off duty.

Alfric knew then that it was useless to strive to be a man in his own right unless he was prepared to break free from the organization. Was he? No. He was wedded to the institution because it was the institution that offered him his chance of power, of influence, of glory.

For a moment, Alfric felt something close to despair.

Then he realized this kind of thinking belonged to his past.

He was no longer a slave of the Bank, for his future was almost upon him, and his future was to be king. Once he had met Herself in combat, once he had made himself a hero, then the Bank would have to support him in his drive for the throne. And even if the Bank did not, why, the Yudonic Knights would put him on the throne regardless. The movement to enthrone Grendelson Danbrog was rapidly gathering momentum, and nothing could stop it now.

Nothing except Alfric's death.

He might die when he went up against Herself.

Oh yes, he might die indeed.

But that was a risk he would have to run.

'Come,' said Xzu, 'we have wasted enough time on this. The directive from the Bank is clear. We ask you for a seven-day delay. You are not to make any attempt to free the Wormlord from Saxo Pall. Not for seven days. Likewise, you are not to make any move against Herself. Not for seven days, and even then not without the Bank's permission. Do you agree to these constraints upon your actions?'

Alfric did not.

But what he actually said was:

'Naturally I am willing to do everything which is possible to further the plans of the Bank, but I scarcely see that what the Bank now demands comes under that heading. The Yudonic Knights have been stirred up. Even now, they are readying themselves for confrontation and battle. To cool their blood is something I think beyond my powers. If the Bank wishes me to undertake this thing, then the Bank must provide me with a suitable strategy, for the task is quite beyond my unaided powers.'

Alfric felt very pleased with himself.

The Bank could demand much, but surely it could not demand the impossible. And stopping the Knights was impossible, wasn't it? Surely.

Banker Xzu smiled.

'Alfric,' said Xzu, 'I'm glad to hear that you're willing to co-operate. Naturally the Bank doesn't expect you to undertake this difficult task unaided. Our best minds have gone to work on the problem, deciding how best we can help you arrange a seven-day delay.'

'And?'

'We have prepared a messenger for you. Our best hypnotists have been working on the man, and he is perfect. He is a peasant by name of Norton Brick. You will take him to an inn which you are in the habit of frequenting. The Green Cricket, that's the one. You will buy this Norton Brick a drink or two. Then, at an appropriate moment, you will say a particular trigger word.'

'Which is?' said Alfric.

'The word is tolfrigdalakaptiko.'

Alfric knew this word. It was from the Janjuladoola tongue, and denoted a specialized dish based on seagull livers.

'So I say the word,' said Alfric. 'A trigger word, I take it. This – this Brick will pour out his story. Is that right?'

'If the hypnotists have done their job correctly,' said Xzu. 'And, as you know, given the right subject, they rarely fail. They judge Brick to be perfect for our purposes.'

'So Brick tells his story,' said Alfric. 'What will that story be?'

'The story,' said Xzu, 'will concern the death of Herself at the hands of a marauding pack of vampires.'

'Oh, come on!' said Alfric. 'Nobody will believe that!'

'Nobody has to believe it,' said Xzu. 'It is an excuse, that's all. Your excuse for asking the Yudonic Knights to call off the release of the Wormlord. After all, the Knights only wish to free the Wormlord so he can march against Herself. Is that not so?'

'You suggest,' said Alfric, 'that the Knights will be ready to accept such an excuse, even if they doubt its veracity. You suggest, then, that the Knights are cowards.'

'Alfric, Alfric,' said Xzu, with a sigh, 'don't be so naive. You know yourself the Knights of Wen Endex are big on boast and small on action. Trust me. Trust us. Trust the Bank. The knightly mentality yielded long ago to our analysis. A little drink, a few songs, and these people can be tempted into committing themselves to the most outrageously heroic causes. But, once the drink

215

wears off, so too does their resolution. Take the peasant, Alfric. Get him drunk. Say the trigger word. Here his story. Then retail it to the Knights with whatever elaborations you see fit. They will happily believe Herself to be dead, at least until we tell them otherwise.'

Well.

What Xzu said had some logic to it.

The plan was at least worth trying, if Alfric really wanted a delay.

'I'll do it,' said Alfric.

'Good,' said Xzu. 'What was the trigger word?'

'Tolfrigdalakaptiko,' said Alfric. 'I won't forget it.'

But, once Alfric had the peasant Norton Brick in his possession, Alfric cast the trigger word from his mind. Because Alfric had made up his mind. He would not do what the Bank wanted. Whatever secret 'political concerns' had led the Bank to seek a delay in the Wormlord's release, Alfric was still going to pursue his own ends.

He was going to see the Wormlord set free and Herself killed, and was then going to make himself king, with or without the support of the Bank.

Thus decided, Alfric took Norton Brick to the Green Cricket, got him drunk then left him there, the trigger word unspoken and the story untold.

Then Alfric went home to his house on Varnvelten Street, and there prepared his gear for the journey which lay ahead. One of his jobs was to clean and sharpen the deathsword Bloodbane, for he had decided this was very much the blade to take to war against Herself.

When Alfric at last went to bed, he slept long, and dreamt his way through many tangled dreams. This was understandable, for he was exhausted by his confrontation with Comptroller Xzu. His recent fever had left him weak, and he needed his sleep.

But the dreams of that sleep were tormented.

Alfric Danbrog dreamt of Herself. Blighted was Her birth and pitiless was Her growth. He dreamt that a company of Yudonic Knights marched against Herself, and in his dreams he saw that even these staunch warriors feared to march against such a shrewd and ruthless foe.

Then dream became nightmare, and he dreamt that his father was dead, killed by Herself. Alfric stood by his father's body, overcome by the cruellest of griefs. The flayed corpse was hideous in death, and Alfric wept over it. His tears fell red-hot to the earth and there became buttons of bronze.

A dreamshift took him.

And Alfric found himself running as a wolf through drenching forests while helmeted men pursued him. Grim was their pursuit, and silent, utterly silent, the whole thing was silent, though he was breaking through branches in his panic, and tearing his way through webworks of thorns. Even though he screamed in anguish, nevertheless his world was silent, for he could not hear himself killed.

Abruptly, Alfric burst from the woods into the streets of Galsh Ebrek, and found himself running between carts piled high with scorlins of seaweed. Then he found himself floundering amidst shellfish and driftwood, his wolf become eel.

Then—

After a series of strange transitions in which he imagined himself first bird and then fox, Alfric dreamt that he was standing in the Imperial Court in Tang, his body days unwashed and his clothes in like condition. With him was the sea dragon Qa, and, to Alfric's distress, the great poet stank of rotten meat and regurgitated fish. Nevertheless, the Emperor of Tang was polite. The Emperor sipped from a cup. Nectar was in that cup, but this drink with blood was blended, and somehow the Emperor's voice was mixed up with that of King Dimple-Dumpling, and—

And another dreamshift took Alfric to a cave deep-delved in the Qinjoks, and there he did battle with the ogre king. Bloodbane was in Alfric's hand, and flames of blood ran bright-burning down the blade as he matched his skills of slaughter against the monsters who confronted him. Then the sword became a horse, and he mounted it, the bit-clenching beast bearing him away to a cave where he stood knee-deep in seawater. There were rings in the water, rings glinting cold and gold in the gloom of the sea. Drowned in the same water were many blades of war, and gilded cups which had once kissed the lips of kings.

And Alfric, in his dream, knew himself to be dreaming of death; and knew that this was because he expected to shortly die.

Then the images changed, though their burden did not; and Alfric dreamt himself to be once more in the Spiderweb Castle, looking upon the blanched faces of princes once bounteous, watched the frozen flesh of a long-dead sage who still bent as if to construe the runes, listening to the echoes of the voices of ghosts . . .

Then the dreams changed again.

And Alfric found himself dreaming that he was trapped in the sagaworld of the songs of the Yudonic Knights of Wen Endex.

In his dreams, Alfric longed to escape to his desk at the Bank, to the clean world of paperwork, the ordered world of interest rates and agiotage. But he could not escape. He was doomed to a world of boiling oceans and wolfhaunt wilderness, of cold forests and turbulent rivers, of mountains gripped by winter's icy binding, of ship and sword, of dare and danger, of slaughter and battle, of heroes and corpses.

Then Alfric woke, for someone was hammering at the door.

It proved to be his father.

'A new night has begun,' said Grendel Danbrog. 'And we are ready to march upon Saxo Pall.'

And Alfric, finding himself doomed to the world of heroes for real, had no option but to buckle on his sword and march forth to face his future.

CHAPTER FOURTEEN

With the deathsword Bloodbane sheathed at his side, Alfric Danbrog joined the Yudonic Knights of Galsh Ebrek who marched upon Saxo Pall.

Under a swollen moon they marched. Their numbers had greatly increased since the meeting in Grendel's barn. Instead of two dozen knights, there were almost two hundred in the army which assaulted the Wormlord's fastness. The gates of the great stronghold were thrown open at their demand, and they tramped, the mud from their boots despoiling the carpets, their hounds loping alongside them as they stormed into the castle.

None tried to stand against them until they got to the Wormlord's sick room. There they found Ursula Major standing on guard. She looked poised and impeccable, her linen clean, her jewels splendorous by lamplight, her hair bound back by bands of silver, all but for one frail strand of blondeness which wisped around her mouth.

'Halt,' said she.

They halted.

'You can go no further,' said Ursula Major, 'for I am of royal blood. To touch me is treason.'

'Not so, sister,' said Grendel, stepping forward from the ranks.

'I acknowledge you not as my brother,' said Ursula Major.

A reasonable statement, this, if appearances were

220

anything to go by. For Grendel Danbrog was a massive man of middle years, coarse in dress and feature, the stench of many unwashed years upon him. Whereas Ursula Major was in her early twenties, the gloss of well-scrubbed health upon her elegant face. Still, all there knew the truth, and Grendel did not bother to restate it. Instead, he shoved the woman out of the way, flung open the sickroom door, and entered.

The Knights followed, though only the first half dozen could actually fit into the room.

In that chamber was the Wormlord. The old man was tucked up in bed, kept warm by flannel pyjamas, his feet comforted by a hot rock wrapped in a towel; but (as always) his head was capped by his horned helmet. Tromso Stavenger looked unspeakably comfortable as he lay there supping upon lukewarm gruel which was being fed to him (a spoonful at a time) by a nubile young serving maid. Unless Alfric was badly mistaken, Stavenger was somewhat disconcerted at the sudden arrival of the Knights, and was not altogether pleased by their advent.

However, when he had been made to understand what was going on, the Wormlord agreed to leave his sickbed, and spoke of his longing for battle as he struggled into his clothes.

'My teeth!' said Stavenger.

His teeth were found and placed in his mouth. Good! It would not do for a king to die without his teeth.

Now that they had freed their liege-lord, the Yudonic Knights were ebullient. They sang and shouted as they hustled their king out of his sickroom. Through the halls they went, ineffectually pursued by Guignol Grangalet, who could do nothing except wring his hands and proclaim his despair. Into the Hall of Shields went the Yudonic

Knights, and detached the shields from the walls before they left the castle and surged down Mobius Kolb.

Through the streets of Galsh Ebrek they went, and the hoi polloi came spilling out of taverns and brothels to join them. Tromping through the mud they went, singing like a bawling mob. And a mob they were in truth.

But when they reached the outskirts of the city, then some orderliness began to assert itself. Horseboys were waiting there with steeds for the Yudonic Knights. The horses were laden with journeypacks holding rations, tentage and bedding, in case they had to hunt Herself through the wilds for days at a time.

The act of sorting out their horses and mounting up sobered the Knights, for it constituted a positive commitment to an arduous and taxing task. Rescuing their king from his sickbed had been but a romp, a game; but this was war, and war was a serious business.

And when they got underway, the drunkards and roistering boys were soon left far behind, and the Yudonic Knights went on alone.

Into the wolf-retreats they ventured, a company of shadows marching through a night which was dark indeed, for clouds were overshrouding the moon. In time, they climbed on to a windswept ridge to escape sundry bogs which would otherwise have claimed them.

Alfric then looked back and, to his surprise, saw that their numbers had diminished considerably. There had been at least two hundred Yudonic Knights at Saxo Pall, and he could have sworn a like number had set forth upon this grand expedition. But, unaccountably, no more than fifty were left.

What had happened to the others?

They could scarcely have vanished.

And there was nothing in Wen Endex which could have silently overwhelmed so great a number.

So they must have gone astray, unless – perish the thought! – they had turned back out of fear.

In the boggy ground below, some fen-creature screamed as it sensed the presence of the warm-blooded humans on the ridge. Hearing that cry, Alfric saw, or imagined he saw, strange portents appear in the murky sky. Unless he was mistaken, the night-sky clouds had turned to the colour of blood. Unless he was imagining it, those clouds were writhing into snake-like entanglements which hinted of some malign disturbance of the sky.

Alfric may have been imagining these symptoms of the world's displeasure. However, he did not imagine the grim despair which settled upon the company of Knights as the trek continued, for the reality of that despair was beyond dispute. While the pace of the expedition did not falter, nevertheless the talk did; and the Knights became taciturn as they rode along with heads bowed. But Alfric, paradoxically, found his mood lightening.

Alfric Danbrog had imagined the worst already, so the reality was almost comforting. Here he was, hunting Herself for real; and, as yet, nothing too terrible had happened. At the moment, he was suffering no more danger than he had endured on any of his solitary journeys through the dark nights of Wen Endex.

Then the high ridge came to an end, and the expedition had to descend a steep slope which ended at a stream. A stream chest-deep at least, thrashing along between banks too steep for horses to climb. There was only one way to cross this churning water, and that was by way of a narrow bridge.

Tromso Stavenger dismounted and walked his horse

across it without fear. Grendel followed. Then Alfric. The bridge was firm enough; it creaked a bit underfoot, yet took the weight of himself and his noble steed without danger.

But, when Alfric looked back, the fifty Knights on the other side seemed to be possessed of a great hesitation.

'What's the matter?' said Alfric.

'They know,' said Tromso Stavenger, 'that once they cross the bridge to join us, then they are well and truly in Her territory.'

Alfric wanted to know how the Knights could know any such thing, since the countryside looked all of a piece to him, and he knew of no border (real or imaginary) which divided off a piece of Wen Endex as Her territory. However, he did not argue.

Despite their hesitation, the Knights did begin to cross the stream, much to Alfric's relief. He had half-feared that the Knights would turn back, leaving the Wormlord to go on with none but his son and grandson for company.

'Gather them here,' said Tromso Stavenger to his son. 'Gather my Knights here, that I may speak to them.'

And Grendel, obedient to this order, marshalled the Knights so Tromso Stavenger could address them. Which the king did once all were across.

When the Wormlord spoke, it seemed that he was possessed of something of the sea-strength of his youth, for his voice was stronger than it had been for years; and this they took to be a good omen. It heartened them to see the Wormlord standing firm in the windwrath night. He looked every bit the hero-king as he stood there in hand-braided byrnie, his helm with dragon adorned. Lavish was the inlay of his ancient iron he held and sharp was the blade of that merciless sword.

'Ahead lies our destiny,' said the Wormlord. 'For this we were born. For this we were raised. This is why Wen Endex has its Knights. So the weak may be protected, the lawless suppressed, and order maintained in the realm. Who will do this, if not us? Nobody. It is the strength of the strong alone which maintains the nation. Let us go now, onward to our destiny.'

Thus it came to pass that in the last year of his reign, the Wormlord rode forth to meet his death; for death was the destiny which had been prepared for him since the day of his birth. In company with Tromso Stavenger there travelled some fifty Yudonic Knights mounted upon their roans; these were the noblest and most loyal of the king's rune-warriors, the few who were prepared to go with their liege lord even to the brink of that fatal mere where they were destined to have a testing of wills with Herself.

And Alfric Danbrog found himself proud to be one of that number. He was proud that his grandfather could hearten his men with but a few simple words, and command them forward even though death was known to be waiting. That was a true measure of kingship!

'Let us have a song,' said the Wormlord. 'Or a story, at least. A voice to lighten the night.'

They had no bard with them, but Grendel Danbrog served as gleeman, and began to rouse the night with a sagasong. However, his choice of subject was somewhat unfortunate, for he began to narrate the story of one of the heroes who had fallen in battle against Herself. This story began with an accounting of what was known of Her lair.

Her lair was said to be a mere overshadowed by a mighty rock. It was claimed that falling streams tumbled

225

down the rockface into Her pool; but that pond was of such size that those cascades did not suffice to churn its surface into turbulence. Rather, a calm persisted despite the onslaughts of the falling waters. Blue fire burnt both beneath and above the water, a cold fire which failed to warm the black waters. Cold were those waters, cold waters overshadowed by towering bluffs, and a chilling mist rose from the surface.

'Perhaps,' said Tromso Stavenger, 'we could hear of something else. We all know where we're going and why.'

Grendel, realizing he might have made a tactical error, did his best to oblige, and began to tell another tale. For the delectation of the Knights, he told a noble story of the deeds of the elven lords of a kingdom long since lost to the world of geography.

But this failed to lighten the depression which had settled upon the expedition.

Alfric sensed the way in which morale had fallen, and was distressed. His own morale was falling itself. As he rode toward his doom in company with the Yudonic Knights, he realized that these brawling swordsmen might be the last people he saw before he died. And, in a mood strangely like panic, he realized he did not know any of these men, these his death-companions.

He did not know them?

Yes, that was the literal truth.

Alfric Danbrog had lived so much in the world of the Bank that he had not seen most of these Knights from one year to the next. He had lived as Izdarbolskobidarbix, Banker Third Class, and the world of the Yudonic Knights had become steadily more foreign to him, year by year.

With difficulty, Alfric hushed his panic down to nothing, and tried to distract himself from the dangers and difficulties of the moment by mentally revising the grammar and vocabulary of Janjuladoola.

As Alfric and the Knights ventured into higher ground, the air became colder, and there was both ice and snow underfoot. And how many memories this brought back! The snorting horses. The crunch of snow. The grinkle-grak of breaking ice. But the memories belonged to happier times alien to this grim expedition.

'How much further?' said Alfric, addressing the question to his king. 'How much further till we get there?'

By 'there', Alfric meant Her lair; and his grandfather knew as much.

'Not much further,' said Tromso Stavenger.

Then said no more.

Alfric longed for more conversation, but did not know how to initiate it. It distressed Alfric that, as he neared his death, his contact with his grandfather was reduced to the trivialities of expedition routine.

For once, Alfric wanted a heart-to-heart talk, a communion of souls, a mutual exposure of the spirit. But he was not able to talk on such a deep and personal level with any member of his family. In fact, Alfric knew his family as a diplomat knows the personages of a foreign state in which he is stationed; and, tonight, he regretted the way in which the Bank had estranged him from his family.

Others must have known they were nearing Her lair, for the Knights began to check the carriage of their weapons. Alfric was glad that he himself was armed with Bloodbane, the work of wonder-smiths, a sword possessed of such inate savagery that it would provide him with the battle-courage he needed to succeed in combat.

All in that company were richly armed. Alfric's father had a spiral-hilted blade of black iron, while the Wormlord bore a serpent-bladed weapon inlaid with runic gold.

It is said that, when a man realizes the nearness of death, this is a good time to review the deeds of his life. For his part, Alfric had lived not the careless life of an idle rake. Instead, he had pursued ambition in the Bank. Doubtless he had lived what was in many ways a cold and ruthless life, but he thought himself none the worse for that. In any case, personal virtue is no consolation in the face of death.

As Alfric was so thinking, he smelt something foul, a deadly taint of flesh-rot and knew they must be near Her lair, or near some place equally as evil, near some hideous secret of the clutching earth, the silent hills. Not for the first time, he shivered at the thought of the ordeal of battle, the possibility of being hideously maimed. But where precisely was the smell coming from? The source appeared to be a stream of utter black; and this they followed uphill to the point where it issued from a cleft rock. Alfric looked uphill further. The source of this stream must be over the rise which lay above – unless the stream was springing from some dark place inside the hill itself.

Tromso Stavenger dismounted and dipped his fingers into the chilling currents of that black water. The Wormlord lifted his fingers to his nose, sniffed at them, then spat in disgust. He got to his feet.

'This stream flows from Her place of darkness,' said the Wormlord. 'Hence its stench. We'll find Her lair just over that rise.'

This news was communicated to the king's rune-warriors, who received it without enthusiasm. They were cold; they were tired; they were hungry; they were afraid. Worse, a skyshadow had obliterated the moon, much to the distress of those Knights who could not see in the dark.

Had they been true to the boasts of the saga songs, the Knights would welcome the opportunity to prove themselves in the ultimate test of courage and manhood, to go up against Herself and subdue the monstrous female thing. But, in the event, the Knights were not able to rise to the standards of the heroes of saga. This is understandable, for death is a savage penalty, ever hard to pay; and glory which seems a surpassing reward in the warmth of a beerhall is cold comfort on a nightside hillside.

The Knights wanted to live, to return to the warmth of the world of the living, to gold-giving halls and woman-warm beds. Yet none wished to run, for none wanted to be branded a coward; and, while their courage was failing, each who faltered feared that death would be the penalty for abandoning his king at such a moment. But each of the Knights grieved for the life he thought himself about to lose.

And, without anyone consciously willing it, it happened that all the horses came to a halt, for the fear and abodement of the Knights was communicating itself to the horses, and the beasts were close to panic. Shortly, the horses were sure to bolt and run, carrying the Knights away with them.

And, while none of the Knights consciously wanted this to happen, it is nevertheless certain that none took any step to calm the horses. The logical thing to do was to dismount; and, if the horses could not be comforted, then to proceed on foot. But the Knights would not do this unless ordered.

And maybe they would not do it even then.

Tromso Stavenger halted when he found himself too far ahead of the others. All the Knights had fallen back, but for his son Grendel and his grandson Alfric. A courageous threesome they made, undoubtedly, but surely fifty would have a better chance against Herself than would three.

'They're falling behind,' said Alfric unnecessarily.

'We should flog one to death to set an example for the rest,' said Grendel. 'We should—'

'Peace,' said Stavenger.

And his son hushed.

Then the Wormlord paused to give his men time to catch up; and, when they had gathered around him, then he addressed them.

'My noble companions,' said Tromso Stavenger.

And the generosity of the Wormlord's heart was such that he accorded his warriors this accolade without letting any hint of sarcasm intrude into his speech.

'My rune-warriors,' said Stavenger, 'it is to you I speak. We are about to approach Her Lair. You have dared much by coming this far. However, I do not ask you to come any further.'

Alfric wanted to protest, then realized that it made no difference what his grandfather said. The horses were about to panic, and their riders meant the beasts to panic, whether they knew it or not. If Tromso Stavenger ordered them to dismount, then he would only precipitate an immediate rout. The king might manage to salvage one or two men from such a debacle, but they would be useless in combat.

For the Yudonic Knights were cravens all.

And Alfric remembered Comptroller Xzu, and the calm certainty with which Xzu had told him that the Knights were big on boast and small on action. As Alfric listened to his grandfather, he began to wish that Xzu was here to audit Stavenger's speech. For the king's unflinching courage was plain to the ear; and there was no doubt that, whatever the deficiency of most of the men of the Families, Wen Endex was possessed of at least one authentic hero.

'Many have fallen away,' said Tromso Stavenger, 'for their dread overcame their judgement. It is true that danger awaits us, for Her reputation was not built out of shadows. It is true that our task is no matter of whimsy but a deadly venture into the realms of fear. We all know of the brave men She has killed. We all know of the skilled warriors She has overcome, tearing their flesh to pieces. We all know that death awaits those who dare their flesh against Herself.'

Yes, Xzu should have been here to listen to this. But . . . maybe the king should have phrased his speech a little differently. For surely such emphasis on death and danger was no way to motivate men to battle. A little encouragement would not have gone astray, surely.

'However,' said Tromso Stavenger, continuing with his rhetoric, 'she is not the only power in Wen Endex. The royal family can supply the courage and strength needed to accomplish her doom. Furthermore, such a deed is the duty of the royal family, whereas it is not the common duty of all the Knights.'

Alfric saw no logic in this at all. Rather, he thought the contrary was the case. Law and tradition surely meant that actually the Knights were doomed to strive beside their king until the common end of all descended upon them. And Tromso Stavenger must know this. Nevertheless, the king was pretending that things were quite otherwise:

'Therefore,' said Stavenger, 'we ask none here to give us aid in this task. You have done your duty by accompanying us this far. By bodyguarding your king through the wilds, you have kept us safe from vampires and marauding shape-changers, from bog fiends and giant vogels, and from all those other things which haunt the night with teeth and talons.'

Belatedly, Alfric realized Tromso Stavenger did not intend to compel the craven to battle, but instead was giving them a chance to escape their duty. Giving them a chance? He was positively encouraging them to escape!

'I have but one command,' said the king. 'And that is that, when you withdraw, you go to no great distance. Rather, I ask that you fortify yourselves in a position of battle-strength, and there hold your ground to wait until we return. For return we will, bearing Her head between us. It is meet that there should be witnesses to the deeds of the royal family. You are those witnesses.'

Silence.

The king was finished.

At length, one of the Knights cleared his throat and said:

'Which position does our lord wish us to fortify?'

Tromso Stavenger nominated a small knoll they had passed some half a league distant from this hillside. Then, without further ado, the Knights departed. They moved off in a close-knit group. No sound of talk came from them, and no snatch of song; but for the jingle of their harness, they might have been ghosts. Their silence was that of men who were bitterly ashamed.

'Was that wise?' said Alfric, unable to restrain himself. 'Was that even – even sensible? To send away the greater part of our numbers?'

'Those cravens would have obeyed no other order,' said Grendel with contempt. 'Except one compelling them to quit this place at the greatest speed possible.'

'But,' persisted Alfric, 'we could have tried.'

'Let's waste no strength on argument,' said Tromso Stavenger. 'Let's move on uphill.'

Then the Wormlord set off, walking on foot and leading his horse uphill. Grendel and Alfric followed him in like manner, trudging uphill in silence; and the loudest sound in the night was the panting which came from their aged leader as he contended with the steepness of the slope.

To his surprise, Alfric found his fear had left him. Perhaps this was not so very strange. Alfric Danbrog had gone through life thinking himself as superior to other people. In truth, he was no more competent than anyone else at dealing with the routine demands of day-to-day life. But, in a crisis, his pride steadied him; for his monstrous ego would not allow him to freely confess to fear. Alfric Danbrog was a scion of a Family indeed, possessed of that lordly arrogance which is one of the greatest battle-assets of a warrior caste.

While the men showed no fear, the horses did; but, with a fair amount of persuasion, the beasts were brought to the top of the rise, and so to the place which was rumoured to be the scene of the doom of many men.

CHAPTER FIFTEEN

From the top of the rise, the king and his two companions looked down a grassy slope which led to the mere which was Her lair. The moon was still masked by cloud, but blue-burning fire above and below and the dark waters lit the scene with a ghastly light.

'Mount up,' said Tromso Stavenger.

'What have you in mind?' said Grendel.

'To ride our horses to the edge of the water,' said his father. 'If She attacks, we flee before Her. If She follows, we lure Herself into the mass of our Knights.'

So saying, the king struggled on to his horse. Alfric and Grendel did likewise. Alfric could not help but admire the king for his mastery of minor tactics. The Wormlord was prepared to die, but was not going to throw away his life without cause. If he could, Tromso Stavenger would tire his enemy by making Her contend against the speed of a horse; then he would lead Herself into the midst of his retreating rune-warriors, so weight of numbers would be on the side of the Knights.

And Alfric remembered an occasion, years ago, when he had met with the Wormlord in private audience, and Tromso Stavenger had said:

'Forget the feats of heroes. A professional soldier always seeks odds of three against one. At the minimum.'

At the time, Alfric's mind had been all on Bank business. Nevertheless, he had remembered those words; their wisdom had stayed with him. Thinking back, he realized there was much he had been taught by the Wormlord. He had taken it all in, memorizing many lessons, the truth of which he would appreciate in the years ahead, when he ruled Wen Endex as king.

If he ruled.

If he survived this night.

If he lived through the encounter with Herself.

'Are we ready?' said Tromso Stavenger.

'We're ready,' said Grendel, answering for himself and his son.

'Then – let us ride!'

Alfric leant forward in the saddle as the three men rode their horses down to the edge of the water. He was breathing quickly. He clutched the reins tightly. He was nerved up. Ready for Her to burst forth from the water. Ready for his horse to rear, then gallop away in headlong panic.

But nothing happened.

Instead, the men sat there on horseback by the side of the waters, watching and waiting to no avail.

Slowly, Alfric straightened up. He still kept tight hold of the reins, just in case, but he began to suspect that nothing was going to happen. Not immediately.

He began to take stock of the pool.

A dark and hideous pool it was, much as the songs had pictured it to be. There was, as the sagas claimed, a tumbling stream pouring into the black waters. And, despite the everfall of the waterfall, the surface of the mere was still and silent. It was backed by towering bluffs, and from those cliffs there grew crag-rooted trees, the sightbare branches of which bore not a single leaf. From those trees, three corpses hung by their heels, victims of Her most recent depredations. Blue fire shimmered in the depths of the waters, in which swam the nicors, the ravaging waterworms.

The blue light from the water made their faces appear to be fleshed with the meat of corpses. That same light was reflected from their eyes, giving each of them a weird and inhuman aspect.

'What now?' said Alfric.

'Someone must dive into the pool,' said Tromso Stavenger. 'That's the only way. She must be brought to battle in the water if She will not come forth upon the land.'

'True,' said Grendel. 'Alfric, you're nominated.'

'But – but—'

Alfric struggled for words to express his dismay. But found none. Cold and clammy with dread, he got down from his horse.

'Alfric!' said Grendel sharply. 'What do you think you're doing?'

'The – the pool,' stammered Alfric.

'Blood of the Gloat!' said his father. 'Make a joke, and the boy is ready to die for it! What next? Will you fly to the moon on command? Get on your horse, fool.'

'But – but you said—'

'You can't breathe water, moron,' said his father impatiently. 'Mount up!'

Alfric complied.

'Don't be hard on the boy,' said Tromso Stavenger. 'It's his first battle, after all.'

Alfric wanted to protest. This was not his first battle by any means. He was a killer of dragons, an enemy of giants, a terrorizer of werehamsters. And he was thirty-three years old! No boy in anyone's language. However,

236

the shock of being commanded into Her pool was still upon him, and he lacked the strength for protest.

'There does remain,' said Tromso Stavenger, 'the problem of bringing Her to battle. I wish we'd thought to bring a goat. That might have lured Her from the water.'

'We could hamstring one of the horses,' said Grendel, not joking now. 'Blood and panic would draw Her forth.'

'Maybe,' said his father. 'But there's something else I'd like to try first.'

Then Tromso Stavenger produced a battle-horn which Alfric had never seen before.

'You know this horn, boy?' said his grandfather.

'No,' said Alfric.

'This battle-horn belonged to Melrik himself. Yes, Melrik, hero of saga.'

And Alfric shivered, for he felt himself to be in the presence of the Great Ones of the past. Then Tromso Stavenger chose to wind that horn. High rose the challenge of that rouser of men. The brazen voice of the battle-horn sent shivers running down Alfric's spine. The blue-flaming waters of the mere shuddered, and echoes rolled back from the high-walled bluffs on the far side of the pool.

But She did not rise to that challenge.

The tableau remained unchanged: three men on horseback waiting by a dark pool beneath a darker sky. It was cold, and a mourning wind was making it colder yet; and Alfric was starting to feel just a tiny bit ridiculous. The horses were starting to get restless again; they had endured this place for as long as they could, and were eager to be gone.

It would be the height of absurdity if the horses were to panic now and bear away their riders. Or if the horses stayed and nothing happened at all. Perhaps they would wait out the whole night without seeing so much as a hair of Herself. Perhaps She was hunting elsewhere. Or was dead, her flesh rotting at the bottom of the mere. Or . . . maybe She had never existed at all.

But . . .

There were real corpses dangling from the crag-rooted trees on the far side of the mere.

Oh yes, the dead were real enough.

But, even so, maybe She was but a tale, Her murders the work of some night-slashing human.

Who?

Grendel Danbrog was a possible candidate. He was big; he was strong; he lived remote from the rest of humanity; he could come and go as he wished. He could have brought those corpses to this place. Perhaps there was a coracle hidden somewhere near the mere. Perhaps—

Alfric looked at his father with obscene surmise, then shuddered.

'The horses will not stay,' said Grendel. 'We must turn them loose.'

Then he dismounted, removed his journeypack from the horse, and slapped the beast on the rump. It turned and fled. Alfric's beast tried to do likewise. Because, in a fit of sudden panic, Alfric was urging it to flight with his knees.

'Ho!' said Grendel, catching the thing by the bridle.

Man fought with horse, and the horse was mastered. Never before had Alfric appreciated his father's true strength. The man must have muscles a blacksmith would envy.

'We almost lost you then,' said Grendel with a chuckle. 'I wouldn't like that to happen.'

And Alfric heard in that chuckle the tones of evil, and knew then that his father was the real killer. His father was the terrorizer of Wen Endex. His father had murdered those hapless humans who now hung from the trees at the far side of the mere. And Alfric stared at the man, eyes bulging in horror.

'You look sick,' said Grendel. 'What is it? The smell? Get down, you'll feel better soon.'

Then he reached up with one of his hands. Alfric had never before realized how massive those hands actually were. The strength of those hands could not be resisted.

—He will have me.

Thus Alfric. In silence. In terror.

Helpless to resist, Alfric got down from his horse. Grendel brought Alfric's journeypack to earth then sent the horse on its way. Then Tromso Stavenger started to dismount.

'Grandfather!' said Alfric.

Meaning to warn the man, to tell him to run.

The Wormlord, startled by the note of panic in Alfric's voice, slipped and fell. Grendel caught him, saving him from doing himself an injury. Then Grendel got down the king's pack, dismissed the old man's horse, and sent the beast on its way.

'Seat yourself,' said Grendel.

Tromso Stavenger lowered himself on to his pack. Watching the studied care with which his grandfather seated himself, Alfric realized what an effort every action was costing the old man. The king was worn out by all this mounting and dismounting, this hill-climbing and horn-blowing. He should have been in bed, feeding on warm soup and watching his favourite cat watching the untunchilamons.

239

Tonight Alfric truly appreciated the age of their white-haired leader; tonight, Alfric began to understand something of what it meant to be old. Tonight, Alfric knew that Tromso Stavenger would be no help at all when Grendel made his Change and became Herself, and fell upon the pair of them to kill them.

'Now,' said Stavenger, once he had seated himself comfortably, 'what was that about, Alfric? What did you want to tell me?'

'I – I thought I saw something,' said Alfric. 'But I was wrong.'

Then, cold with terror, Alfric sat on his pack and watched his father. When would the man make his move against them? Maybe the eyes would give warning. It was said that from Her eyes a hellish light outshone, a light which blinded Her enemies in battle.

Abruptly, Grendel stood.

And Alfric thought, in panic:

—This is it!

Grendel stumped uphill. Alfric watched him. Twenty paces he went, then began to pull down his trousers. This was it! Grendel was disrobing so he could Change, so his flesh could swell and girth, so he could become Herself!

Suddenly, Grendel became aware of Alfric's unblinking watch.

'Alfric,' said Grendel, 'can't you give me a little privacy?'

'What – what are you doing?' said Alfric.

'What do you think I'm doing?' said Grendel. 'Blood of the Gloat! Has the boy lost his wits entirely?'

'Alfric,' said Tromso Stavenger, 'look to the pool. Our watch we must keep.'

Alfric tried to find the will to protest. But failed. He

could not disobey a direct order from his king. He turned to the pool. Behind him, he heard Grendel grunt. The sound was low-pitched. An animal sound. Hideous with menace. Grendel must be Changing. Surely. Changing into Herself.

Then—

Heavy footsteps lurched toward them.

Alfric jerked his head around, and saw—

Saw his father walking toward him, Grendel Danbrog as yet unchanged, buckling his belt as he came. Alfric sat back, weak with relief.

'Ah,' said Grendel, with happy satisfaction. 'That feels better. Now. I had something in here.'

So saying, Grendel undid his journeypack and pulled out a heavy four-buckle bag of alien make. What was it? With renewed terror, Alfric remembered tales of Herself, and feared this satchel to be a glof, a bag of devils' skins which She carried, and into which She was wont to stuff the tripes of those She slaughtered.

But, when Grendel unbuckled the bag, no smell of dead meat issued from within. Instead . . . was that cheese?

'Cheese,' said Grendel, as if he had been reading his son's mind.

Grendel took a big fat wheel of the stuff from his satchel and passed it to his father. Tromso Stavenger pulled out a dirk and started to cut slices for the three of them. He then produced three small cups and a skin which yielded rough red wine. Then – miracle of miracles – a loaf of crusted bread.

The wine was good, and the bread likewise, and Alfric was soon tearing into the goodness of the breadflesh. His terror began to ease, and he sat back on his pack, relaxing somewhat. Then—

Where were his spare spectacles?

For a moment, Alfric feared he might be sitting on them. Then remembered they were in the top of his pack, inside a hardwood casket.

'Maybe we should put up a tent,' said Tromso Stavenger.

'A tent?' said Alfric in amazement.

'Well, yes, we have to sleep sometime,' said the king.

'You can sleep now if you wish,' said Grendel. 'Both of you. I'll keep watch.'

This declaration stirred Alfric's fear to life. While his eyelids had been nodding, now he was wide awake indeed.

'No,' said Alfric. 'No thank you. We're all right.'

'Speak for yourself!' said Grendel. 'Your grandfather may not be so ready to wait out the night.'

'I'm fine for the moment,' said Tromso Stavenger.

But Alfric suspected it was pride which did the speaking, for the king's voice was weary. Certainly they would both of them have to sleep sooner or later. And then – then they would be utterly at Grendel's mercy.

Alfric straightened his back and concentrated his efforts on staying both awake and alert. He was helped by the cold of the night and the occasional menacing sounds which stirred in the poolside grass. Living indoors, one always forgets how very large the night actually is, and how menacing.

Once, a nicor raised its hideous head from the blue-burning waters of the mere then slipped beneath the surface again. Could the things crawl out of the water? Maybe they could. As Alfric was thus thinking, a ripple spread across the pool. Alfric's hand dropped to the hilt of Bloodbane. He glanced at his father and grandfather. They appeared to have noticed nothing.

Then, without warning, a head broke free from the water.

Alfric was so terrified he could not speak.

The head was huge, hideous, armed with teeth. Shaggy was the hair which clothed it. And—

And it was making for the shore!

To the shore came the head, then the body which supported it dragged itself from the water, revealing itself to be a rat, a huge and hideous rat some four times the size of a dog. The rat swaggered toward the three men.

Alfric got to his feet.

'Ho!' he cried.

The rat paused.

It was a monster, yes, but it was only a rodent when all was said and done. Alfric drew the deathsword Blood-bane and advanced upon the rat in a mood of marauding murder. For a moment, the thing stood its ground. Then it fled, scuttling back to the water. Alfric swung at it once, but missed. Then the brute splashed into the water, dived, and was gone.

Alfric stood by the side of the mere, panting. He stared into the dark waters, trying to see where the rat had gone. If rats grew to such size in these dominions of darkness, what else might have obtained monstrosity?

Behind him, his father and grandfather laughed.

'Bravo,' said Grendel softly.

Alfric turned.

The rage of Bloodbane possessed him.

Driven by the murder-lust of the weapon, Alfric Danbrog strode toward his father and grandfather, his sword ready for the kill.

'Ho,' said his father. 'He walks like a hero.'

Then both Grendel and Tromso Stavenger laughed at what they took to be Alfric's posturing; and their laughter deflated his anger; and he felt somewhat sheepish.

His sword was angry.

Murder-thoughts from the weapon stirred to life again in Alfric's mind.

But he could not kill his father, not yet, for as yet the man had made no move against them, and they were family, were they not? And it was possible, was it not, that Grendel might spare them because they were family?

Alfric resisted the claims of the weapon, sheathed it, released his hand from the hilt, and felt easier.

He returned to his pack.

A twinge of pain stabbed through Alfric's right hip as he settled himself. This pain he had felt often over the years; and, though he did his best to ignore it, every year it got worse and more frequent. Though he was only thirty-three, arthritis was already making claims on his health. As Alfric tried to get comfortable on his pack, his back protested. He had sudden visions of putting his back out. He imagined himself lying on the ground, writhing in helpless agony, while Grendel went through his Change and became Herself, devoured Tromso Stavenger then turned his attentions to Alfric himself.

—No!

So thought Alfric, strenuously, wilfully, denying the validity of this vision, and denying too that his father was actually Herself.

But Alfric did not believe his own denials.

He kept glancing sideways at his father, expecting to see some sign of a monstrous Change.

244

As Alfric waited for the moment of disaster, Grendel said:

'I want you to know something.'

Alfric was about to ask 'what' when he realized his father was not speaking to Alfric but to the Wormlord.

'Speak,' said Tromso Stavenger.

'I want you to know,' said Grendel, 'that I was never a werewolf. There was no truth at all to that rumour.'

What was this?

Was Grendel about to admit the truth? Was Grendel about to admit that he was no mere wolf but, in truth, Herself? Alfric fingered the hilt of Bloodbane.

'I know, I know,' said the Wormlord. 'I've always know as much.'

'Then . . . then why did you cast me out? All these . . . these years in exile, these . . .'

'Hard times demanded hard decisions,' said Tromso Stavenger.

'How so?'

The Wormlord sighed, then said:

'It was the Bank which forced my hand.'

'The Bank?' said Grendel. 'They told you to name me as a werewolf?'

'No,' said the Wormlord. 'They threatened to do as much themselves. You don't know what it's like, dealing with the Bank. They've so much power, so much . . . ah, you wouldn't understand. But believe me. They were . . . oh, but it's a long story.'

But, as the night lengthened, Grendel Danbrog got the rest of the story out of his father. Grendel and Alfric listened as the Wormlord told them of the varied threats the Bank had used to try to make the king grant fresh concessions to the Izdimir Empire.

'At last,' said Tromso Stavenger, 'they schemed against my own family. They forged medical reports and prepared false witnesses to testify against you. It is said that the Bank has hypnotists, men who can work upon the minds of their victims until those victims firmly believe stories which have no foundation in fact. Such victims were prepared.'

'And?' said Grendel.

'And the Bank threatened me,' said Tromso Stavenger. 'I must do what the Bank wanted. I must allow the Izdimir Empire to station troops in Wen Endex and place its bureaucrats in Saxo Pall itself to guide my deliberations. I must enforce the same laws that govern the people in Ang and Obooloo. I must – well, in a word, surrender.'

'They really thought they could make you do that?' said Grendel.

'They thought they had prepared a strong position for themselves,' said Tromso Stavenger, 'since they could so easily prove you to be a werewolf.'

'But I was never such a creature!'

'I always knew that,' said Tromso Stavenger. 'I knew all the evidence was forged. I knew, too, that, in time, I could have proved your innocence to the people of Wen Endex. But, had the Bank moved against you, I would not have had time. The mob would have believed you a shape-changer. Worse, they might have believed me to be a werewolf myself. Urged by the Bank, the mob would doubtless have killed you. Equally, the mob might have overwhelmed myself. We might all have died.'

'So the Bank had you by the oysters,' said Grendel.

'So thought the Bank,' said Tromso Stavenger. 'But I did what the Bank did not expect. I moved against you

246

myself. I myself named you as a werewolf, thus proving my own innocence of any such charge. For, as is well known, all shape-changers cling together; so it follows that a father who casts out a shape-changing son cannot be a shape-changer himself.'

'That was a cruel thing to do, even so,' said Grendel softly.

'Cruel, yes,' said Tromso Stavenger. 'But it preserved the freedoms of the state. Oh, and I took revenge, believe me. The Bank had grown bold. They were expecting my collapse, my surrender. They were not expecting me to strike. But I did. Immediately. Two dozen bankers died. Private murders, streetcorner butchery. You know how it's done. In like manner, I disposed of agents from the Izdimir Empire who had exposed themselves through carelessness.'

'That won you the moment,' said Grendel.

'The moment, yes,' said Tromso Stavenger. 'But what of the future? The Bank is strong. How could my line be protected against the Bank? I chose to let the Bank think I really did believe you to be a werewolf. I chose to foster difference and disagreement between us. I made you my enemy. Because you were my enemy, your son was likewise my natural enemy.'

'I never thought thus,' said Alfric.

'Didn't you?' said Tromso Stavenger. 'Whatever you thought, the Bank thought of you as a weapon which could be used against me. The Bank took hold of you. Sought to train you to be a weapon which could one day be used to win power for the Bank. Ah, what a risk I ran! For the danger was that you would ultimately prove true to the Bank.'

'And?' said Alfric. 'Have I? Or haven't I?'

'That . . . that I don't know,' said his grandfather. 'Not for certain. But . . . I have measured you over these years. I have seen you grow, and I have seen the potential for kingship grow with you. I believe you will rule Wen Endex for the benefit of the nation, not for the benefit of the Bank. When you sit on the throne, then Galsh Ebrek will have a king who understands the Bank, who can control its power, and who can break the Bank, and make it a mere tool of the state. That is what I hope for. When you are wormlord, Alfric, my long revenge against the Bank will be complete.'

'This . . . this is much to learn at once,' said Grendel in a wondering voice.

'Much indeed,' acknowledged Tromso Stavenger. 'I . . . I only hope you can forgive me for following the necessities which were placed upon me.'

Then Tromso Stavenger embraced Grendel, and father and son clung to each other, and then both began to weep.

And Alfric for his own part wondered.

Was this true?

Could it possibly be true?

Was his father really not a werewolf?

And—

Wah!

What an amazing old man was Tromso Stavenger! A wicked enemy, a wily foe, one of the few men to out-think and out-smart the Bank. How had he done it? Why, by thinking of the long result, and hatching a plan which would only be brought to fruition by the work of generations.

Once again, Alfric had a glimpse of the burdens of kingship. To think not just for the moment and not just for the day, but to plan for the generations. Tromso Stavenger had done just that; had out-thought and out-manoeuvred the Bank; and had tricked the Bank itself into shaping the weapon he needed to fulfil his purposes.

Right then, Alfric Danbrog knew that he was that weapon indeed.

Tromso Stavenger had won his great gamble.

For Alfric was filled with rage at the thought of what the Bank had done to his family. When he became king, he would exact vengeance. The Bank would be brought to heel and made an instrument of the state. Then Alfric would use the power of the Banking Circle to bring the Izdimir Empire itself to heel, and end for ever the threat which that empire posed to the liberties of Galsh Ebrek and the nation of Wen Endex.

Alfric wished he was in the Bank already, cleaving heads and opening bellies with the deathblade Blood-bane. His fingers lingered over the hilt of that weapon, and he longed to draw it in earnest against his foes, to hold that living fury in his hands and run beserk, giving himself to the possession of a beserker rage.

These imaginings were so engrossing that Alfric did not notice something stirring in the water. Then his father swore, and Alfric looked up abruptly, and saw Herself rising from the mere.

'Stroth!' screamed Alfric, leaping to his feet.

He slipped in the mud, his feet went from under him, and down he went. And She was already striding toward them, water slathering from Her loins, the burning light of Her eyes blazing from the shapeless shadows of Her face.

Alfric scrabbled for balance, slipped again, went down, and he was going to die, to die, but—

But Grendel was there.

Grendel Danbrog stood between Herself and Her victims. Old iron was in the warrior's hands. With his sword he struck. But the hag dismissed the warrior's weapon with a swipe of one of her mighty paws. Then Grendel was down, and She was upon him. There was a scream of tortured metal as Her talons clawed iron, tore through Grendel's armour and ripped into his bowels.

'No!' cried Tromso Stavenger.

Thus cried the old man.

And made as if to advance.

'Stand back,' said Alfric to his grandfather. And then, loudly, to Herself: 'Stand back from my father!'

His words were savage, for Bloodbane was in his hands, and Alfric was buoyed up by his own rage and the bloodlust of the weapon.

Certainly his challenge made Her pause.

She turned Her face from Grendel's bleeding body. She looked upon Alfric with Her burning eyes. Then She made a sound in her throat, a hideous noise like mud slithering down a monstrous swampland suckhole. Alfric realized she was laughing. At him!

'Laugh, bitch,' said Alfric coldly. 'Laugh while you can. For your end is upon you. For this is the deathblade Bloodbane.'

But She knew that weapon not, and, in any case, She feared no sword, regardless of its reputation.

She smashed Grendel with her monstrous fist, killing him, then She gathered Her shadows and advanced upon Alfric. Hot with murderlust stood that warrior, braving himself against Herself like a hero from out of the sage songs.

She leapt.

Alfric struck.

The deathblade Bloodbane sang through the air, joyful its slaughtersong.

'Die!' screamed Alfric.

Hacking Her flesh.

She screamed.

The blade slashed Her flesh wide open.

But even as it did so, the blade bucked and buckled. And, as She flailed at the air in frenzied agony, the metal bubbled and boiled, melted and vaporized.

And Alfric—

Astonished—

Disbelieving—

Found himself holding nothing more than the hilt of his weapon.

Then she smashed him.

It was like being hit by a charging bull.

Down in the mud went Alfric Danbrog.

He did not scream, he had no breath to scream, but he fought as best he could. She tore him, ripped him, scragged away his clothes, then picked him up. He swooned as she lifted him. Then She hurled him into the mud.

He lay there, alive.

Just.

He had wit enough to grope for a weapon, any weapon. All he found was a branch, and that was rotten. But it would have to serve.

'Mork,' muttered Alfric.

And what he was saying, what he meant to say, why, that was a mystery even to him.

He struggled to his feet.

'Yoth,' he said.

Faintly.

But, though his voice was not working properly, his legs were. And he was walking toward Her, walking knee-deep through what felt like glue. She screamed in defiance. Standing. Waiting. A shadow amidst shadows. Alfric could not see Her properly, for his spectacles were gone, and his world was little more than a blurred mist of darkness.

Then She attacked.

Alfric's stick was knocked aside in a moment.

Screaming, she clutched Alfric to Her hairy chest and started to crush the life from his body. The hard tips of Her paps were grinding into his cheek. Desperately, he turned his head and bit into one of those paps, bit as hard as he could, and broke one of his teeth on the hideous thing.

She laughed.

'Shon,' she said. 'Mona shon.'

Alfric sensed that this was a threat.

But what did it mean?

Moments later, he thought he knew.

For She pushed the hapless Alfric down to the heat between Her thighs. The hot breath of Her lower lips billowed out around him. And he saw the teeth which worked in Her privacy, teeth burning with the same fire which possessed Her eyes. The rancid stench of Her desire belched out from Her wound.

And She was forcing him inwards.

Alfric twisted, struggled, fought, but it was no use. He was being forced toward those teeth. Slowly. Remorselessly. She was taking Her time, for She was enjoying this.

In desperation, Alfric tried to Change. But that was impossible in the heat of combat. In moments he would be mutilated, would be—

She dropped him.

Just like that.

Alfric lay still.

Did She think him dead?

She was standing up.

Looking around.

At what?

For what?

Then Alfric heard some creature howl.

That sound was hideous, the bloodlust slaughtervoice of some blood-crazed animal, the sound of a thing which gave itself entirely to appetite. It was the sound of a tongue being uprooted, of a leg being wrenched free from a man's buttock, of a horse screaming as it was slaughtered. And, in a sudden thoughtflash, Alfric realized that She might have a mate, and that this might be the cry of Her mate.

Then—

Then he saw it.

Something white, charging out of the night.

It leapt upon Her, and She was overthrown.

Down She went, with the white thing on top of her.

And Alfric, scarcely a skin away from the combatants, was close enough to see that the white thing was a wolf.

This was the thing which had howled, which had saved him.

Saved him?

Whoever won this mortal combat would surely fall upon Alfric Danbrog and eat him.

So—

Slowly, painfully, Alfric began to crawl away from the struggling combatants.

He moved.

Paused.

Moved.

Rested.

Moved.

It hurt to move, but he must.

He—

The pain was too much.

He could not move.

Could not even crawl.

He lay in the mud, shuddering.

Then—

Then the moon emerged as the clouds cleared.

And—

And Alfric knew what last chance was left to him.

Alfric gazed upon the moon, upon the blurred white disk of the moon, and, as he did so, that disk sharpened as it came into focus. And he smelt the moonlight shining upon the waters of the mere, and the smell was a high thin smell vaguely reminiscent of onions. And he smelt the blood of combat, the blood of a dead human and the blood of a wounded wolf and the foul clotted blood of Herself, and—

And his teeth were sharpening for the blood, his jaw was lengthening, his belly becoming lean, his muscles strengthening, girthing, lengthening.

And the sounds were changing, and he heard much more, now, as he stood up on his four feet, and—

And She had won against the white wolf, and the creature was mortally wounded, and She looked up from her prey to see a black wolf of monstrous size bruting toward Her.

Alfric leapt.

She was thrown backwards as Alfric took Her with his monstrous strength. His throat rending at Her throat. One of Her hands scrabbled for his eyes, sought, almost found, but—

His teeth tore, crunching, munching—

And black blood ran from Her throat, blood black by the light of the moon, and spasms shook Her body, and She died.

And Alfric threw back his head and howled.

Then—

He could not help himself.

He ate.

He fed.

He was animal, he was appetite, he was a brute ravening, shameless, shameless, giving himself to his greed, to the gluttony of the blood. And She was torn open before he could stop himself, She was torn from throat to crotch, Her intestines spilt to the night, and much of Her gut in Alfric's belly.

Then he shuddered, and stepped back from the corpse, back-pacing neatly with his four feet.

Then he dipped his muzzle into the black waters of the mere and he drank, though the water stank he drank of it, drank deeply, slaking his thirst.

And only then did he force himself to Change, discarding wolf for human.

When Alfric had two feet again, his first thought was to seek his second-best spectacles. He recovered them from his pack, then rummaged in the same pack for his spare clothes, the change of clothes a traveller always carries in case he becomes soaked by rain or river. Alfric dressed himself, and that was enough, for the moment, enough for him to go into action.

'Grandfather?'

Where was his grandfather?

Had the white wolf killed it?

And was the wolf yet dead?

To his surprise, Alfric saw there was life in the white-haired brute.

Alfric dared himself toward it in time to see it writhe, distort, deform, and—

Change.

Though it was dying, the wolf possessed strength of will sufficient to make itself Change, and this it did, bloodfroth pain spewed forth on its bubbling breath as haunch became leg, as fur became skin, as the jawbone shrank, as the face became that of Tromso Stavenger.

'Grandfather . . .'

Alfric knelt by the old man.

Stavenger's mouth moved.

'Am—'

The Wormlord said no more.

But Alfric knew what question would be in the mind of the dying man. Had he managed to Change back into human form? Or was he dying as a wolf?

'You die as a hero,' said Alfric. 'A human hero.'

Tromso Stavenger smiled, glad that he would not bring shame on his Family, glad that he would die without the world at large ever knowing his secret, that secret which he had for so long concealed even from his son and his grandson, the secret being, of course, that he was in fact a shape-changer, a werewolf.

Then a gut-wrenching spasm of agony contorted the old man's face, and he snarled, trying to fight free of the pain, and Alfric suddenly wished he would die, for it was hard to watch such agony.

But the old man did not die, not then.

No.

His dying was long, and his dying was hard, and Alfric, to his shame, felt something like relief by the time the old man was finally gone.

Alfric kissed his grandfather, kissed the lips of the corpse, then went and sat on his pack.

The night was very calm, its details crisp and crystalline. The clouds had cleared away from the sky entirely, driven by a wind high in the heavens, but by the side of the mere no wind at all was now blowing.

The stars shone down, poisonous nightfruit, reflected in the black of the waters.

No blue fire burnt above or beneath the dark waters of the mere. Had the fire died because She had died? Or was the blue fire a transitory phenomenon, a—

'Shut up,' said Alfric, to the investigative part of his mind which was trying to pursue these questions.

Then he closed his eyes.

But as soon as he did so, memories assailed. Memories of his murder of the sea dragon Qa, of the torments he had inflicted upon the swamp giant Kralch, of the shameful bargain he had struck with the vampires on behalf of the Bank, and, perhaps hardest to live with of all, the grandiloquent pride he had felt when he had subdued and terrorized the moth-eaten old werehamster which had once tried to ambush him in the forest.

Alfric opened his eyes again and shuddered, trying to shake off the past.

The present was surely enough to deal with.

As he stared at the darkened mere, a snake came sliding from the water, sibilant moonlight glissading from its scales as it ventured on to the land.

'Pa!' said Alfric in disgust.

And the snake fled.

If Alfric had not spoken, the creature would have fed upon the flesh of Tromso Stavenger or Grendel Danbrog. The torn corpses lay in the welter of mud and muck which was the aftermath of battle. What to do with them?

Should Alfric guard the dead or leave them?

As he was trying to work out what to do, something else crept from the waters beneath the cold and silent moon. It was the rat. And now Alfric knew why he hated the thing so fiercely. The very first time he had seen the brute, he had suspected that it would soon be feeding upon the flesh of the dead.

The rat lifted its head.

Gazed upon Alfric.

Then started toward him.

Forget the flesh of the dead!

This thing had a taste for the living!

Alfric, war-battered and weaponless, stumbled backwards. Then tripped over a pile of clothing. Down he went, landing on something hard. The rat stalked toward him. And Alfric rolled over, scrabbled for the hard thing, and found it was just what he thought it was.

On came the rat.

And Alfric stood up, kicked away his grandfather's clothes, and braced himself, and the hard thing was in his hands, and the hard thing was his grandfather's sword.

And the rat leapt.

And Alfric screamed as he met the thing with the blade of old iron, and he screamed again and again as he hacked it, slaughtered it, killed it, murdered it.

Then he stood there panting.

Something else stirred in the water.

A nicor?

Or what?

Suddenly, Alfric realized he was almost completely exhausted. If something else came from the depths, he would have no chance of defeating it. And who could say what limit there was to the horrors of this place? One might almost think She had treasured the company of hideous things during Her life. Perhaps that was why She brought corpses to this place. Perhaps the dead meat was food for Her pets, and these pets the measure of Her loneliness. Perhaps—

Alfric shuddered, then—

He had no choice—

Walked away from the mere, taking nothing with him but his grandfather's bloody sword.

After a long and weary trek, Alfric came to the knoll which the Yudonic Knights had fortified in obedience to their king's wishes. There the Knights sat by their fires, toasting the wings of chickens and the legs of ducks, stewing up rabbit and reheating fish chowder.

The Knights stared at Alfric in silent amazement as he came into the firelight. There was blood on his hands and blood on his face and there was a bloody sword in his hands.

'She is dead,' said Alfric. 'The king is dead also. My father lies dead beside him.'

The Knights still stared at him, and he realized they were afraid of him, thinking him perhaps a ghost or a revenant. So he looked among the horses and found the Knights had secured the horse which was his own, and he climbed into the saddle and rode off through the night, making for Galsh Ebrek with a bloody sword in his hand.

CHAPTER SIXTEEN

Perhaps it was the water he had drunk, or perhaps it was the wounds inflicted by Her claws. Whatever the cause, Alfric was feverish long before he reached the Stanch Gates. And whatever his fever, such was the virulence of its onset that he collapsed in the muck scarcely a hundred paces from those Gates, and was picked up and taken to the city hospital by the gate guards.

A hospital bed claimed him. The sheets of the bed were stiff with the blood of whoever had died in it last, but this did nothing whatsoever to discourage the lice and bedbugs.

Alfric paid no heed to insectile assaults, for fever was the world in which he lived. He grappled with demons which strove to pulverize his liver with starhammers and dragon gongs. The dead came to him, and the unborn, their animating spirits stirring through the jaded air. Often he talked with them, or listened to politicking ghosts bickering in his nostrils, or to the worms which he imagined to be hollowing their way through his bones.

In lucid moments, Alfric listened to his neighbour, a demented old man who, believing himself a historian of the ruling oligarchies of the universe, lectured the world at length on the cornerstones of time itself and the flamboyant mysteries of the sun.

But always fever returned.

Living in a world which owed more to hallucination

than to anything else, Alfric began to believe that the air itself had turned to liquid fire, and he made frantic efforts to brush it away with his hands before it could flow into his lungs.

But always the air got in, and the pain of breathing suggested the air was fire indeed. This agony was part of the ever-accumulating evidence which suggested to Alfric that he was going to die. His symptoms were so various that, in time, he accumulated encyclopedic evidence to that effect. His hands crabbed; his joints ached; his intestines writhed; his muscles cramped; and he had visions of Herself, Her flesh swollen to corpse-green yellow, and flickering fire kicking in dragon-spasms from her ears.

In time, Alfric recovered, after a fashion. But he was still weak and slightly feverish when agents from the Bank arrived without warning and removed him from the hospital. Since Alfric was barely recovered from his hallucinations, he was too sick to argue against this abduction; and, lack of argument being taken as health sufficient, he was put aboard a cart and conveyed through the streets of Galsh Ebrek to the slopes of Mobius Kolb.

Then up those slopes.

Past the battlements of Saxo Pall.

And to (then into) the Bank itself. Alfric did not know whether he was honoured guest or prisoner, valued employee or uncrowned king. However, when servitors started helping him into his robes, he supposed that he was being accepted back into the organization on some level. His fears of immediate execution faded, though he was still somewhat confused and disorientated.

'Would you like a meal before your meeting?'

'My meeting?'

'Your meeting with Comptroller Xzu. Well? Would you like a meal?'

'Just a cup of tea, thanks,' said Alfric.

So tea they brought him, jade tea imported from Obooloo by way of the Circle. It helped settle his stomach; and he felt calm and self-controlled by the time he had finished it.

Then he was taken to see Comptroller Xzu.

Before Alfric had marched against Herself, Xzu had asked him to delay that expedition for seven days. What had been the reason for that? Was Alfric going to find out? And would the Bank be pleased or displeased with the ultimate outcome of the expedition? And did it matter? Did Alfric need the Bank's help, or could he make himself king without it?

All these questions and more were confused together in Alfric's head.

(He had more questions? Yes, he had more indeed. He wondered what rate of interest he was getting on his call account with the Morgrim Bank of Chi'ash-lan, and how tea was faring on the commodities market, and whether there was an end to the drought in Tang; and, indeed, he wondered about half a thousand similar questions.)

Then he was entering Comptroller Xzu's office.

'Ah, Alfric, Alfric,' said Xzu. And then, correcting himself without prompting: 'My dear Izdarbolskobidarbix, how nice it is to have you back in the fold.'

'I'm glad you're glad to have me back,' said Alfric stiffly. 'I'm aware that the Bank cautioned me not to dare myself against Herself. Now that I have, and now that She is dead, I trust that there will be no long-term repercussions as a result of this act of mine.'

'You trust correctly,' said Xzu. 'The Bank does not engage in childish vengeance. One does not throw away a sharp knife merely because it has happened to take a nick out of one's finger. While your disobedience disappoints us, your disobedience is not crucial in determining your fate. What matters is your overall performance. Overall, you have performed very well, and have proved an asset to the organization.'

'I'm glad to hear it,' said Alfric.

'Furthermore,' said Xzu, 'please be assured that exemplary work always attracts recognition and reward. We are certainly possessed of no superabundance of talent, hence we do our best to encourage and retain the talented. In your case, the Bank sees fit to reward you for all the good work you have put in over the last few years. Accordingly, we hereby create you Banker Second Class.'

'That is appreciated,' said Alfric dryly. Then: 'I will remember this courtesy once I have made myself king.'

'Ah, my dear Izdarbolskobidarbix,' said Banker Xzu. 'As I remember it, the case was not one of you making yourself king. Rather, you were going to ally yourself with the Bank in a campaign for that position. There is a difference, you know.'

'I am sensible of the fact that it would be difficult for me to obtain the throne without assistance from the Bank,' said Alfric, doing his best to suppress his impatience. 'I am grateful to know that the Bank supports me in this endeavour.'

'Good,' said Banker Xzu. 'That speaks of a very mature attitude on your part toward politics and its complexities. Since you are possessed of such an attitude, you will surely not take it amiss if I remind you of the fact that, in politics, what seems an appropriate enterprise today may come to seem quite the opposite on the morrow.'

'That I grant,' said Alfric cautiously.

Already, from the tenor of Banker Xzu's speech, Alfric guessed that the Bank was not going to support him in his drive for the throne. Alfric's promotion also suggested as much. After all, the Bank would scarcely have gone to the trouble to promote Alfric Danbrog to the rank of Banker Second Class if he were going to be king on the morrow. If the Bank truly expected him to be king, it would either not have bothered with the promotion, or else it would have promoted him straight to Banker First Class as a token of respect and esteem.

So.

After taking so much trouble to help Alfric complete his three quests, the Bank was finally withdrawing its support.

But why?

Why now?

'As I have said,' said Xzu, 'today may think yesterday's ambitions to be an error. In this case, the Bank's ambition, which was to make you king, now seems to be such an error. The fault, of course, lies with the Bank itself, since the ambition was conceived by the Bank and was forced upon you against your will. We acknowledge that the error is ours, hence your promotion.'

'I see,' said Alfric. Then, delicately: 'But I have always found clarity of vision to benefit from professional attentions. Would you care to serve as my oculist in this matter? To play the ogre to a half-blind Banker Second Class? To instruct me, in other words, in the actual reasons for this change of heart on the Bank's part?'

Xzu sighed.

'What you ask is very difficult,' said Xzu. 'Were I a glibly nimble master of fiction, I could conjure up a fetching lie for your delectation. However, the truth is that I am not in a position to elucidate the entanglements which constrain the actions of the Bank in this matter. While portentousness is not natural to my nature, I must confess that we have a very, very delicate stage in the existence of the Banking Circle itself, the intricacies of which I am not free to mention; and questions concerning the kingship of Wen Endex have a bearing on these intricacies.'

Here an ambiguity.

Exactly what was Banker Xzu trying to say? That Alfric did not possess a security clearance high enough to allow him to know exactly what 'intricacies' currently obsessed the Partnership Banks? Or that Comptroller Xzu himself had not been briefed, and so could not instruct his guest?

'Hmmm,' said Alfric. 'All this would be much easier to accept if I knew more of what was going on. I appreciate the delicacy of all relationships concerning the Partnership Banks. I know the difficulty of maintaining good and workable relationships between our various and variegated worlds. However, I fail to see quite how the Circle comes to concern itself with the kingship of Wen Endex, a matter which, to the best of my knowledge, has never troubled the Circle before.'

Xzu sighed again.

Then:

'Let me be frank,' said Xzu. 'The problem is not with

the Banks of the Circle. Rather, the problem is with the Izdimir Empire. The Empire does not accept you as a suitable candidate for the throne. Instead, Obooloo demands that Ursula Major attain the throne. Aldarch the Third will not have it any other way.'

'I see,' said Alfric.

His tone made his displeasure plain.

'Izdarbolskobidarbix, my friend, this is something you will have to endure. We none of us find ourselves living in a perfect world. We all have our little peeves and crotchets, our lists of things we would change were we given godly powers. But we none of us are gods, and so . . .'

'It seems,' said Alfric, 'that we are giving in to the Izdimir Empire with remarkably little struggle.'

'That is the nature of empires, is it not?' said Xzu. 'That they can terrorize minor powers by the most shadowy of threats? We know it would be difficult for the empire to make war upon Wen Endex. Nevertheless, it is by no means impossible. It might not be reasonable, but nobody has ever claimed Aldarch the Third to be a slave to reason. Alfric, we cannot afford to risk having our world plunged into war.'

For a moment, Alfric was almost convinced.

Then he wondered:

Was it true?

Was any of what Xzu was telling him actually true?

Furthermore:

Could it be true?

Communications between Galsh Ebrek and Obooloo were slow and tortuous, for the Izdimir Empire had no use of the Door which was located in Obooloo. That Secret was guarded by the Bondsman's Guild of

Obooloo, which was at particular pains to protect its Secret now that Aldarch the Third ruled the Empire. Had Al'three known of the Circle of the Partnership Banks, those Doors which linked places as far apart as Stokos and Chi'ash-lan, he would doubtless have sought to launch himself upon a conquest of the world.

'I find it hard,' said Alfric, 'to know how we can be in communication with Aldarch the Third, unless one is to presume that he has mastered the Secret of the Partnership Banks.'

Xzu looked at him intently.

Then:

'Izdarbolskobidarbix, my friend,' said Xzu, 'I am going to tell you a great secret. The Partnership Banks have given Aldarch the Third limited use of communication facilities routed through the Doors of the Circle.'

'What!?'

Thus Alfric.

Shocked.

Appalled.

This was the one thing which must never happen! No ruler of empire must ever learn of the existence of the Doors. Otherwise the world would be plunged into a terrifying war as imperial ambition strove to master the Circle.

Xzu smiled.

'Relax, Iz'bix. It's not as bad as it sounds. Are you familiar with mediums? I mean, with those charlatans who pretend to communicate with the unborn and the dead at seances?'

'I have never dabbled in such rubbish,' said Alfric stiffly.

'But Aldarch the Third does,' said Xzu. 'Through one

of his most trusted mediums, he receives intelligence from spies in the World Beyond. He trusts this intelligence, because it regularly proves accurate, at least as far as events in Wen Endex are concerned.'

Alfric frowned.

'It seems,' said Alfric, 'that you are playing a very dangerous game.'

'Dangerous, yes,' said Xzu. 'But very profitable. Aldarch the Third pays highly for the intelligence he receives. Furthermore, even if we wished to avoid the danger, we could not. The Bank in Obooloo came up with this idea, and that Bank has forced this idea upon us. We must co-operate. You know how things are.'

The two men looked at each other.

For a moment, Alfric was almost convinced.

Then:

'No,' said Alfric. 'I don't believe what you're telling me.'

'You don't? Believe me! It's all true! Aldarch the Third really does have a medium. He really does believe!'

'Perhaps,' said Alfric. 'But basic logic tells me it makes no difference to Aldarch the Third whether I sit upon the throne of Wen Endex or whether Ursula Major rules. I am the Wormlord's grandson. She is the Wormlord's daughter. We are of the same blood, the same line. If Al'three thinks of us at all, he thinks of us equally as enemies. Surely. Therefore I deduce this to be no decision of the Izdimir Empire. Rather, it is the Bank's decision. It is not Aldarch the Third who wants to deny me the throne. It is you!'

Alfric had grown heated while making this accusation. But Xzu did not respond with any anger of his own. Instead, he smiled, somewhat sadly.

Then:

'Izdarbolskobidarbix,' said Comptroller Xzu, 'I'm disappointed with you. You are right, of course. Nevertheless, it would have been more diplomatic for you to have gone along with our little fiction. That would have preserved our good relationships, would it not?'

'So you admit it,' said Alfric. 'It is the Bank which wants to deny me the throne.'

'Is that not our privilege?' said Xzu. 'Are you not our creature? Did we not make you? Was it not the Bank which first urged you to quest for the three saga swords? Was it not the Bank which showed you how these swords might be won? Naturally you're angry. But don't fool yourself, friend Iz'bix. You didn't make yourself into a contender for the throne. It was the Bank which made you that.'

'Indubitably,' said Alfric coldly. 'But why the change of heart? Or was the whole thing an empty exercise right from the very beginning? Did you expect me to die on the quests?'

'No, no, not at all. We did seriously consider making you king. We wanted you to succeed on those quests. But . . .'

'But?'

'But, before allowing you to claim the throne itself, we had to be sure of you. Our decision was that we wanted to test your ability to manipulate the Knights, for such a skill is essential to a king. So we set you a two-fold task. You were first to rouse the Yudonic Knights to action and second to stop them carrying out the very action to which you had roused them.'

'That put me in a very difficult position,' said Alfric, struggling to control his temper.

'Agreed,' said Xzu. 'A position which was almost impossible. That was part of the test. We wanted to measure your true loyalties. To the Bank? Or to your family? Unfortunately, you betrayed the Bank. We told you we needed a seven day delay. You denied it to us.'

'But I killed Herself.'

'That is neither here nor there,' said Xzu. 'The Bank never cared whether She lived or died. What mattered to the Bank was whether you would obey us when we commanded you. That was what the test was all about. As far as the Bank is concerned, you failed the test, for you proved disloyal and disobedient. Therefore we will not have you as king. That is our decision.'

'The decision is not yours to make,' said Alfric.

'Isn't it?' said Comptroller Xzu.

'The Bank does not make or break the kings of Wen Endex,' said Alfric coldly.

'Doesn't it?' said Xzu. 'Is that what you really think?'

'I think,' said Alfric, 'that I'm going to find out. One way or another.'

Then he got to his feet and went to the door.

'Iz'bix.'

Alfric turned.

'What?'

'Iz'bix, are you formally resigning from the Bank?'

'Are you asking me to?' said Alfric.

'Iz'bix, we're happy to have you stay. We are disappointed with you. But, as I said before, the Bank is not given to childish vengeance. You do have talent. You can be of great use to us. Your promotion to Banker Second Class is good and valid. In time, you can rise further. But . . . Alfric . . . if you strive for the throne then . . . then we will have to reconsider our position.'

Alfric paused.

'May I . . . may I have time to think about it?'

'Certainly,' said Xzu. 'You've been mauled in battle, and you've been very ill. Go home, Iz'bix. Rest. Sleep. Think it over. Then come back and tell us what you've decided.'

'I will,' said Alfric.

But he was lying.

He had already decided that he would strive for the throne, regardless of the consequences.

The only question was:

How?

CHAPTER SEVENTEEN

She was dead.

She would never again haunt the nights of Wen Endex.

With Her death, the Yudonic Knights were no longer governed by their duty to command the night against Her depredations. They were free to reclaim the day.

But—

In honour of the fallen king, Ursula Major decreed that the Knights should continue to live by night until she commanded otherwise. Ursula Major further ruled that, as a token of respect to her dead father, no official business would be conducted in Galsh Ebrek until thee nights after the Wormlord's funeral.

Ursula Major issued these decrees as regent.

A subtle move, this.

No Knight could rightly disobey such commands, for Tromso Stavenger was surely due such honours. Since Ursula Major's commands were meant to honour the dead, to abandon night for day would be to insult the fallen king; and, likewise, to insist upon certain outstanding administrative matters being settled immediately would also be an insult. No Knight could bring himself to thus profane the dead. Thus the Knights continued to live by night, out of fealty to the deceased Wormlord if for no other reason. And, for like reason, the question of the succession to the throne was left in abeyance for the moment.

Ursula Major, having very carefully chosen her ground, was obeyed without protest.

There was no way Alfric Danbrog could persuade people to rebel against his aunt's commands. Such rebellion was nearly unthinkable. If he had tried to stir the Knights into revolt, if he had pleaded that Ursula's rule as regent was unlawful and that she must be replaced immediately, then he would have shocked one and all by his impious attitude to the dead.

The dead were due the honours which were being paid to them; and, whether Ursula Major was strictly entitled to command those honours or not, nevertheless all must obey Ursula's orders lest they scandalize their peers.

Alfric was frustrated.

He wanted to bring Ursula Major to battle, and soon. He wanted to stage a confrontation. He wanted to march up to Saxo Pall and say:

'Get off my throne!'

But he could not move, not until the funeral had taken place, and not until another three nights had passed.

This meant that Ursula Major had days in which to consolidate her position. Alfric knew that questions of power are largely settled by public perception. He had learnt from the Bank that power is an intellectual conjuring trick. While people believe it exists, it does exist. When belief falters, then power melts faster than ice in a blazing furnace.

By ruling from Saxo Pall as regent, Ursula Major was consolidating her position. She was teaching Galsh Ebrek to think of her as its customary ruler.

Alfric sat at home, wondering what he should do.

He was still sitting at home when the news reached him. Guignol Grangalet came personally to Varnvelten Street to bring Alfric the news.

The earthly remains of Tromso Stavenger and Grendel Danbrog had been recovered from the place of slaughter, and had been conveyed to the seashore, there to be cremated.

'The seashore?' said Alfric, startled. 'Why?'

'Because,' said Grangalet, 'Ursula Major has commanded that it be done so.'

'But,' protested Alfric, 'the bodies of the kings of Wen Endex are burnt in the marketplace in the presence of the people. That is the custom.'

'It has been the recent custom,' acknowledged the Chief of Protocol, 'but that does not mean that it is a good custom. Ursula Major thinks it to be a lazy, slothful thing to do. She says it constitutes a discourtesy to the dead. She says the Knights should prove their honour by making the march to the seashore.'

'But—'

'Furthermore,' said Guignol Grangalet, 'the practice of seaside cremation has an honourable place in our tradition. It is the older custom, is it not? Long before bodies were ever burnt in the marketplace, our kings were consumed by fire by the shores of the Winter Sea.'

Alfric protested, but Guignol Grangalet told him there was nothing he could do. The bodies had already been taken to the seashore, and were being held there under guard in preparation for the funeral on the following night.

Once the Chief of Protocol had departed, Alfric raged around his house, kicking at the furniture in incoherent fury.

274

Now he realized his mistake!

Instead of sitting at home, he should have been taking active steps to seize control of any instruments which might have helped him win power. And, without a doubt, the corpses of his father and grandfather were such instruments.

Alfric should have gone personally to the mere to recover those battle-battered bodies. Nobody could rightly have denied him that privilege. He should have brought the corpses back to his house. Had he done that, Ursula Major could scarcely have wrested them away from him by brute force, for such an action would have scandalized Galsh Ebrek and would have turned the Knights against her.

Then Alfric should have personally made arrangements for the funerals of the fallen, and should have made sure – very, very sure – that the bodies were burnt in the marketplace.

Because the marketplace was in the middle of Galsh Ebrek, so any crowd which gathered for the funeral could then be marched to Saxo Pall by any orator who had the wit to rouse the mob.

Only now did Alfric begin to imagine the speeches he could have made.

It was obvious, wasn't it?

This is what he should have said:

'Here lies my grandfather in company with his son. In death, father and son are united, as they were in the last days of their life. When great peril threatened the nation . . .'

Oh yes, Alfric could see precisely how such a speech should be phrased. First, emphasize the unity of father and son, a unity which made a nullity of the banishment

Tromso Stavenger had imposed upon Grendel Danbrog. Then praise the courage of the dead. Then speak frankly of his own part in the slaughter of Herself.

Thus:

'Much have I dared already. I killed the dragon which long denied Island Thodrun to our race. I dared the wrath of the swamp giant Kralch to rescue the saga sword Sulamith's Grief from the Spiderweb Castle. I wrested the brave sword Kinskorn from the grip of the vampires. But, not content with this, I joined my father and my grandfather for the greatest test of all, that test being open combat with Herself.'

Yes, yes.

Alfric should have made such speeches in the marketplace, and then he should have proclaimed himself king, and then he should have marched the mob to Saxo Pall, and he should have used the mob as an army to overthrow Ursula Major's guards and put him on the throne.

'Well,' said Alfric at last. 'What is, is. I'll have to work with what I've got.'

Unfortunately, it was unlikely that any of the commoners of Galsh Ebrek were likely to make the trek to the seaside merely to see a couple of corpses burnt by night. The Yudonic Knights would be there in force – none would dare to stay away unless mortally ill – but the Knights would not be easily moved to precipitate action.

'But I must try,' said Alfric. 'With every day that woman sits on the throne, it gets harder for me to displace her.'

So Alfric sat down and began to work on a speech which he could give at the funeral on the following night.

How should he phrase his claim to the throne?

Why, there were all kinds of approaches he should take.

For a start, it was the Wormlord's will. Tromso Stavenger had explicitly stated that he would give the throne to Alfric as soon as the three quests had been completed. Well, the quests were well and truly completed, nobody doubted it. So it was time for the king's will to be fulfilled. Yes, in constitutional terms, there was no doubt about it at all: Alfric Danbrog was the rightful king of Wen Endex as of now.

Furthermore, he was a hero, a genuine legitimate hero, for he had personally killed Herself, and that was a fact. Moreover, Galsh Ebrek acknowledged that fact.

Also in his favour was the fact that Ursula Major was a woman; for the Yudonic Knights of Wen Endex had certain fundamental objections to the rule of women over men.

'Prejudice,' muttered Alfric. 'Yes, prejudice, that's the way.'

The validity of his claim in constitutional terms . . . his personal heroism . . . the fact that his aunt was a woman . . .

'Yes,' said Alfric. 'I'll talk them over to my side with no trouble at all.'

And he worked long and hard on his speech, until at last he was disturbed by a brick which came crashing through his window.

'Stroth!' said Alfric.

He almost rushed out into the street, but restrained himself. This might be an ambush of sorts.

Instead, Alfric went upstairs, opened the shutters of a second-storey window and looked out. Below, he saw a couple of drunken yokel-louts.

'What the hell do you want?' said Alfric.

'To bugger your arse with a hatchet,' said one.

'For what and for why?' said Alfric.

'Because you cursed your father and mock him now,' said one.

'Because you dishonoured the Wormlord in death,' said the other.

'Get away with you,' said Alfric. 'Or I'll come down and thrash you thoroughly.'

'Oh, it's you who'll be thrashed,' said one of the drunks. 'The Knights themselves will do it when they get back from the funeral.'

'We'll see about that,' said Alfric steadily. Then, unable to keep from boasting: 'I've a speech to make at that funeral. It may change their minds.'

'Change their minds?' said one drunk.

'A speech?' said the other.

'They won't hear it from here, you know,' said the other.

Then both fell about laughing.

'What are you talking about?' said Alfric.

Then he guessed.

And was shocked by fear.

He shuddered, as if a bucket of cold water had been dumped all over him.

He left the window and pounded downstairs. He threw open the door and stalked forth to interrogate the drunken yokels. And when he had finished with them he went to the Green Cricket to hire himself a horse. And on the way out of Galsh Ebrek, he stopped at the Stanch Gates to interrogate the guards.

It was true.

The worst had happened.

278

Guignol Grangalet had been around the town, telling all and sundry that Alfric Danbrog had cursed his father and his grandfather both, and was keeping to his house in insolence, refusing to attend the funeral that was being held by the seashore that very night.

'Stroth!' said Alfric.

'Don't talk so harsh,' said one of the guards. 'You'll upset your horse. Would your horse like an apple? Would you like to eat, horsey my darling?'

Then, to Alfric's surprise, the guard produced a wizened old apple and fed it to the horse, which munched it down greedily. At this end of the cold weather, all the horses of the city were on short commons, with the last of the hay close to running out and precious little else for them to eat.

'My horse thanks you for your kindness,' said Alfric coldly. 'And now I must go.'

Then he set off for the shore.

He was consumed by fury.

How dare they!

How dare they stoop so low!

And – what could he do to repair the damage?

Guignol Grangalet was a sober citizen, a man of impeccable reputation. Ninety-nine people in a hundred would believe him. And Alfric? Why, many people feared him to be a werewolf, because his father had long been thought to be such a shape-changer; and, besides, he was a banker, and hence had lived most of his life at a remove from his peers; and—

'Pox!' said Alfric.

One of the Bank's teachings came to him, but late, far too late:

'First secure your lines of intelligence.'

Alfric should have had a spy in Saxo Pall. Who? It mattered not. A guard, a serving maid, a slave who went round collecting night soil. Anyone, anyone. Just one set of ears in the castle might have saved the day for him. He should have known where his father's body was, and when the funeral was.

And now—

'Faster, blast you!' said Alfric to his horse.

But the beast had its limits, and all Alfric's strength of will could not extend them, and long before he got to the seashore he started to meet Knights returning from the bonfire.

'So!' said one, recognizing him. 'Danbrog! You repent of your insolence, do you?'

'I've nothing to repent of,' said Alfric defiantly. 'Guignol Grangalet told me the funeral was scheduled for the morrow. He lied as to my reaction.'

'You call him a liar, do you?'

'That I do,' said Alfric. 'I'll say as much in public. If he wants to make a fight of it, then that's fine by me.'

'If you make a fight of it,' said the Knight grimly, 'you may well find that friend Grangalet has heroes to champion him.'

Then rode on, without listening to Alfric's protestations any further.

Other Knights he stopped. Some, after listening to his explanations, were prepared to allow that there might have been a misunderstanding between Alfric and Grangalet.

'Perhaps you were drunk,' said one of them. 'You sound a little drunk at the moment, if truth be told.'

But none would countenance the idea that Grangalet had deliberately deceived Alfric, or that Grangalet had wilfully besmirched Alfric's reputation. The thought was too monstrous to be believable.

'Drunk!' said Alfric to himself. 'So that's what they'll think, is it?'

Well, yes.

Once Alfric had worked long and hard at salvaging his reputation, the Knights of Galsh Ebrek might be prepared to forgive him for saying foolish things while drunk. That was the very best he could hope for.

And even to achieve that outcome would take time.

And time was of the essence.

'I don't have time,' said Alfric.

At last, Alfric reached the shores of the Winter Sea, and found the funeral was at an end. All the Knights had departed. A huge pyre still smouldered in the dunes; and, by the firelight, Alfric saw the hoofmarks and footprints which spoke of a great gathering. Doubtless, speeches had been made and hearts hardened; doubtless, hard words had been said and curses had been heaped on his throat.

'She plays hard,' said Alfric bitterly, speaking of Ursula Major.

But what had he expected?

There had never been any love lost between the two of them.

But whose was the mind which had done the necessary malicious scheming? Who precisely had cooked up Grangalet's breath-taking untruths? Who had the daring, the wit? Who was ruthless enough? Not Ursula herself, surely; for she was a woman of much beauty but little mind.

'I'll find out,' said Alfric grimly. 'I'll find out. Then take revenge.'

Right then and there, he felt every bit the werewolf, a bloody outcast full of hate, rapacious and desperate, bent for revenge upon humankind. He sat down by the smouldering embers of the fire and began to brood upon his misery.

Right now, Guignol Grangalet . . .

Right now, Grangalet was in Galsh Ebrek.

—And what would I do if I were Grangalet?

Belatedly, Alfric started to think.

—If I were Grangalet, I'd know young Danbrog had gone riding. I'd know he'd speak to as many Knights as he could. So I'd place myself or my ears at the Stanch Gates to meet the Knights as they returned to Galsh Ebrek. Myself would be best, for then I could meet truth with fresh lies.

—Stroth!

Alfric swore thus, then swore again. He began to suspect manoeuvres within manoeuvres. How had those men come to be outside his house? Had they come there spontaneously? Or had they been paid to go there and throw a brick through his window? And had they really been as drunk as they seemed?

'Blood of the Gloat!' said Alfric. 'Maybe he planned this too!'

Whatever Guignol Grangalet had planned, the outcome was all in his favour. Here sat Alfric Danbrog by the ruins of a big bonfire, leagues away from Galsh Ebrek. Meanwhile, back in the city, Grangalet was free to tell, retell and modify his lies, to soothe doubts and extract pledges of loyalty and allegiance, to tell fresh lies, distribute forged documents, cast doubts upon Alfric's part in the death of Herself, and do anything else he wished to do to secure Ursula Major's position.

'How are you feeling, horse?' said Alfric, turning to his noble steed. 'I hope you're feeling fit and hearty, because we've a good long ride ahead of us.'

Then Alfric mounted up, intending to gallop back to Galsh Ebrek and plunge into the heart of the city's turbulent politics.

But his horse gently subsided beneath him.

'Get up!' said Alfric, kicking the beast.

But kicking was no good, for the thing was dead.

Then Alfric remembered the guard at the Stanch Gates who had fed his horse an apple. A poisoned apple? Or was it just coincidence that his horse had dropped dead?

'Apples, apples,' said Alfric. 'What's the price of apples?'

He didn't know.

Why didn't he know?

For a very simple reason: he never did the shopping.

His wife Vanaletta had always bought in their provisions.

But Alfric guessed that, at this end of the cold weather, the price of apples was likely to be monstrous, even the price of dried-up time-shrivelled apples such as that which had been fed to the horse.

'They haven't missed a trick,' said Alfric bitterly.

What should he do?

—Stop!

—Think, for once.

—What would Grangalet expect me to do?

—Why, walk back to the city, of course. A dead horse is no bar to locomotion.

Suddenly, Alfric realized that his position was somewhat precarious. He was all alone and far from the city.

283

He had no horse. Also, if he died tonight, there would be nobody in Galsh Ebrek to avenge him. Rather, the Knights would probably think themselves well rid of him.

'A good time, then, for murder.'

Ursula Major and Guignol Grangalet had dared so much already that they were scarcely likely to shy away from acts of precipitate violence.

They would expect him to head back to the city. And they might well have arranged for an ambush along the way.

—So what should I do?

—Preserve my life.

—But how?

—Well . . .

—What would they think me least likely to do?

—Why, to stay here and do nothing.

So Alfric did just that, and sat long by the sea, alone with his thoughts and his sorrows.

Time and time again the suthering seas rose from the drenching depths of the ocean, ran up the beach then retreated. And Alfric was almost minded to cast himself into the waters of the Winter Sea and to be swept away by that power which playthinged wrecked ships and rubbled the rocks of sunken cities.

But:

'I won't surrender. Not so easily.'

So said Alfric to himself.

'I am king,' whispered Alfric.

Thinking that surely true, true, at least in terms of legal entitlement. For he had really and truly gone on the three quests, against dragon, giant and vampires. He had won the three saga swords, Edda, Sulamith's Grief and

Kinskorn. He had dared his strength against Herself, and had slaughtered the monster who had for so long afflicted Wen Endex with terror.

All this he had done.

The throne should be his.

So:

'How dare the woman deny me mine!'

So thought Alfric, then got to his feet. He had lingered here long enough. It was time to be going, whatever the dangers.

'If she sends murderers, who will they be?'

The most likely assassin was Ciranoush Zaxilian Norn. Alfric had never wished to have the blood of any of the Norn brothers on his hands. He certainly had not wished Pig Norn to die as he had at banquet, strangled by Nappy. But Pig was dead. And Alfric had killed Muscleman Wu himself, and all of Wen Endex knew it. Whether he liked it or not, he was locked into a feud with the surviving Norn brother, Ciranoush Zaxilian.

Ursula Major knew as much, so, if she wanted Alfric dead, her most obvious step was to urge Ciranoush to seize his opportunity.

'But Ciranoush,' said Alfric, thinking what he knew of the man, 'is a city person. I don't think he'd hunt me through the woods. I think, rather, that he'd wait for my return. In my own house, maybe.'

So thinking, Alfric started back for Galsh Ebrek. And, though he went cautiously indeed, he did not truly expect to be attacked, not in the wilderness.

He only started to look for murderers in earnest when he came in through the Stanch Gates.

The guards at the Gates had been changed, so Alfric asked no questions about apples and the poisoning of horses thereby. Nor did he ask after Ciranoush Norn, for he thought the guards might have been primed with lies. Alfric's enemies hadn't missed a trick so far, and he doubted that he had seen the last of their tricks.

—Where now?

—Home?

It would be safer, surely, to go somewhere more populous. His home was dark and empty. It would be easy for Ciranoush to murder him there. More difficult, though, if he sheltered in the Green Cricket.

—Besides, I have to tell Anna Blaume about her horse.

Blaume was not going to be happy to know that another of her mounts was dead, even though Alfric could easily pay for the horseflesh.

—Still, I don't think I'll have cause to hire another horse in a hurry.

—Unless it's to take me in flight from the city.

So thinking, Alfric started out for the Green Cricket, cursing the heavy mud of the city streets. Those streets should by rights be paved with good stone. That would cost money, of course; but money there would be if the wealth of the Bank was properly taxed. The Bank itself taxed everything which moved through the Bank's part of the Circle; but precious little of the wealth so won came into Galsh Ebrek. Rather, the Bankers invested their wealth in estates in foreign parts, and retired in their old age to Dalar ken Halvar or Chi'ash-lan, spending their fortunes on the cosmopolitan pleasures available in those places.

Such behaviour was only natural when Wen Endex was nothing but a muddy province of swamp and ghosts, but, when Alfric became king, it would change. He would have the streets paved. Or he would move the city

286

from the river, for the lowlands were unhealthy. Or he would at least see the city's buildings put up on stilts, as was done in foreign places he had heard of, such as Bolfrigalaskaptiko, a famous city in the tropics.

Bolfrigalaskaptiko.

He would like to see that place one day. It lay by the River Ka, did it not? Just upstream from the great lagoon of Manamalargo. There were many worthy places a man could visit if once he . . .

Alfric sternly counselled himself against thinking such thoughts. They were defeat-thoughts. He was already beginning to imagine defeat and exile.

—Which will not happen!
—The game is not yet played out!
—I will fight.
—I will!
—And I will win!

Thus thinking, Alfric gained the door of the Green Cricket, and was about to knock upon that door when he heard the sound of a boot sklurching out of the mud behind him. He turned, drawing his sword as he turned, and was just in time to meet a blade with his.

Steel clashed with steel, then the door was thrown open and the orks Cod and Morgenstern came shouldering out into the night, with the dwarves Du Deiner and Mich Dir nimbling at their ankles. And Alfric's assailant panicked, and fled.

'Who was it?' said Cod, staring into the dark.

'I don't know,' said Alfric, panting.

He had seen the man clearly enough, but had not recognized him. Which was a bad sign. He had thought Ciranoush Zaxilian Norn to be the only assassin he would have to deal with, but another had been found.

Either Ursula Major had recruited the fellow, or else the man had recruited himself. Either way—

'Come inside,' said Morgenstern.

And led Alfric inside, and sat him down.

'Drink this,' said Anna Blaume, materializing at Alfric's side.

She pressed a mug into his hands. Alfric thought it was ale, and drank deeply. Brandy flamed down his throat, and he gasped.

'Brandy,' said Blaume. 'A drink for heroes.'

'Tonight,' said Alfric, carefully putting down the mug, 'I'm not feeling quite that heroic.'

A greeding untunchilamon settled upon the side of the mug and dipped its head into the fiery brew. Anna Blaume knocked the dragon away. It took to the air, circled thrice, then settled upon her head.

'Some of those things are becoming positively alcoholic,' said Blaume. 'But never mind. Let's talk of what's really important. Who was it who tried to kill you? And how can we stop them?'

'I don't know who it was,' said Alfric. 'As for how you can stop them, why, the only way for me to save my life now is for me to make myself king. But I don't know that I can hope to survive the next few days.'

'Of course you can,' said Anna Blaume.

'Listen,' said Cod, 'we're to present ourselves to Saxo Pall some four nights from now.'

'So?' said Alfric.

'So, come with us,' said Cod. 'We're ambassadors, aren't we? Whoever's out to kill you, they're not likely to attack you while you're with two ambassadors.'

'I wouldn't be so sure,' said Alfric.

But, on reflection, he saw that the ork's plan had a lot

to recommend it. Alfric's main danger was from Ursula Major. She would move cautiously where the ogre king's ambassadors were concerned.

'It's a good plan,' said Anna Blaume. 'You stay here, Alfric. We'll keep you safe with the orks. Nobody will dare to move against you.'

And so it was that, shortly, an exhausted Alfric Danbrog was asleep in Anna Blaume's big bed, with an ork keeping watch over him. While Alfric slept, untunchilamons descended to his pillow, and ravaged the few lice that were to be found in his hair. Then settled there to sleep themselves, liking the warmth of his body.

Thus the rightful king of Galsh Ebrek slept in the house of one of his loyal subjects, guarded by the minions of the lord of the Qinjoks and by the valour of the dragons of Wen Endex.

CHAPTER EIGHTEEN

The rightful king of Wen Endex spent three nights sheltering in the Green Cricket with the ambassadors from the Qinjoks. Then, on the fourth night, he accompanied them to Saxo Pall, where the orks were to have an audience with Ursula Major.

There was some trouble when the three-strong party arrived at Saxo Pall, for Guignol Grangalet sought to separate Alfric from the orks. But Cod and Morgenstern stood firm, and insisted that Alfric be allowed to accompany them into the throneroom.

Which, at last, he was allowed to do.

Though Ursula Major had ruled Saxo Pall but briefly, she had made her mark on it in a mixed way. The throneroom had been massively renovated since Alfric had been there last. It blazed with light, for the number of lanterns in the place had been tripled. Everything had been washed, polished, scrubbed or refurbished; and, to his surprise, Alfric found he could see his reflection in the unstained floor. He had always thought it roughwork granite of some kind; but, now the muck of generations had been scoured away, he saw the floor was made of the smoothest white-veined black marble.

Sitting on the throne was Ursula Major, as poised as ever. She was wearing silks; and her nipples flowered against her silks. Something in the way she sat suggested that she was fully conscious of the perfection of her breasts and the effect it had on the susceptible; and, little as Alfric wanted to admit it, in truth he was one of the susceptible.

'Stand here,' said Guignol Grangalet.

'Where?' said Alfric, taking his eyes off Ursula Major.

'Never mind where he says,' said Cod firmly. 'You're staying with us.'

Again the orks stood firm; and Alfric stayed in the company of those ambassadors from the Qinjoks as they made between them an interminable and wearisome speech about the long friendship which had endured between that king and the lords of Galsh Ebrek.

The witnesses to this speech were many; but Alfric felt very much alone and isolated, for the many were Yudonic Knights to a man, and fear of assassins had kept him from making any effort to repair his relationships with the breed.

While listening to Cod and Morgenstern enlarge upon their theme, Alfric had ample time to watch Ursula Major, and to think, and to wonder. Was she still ruling as regent? Or had she declared herself to be the new king? Really, the question was immaterial. Obviously, she was now the ruling power in Wen Endex: and that was what really mattered. He observed the way she teased a strand of her hair through her fingers. She was bored with this, he could tell. Boredom betrays itself swiftly. So was she unhappy sitting on the throne? Perhaps. But perhaps it was her nature to be bored with life; and, in any case, since when did anyone surrender a throne out of mere ennui?

As Alfric watched Ursula Major, admiring the elegance of the hair which flowed in ripples about her neck, he knew that he wanted her; but greater than lust was the desire to kill. But if anyone was going to do any killing in Saxo Pall, it was more likely to be Ursula than Alfric.

At last, Ursula Major was finished with the orks.

'We will deliberate,' she said, thus sidelining the petition which the orks had just made, which was for them to be allowed to address a general assembly of the Yudonic Knights of Galsh Ebrek.

Now Ursula was ready to deal with Alfric.

'Alfric,' she said.

'Greetings, aunt,' said Alfric.

He chose to address her thus for two reasons. First, because he knew she hated to be thus addressed. Second, because he wanted to stress the family connection. Surely Ursula Major could not order the death of a family member without shaming herself beyond redemption.

Or could she?

In Obooloo, Aldarch the Third had celebrated his victory in a seven-year civil war by disembowelling his forty-seven brothers and feeding his twenty-nine sisters to the Favoured Rats; but nobody thought any the worse of him for that.

'We hear,' said Ursula Major coldly, 'that you were the man who got my father killed.'

Alfric had been ready for many accusations. He thought Ursula Major might have tried to accuse him, for example, of being a werewolf. But never in his wildest dreams had he imagined that she would blame him for Tromso Stavenger's death; and he was so taken aback that he could hardly believe this charge was seriously intended.

'We see,' said Ursula, 'that you make no effort to deny the charge.'

292

Alfric recovered the use of his voice and said:

'The man met his end as a hero should. Fighting against Herself.'

'You got him killed,' said Ursula.

Her debating style was clumsy; but, for that very reason, it was going to be difficult to deal with. Alfric had honed his speaking abilities in moots conducted by the Bank; and, in such debates, a speaker dropped a line of argument once it had been decisively refuted. Alfric, believing that he had so refuted his aunt's accusation, was more than irritated to find her staunchly repeating it.

'We killed the Hag,' said Alfric.

'So?' said Ursula. 'A dozen men with crossbows could have done as much with less fuss and no deaths whatsoever.'

'I believe She would not have fallen easily to any hunters,' said Alfric. 'Anyway, the matter is closed. She is dead, and there's an end to it.'

'The issue is not closed,' said Ursula. 'Her death is greatly regretted, for She was an asset to the state.'

'That,' said Alfric, 'is the most nonsense I've heard in one breath since the day I was born.'

'What you fail to understand,' said Ursula, 'is that our monsters are assets. Amongst other things, they discourage invasion. You have done much to wreck the reputation of Wen Endex. Lusting for personal gain, you slaughtered the dragon Qa. Poor Kralch you humiliated. You dared the lair of the very vampires themselves and returned unscathed, much to the diminishment of the stature of those valued allies of ours. Finally, you have participated in the murder of Herself.'

'She was a killer,' said Alfric.

'So She was,' said Ursula. 'That was Her purpose. To stalk the night and kill. To be a thing of terror. A thing to make hideous all beyond our walls. You understand?'

'No,' said Alfric.

'Of course you don't understand,' said Ursula scornfully. 'But it is true. She did us a great service. She bound all of Wen Endex in a great alliance. Thanks to Her, the commoners ever found the swords of the Yudonic Knights a welcome asset rather than an irksome imposition. By killing as She did, She made our people see the ruling hierarchy as a chivalrous and self-sacrificing order, as an asset rather than a burdensome ruling class.'

'You seem to be accusing me,' said Alfric, 'of stirring up revolution.'

'Your actions, witted or witless, present us with that possibility,' said Ursula.

'I do not believe for one moment that there will be a revolution.'

'Of course there will be no revolution,' said Ursula. 'For we will do what we must to prevent it. She helped secure our ruling order, and could help us yet; therefore, we will reinvent Her. As for the dragon, why, no doubt we can get another one, somewhere. In due course, we can also assist the swamp giant and the vampires to recover their reputations.'

'You're mad,' said Alfric, in disbelief.

'No,' said Ursula. 'I am not mad. I am simply better educated than yourself. You think yourself a cold-blooded banker, whereas in fact you see the world through a haze of romance. Your vision of power is blurred by the glamorous impracticalities of legend and myth. You still think that power exists as a service to the people. In this you are a child.'

'For what then does power exist?' said Alfric.

'To serve itself,' answered Ursula Major.

Alfric looked around at the silent assembly.

'You dare say that?' said he. 'Here? In front of witnesses?'

'All those here today are gathered together in an alliance of power,' said Ursula Major. 'In other times it may be politic to speak with greater circumspection. But today, this once, we can indulge ourselves in the truth.'

So she spoke. Then studied Alfric with a cold calculation which made him suddenly afraid, terribly afraid. She had planned his doom; he was sure of it. Her speech was just a preface to his death, or – or to something worse.

He had thought to come here to throw her off her throne, to dismiss her with a word. He must have been mad. Completely deluded. He should have fled from Wen Endex immediately after his father's funeral. He would have been safer in Obooloo than here.

Suddenly, Ursula Major smiled.

Was Alfric reprieved?

No!

For Ursula said:

'You are a criminal, for you have wilfully destroyed state assets to further your own ambition, and you have led an old and senile man to a hideous death. This amounts to treason. Therefore we pronounce your doom. You are guilty of treason. Therefore, you must die.'

That proved what Alfric had already guessed: he had hopelessly misjudged the situation.

Alfric had guessed that Ursula Major was prepared to destroy him, but not that she was ready to do so in public view. He had expected backstreet murder, knives in the dark, arson, poison, arrows fired from the shadows. He had feared death at the hands of Ciranoush Zaxilian Norn. But not this! Not a formal condemnation from the throne.

'But,' continued Ursula Major, 'while you must die, we do give you the chance to die as a Yudonic Knight. If you wish, you can seek to prove your innocence by trial by combat. If you do not wish to be dragged away by the executioner, then you can seek to prove your innocence in challenge against this hall.'

'Against the hall?' said Alfric in astonishment.

'Yes,' said Ursula. 'Do you need an explanation of what that means?'

Alfric made no answer, for the question was purely rhetorical. Of course he knew what it meant.

In trial by combat, one fights and kills to prove one's innocence. The state puts forward one or more champions, and the accused criminal must murder all those champions to prove himself not guilty. On this occasion, Ursula Major had volunteered every single person in the hall to champion the state.

Which meant that Alfric would have to kill off the entire hall, man by man, to prove his innocence.

An impossible task.

But he did have one advantage.

It was his privilege to choose who he would fight first.

Alfric looked around, seeking a suitably weak victim. But he saw none. He suspected this had been planned long in advance. None of the old, the weak and the crippled was in this throneroom, though such people existed in the ranks of the Yudonic Knights.

However, there was Guignol Grangalet.

Alfric caught Grangalet's eye, and the Chief of Protocol looked away nervously. He knew Alfric could kill him easily. But, what was the point of that? Who cared whether a civil servant like Grangalet lived or died? Ursula Major could get another Chief of Protocol easily.

Nothing would be served by murdering Grangalet.

So . . .

Alfric was doomed.

He might kill the first man to champion the cause of the state; and he might kill the second, the third, maybe even the fourth – but sooner or later, one of his foes would kill him.

Or was he doomed?

Surely . . . surely Ursula Major had made an error.

Alfric cleared his throat.

'If I heard you rightly,' said Alfric, 'you volunteered everyone in this hall to fight for the state.'

'So I did,' said Ursula Major. 'Such is my privilege.'

'But surely you exclude yourself from that number,' said Alfric.

'I do not,' said Ursula Major in a level voice. 'I stand ready to meet you in combat if you satisfy the necessary protocol.'

'And the necessary protocol is?' said Alfric.

'Very simply, that you prove yourself to be a woman,' said Ursula Major. 'For it is the law of the Yudonic Knights that a female cannot meet anyone in trial by combat excepting another female. If you can prove yourself to be a woman, Alfric, I'll happily fight you.'

This roused a laugh from the Yudonic Knights.

Alfric let that laugh die away, then said:

'So, if I'm not a woman, I have to fight the men. The males.'

'Such is your destiny,' said Ursula.

'And I can choose . . . I can choose any male in this hall to be the state's first champion.'

'That is your privilege,' said Ursula.

'Since that is the case,' said Alfric, 'it would appear that you have put the lives of King Dimple-Dumpling's ambassadors in peril.'

A babble of protest uprose from the Yudonic Knights. Ursula Major called for silence. She was not granted it.

'Silence!' she said. Then, shouting, this time: 'Silence! Shut up, or else!'

Slowly, the noise from the Knights muttered down to almost nothing.

But Alfric knew he had unsettled them.

Ursula Major had designated 'the hall' to meet Alfric in challenge. Which meant that Alfric was entitled to choose any person in the hall to fight him.

If he chose one of the orks, then the ork would doubtless die, for any Yudonic Knight could cut such a blubbery creature to pieces with no trouble at all, regardless of what weapons the soft-natured thing might have in its hands.

Alfric could easily kill both of King Dimple-Dumpling's ambassadors.

Which would mean war between the Qinjoks and Wen Endex.

Ursula Major now had no choice.

She would have to cancel the trial by combat.

Or Alfric would kill the orks and plunge Wen Endex into a ruinous war.

Ursula stared at Alfric in fury, then said:

'You want to kill the orks? Very well! Kill them!'

Again there was an uproar from the Yudonic Knights. It did not cease until Guignol Grangalet joined Ursula Major in shouting the Knights down to silence.

'As I said,' said Ursula Major, 'kill the orks if that's what you wish.'

Alfric glanced at the orks. The grey-skinned creatures had shrunk away from him. They were huddled together, holding hands. And both were crying. He was embarrassed.

Well?

Should he murder them?

Alfric made a cold-blooded calculation, and decided there was no profit in killing orks. It would win him no prestige with the Yudonic Knights. It would not serve to prove his courage; which, in any case, had been adequately proved already. He had threatened to plunge Wen Endex into war, and Ursula Major—

But wait!

Was she bluffing?

Was she waiting to see whether he really would go ahead and challenge one of the orks?

Alfric looked again at Ursula Major, saw the depth of her frustrated rage, and decided that, no, she was not bluffing. She wanted him dead. Even if a war with the ogres was the price of his death.

Alfric cleared his throat.

'You invite me,' said Alfric, 'to murder two ambassadors. I do not think such an invitation civilized, nor do I intend to accept that invitation. Nevertheless, let all here bear witness to the fact that you extended such an invitation to me.'

'You were the one who suggested it!' shouted Ursula Major, unable to contain herself.

'I felt it my duty to point out the grievous error you had made,' said Alfric coldly. 'I would never take advantage of such an error, for I love my country. But others would not be scrupulous. Whether I live or die today, I do not want you to repeat your error. I do not want Wen Endex driven to war on account of your foolishness.'

This excited the Yudonic Knights again, and Guignol Grangalet had difficulty in silencing them. Alfric knew he had scored a decisive blow in this battle of wits. The odds were against him, but maybe, just maybe, he could undermine Ursula Major's authority to the point where she got laughed off the throne.

As Alfric was so thinking, he was engulfed in the arms of an ork. It was Morgenstern.

'Thank you, Alfric,' said Morgenstern, giving him a big slubbering kiss. 'Oh thank you, thank you, thank you so much for sparing us.'

The Yudonic Knights broke into open laughter, and Alfric knew all the ground he had made up was lost. He was enraged. He wanted to break Morgenstern in half, to smash the soft and slobbery creature. But he knew it was too late. The ork had made him look ridiculous, and he could not recover his dignity by killing the thing, an action which would only lead to an embarrassing scene with Cod.

'So,' said Ursula, as Morgenstern released Alfric, 'we see this thing for what it is. A lover of orks.'

More laughter from the Knights.

'We wonder what other strange passions it learnt in the Qinjoks,' said Ursula. 'Many times it went there, did it not? Many dealings it had with the ogres. Secret, those dealings, but we won't ask it what happened in those meetings.'

What was this? A subtle accusation of treachery?

'I went to the Qinjoks at the behest of the Bank,' said Alfric. 'All men know that, and women too. I brought back a treasure of jade, tribute to be handed over to the ambassador from the Izdimir Empire.'

'Yet the treasure every year became leaves and sticks,' said Ursula. 'Strange, is it not? What really happened, Alfric? And does what happened help to explain your fine rich house on Varnvelten Street? Never mind, we—'

'I mind!' said Alfric. 'How much more nonsense can we listen to? Do you really think I took the ogres' treasure? Are you really accusing me of theft?'

'You stand guilty of treason,' said Ursula Major. 'Therefore there is no point in us trifling with lesser crimes. Let it be noted, however, that you appear to love the denizens of the Qinjoks more than your own kind. These last three nights, you've sheltered with orks when no house of humans would have you.'

'Orks took me in,' said Alfric. 'True. Orks sheltered me. I could quibble, oh yes, I could quibble with a minor point, and say the house in question was not a place of orks but, rather, an inn owned by one Anna Blaume. But I won't trifle with such points. Rather, I'll ask the big question. Why have orks proved more constant in friendship than humans? I believe it is because the humans have erred in their judgement.'

Alfric took a deep breath.

If he was going to talk himself out of this one, he must make himself acceptable to the Knights. He could not repudiate the orks, because the evidence of his affiliation

301

with those blubber-oil beasts was too strong. But he could stress that he was in truth a Yudonic Knight, a hero equal to any out of saga.

'Humans have erred,' said Alfric, 'and any who think on what I am and who I am will realize the depth of that error. I am a patriot. I am Alfric Danbrog. A hero! The killer of Herself! Whatever you think of – of the political advantages of having a monster on the loose, I'm entitled to the gratitude of the nation.'

Alfric paused.

Actually, his heart was not really in this. While he had always had a very high opinion of himself, he had never been one for open boasting. And, what was more, he was starting to despair of winning victory through words.

'The gratitude of the nation,' said Ursula Major, sneering as she said it.

'Yes!' said Alfric. 'And – and I tell you this. You want me dead? Very well. You can have me dead. But I won't die alone. I gladly take the opportunity to prove my innocence in trial by combat. Naturally, I'll die. Sooner or later. But this I promise: I'll kill the first man who comes against me.'

So saying, Alfric looked as fiercely as he could upon the Yudonic Knights. They looked back with undisguised hostility. Indeed, with hate.

But why?

Why did they hate him?

His association with orks could make him look ridiculous, but it could scarcely make him hateful. And surely nobody could believe the accusations of crime which had been made against him. Something else had caused the breach between Alfric and the Knights. Did they really believe that he had deliberately shunned the funeral of his father and grandfather? And even if they did believe that, was that enough to condemn him to death? And could they not see that he would make a good king, maybe even a great king?

Many of these Knights were the very same men who had marched with Tromso Stavenger to do battle against Herself, yet Alfric saw not a hint of sympathy on any of their faces. He started to suspect that they were ashamed of their cowardice (as well they should be!) and that their hostility was consequent upon their shame.

Their cowardice haunted them, and so they wanted to forget the past. They did not value Alfric Danbrog for his heroism; rather, they resented his triumph and what that triumph said about their own timidity. Thus the momentum of the movement to put a Danbrog on the throne had been killed entirely. For the Yudonic Knights it was far better (as far as their egos were concerned) that Alfric be known as a murderous fool, an anarchic underminer of stability, a self-serving careerist, an enemy of the State.

Thus Ursula Major's smooth-voiced logic had a potent appeal for the Knights, and there was no way Alfric could argue effectively against it.

He saw that, now.

All his rhetorical efforts had failed, and had always been doomed to fail.

So.

It had come to this.

He must meet the Yudonic Knights of the hall in combat. One by one he must meet them and kill them. Naturally, if he tried to do any such thing he would surely die himself, on his first duel or his second, or the sixth or the seventh. So he could give up. Now. He could let himself be dragged away by the executioner. He could submit himself to a coward's death.

Or—

He had another option, yes.

He was a shape-changer, yes, and so he could Change, and once he had Changed he could fight his way out of this place.

In a moment of bloody battle-lust, Alfric longed to do just that and have done with pretence. He would become wolf for real and forever. He would become what he truly was, and would savage any and all who stood in his way as he fought free from Saxo Pall. Nobody would be able to stand against his strength. And once he had fought his way out of Saxo Pall—

Why, then he would flee for the wilds, and live as an outcast ravager, a lawless marauder. He would have done with civilized restraint. He would put an end to his life of lies and deceits. For him, no more the life of studied smiles and careful diplomacy. He would make himself one with the appetites of his blood. He would be a haunter of shadows, a lurching fear which made nightmares come true beneath the moon.

Then, suddenly, Alfric realized that this was exactly what Ursula Major wanted. The Hag was dead, so the state desired a monster. Unless Alfric was badly mistaken, Ursula Major knew what he was and what he could do. She knew he could Change and fight his way free. Ursula Major had said she would reinvent Herself; and she was fast on the way to doing just that.

Alfric steadied himself.

—Whatever I do, it will not be what my aunt wants.

So what options did he have?

Three.

First, to submit to the executioner.

Second, to fight the Knights, one by one, seeking to prove his innocence in trial by combat.

Third, to Change, and fight his way out of Saxo Pall.

The first two options would see him die, and the third was nearly as disastrous. So.

What was it the Bank advised?

—When all else fails, seek delay.

Alfric smoothed a smile on to his face. The rage which had almost brought his Change upon him was over. In the aftermath of that rage, his limbs were weak and trembling. But his voice was steady.

'My lady,' said Alfric, smoothing honey into his voice. 'Much is often spoken in haste which is regretted at leisure. You have given me the opportunity of proving my innocence in trial by combat. This I can do, and will do if I must. However . . . is it not the custom that I have the opportunity of asking someone to champion me in such combat?'

'That has happened in the past,' acknowledged Ursula Major.

'Then,' said Alfric, 'I ask that these proceedings be delayed until tomorrow night, to give me the opportunity of seeking such a champion.'

'The flower of chivalry is gathered together in this throneroom,' said Ursula, indicating the Yudonic Knights. 'If you wish to have a champion, then seek one here.'

Alfric turned to the Yudonic Knights. He knew there was no hope that any of the Knights would volunteer himself as Alfric's champion, but the gesture at least gave him time in which to think.

But all he could think of was that single word:

—Think!

—Think!

Alfric had exhausted all his ideas, and was close to panic.

Then, as he surveyed the hard-faced Knights, he heard someone say:

'I will champion him.'

Alfric turned in astonishment.

It was Morgenstern!

How absurd!

Already the Yudonic Knights were laughing. Alfric was furious. Morgenstern must be mad. What did the foolish creature think it was doing? A blubbery ork would not have a hope in the world against the least of the Knights.

But he kept his fury from his face.

Oh well.

That was it, then.

He had no option left to him but to Change.

He looked around the throneroom and saw a side-door which was ajar. That was the one he'd make for. When should he Change? Now? No! Wait! Wait for the ork to go into battle. Once combat began, all eyes would be on the fight. That would be the time to start to Change . . .

'Peace!' said Guignol Grangalet. 'Hush down, all of you! We have a champion for Alfric Danbrog. The champion is an ork. The name of the ork is Cod.'

'No,' said Cod.

'That's Cod,' said Morgenstern, pointing. 'I'm Morgenstern.'

'My apologies,' said Grangalet. Then, turning to Ursula Major: 'My lady, Alfric's champion is the ork Morgenstern.'

306

Ursula smiled.

'This will be interesting,' said she. 'Very well, ork. Who do you want to fight first?'

'You,' said Morgenstern.

Ursula laughed, and so did the Knights. When the laughter had died away, Ursula spoke:

'You want to fight me? I'm sorry, Mister Blubber, but I'm not for fighting.'

'The challenge is against the hall,' said Morgenstern, with surprising firmness of voice. 'You said so. That means I can choose to fight against anyone in the hall.'

'Poor orky!' said Ursula. 'Weren't you listening, little orky thing? We went through that earlier. I can't fight you even if I wanted to. Only females can fight females. That's our law.'

'But the women of Wen Endex do fight,' said Morgenstern stubbornly. 'Both the laws and the traditions of the land say as much. Many are the shield maidens who have fallen in battle for the honour of the Families, and mighty are the legends which surround them.'

'Yes, yes,' said Ursula, with a touch of impatience. 'Doubtless such things have happened. However, we are not on a battlefield.'

'Nevertheless,' said Morgenstern, 'the law is what the law is, and tradition likewise.'

'Orky thing,' said Ursula, 'you're starting to annoy me. We've been through this once, we've been through this twice, now we're going through it thrice. Here, only a woman can fight a woman. Please believe me, Mister Oil-for-brains. What I tell you three times is true. Were you female, I'd have to fight you. But you're not, so I don't and won't. Choose someone else.'

307

'But—'

'But me no buts,' said Ursula. 'Choose a man.'

'But I'm a woman,' said Morgenstern.

Ursula gaped. She really did. Her jaw fell. Then she closed it abruptly.

'Don't be absurd,' said Ursula Major. 'You cannot possibly be a female. The ethnology texts are very clear. Female orks are small and shy. You're neither. You're big and bulky. So you're a male. The females run around in pleated skirts. I don't see you in a skirt.'

'The textbooks,' said Morgenstern, 'are wrong.'

Then, in support of this thesis, the ork began to strip. Off came the ork's heavy woollen shirt. Revealing sluggardly low-slung breasts. Off came the ork's woollen trousers, revealing—

'You – you must be a freak,' said Ursula desperately.

'Not so,' said Cod, starting to strip in sympathy. 'We're not freaks. We're females.'

'That's right,' said Morgenstern. 'We're not freaks. We're fact. Your ethnology texts lie. What is more, you know full well why they lie.'

That loud-voiced accusation rang through the hall. It was received by the Yudonic Knights in utter silence. For both orks were now bare-arse naked, and the proof of their anatomy could not be denied.

And this shocked the Knights to the core.

It was no secret that the wealth of the Families was based on the slaughter of orks. While the ork-killing days were long since over, it was acknowledged that it was wealth won from ork-oil which had made the Families great, and which also made the Flesh Traders' Financial Association a power to be reckoned with.

Every Knight knew that his family had risen to

308

greatness as a result of the murder of many orks.

But, in Wen Endex it was an article faith that the killers of orks had always, as a chivalrous gesture, spared the females. Now the horrors of the past were revealed in full force. The victims of the orking days had been exclusively female; and those who killed them for fun and profit must have been fully aware of the fact. It was the big, blubbery females who were full of oil, for the timid little males were too small to have commercial potential.

As the Knights were absorbing this shock, Morgenstern spoke:

'Come to me, Ursy-thing. Come here, prattle-head. Bring me your perfumed lips, the pink of your underwear. Come to me, Ursy-thing. I want to strangle you.'

'We – we fight with swords here,' said Ursula Major unsteadily.

'My champion is free to opt for unarmed combat if my champion so wishes it,' said Alfric loudly. 'That is the law, and you know it.'

Ursula Major looked on him with hatred.

There was no way Ursula Major could best an ork in combat, and she knew it. Ursula Major was a clothes horse, not a woman warrior in the shield maiden tradition. If Morgenstern insisted on unarmed combat, then Morgenstern must necessarily win, for the ork was at least twice the weight of the human female.

'So,' said Ursula. 'So, they are females. The orks are females. Very well. Then let it be so written. Alfric Danbrog was championed by a woman. Thus he lived.'

Then the Yudonic Knights began to laugh, for of course it was a great joke to think of Alfric being saved by an ork, and a female ork at that. As the Knights collapsed in paroxysms of backslapping and kneeslapping, Alfric realized his public humiliation was complete. Lower than this he could not go.

When the laughter at last died down, the throneseated Ursula Major said:

'Your doom is withdrawn. You are free to go.' Then, to her Chief of Protocol: 'Show our guest out.'

Whereupon Guignol Grangalet invited Alfric to leave. He agreed that he would leave. There was, after all, nothing he could win by staying.

'We'll come with you,' said Morgenstern, who was in the process of getting dressed again.

'No,' said Ursula Major. 'I command you to attend a banquet to celebrate your victory today. You and your friend. Both the orks.'

A half-dressed Morgenstern looked at Alfric.

'I'll be all right,' said Alfric, who felt so miserable and humiliated that all he wanted was to escape from Saxo Pall.

'Good speed,' said Cod.

'Thank you,' said Alfric. 'Thank you.'

Then he bowed to the orks, bowed to the Knights, bowed to Ursula Major herself, then allowed the Chief of Protocol to lead him away.

Through halls and corridors went Alfric Danbrog and Guignol Grangalet, down echoing stairwells and then through tunnelling dark. Alfric realized Grangalet was taking him into an unfamiliar part of the castle. Alfric meant to ask about this, but—

When he looked around, Grangalet had vanished.

'My lord?' said Alfric, uncertainly.

He was sure the man had been behind him but a dozen footsteps previously.

310

Cautiously, Alfric retraced his steps. Slipped through an archway. And—

And there was Nappy, and for Alfric there was no time to retreat, no time to run, and certainly no time to Change, for he would be dead before he could do any such thing.

'Good evening, sir,' said Nappy.

Nappy's happy brown eyes held no hint of menace, but the stiletto in his hands was living a life of its own, the quicksilver blade flickering as it danced by the light of an overhead lantern, its agility confirming what Alfric knew already. If Alfric were to Change, he would be dead before the first shadows had possessed his flesh. If he were to draw his sword, he would fall with that needle of steel buried in his heart. He could not run, he could not dodge or duck, he could not – would not – beg for mercy.

He was a dead man.

But he managed manners sufficient to say:

'A good evening indeed. And how would you be on this night of nights?'

'Very well, thank you sir,' said Nappy. 'May I invite you to step this way?'

'By all means,' said Alfric.

And, commanded by a negligent gesture, Alfric Danbrog walked in front of Nappy. Waiting as he walked. Waiting for the knife. Between the vertebrae, doubtless. One blow to paralyse, another to kill. Or would it be in the back of the neck? Then one single strike would suffice to make death certain.

Wherever the blow fell, this much was certain:

Alfric Danbrog was a dead man.

CHAPTER NINETEEN

'Something wrong with your legs, sir?'

'No,' said Alfric, who had been deliberately slowing his pace to try to delay his arrival at his place of execution, wherever that might be. 'No, not at all, nothing wrong, nothing.'

And he lengthened his pace exceedingly.

'That's enough, sir.'

'What?'

'I mean, sir, we're here.'

Alfric stopped still. Trembling. He waited. For the bite of the blade, the shrill agony, the murder-strike.

'On your right, sir. The door on your right. Open it, if you would.'

Alfric looked to his right. There was a door. An old, immensely heavy door made of polished oak. He could smell the polish. He even recognized the odour as that of Brondlord's Furniture Polish, which was based on the oil of riverworms caught in the Riga Rimur. Viola Vanaleta used to use it regularly on all wooden furniture in Alfric's house in Varnvelten Street.

'The door, please. Open it, if you would.'

There was a heavy iron ring set in the door. It was jet black, not from age but because it had been painted that colour. Reluctantly, Alfric's fingers closed on the iron ring. It was cold, cold, cold as death and as heavy. What was beyond this door?

Suddenly, Alfric knew.

A psychic intuition told him.

Never before had he had such a vivid premonition. But, under the stresses of the moment, unexpected powers were coming to life. He knew, then, that he could see the future. He could see what lay beyond that door, and what was going to happen to him. On the other side of the door there was a sickening drop to a pit full of slicing knives. And, as soon as Alfric opened the door, Nappy would kick him in the small of the back and precipitate him into that pit.

Alfric felt sick.

He urged himself to turn, to turn and fight, to die in combat, to die like a man.

—But I cannot.

—It is the future. I have seen it. Therefore it is fated. It is fixed. I cannot alter the future.

So thinking, Alfric turned the heavy iron ring and pushed open the door. It screamed on its hinges. And revealed:

A small room, lit by three lamps.

A very warm, cosy room, heated by a small charcoal brazier.

There was a faded red carpet on the floor; a truckle bed on the right side of the room, neatly made up with a featherdown duvet; there were two armchairs, each upholstered with a shaggy brown animal skin which might have been that of a yak; there was a small liquor-table sitting between the armchairs; and there were any number of oddments and knick-knacks on the wooden shelves affixed to the walls with skewering iron.

'Take a seat, sir,' said Nappy genially.

Alfric stumbled into the room. As he did so, something

flew up from the floor. He started, then saw it was only an untunchilamon, fleeing from a saucer of milk. Did Nappy put down milk especially for dragons? For a moment Alfric thought so, then saw the kitten curled up on the bed. He found his way to one of the chairs and sat down. The door screamed on its hinges as Nappy closed it.

'I thought you might like a drink before you go,' said Nappy, seating himself in the other armchair.

Before you go? What did that mean. Doubtless it was a new euphemism for dying. But, even so, a drink would not be out of place.

'Yes,' said Alfric. 'Yes.'

Gladly accepting Nappy's hospitality.

Nappy poured liquor into two thimble-skulls, and passed one of them to Alfric. He swallowed the contents at a gulp.

'Would you like another one, sir?'

'Yes, thank you.'

While Nappy poured Alfric a second drink, an untunchilamon (maybe the very one Alfric had scared away from the saucer of milk) alighted on the liquor-table. Indulgently, Nappy poured the thing a thimble-skull of strong drink all for its very own. Alfric watched, fascinated, as the fingerlength dragon plunged its entire head into the thimble-skull. It stayed under for quite some time, while the level of liquor steadily sank.

Then the dragon's head emerged from the drink. Liquor gleamed wet and slick against its scales. The untunchilamon burped. Unfortunately, this action conjured forth a single spark of dragonfire. The dragon-spark ignited the liquor. Next moment, the little beast was wreathed in writhing fire.

Instantly, Alfric saw that the dragon was doomed to be burnt alive, or at least badly injured. For, while dragons are firebreathers, they cannot live amidst fire, any more than can the human firebreather who performs at village festivals. So Alfric knew at once that the untunchilamon was in big trouble.

Then the dragon was gone.

Nappy had snatched the thing away and had plunged it into a pitcher of milk, reacting so swiftly to the unexpected that the thing was done even before Alfric had time to gape in dismay.

'That's the thing with them dragons, sir,' said Nappy. 'They like their liquor, but they don't know the dangers of the stuff.'

The pink-faced little man peered into the pitcher where the untunchilamon was swimming around in drunken circles. He hoicked it out and dumped it down on the liquor-table. The disgruntled dragon shook itself, throwing flecks of milk in all directions. Some splattered against the lenses of Alfric's spectacles. He tried to take them off and clean them.

'Here, sir,' said Nappy, handing him a clean white handkerchief.

'Thank you,' said Alfric.

He cleaned his spectacles then put them back on.

'I've got cancer,' said Nappy.

But the words were said so casually that Alfric was not sure whether he had heard correctly.

'It's . . . it's good drink,' said Alfric, draining his.

'Cancer,' repeated Nappy.

'You don't mind if I pour myself another one?' said Alfric.

'In my gut it is. Started on the skin then ate its way in.'

315

'A very, very nice drop,' said Alfric, draining his thimble-skull.

'Here,' said Nappy, pulling his clothes away from his midriff.

Then Alfric had to look, had to, he had no choice, and it was cancer all right, cancer or some kind of lethal ulcer or something worse, yellow at the margins, yellow becoming brown, brown becoming wet black in the centre, and the centre was a kind of funnel that descended inward, inward to the wet pain and the glistening ooze.

Then Nappy covered the thing once more.

'A drink,' said Alfric. 'Maybe you'd like a drink.'

He poured one for himself, one for Nappy.

Then said:

'How long have you got?'

'The doctors, they gave me six months,' said Nappy. 'But that was last year. I won good money off Olaf Offorum. He bet I'd be dead by now. But, well, let's put it this way. I've made no wagers since. I won't last long, sir, not now.'

'Do you take anything for it?'

'Laudanum, sir. At nights. So I can sleep. But nothing during the day, no, have to stay sharp, you know. So it hurts, oh, it hurts, I won't say it doesn't hurt.'

A pause.

The untunchilamon took to the air, circled, then settled on Alfric's head. He felt its claws seeking purchase. There was a tiny twinge of pain as its talons momentarily dug into his scalp. Then it settled, content with the grip it had established on the hairs of his head.

Pain is the worse thing.

'They want you dead, you know,' said Nappy in a conspiratorial whisper.

'I had suspected as much,' said Alfric.

Another pause.

Then:

'Yes,' said Alfric.

'That's nice to know,' said Nappy. 'I was never sure, you see. I was always too . . . well, too shy to ask, if you know what I mean. They said I had a reputation, but I never really knew whether to believe them. It's nice to know, now that . . . now that it's all coming to an end.'

'You're – you're not going to kill yourself, are you?'

'Kill myself?' said Nappy in wonderment. He thought about it, then laughed: 'Oh, I see what you mean. No. No, sir. I'm not going to kill myself. Oh no, there's no need for that. It'll all end soon enough, without me doing anything about it. Would you like this, sir? As a souvenir, I mean.'

So saying, Nappy offered Alfric his stiletto. Alfric blinked at the weapon. It had been gone from sight ever since they came into the room, but here it was again, back in Nappy's hand, and Alfric was prepared to swear by a complete list of all his known ancestors that he had not seen Nappy sheath or unsheath the thing. The steel simply came and went. Like magic.

'Thank you,' said Alfric, gingerly reaching out and taking the stiletto. 'It's very kind of you to give me this.'

'Oh, you've earnt it, you've earnt it. It's my father, see.'

'This?' said Alfric, looking at the knife.

The room no longer seemed cosy. Rather, it was hot, hot, overheated by the brazier. Alfric wanted to get out, to escape from Nappy, from Nappy's cancer, from Nappy's madness. He wanted to be out in the night, alone, utterly free from all the demands of the rest of humanity.

'No, young sir, it's not the knife I'm talking about,' said Nappy. 'It's my dad. You met him, you see. He's a werehamster.'

'Ah,' said Alfric, enlightened.

'He was most impressed with you, he was. You leaving him the most of his treasure. As for what you took, why, I found out about that. What you wanted it for, I mean. That was very handsome of you.'

'It was nothing, really,' said Alfric, mystified as to why he should be getting such praise for such trivial acts of courtesy and (minimal) kindness.

'It shows you as a generous man,' said Nappy.

'But I'm not,' said Alfric, speaking the truth. 'I'm narrow, intolerant and selfish to boot.'

'Oh, that's how you see yourself, doubtless,' said Nappy. 'That's how you may be, too, set up against some absolute good. But people – people, young sir, I wouldn't rightly like to speak of them, not the truth of them. It's ugly, that's what it is. But you're not ugly, not ugly-evil at least.'

'Thank you,' said Alfric, wishing he could believe this were true.

'So I've given you the knife,' said Nappy. 'I'd like you to have this, too.'

With that, Nappy gouged out his right eye. Alfric locked his jaws together, choking off a scream. Nappy reached out. He had the eye in his hand. He wanted Alfric to take it. Carefully, Alfric put down the stiletto. He forced his fingers open. He extended his palm. Nappy pressed the eye into Alfric's open palm.

'Thank you,' said Alfric.

318

Then closed his fist on the eye, expecting it to sklish and squash, to splatter and spurt.

But the eye was of glass, warm where it had been in contact with Nappy's flesh, cool where it had been exposed to the night air. Alfric took a good long look at Nappy's face. The gaping eyesocket was dark, and gave an unexpected touch of malevolence to Nappy's countenance. But it was bloodless. The injury was years old.

'Thank you,' said Alfric. 'Thank you very much.'

'I thought . . . I thought you'd appreciate the gesture,' said Nappy. 'Something to remember me by. Now, young sir, I don't want to impose on you, but I do need someone to take over when I die.'

'But of course,' said Alfric, as if in a dream.

He had no wish to be a killer, but he would be, if that was the only way for him to live.

'I've got a list,' said Nappy, opening a snuff box and taking out several sheets of onionskin which were almost covered by crabbed handwriting. 'I wrote this out. I can write. There's not many who can write, but I wouldn't be wrong in taking you for one of them.'

'I'm a Banker Third Class,' said Alfric. Then, remembering his recent promotion: 'No, Second Class. Anyway. All bankers can read.'

'That's what I thought,' said Nappy. 'So here's the things, all the things, and what to do about them. There's the asylum committee, that's for the lunatics. The abortion clinic, not that I approve of it, it's murder if you ask me, but if we don't then others will, and better for it to be run on a non-profit basis, that's what I always say. It's a crime to make money out of something like that, don't you think?'

'Agreed,' said Alfric weakly.

'Then there's the charity school.'

'School?' said Alfric. 'What school?'

'Oh, it's a new project, you won't have heard of it. Funding, that's the problem. Not much money in Galsh Ebrek, you know. Not money enough for all the things that have to be done. But we have our sources. Begging, that's what it is when you come right down to it. But the Knights don't pay taxes, and it's them that has the money, so how else can we get it?'

Then Nappy led Alfric step by step through the intricacies of all the charity work he was involved in; then he passed his lists to Alfric; then Alfric swore himself to continue Nappy's good deeds.

'But,' said Alfric, 'what about the killing?'

'Killing?' said Nappy in surprise.

'Yes,' said Alfric. 'I mean, someone has to do it.'

'Oh, don't worry your head about that, young master. Killing's no problem. There's always someone ready to kill. It's looking after widows and children, that's where the problem is. No, don't you worry your head about any killing. They'll find a killer with no trouble at all. Well, sir, that takes me to the end of it. I'll show you to the Polta Door.'

'The Polta Door?' said Alfric, who had never heard of any such thing.

'A secret way,' said Nappy. 'A secret way in and out of Saxo Pall. My secret, sir, known to me and now to you. Not to anyone else.'

'I'd rather leave by the main gate.'

'Oh, I wouldn't do that,' said Nappy. 'They're waiting for your body. Ursula Major, I mean. Oh, and Ciranoush Norn. They're expecting it. They won't come looking for it, not yet, they know my work's not always quick. But they do want the body, oh yes, and they wouldn't let it out of their gates, not if they had a choice in the matter.'

'So they want to kill me,' said Alfric. 'So how do I survive hereafter?'

'I can't help you there,' said Nappy. 'I'm sorry. I've done what I can, but the rest is up to you.'

Nappy guided Alfric to the Polta Door and showed him out into the night. Then Nappy let the door close behind them.

'Where did it go?' said Alfric, staring at the rock walls of Saxo Pall. 'It's vanished!'

'It's closed, that's all,' said Nappy. 'Here, young sir. Put your hand here. That's right. And the other one there, just there. Now. Push inward and downward with the left hand, inward and upward with the right. See?'

What appeared to be solid rock gave beneath Alfric's hands, and the Polta Door opened.

'Finding the place,' said Nappy, 'that's the thing. Finding the place. Landmarks, that's the thing. Line up landmarks.'

Alfric orientated himself. Looked up the slopes of Mobius Kolb to the walls of the Bank and to the moonshining Gloat on the heights beyond.

'I can find the place again,' said Alfric.

'I hope you can, young sir,' said Nappy calmly. 'Because I won't be here to help you.'

Then Nappy said one final goodbye, went into Saxo Pall through the Polta Door, and let that secret portal close behind him.

Alfric was left alone in the night, which was bitterly cold. The moon was null, but the uncanny light of the Oracle of Ob still shone bright and strong, serving as an acceptable substitute.

But Alfric needed no substitute. Nor did he need the moon itself. Tonight, he knew. He was not the moon's minion but the Commander of his own Powers, the Commander of the Power to Change. He could do so now, if he wished. Wrists thickening, hairs darkening, teeth lengthening, body girthing and strengthening.

He had the choice.

He could Change, and flee Galsh Ebrek, and live wild as a ravening enemy of the city, live wild in the forest, savaging and destroying at will.

But:

'That is not my choice.'

So said Alfric Danbrog, then turned his back on the Oracle of Ob and started walking down Mobius Kolb, making for Varnvelten Street and his home.

Of course, this was not the end of the matter. There would always be the moon, and the temptations of the moon. There would always be the memory of those three months in the Qinjoks when he had lived as a wolf, running wild and shameless through the wilderness.

But . . .

He had faced his great crisis and had survived it. While he was a shape-changer, he knew himself to be fit to live among humans. He had never been entirely sure of that till now. The great burden of his life had been the fear that the madness of the moon would one day overcome him; that his efforts to restrain himself would fail; that he would become one with the ravening beasts, gladly slaughtering any and all without thought for the consequences.

Now he knew otherwise.

He would never yield to such temptation, except by an act of untrammelled free will; and this knowledge of self-possession compensated for whatever he had lost. Though he had been defeated in his efforts to win the throne of Galsh Ebrek, at least he had full possession of himself.

'Besides,' said Alfric, 'the game is not yet played out.'

He was still alive.

And Ursula Major could not kill him openly, for she had granted him a pardon in the presence of many witnessing Yudonic Knights. When challenged to combat by the ork Morgenstern, Ursula had pardoned Alfric; and law and tradition did not allow such a mercy to be withdrawn.

'She wants to kill me,' said Alfric to himself, 'but it must be done by stealth. Well. I have eyes and ears and hands and feet, and a sword to guard myself, and a stiletto, and a glass eye besides, so what fear have I of assassins?'

He realized that, though he was speaking to himself, his voice was loud. He must be a little drunk.

'What of it?' said Alfric. 'A man may have a little drink to celebrate a victory, may he not?'

Then he went down Mobius Kolb, walking boldly through the night, careless of any danger he might encounter. He went directly to Varnvelten Street. As far as he was concerned, that was enough. His enemies thought Nappy to be killing him slowly in some secret place of screaming horror. They would not look for him in his home or elsewhere, not tonight.

When Alfric got home, he found his house had been looted. Candles lit by the looters were still burning.

'Robbers!' said Alfric.

And tried to work out exactly what had been stolen.

Viola Vanaleta's favourite chair. Viola Vanaleta's

favourite table. Vanaleta's spare clothes. Vanaleta's lantern, the special stained-glass lantern which had been a wedding gift from her grandmother.

No, the house had not been burgled.

Rather, Alfric's wife had come and had removed all that belonged to her, together with all those items of jointly held property to which she had some special claim.

'So this is it,' muttered Alfric. 'This is final. What next? Divorce papers, I suppose.'

And he began to feel weary, very weary, so weary that he wondered if perhaps Nappy had poisoned him. Reeling with fatigue, he stumbled to his bed, and laid himself down without bothering to take off his boots. And when he woke it was morning, and sun was streaming in through a small glass window near his head, and at first he was puzzled by that light, for it was so long since he had seen the sun that he was almost ready to deny the reality of the sun's existence.

'A new day,' said Alfric.

Yes, a new day.

And now he had his problems to attend to.

CHAPTER TWENTY

Alfric scavenged around for a meal, and was rewarded by the discovery of three small cakes of cooked oatmeal and a lump of dried fish. While he was taking breakfast, he schemed diligently. The game of power was not played out yet; but, if Alfric was going to survive to play much longer, he would have to make Ursula Major understand that she needed him.

What did he have that she wanted? Or might be made to want? Of course! His knowledge of finance!

Alfric had long observed that the government of Wen Endex was deficient in that it had no properly organized system of taxes. Given such a system, the streets of Galsh Ebrek could be properly paved; roads could be built across the nation; the swamps could be drained; and many other things equally as marvellous could be accomplished.

Once Ursula Major understood that Alfric could arrange all this on her behalf, surely she would rather have him as an ally than as an enemy. And once installed in the power system, he could work to put himself on the throne.

'It will work,' said Alfric to himself.

Then was startled by a knock on the door.

Alfric feared this might signal the advent of Ciranoush Zaxilian Norn at the head of a gang of headhunters. But his visitors proved to be the orks, Cod and Morgenstern.

'Hello,' said Alfric.

'Hello Alfric,' said Morgenstern.

'May we come in?' said Cod. 'There's something we'd like to talk about.'

'I'm afraid,' said Alfric, 'that this isn't a convenient moment for a talk.'

'Why not?' said Cod.

'Because,' said Alfric, 'I'm going to Saxo Pall.'

'Oh,' said Morgenstern. 'Do you think that's wise?'

'I don't care if it's wise or not,' said Alfric. 'I'm going.'

'There's things going on in that castle which aren't really nice,' said Morgenstern.

'Such as what?' said Alfric.

'Such as people dying,' said Morgenstern. 'Nappy, for instance.'

'What happened to him?' said Alfric.

'He died,' said Morgenstern. 'He died in his sleep last night.'

Alfric knew what it meant 'to die in one's sleep'. Alfric could not help himself. He shuddered, imagining the wet bone, the shattered teeth, the eyes avulsed, the intestines spraddled across the room. 'To die in your sleep' – in Wen Endex, that denoted the most hideous of all possible deaths. Who had commanded such a death? The smooth-breasted Ursula Major? Or the female Thrug? Or had the execution been commanded by Ciranoush Zaxilian Norn?

Whatever the truth, Nappy's death served to increase Alfric's sense of personal danger. Unless he could secure himself the protection of some kind of power base, he had best leave Wen Endex to preserve his own life.

'I'm sorry to hear about Nappy,' said Alfric, 'but it doesn't change the facts. I'm still going. I've got a clear choice. Either I do a deal with Ursula Major or I flee the city.'

'What kind of deal are you thinking of doing?' said Cod.

'I'm going to offer to run her inland revenue department,' said Alfric.

'But she doesn't have an inland revenue department!' said Cod.

'A deficiency,' said Alfric, 'which I hope to remedy.'

'Can we come with you?' said Cod. 'To Saxo Pall, I mean.'

'Of course,' said Alfric. 'If you want to.'

'Good,' said Cod. 'If they threaten you, we'll say we've made you part of our diplomatic staff.'

'Thank you,' said Alfric, genuinely touched to find the orks selflessly prepared to go to such efforts on his behalf.

In company with the orks, Alfric went through the streets of Galsh Ebrek.

It was hot.

Hot?

Yes, it was hot!

The sun was high in the sky, for it was not morning at all, it was early afternoon. Which meant that Alfric had not just eaten breakfast. Rather, he had consumed lunch.

Rooftop snow, slushed by sun, was melting fast. Already, flowers were unfolding, life ressurecting itself from the mud, pushing outward to the sun in a flamboyance of purple, a roseburst of red. Alfric saw no miracle in this, for he had lived in Wen Endex all his life, and was accustomed to the violence of the onset of spring. Nevertheless, he was pleased to find the cold weather broken, and the sun ruling in splendour in the heavens above.

Up the slopes of Mobius Kolb went Alfric Danbrog, then into Saxo Pall went he with the orks Cod and Morgenstern in tow. Alfric demanded an audience with Ursula Major.

'I'll see what I can arrange,' said a very nervous Guignol Grangalet.

'You do that,' said Cod the ork. 'And make sure you don't accidentally arrange Alfric's death, because the ogre king wouldn't like that at all, oh no, King Dimple-Dumpling would be very upset with you if you did a thing like that.'

Guignol Grangalet looked more nervous than ever.

'Go!' said Cod. 'Don't keep us waiting!'

And the Chief of Protocol fled.

Alfric and the orks were shortly shown into the Council Chamber. This was a big room dominated by a horseshoe table of polished oak. The windows of that room made no concession to the requirements of defence, for they were wide and tall. They had been unshuttered, so the sun splashed into the Council Chamber.

Several people were sitting at the horseshoe table, but there was no sign of Ursula Major. Alfric turned to the person who sat in the Chair of Honour. That person was Justina Thrug, daughter of Lonstantine Thrug and sometime ruler of the distant island of Untunchilamon.

'I have come here,' said Alfric, 'to see Ursula Major. Where is she?'

Justina Thrug looked at him. A small smile played about her lips. The pet owl which sat upon Justina's shoulder opened one eye – huge, orange, malevolent –

and stared at Alfric for a moment before lidding its vision once more.

'Ursula,' said Justina, choosing her words carefully, 'is sitting in the throneroom, playing at being king of Galsh Ebrek.'

'I want to see her,' said Alfric harshly.

Justina smiled again.

Sun shone bright on an ornamental bronze comb placed in her hair. Sun glinted from the heavy gold rings on her fingers, and dazzled from the cut diamonds which adorned those rings. Her father's battle-shield was hung on the wall behind her, and the reflected glory of this aegis shone around her.

'Izzy, my darling,' said Justina. 'I don't think you really want to see little Ursula. I think you want to see the ruler of Galsh Ebrek.'

'Which is?' said Alfric.

Justina Thrug smiled. Like a cat with cream. Alfric looked around the table. There sat Ciranoush Zaxilian Norn. And there sat the elderly Banker Eg. And there, Comptroller Xzu. And, besides, five Yudonic Knights from the greatest of the Families.

Only then did Alfric remember how he had seen Justina Thrug in the precincts of the Bank shortly after his return from his latest visit to the Qinjoks. He had asked what she had been doing there. He had been told she had been arranging a loan. He had believed it. But now he knew differently. She had been playing politics, even then.

This was the most devastating revelation Alfric had ever endured in his whole life.

Never before had he felt so totally outclassed.

He had thought himself to be right at the centre of the

politics of Galsh Ebrek, whereas in fact he had been a peripheral figure on the fringes of political life. While he killed dragons, dared giants and dealt with vampires, he had imagined himself to be winning the throne of Wen Endex. In fact, the true power brokers had been wheeling and dealing right in the heart of Galsh Ebrek itself.

So . . .

Had the Bank ever truly intended Alfric to become Wormlord?

He knew, now, that he would never know. More likely, the Bank had threatened from time to time to make Alfric king, using this threat for political leverage. Or . . .

Alfric gave up.

He would never work out all the intricacies of the power game which had been played in Galsh Ebrek.

But one thing was for certain. He had thought himself the complete politician: but he had been as a child compared to these people.

'Well, Izzy my darling,' said Justina, breaking into Alfric's long silence. 'You've had time enough to think. Has your thinking proved profitable? Do you understand a little better now?'

'I do,' said Alfric thickly.

The Thrug smiled, showing remarkably few teeth but a good deal of tongue and gum.

'Well then, Izzy my darling,' said she. 'What can we do for you?'

'I would like to have a word with Banker Xzu in private,' said Alfric.

'You may,' said Justina. 'Your orks can wait here.'

'They're not my orks,' said Alfric. 'They're King Dimple-Dumpling's orks.'

330

'Relax,' said Justina. 'We know your orks to be ambassadors. We're hardly going to kill diplomats for their blubber, are we now?'

This comment was so shockingly offensive that it left Alfric wordless. So he made no further remarks as he accompanied Comptroller Xzu from the Council Chamber.

Xzu led Alfric to a small office near the Council Chamber. As they seated themselves on either side of a rosewood desk, Alfric looked round the office, seeing abaci, foreign-language books and paperweights which he guessed to have been manufactured in Chi'ash-lan.

Alfric guessed this to be Xzu's private office. And judged, moreover, that the office had been long occupied.

'Perhaps you think,' said Xzu, 'that this office bespeaks a very close relationship between Saxo Pall and the Flesh Traders' Financial Association. If that is indeed what you think, then you are entirely correct. The relationship between the Bank and the throne is very close, much closer than low-ranked bankers imagine it to be. Tell me, Alfric, what did you come here for?'

'I came here,' said Alfric, 'to suggest to Ursula Major that I be appointed head of her inland revenue department.'

Xzu laughed.

His laugh was mirthless.

'A poor joke, Alfric,' said Xzu. 'If that's what you really intended, I suggest you've taken leave of your senses. You know where you should be right now, Alfric?'

'Where?' said Alfric.

'On your way to Port Domax, that's where. Another city, another country, another continent. A new start. Take my advice, Alfric. Run. If you stay, you die. Nappy died last night.'

'So I heard,' said Alfric.

'And?' said Xzu. 'Are you going to run? I can assist you with passage money if you're short of cash.'

'No thank you,' said Alfric. 'I'm not going. I want you to convene a formal meeting of the Governors of the Bank. I want to ask for the Bank's support and protection.'

'You won't get it,' said Xzu.

'Even so,' said Alfric, 'I still want you to convene that meeting. I am a Banker Second Class. I have a right to be heard.'

'Alfric,' said Comptroller Xzu, 'I have news for you. You're not a banker of any class. The Bank has expelled you. Your place in the Flesh Traders' Financial Association has been given to Ciranoush Zaxilian Norn.'

Alfric stared at Xzu.

'It's true, Alfric,' said Comptroller Xzu. 'I'm not joking. You're out. Norn is in.'

'You – you must help me,' said Alfric thickly. 'You must help me to fight back. You must!'

'Must?' said Xzu. 'I couldn't, even if I wanted to.'

'You must!' said Alfric. 'Or – or I'll expose you.'

'Expose me?' said Xzu.

'Yes! I'll tell them what you did!'

'And what did I do?' said Xzu.

'You – you took bribes,' said Alfric. 'You took bribes from me.'

Xzu looked at Alfric, pitying the poor fool.

'I was authorized to accept your bribes,' said Xzu.

'And to accept your forged medical reports. The Bank gave me written orders to do as much. You see, we thought we might have a use for you.'

Alfric opened his mouth, closed it, then opened it again. Like a fish dragged from the water, a fish trying to breathe in a world suddenly become inimical and incomprehensible.

'You see,' said Xzu softly, 'the Bank cannot predict the future, nor does it attempt to do so. But it does make contingency plans a long, long time in advance. We think long term, you see.'

Alfric bowed his head, as if ashamed of himself.

He was ashamed of himself.

He had been totally outclassed, out-thought and outmanoeuvred; and such was the blindness of his pride that he had never suspected this for even a moment, not until the revelations of this day of disaster.

Then Alfric straightened up. He picked up a paperweight, a glass bauble with a yellow flower encapsulated in its depths.

'May I have this?' said Alfric.

Xzu looked at him in surprise.

'What for?'

'A gift,' said Alfric. 'A gift for my mother.'

Xzu studied Alfric and the paperweight both, tried to figure out what Alfric's tactics were, then said abruptly:

'Take it.'

'Thank you,' said Alfric.

And withdrew.

Alfric collected the orks from the Council Chamber then left Saxo Pall, making for the Green Cricket.

'Where are we going?' said Cod.

'To Anna Blaume's,' said Alfric.

'Oh, that's good,' said Morgenstern. 'You'll have a chance to have a drink with us, and we can have a good talk.'

'Sorry, but no,' said Alfric. 'When we get to the Cricket, I'm going to buy horses and be gone. I have to get out of Galsh Ebrek soon, now, today. Because those who rule from Saxo Pall most definitely intend to kill me.'

CHAPTER TWENTY-ONE

As Alfric walked through the streets of Galsh Ebrek, he began to consider what kind of future he might make for himself in Port Domax. His years of strength were half over, but in all probability another thirty-three years of health remained to him. In that time, could he raise the army he would need to recover the throne of Wen Endex?

As Alfric was so thinking, he turned into Fraudenzimmer Street. And there was the Green Cricket, a two-storey building painted pink. Yes, it had always been pink. But Alfric had seen it so often by night that he had quite forgotten its colour till now.

'Flowers, mister?' said a girlchild, coming up to him with a bouquet.

'How much?' said Alfric.

She named the price; he paid. Where women were concerned, flowers were a most effective weapon of diplomacy. They might sweeten Anna Blaume's temper and lower the price of the horses Alfric wished to buy from her.

Thus armed, Alfric advanced upon the Green Cricket. The slovenly thatch was steaming in the hot sun. A few icicles yet clung to the eves; but, even as Alfric approached, one fell off and dagger-darted to the mud below. The front door was open, and the dwarves Du Deiner and Mich Dir were fighting in the doorway. They were supposed to be scrubbing the front step, but, instead, Du Deiner was trying to force Mich Dir's head into a bucket of hot soapy water.

'Hey,' said Alfric. 'Stop that.'

At which the struggling dwarves knocked over the bucket of water, which went all over Alfric's boots. He didn't worry. He had other things to worry about.

With Cod and Morgenstern on his heels, Alfric went inside, into the Green Cricket. He looked around, as if he had never seen it before by daylight. Skaps the vogel hung upside down from one of the rafters overhead, sleeping. Alfric reached up and chucked the vogel under the chin, whereupon it opened one purple eye and looked at him in a malevolent fashion which was disconcerting in the extreme.

'For a parrot-bat,' said Alfric, trying to recover his composure, 'you don't talk very much.'

'Some of us,' said Skaps, 'prefer to think.'

Then the vogel closed its eye and went back to sleep, leaving Alfric unsure whether he had actually heard that little speech or not. He concealed his discomfiture by pretending an interest in the cradle which sat on one of the tables. Inside was the baby Alfric had rescued from the swamp giant Kralch. Much to Alfric's surprise, the infant was giggling. When Alfric thought of babies, he thought of them as perpetually operating in the crying mode. The idea that they could sometimes be happy was an alien notion indeed.

'Isn't it cute?' said Morgenstern.

'I love it,' said Cod.

'I'd love a drink,' said Alfric, turning from the baby to the bar.

Nobody stood behind the bar. But on top of the bar

stood a huge hissing cockroach, which was doing its best to deal with the repeated onslaughts of a determined untunchilamon. Alfric moved closer, fascinated by this scene of combat. Though the miniscule dragon was no larger than the massive orthopterous insect, Alfric thought the firedrake would surely conquer.

As Alfric watched, the dragon spat sparks and closed with the cockroach. The roach hissed and outsquirted a fine spray of a vile and stinging fluid. The untunchilamon squeaked in rage and threw itself upon its manxome foe. The two creatures grappled with each other, rolled over and over, then tumbled to the floor and broke apart. Making a rapid recovery, they confronted each other, ready for a second round.

Then the floorboards began to creak and tremble as someone came tromping down the stairs, and the cockroach scuttled away to the nearest mousehole while the untunchilamon took to the air.

Who was it who was coming down those stairs?

Why, it was Anna Blaume herself, she of the larded skin, the blue-green yellow hair.

'For you,' said Alfric, handing her the flowers.

'Thank you,' said Anna Blaume.

Then kissed the flowers.

One of the petals came away, and she ate it, her strong white teeth crunching its force-grown beauty into little pieces. Then she swallowed it, grinning. She was strong and virile, the promise of many children dwelling between her stalwart thighs.

'Is Viola here?' said Alfric.

'Viola has taken herself off to the convent,' said Anna Blaume.

'You must be joking,' said Alfric in astonishment.

'No,' said Anna Blaume. 'It's the truth.'

Alfric thought a convent was the last place in the world where Viola Vanaleta would be happy. Galsh Ebrek's convent was the refuge of all those women who were dissatisfied with life in a world of men; and, if there was any truth in the rumours Alfric had heard, their days were largely given over to drinking bouts, wrestling matches and shameless indulgence in other uncouth pleasures.

'She's divorcing me, I take it,' said Alfric.

'She's divorced you already,' said Anna Blaume.

'What?'

'Go to the divorce court if you don't believe me,' said Anna Blaume. 'It's all finished.'

'But – but—'

'She forged your signature on certain documents, of course,' said Anna Blaume. 'Otherwise the whole thing might have taken much more time. You don't object, do you?'

'It is but a trifle,' said Alfric heavily. Then, realizing he was a free man: 'Will you marry me?'

'No,' said Anna Blaume.

'Why not?'

'You had your chance.'

This was true. When Alfric had been engaged to Viola Vanaleta, Anna Blaume had asked him to break the engagement and marry her instead. But he had refused. A mistake.

'Your mother's here,' said Anna Blaume.

'Gertrude?' said Alfric, again startled.

'Yes,' said Blaume. 'You don't have any other mother, do you?'

'Not that I'm aware of,' said Alfric. 'Where is she?'

338

'In the beer garden,' said Anna Blaume.

So Alfric went out of the back door to greet his mother. She was sitting at a table which rested on the flagstones which paved the beer garden. She was drinking gin. Little Ben Zvanzig was sitting under the table, playing with his pet frog, while Anna Blaume's daughter Sheila, with half a dozen dolls at her disposal, was playing at being a brothel keeper.

'Mother,' said Alfric.

Greeting Gertrude with a kiss on her cheek.

'Alfric, my boy,' said Gertrude. 'Sit down. Sit down.'

Alfric sat. And the orks Cod and Morgenstern, who had followed him outside, sat down also.

'I've got something for you,' said Alfric, producing the paperweight.

'Alfric,' said Gertrude. 'That's very nice of you.'

A tear glistened in her eye, and Alfric hoped she wasn't going to cry.

'Where have you been today?' said Gertrude.

Alfric was about to answer when he realized the question was being directed at the orks.

'Up at Saxo Pall,' said Cod.

'How did it go?' said Gertrude.

'Not too bad,' said Cod. 'Yes. All in all, things aren't going too badly.'

'By which we mean,' said Morgenstern, glumly, 'that things could be worse. Much worse. We could have come down with bubonic plague by now.'

'But we haven't,' said Cod.

'But we will,' said Morgenstern. 'If we stay in Galsh Ebrek we surely will. It's only a matter of time.'

'Ah well,' said Gertrude, 'I'm sure it'll all come right for you in time.'

339

Then she excused herself from the table and toddled into the Green Cricket. Alfric knew he should be moving. He should buy horses from Anna Blaume and be gone. Instantly. But he was finding himself possessed by lethargy.

'What happened between you and Banker Xzu?' said Cod.

'Nothing much,' said Alfric.

'Did he offer to help you?' said Morgenstern. 'Help you win the throne, I mean.'

'No,' said Alfric. 'He told me to get out of Galsh Ebrek lest I die in my sleep. He told me I've been kicked out of the Bank. I'm not welcome here.'

'So . . . so who is actually going to rule in Galsh Ebrek?' said Cod.

'Unless I'm very much mistaken,' said Alfric, 'Justina Thrug has come out on top, with Ursula Major as her puppet.'

Then he elaborated.

'That's nice to hear,' said Cod. 'At least it means there won't be a war in the city. Political stability makes things easier for us ambassadors. In theory, at least.'

'But in practice, probably not,' said Morgenstern.

'What's the problem?' said Alfric.

'Nobody takes us seriously, that's the problem,' said Cod. 'Because we're orks. It makes it very hard to get business done.'

'And,' said Morgenstern, 'we find it hard to settle to business in any kind.'

'Why?' said Alfric.

'Because,' said Morgenstern, the eyes of the big lubbery creature growing wet with tears, 'we're afraid. Afraid of living here. Afraid of the Knights and the commoners.'

340

'Afraid?' said Alfric. 'I don't believe it! You were heroes up in Saxo Pall. Challenging Ursula Major like that. I was ever so impressed.'

'Were you?' said Cod.

'Yes,' said Alfric. 'Really.'

'I'm glad to hear that,' said Cod. 'We did . . . we did rise to the occasion, and we know it. We're proud of it. But it's the routine that's wearing us down.'

'The routine,' said Morgenstern, 'of just living in this city.'

'They make jokes about us, you see,' said Cod. 'Jokes about eating us. I can take a joke. But it's not a joke, not really. They really do want to eat us. I can't sleep at night for the bad dreams.'

'Sleep by day, then,' said Alfric carelessly

'Oh, it's all right for you,' said Morgenstern. 'You're not an ork. Nobody ever threatened to boil you down for your blubber oil.'

'Well . . . no,' said Alfric, conceding the point.

'If you were ambassador,' said Cod, 'King Dimple-Dumpling's ambassador, I mean, then people would take you seriously. You could get things done. Not like us orks.'

'I wouldn't count on it,' said Alfric. 'The Izdimir Empire has an ambassador here, but nobody takes him too seriously. They make jokes about him too, you know. It's not just because you're orks. It's because you're outsiders. Anyway, if it's getting too much for you, why don't you go back to the Qinjoks?'

'King Dimple-Dumpling wouldn't like that,' said Morgenstern. 'He has to have an ambassador in Galsh Ebrek.'

'Then let him send an ogre,' said Alfric. 'One of his

sons, perhaps. This just isn't the place for orks. I'm quite happy to come along to the Qinjoks and tell the king that myself.'

'Oh,' said Cod, 'that's awfully kind of you. But it wouldn't really be a good idea. The king's most awfully keen to keep an ambassador here. We're under orders. We can't leave unless we can find someone to substitute for us.'

Cod paused.

Looked at Alfric.

Morgenstern did likewise.

And Alfric thought to himself, in amusement:

—They want me to be ambassador?

Oh no.

That was impossible.

Or was it?

Technically . . . technically it might be possible. If Alfric became the ogre-king's ambassador in Galsh Ebrek, then the Powers That Be would not dare murder him, lest they start a war with the Qinjoks. But . . . but Alfric planned to leave the continent of Yestron for the continent of Tameran. To make a new life for himself in Port Domax. There, life would be a struggle, but there was no limit to what he might achieve, given time.

Whereas to be the ogre-king's ambassador in Galsh Ebrek would surely be a dead end.

'Maybe you're mistaken about the importance the king attaches to diplomatic representation in Galsh Ebrek,' said Alfric. 'I don't see why King Dimple-Dumpling really needs an ambassador here at all. Our relations are perfectly cordial, and will remain so as long as the annual tribute is paid.'

Alfric frankly did not think that payment of that

342

annual tribute represented much of a strain on the treasury of the king of the Qinjoks.

Cod looked at Morgenstern.

Morgenstern looked at Cod.

'Shall we tell him?' said Morgenstern.

'Let's,' said Cod.

So Morgenstern said to Alfric:

'King Dimple-Dumpling wants to open a bank. Here. In Galsh Ebrek.'

'A bank?' said Alfric, not bothering to conceal his surprise.

'Yes,' said Morgenstern. 'A bank.'

'But why?' said Alfric.

'Why does anyone open a bank?' said Cod. 'To make money. The king's got all that treasure up in the Qinjoks with no place to invest it. The stuff just sits there getting warm in spring and cold in autumn. If the king had a bank, he could lend out his money for interest. Invest. Land, ships, insurance. You know. You're a banker. I don't have to tell you all this stuff, you know it already.'

'It's a nice idea,' said Alfric cautiously. 'But investment opportunities in Galsh Ebrek are somewhat limited. I don't know that there's room enough for another bank. Not here.'

'Of course there is,' said Cod. 'After all, you trade with the world.'

A fever-flush burnt through Alfric's veins. He felt dizzy. Did the orks know about that? But how? How could they?

—Careful now.

—This could be a trap.

Then Alfric chided himself for being so foolish. Of course the orks knew nothing of the Bank's secret. They

343

couldn't. It just wasn't possible. When the orks said that Galsh Ebrek traded with the world, all they meant was that ships came and went, and those ships could go anywhere in the world to do their trading.

'Let's have some wine,' said Alfric abruptly.

He raised his voice, and, by dint of a little shouting, summoned Du Deiner from inside the Green Cricket. Orders were placed, and, shortly, Alfric was sipping on some delicate lemon-flavoured wine. By now he had quite recovered himself, so he said:

'With reference to trade, you know as well as I do that a few ships come and go to and from Wen Endex. So, yes, certainly, we trade with the world. But it's a lean tradeline, isn't it?'

'Ah,' said Cod. 'But it's not ships I'm talking about. I'm talking about the Door.'

Alfric felt as if he had been abruptly dumped into a barrel of boiling water. They knew! They knew! The orks were privy to the Secret! This was a thunderbolt upset if ever there was one.

But Alfric masked his face with a diplomat's blandness and said, lightly, lightly, making a joke of it:

'Door? Yes, the Bank's got a Door for sure, otherwise we'd have to climb over the walls every time we went in and out.'

Thus he spoke, then felt a pang of anguish when he realized that 'we' no longer included himself. He was an outcast, excluded from the company of his fellows. And, for a moment, he almost wanted to weep.

'It's not that I'm talking of,' said Cod. 'I'm talking of a Door which goes from here to Elsewhere. To Chi'ashlan, Parengarenga and Tang. To Argan. To Ashmolea.'

Alfric almost declared Cod to be in error; for of course

344

the Circle of the Partnership Banks did not give them access to Ashmolea. However, he restrained his tongue. Took the time to think. Then answered, trying to make his answer seem careless:

'A pretty tale, methinks, and one you must fabricate for me in full, for I warrant it worth the telling. But of your mysterious Door I know nothing.'

'See?' said Morgenstern. 'I told you he was a liar.'

'Don't be too hard on him,' said Cod. 'It's his upbringing.'

'What do you mean, I'm a liar?' said Alfric. 'I'm telling you the truth.'

'We'd believe you if we could,' said Cod, 'but we know better. Ogres and orks have always known about the Door, you see. We go back to the days before Galsh Ebrek, you see. Before the city was ever founded. Before the Bank built on Mobius Kolb.'

'You have legends, doubtless,' said Alfric.

'Legends, yes,' said Cod. 'And truths to go with them. We know the Door to stand in the Rock of Rocks, the Keeper of Secrets. We know it to be a grey screen through which an ork can step to be Elsewhere.'

'I know nothing of this Door,' said Alfric. 'But suppose such a thing to exist. Certain things follow. First, the Bank would never acknowledge its existence, for it would be a secret too great for the world to be trusted with. Second, the Bank would never allow its use by orks.'

'And why not?' said Morgenstern.

'Because, um—'

'Prejudice,' said Morgenstern heavily. 'That's what you're talking about. We're orks, so they hate us. If only because we make them remember. That's all. You'd like to wage genocide on the lot of us. Then you could forget the crimes of your ancestors. You could forget we ever existed.'

'I don't know that that's entirely fair,' said Alfric. 'But the truth is that your Door doesn't exist, and if it did you wouldn't have access to it, nor would your bank.'

'But,' said Cod, 'what if our bank was run by one who already shared the secret of the Door?'

Alfric frowned.

The ork was hinting at—

At . . . ?

Grief!

But—

Alfric was cautious.

Maybe Cod wasn't actually offering him anything. And there was no guarantee that any offer made by the orks would be made in good faith. Best that Alfric be cautious; for it was quite possible that the orks' sole purpose was to spy out the secrets of the Bank.

'I think,' said Cod, 'that you think I'm trying to trick you into telling of something you'd rather not talk about.'

'He doesn't trust us,' said Morgenstern gloomily.

'But maybe he could learn to trust us,' said Cod. 'If we brought him money enough, I mean. Five pack-trains of gold to establish his bank. A formal treaty with the king of the Qinjoks. Does the idea appeal, Alfric my friend?'

'You tell an interesting story,' said Alfric.

'It's not just a story,' said Morgenstern. 'What we're getting at – and I must say you seem awfully slow on the uptake – is that we want you to run our bank. You're the perfect candidate.'

'So you tell me,' said Alfric. 'But that's only your opinion. Your king may think otherwise.'

'Oh no,' said Cod. 'We had a long talk about that before we left the Qinjoks. He likes you, Alfric. He's watched you every year in interview. He thinks highly of you. We're authorized to offer you full management of the bank, with a baseline salary of five thousand saladins per annum plus 25 per cent of the profits.'

Alfric was staggered.

But—

The Bank would kill him if he so much as breathed of the Bank's secrets.

'As I keep trying to tell you,' said Alfric, 'it's no good. Your offer's based on a fallacy. There's actually no Door in the Bank, and even if there was, it would be far too dangerous for anyone to confess knowledge to such.'

'That's all right,' said Cod, patting Alfric's hand. 'You can pretend with us if that's what you want to do. It doesn't make any difference to us. Just accept the job, that's all we're asking. As for danger – with powerful friends you'll have nothing to worry about.'

'It's a long, long way from here to the Qinjoks,' said Alfric.

'Yes,' said Cod. 'But we'll make you an ambassador as well as the head of your own bank. Besides, it's no distance at all to Saxo Pall. Justina Thrug's done well for herself, hasn't she? Even so, she may not be immune to . . . to the lure of financial incentive.'

'Justina?' said Alfric. 'How does she come into it?'

'That's for you to say,' said Cod. 'But I venture to suggest that you could reward her most handsomely with but a fraction of your 25 per cent of the profits.'

'I don't think she'd want to deal with me,' said Alfric.

'Oh, but she does, she does,' said Cod calmly. 'She told us as much herself.'

'What?!'

'We had a brief conclave,' said Cod. 'With Justina, I mean. While you were talking with Comptroller Xzu. The three of us. Justina and us two. We went to the stench pits together. We told Justina that you had the favour of King Dimple-Dumpling. She's agreed to see you in private interview at noon tomorrow, though as yet she doesn't know what's at stake.'

Alfric was staggered. He had grossly underestimated these orks, who were far better diplomats than he had thought. Earlier, he had seen fit to lecture them on the power politics of Wen Endex. Had even told them of Justina Thrug's freshly won supremacy. And they had listened like little children receiving instruction – though they had known all about it all along.

'So,' said Cod. 'It's all set up. Almost. All you have to do is to agree to be our banker.'

Alfric thought about it.

'You tell a pretty fairy tale,' he said at last. 'But there's one thing I don't understand. Why me? If your offer is as it is, why would you freely give me such wealth and such power?'

'He's a bit slow today,' said Morgenstern.

'That's forgiveable,' said Cod. 'He's been overworked these last few days.' Then, to Alfric: 'First, you're a Yudonic Knight, not a commoner, so you can get things done in Galsh Ebrek. But you're less of a barbarian than most Knights, so we feel comfortable dealing with you. You're already privy to the secrets of the Flesh Traders' Financial Association, which is the greatest of advantages. And – you've nowhere left to go.'

'What do you mean?'

'He means,' said Morgenstern, 'this is your last chance in Galsh Ebrek. Otherwise, you're finished. So you're ours or you're nothing.'

Cod smacked Morgenstern sharply on the shoulder, and said:

'Diplomacy, remember?'

'I remember,' said Morgenstern. 'But talking in circles isn't getting us anywhere in a hurry, is it?'

'Maybe not,' said Cod. 'But at least we've got his attention.'

The orks had Alfric's attention indeed. If he was made an ambassador, that would guarantee his personal safety. And, if he cut Justina Thrug in on the deal, he could set up a bank in Galsh Ebrek with no trouble at all. And, with the wealth of the Qinjoks behind him, he could swiftly become rich. He would have his power base, and nobody would be able to touch him. Unless Galsh Ebrek's Bank . . . but on consideration, in all probability the Flesh Traders' Financial Association would be more than happy to deal with him. Access to the resources of the Qinjoks would mean a permanent solution to the Bank's intermittent liquidity problems.

No small matter, this. In theory the Partnership Banks were equal allies working to mutual advantage. In theory, a run on the Bank in Dalar ken Halvar could be met by funds in Chi'ash-lan or vice versa; and the intricate treaties which bound the Banks together alleged that such support would be forthcoming automatically. But in practice, the larger Banks would happily combine to wreck one of their weaker associates if a profitable opportunity ever became available.

The wealth of the Qinjoks was a financial weapon which would make Galsh Ebrek great. The Flesh Traders' Financial Association would acknowledge as much, and Banker Xzu and his fellows would have to deal with Alfric Danbrog as an equal. Between them, they would finance coal mines on Stokos, wars in the Cold West, forestry in Quilth, poetry in Tang . . .

As Alfric luxuriated in the possibilities, he realized that already he was committed. Cod was right. For Alfric, there were no options. The challenge would be great, and the dangers greater yet; but the bait was irresistible.

'Well?' said Cod. 'Tell us your thoughts.'

'I'm thinking,' said Alfric gravely, 'that the proposal you're making would have to be subject to the negotiation of suitable terms. After all, 25 per cent is small recompense for the personal risks I'd be running, particularly when so much of the money would be going in bribes.'

'You're lucky to be getting anything!' said Morgenstern, in a rare display of explosive anger. 'At best, I thought you worth 5 per cent, not 25.'

'Perhaps I know my own worth better than you,' said Alfric calmly. 'I'm thinking more along the lines of a 60–40 split.'

'In your favour, I suppose,' said Morgenstern sarcastically.

'Yes,' said Alfric.

This insolent audacity left Morgenstern temporarily dumbfounded, but Cod found tongue enough to say:

'If thus you think, then please to think again, for 25 is our absolute maximum.'

'Think I will,' said Alfric solemnly.

But his head was filled not with percentages but with visions of glory. At whatever percentage, he would do a deal with these orks; and he would open his bank, and become rich, and great, and glorious. Already he was filled with a lust for enterprise, an enthusiasm for battle, and with savage hopes of ultimate triumph. Kingship of Wen Endex? His bank would give him a powerbase for making himself king, thus redeeming his father's name and fulfilling his grandfather's wishes.

Youth was over, yes; but all of manhood lay ahead. And, for Alfric, anything was possible.

Then Anna Blaume emerged from inside the Green Cricket to say:

'There's someone at the door. They want to see you.'

'People?' said Alfric, immediately beset by blood-stained visions of death and disaster.

'Not dangerous people,' said Anna Blaume. 'People people.'

So Alfric went to the front door and found a most motley crew assembling outside. There were beggars and lepers, and widows in rags with bawling babies, and cripples and mutants, and more than a few people who were frankly insane.

Alfric realized then who these people were.

These people were Nappy's constituency, those whose care Nappy had imposed upon him as the price of his life. Nappy must have spread the word before he 'died in his sleep', and obviously all of Galsk Ebrek knew by now.

Alfric began to suspect that he was going to pay a

very, very heavy price for escaping murder at Nappy's hands.

But he had no choice in the matter.

So he sighed, then said:

'Come in.'

THE END